HIS HAND BEGAN TO MOVE, SKIMMED ACROSS her breast, thrilling her. Her breath hitched, and for an instant he froze.

Zach released her mouth and his arms fell away as he jerked back and stepped away. Her stomach dropped with an instant of loss before good sense prevailed. For a long, humming moment he stared at her with eyes gone dark and edgy, the angles and planes of his face pronounced. *I did get to him*, she thought, pleased.

He got to you, too. And he's the sheriff! He knows about you. It's only a matter of time before he tells everyone in town.

Savannah wasn't nearly as pleased as she'd been a moment before.

Maybe her displeasure showed in her expression, because all of a sudden Zach relaxed. That oh-so-talented mouth of his lifted in a smug, knowing smile. He tipped an imaginary hat and turned to leave. "See you later, Peach."

BY EMILY MARCH

Angel's Rest
Hummingbird Lake
Heartache Falls
Mistletoe Mine
Lover's Leap
Nightingale Way
Reflection Point

Books published by The Random House Publishing Group are available at quantity discounts on bulk purchases for premium, educational, fund-raising, and special sales use. For details, please call 1-800-733-3000.

Reflection Point

An
Eternity Springs
Novel

EMILY MARCH

BALLANTINE BOOKS • NEW YORK

Sale of this book without a front cover may be unauthorized. If this book is coverless, it may have been reported to the publisher as "unsold or destroyed" and neither the author nor the publisher may have received payment for it.

Reflection Point is a work of fiction. Names, characters, places, and incidents are the products of the author's imagination or are used fictitiously. Any resemblance to actual events, locales, or persons, living or dead, is entirely coincidental.

A Ballantine Books Mass Market Original

Copyright © 2013 by Geralyn Dawson Williams
Excerpt from *Miracle Road* by Emily March © 2013 by Geralyn Dawson Williams

All rights reserved.

Published in the United States by Ballantine Books, an imprint of The Random House Publishing Group, a division of Random House, Inc., New York.

BALLANTINE and colophon are registered trademarks of Random House, Inc.

This book contains an excerpt from the forthcoming book *Miracle Road* by Emily March. This excerpt has been set for this edition only and may not reflect the final content of the forthcoming edition.

ISBN: 978-0-345-54226-7
eBook ISBN: 978-0-345-54227-4

Cover design: Lynn Andreozzi
Cover illustration: Robert Steele

Printed in the United States of America

www.ballantinebooks.com

9 8 7 6 5 4 3 2 1

Ballantine mass market edition: April 2013

For the angels who bless my life

Reflection Point

ONE

༒

"There's a new girl in town."

Sheriff Zach Turner first heard the news from Cam Murphy when he arrived at the man's outdoor-sports shop, Refresh, on his day off. The fly rod he'd noticed on his previous visit was proving to be quite a temptation. A sports equipment junkie, Zach had been both delighted and dismayed when Murphy's shop opened this past winter. Having such a great selection of gear within spitting distance of the sheriff's office was playing hell with his wallet.

Zach lifted the rod from the rack, tested its feel, and replied, "A troublemaker?"

"A looker."

Ah. "And you are compelled to share this information why? Still threatened that Sarah will come to her senses and decide that she can't live without my superior kisses after all, Murphy?"

Cam flashed the shark's smile he'd become known for since his return to Eternity Springs from Australia, and his blue eyes gleamed with contentment. "I'm too sexually satisfied to respond to that dig, Sheriff."

"Ouch." Zach set the rod on the counter, then wandered over to the bicycles, where a red Enduro EVO caught his eye. He'd been wanting to move up from his

Stumpjumper, but he couldn't justify the cost. Not now, anyway. Maybe this summer . . .

"Actually, I'm giving you a heads-up," Cam continued. "The quilt group met at my house last night, and your love life—specifically, your lack of a love life—was one of the main topics of conversation."

Zach glanced up from the bike and fastened a frustrated look upon his friend. "You're kidding me."

"Nope. The women have matchmaking on their minds."

Zach groaned aloud. "Does it never occur to them that they don't know everything they think they know about my love life?"

Cam folded his arms and arched an inquisitive brow. "You have a fish on the line we don't know about, Turner?"

Zach's thoughts went to the ski instructor he'd been seeing over at Wolf Creek. Inga Christiansen was a lovely, tall, talented woman who was as athletic in bed as she was out of it. He'd enjoyed the time they'd spent together, but they'd both gone into the relationship knowing it was seasonal. "Actually, I recently cut one loose."

"Someone I know?"

Zach gave a slow smile. "Inga."

"Inga?"

"She's going home to Sweden, and I just didn't want to move with her."

"Ah, a Scandinavian! I used to love it when we had snow bunny Scandinavians sign up for dive trips," he said, referring to the reef diving tour business he'd owned when he lived in Australia. "Nice scenery."

Zach mentally envisioned Inga the last time he'd seen her naked. "Very."

"Although I will repeat that the new southern comfort we have to enjoy is pretty scenic."

"Southern comfort?"

"Ms. Savannah Sophia Moore, from Georgia. Wait until you hear her accent. I told Sarah that the way she says 'sugah' sorta licks up and down a man's spine."

"And your bride didn't take a knife to you?"

"No. She was too busy trying to figure out a way to set the two of you up."

Zach snorted and decided it was time to change the subject. "So have you heard how the rainbows are biting on the Taylor River this week?"

The conversation turned to fishing, and Zach forgot about the newcomer to town as he went about his errands. His next stop was the local vet's office to pick up his whippet, Ace, whom he'd left with Nic Callahan first thing that morning. The tall, blond mother of twin daughters had an appealing girl-next-door beauty and a friendly demeanor, and she gave him a welcoming smile as he opened her office door and strode inside. "Hey, Zach."

"How's my dog?"

"Ace is a doll, and I'm happy to say that he's doing just great. Even better, he seems to have gotten his spirit back. You've done a great job with him, Zach. Aren't you glad we talked you into keeping him?"

Ace had been in pitiful shape when Nic and her friends rescued him from a bad situation the previous summer. Scarred, starved, and scared, he'd required extra doses of TLC to nurture him back to health. Surgery had helped his hip injury, the likely result of being hit by a car, but the speed-demon escape-artist days enjoyed by most whippets were behind him. "He's a good dog. Good company."

Nic snapped her fingers. "Speaking of which, have you heard the news? Eternity Springs has a new permanent resident. Savannah Sophia Moore. Isn't that a lovely name? She's from Georgia and is a dog person.

She adopted the cutest little mutt recently. A mini. Savannah brought her to me for a checkup."

"Purse pets," Zach said with a disdainful snort.

"Don't be snotty." Nic frowned at him. "The world
needs small dogs, too. She's opening a business in town,
and that's good for Eternity Springs."

"What does she do?"

"Handmade soaps and lotions. She's rented Harry
Golightly's old place on Fourth Street. She's planning to
use the first floor as retail space and the carriage house
in back as her workshop. She said she mostly sells her
stuff at street festivals and craft fairs, as well as online.
She plans to open the retail shop only during tourist season."

Zach considered the space. The Golightly place was
one of the old Victorian houses in town. The house had
good bones, and with a coat of paint and some land-
scaping, it could be a tourist draw. The location worked
since it was cattycorner to Sage Rafferty's art gallery,
Vistas, one of the town's biggest tourist draws. "What is
she like?"

"Honestly, I thought she was a little quiet and reserved
at first, but once I got her talking, she opened up. I like
her. I think she's a great new addition to Eternity Springs.
I'm excited about the new shop."

"Me too," Zach replied in a tone that clearly suggested the opposite.

"Now, Zach," Nic chided. "It *is* exciting."

"You are such a girl, Nic. Having Cam open a sporting goods shop was exciting. A soap shop? I don't think
so."

Nic's expression turned knowing. "Want to make a
bet you're singing a different tune after you meet her?"

Zach decided to put a stop to this matchmaking business here and now. Choosing his words carefully—he
didn't like to lie to his friends—he said, "The ski instruc-

tor I've been seeing wouldn't be amused to learn that I found a soap shop exciting."

"You're seeing someone?" Nic asked, shock in her tone. She folded her arms and scowled. "I didn't know that. Why don't we know about this?"

"'We'? Do you mean your coven?"

She sniffed with disdain. "Now, that's just mean, Zach Turner."

He reached out and thumped her on the nose. "I adore you, Mrs. Callahan, but I don't need you and your friends sticking your noses into my love life."

"We care about you, Zach. We don't like seeing you alone."

Zach was accustomed to being alone. An only child whose parents had died almost a decade ago, he'd adjusted to solitude. In fact, he relished it. Solitude was one of the appeals of Eternity Springs, in his opinion. "In that case, rest easy. I'm not alone. I have a dog. And a new fly rod. You and the girls can turn your attentions to somebody else. Now, let's talk dog food. The Trading Post has begun stocking a new specialty brand." He named it, then asked, "In your opinion, is it worth the extra money?"

Zach left Nic's office ten minutes later with Ace on a leash and a spring in his step, telling himself he wasn't the least bit curious about a soap maker from Georgia. He had more important things than women on his mind—namely, a free afternoon breaking in his new fly rod at his favorite fishing hole up above Lover's Leap. When he strolled into the Mocha Moose a few minutes later with the intention of getting a boxed lunch to go, he almost pivoted on his heel and marched out. Sarah Murphy, Sage Rafferty, Ali Timberlake, and Cat Davenport sat at one of the tables eating lunch. During his split second of indecision, Sarah spied him, though, and then it was too late.

"Zach!" she said, waving him over to the table. "We were just talking about you. Have you heard the news?"

He swallowed a groan and ordered a sandwich.

On a sun-kissed spring afternoon, Savannah Moore sat atop a picnic bench at an isolated landmark outside Eternity Springs called Lover's Leap. Lifting her gaze from the rainbow of wildflowers adorning the valley below, she looked toward the mountain range rising beyond, where patches of snow clung stubbornly to shady spots. "It's a feast for the eyes," she murmured, speaking to herself as much as to the dog in her lap.

The day was a banquet for all the senses, in fact. Birdsong drifted on air perfumed with the clean, crisp scent of pine, its slight chill offset by the warmth of afternoon sunshine. When Savannah had mentioned she wanted to visit a high, peaceful, isolated place where she could meditate, her new friend Sarah Murphy had directed her here. "It's one of my favorite places in the entire world," Sarah had told her, a secret smile playing on her face.

No dummy, Savannah had concluded that Sarah and her husband, Cam, must use the remote spot for trysts, so when she'd asked for directions this morning, she'd made sure Cam and Sarah's plans for the day didn't include Lover's Leap.

Savannah hadn't confessed the real reason she wanted to visit such a place. What she planned to do here today was private; knowing her luck, she figured it probably broke a law or a regulation or a rule of some sort. All she needed was to get caught doing something illegal; this new life she was building could disappear in a heartbeat. So until she knew her new neighbors better, she didn't dare let on that she was anything less than a straight-arrow kind of woman.

Snorting, she said, "If they only knew."

At the sound of her voice her dog, Innocent, Inny for

short, lifted her head, her long ears perking up. Inny was a ten-pound, short-haired, white-with-brown-spots bundle of love. Savannah had found her abandoned at a rest area in Oklahoma three months ago, and it had been love at first sight for them both.

"I guess it's time to get started," Savannah told her. The dog's tiny tail wagged.

Savannah rose from the bench and glanced around, confirming that their privacy remained intact. The only other sign of life was a lone hawk sailing a thermal high above. Yet despite the secluded nature of the spot—or perhaps because of it—she felt her grandmother's spirit all around her.

"It's a beautiful place, Grams. The sky is a lovely blue and the air is crisp and clean. It reminds me of home. It's the prettiest of all the places we've visited since we left Georgia."

Savannah blinked back tears. Before she died, Rebecca Aldrich had sent her granddaughter a letter containing a request for the disposal of her remains should Savannah decide to leave the state. Previously she'd always intended to be buried at home on Firefly Mountain, but after everything that had happened, she couldn't bear the thought of being so close to the Vaughns. She'd asked Savannah to take her to . . . and leave her at . . . places that Savannah thought she would enjoy.

Savannah had begun planning her route since receiving news of her grandmother's death almost three years ago. She'd left Georgia with six different containers filled with her grandmother's remains. After stops at a beautiful beach, a lake in the Ozarks, a riverboat on the Mississippi, a wheat field in Kansas, and the courtyard of a Mexican food restaurant in Texas, she had arrived here today with a single muslin bag tucked into a button tin.

"This place is called Lover's Leap. It's not the highest

elevation around, but the canyon floor below us is a long way down. I think it's a perfect place for an angel to fly, Grams."

And now the final good-bye was upon her.

Savannah opened the large wicker picnic basket lined in a red bandanna print. She removed a Mason jar of clear liquid, two shot glasses, two Haviland china plates, a dinner knife, a yellow gingham napkin, a homemade pimento cheese sandwich—Grams' recipe—and an apple. Then she opened her tote bag and withdrew the battered cookie tin that Grams had used as a button box for as long as Savannah could remember.

Setting the tin in the middle of the picnic table, she used the knife to cut both the sandwich and the apple in half, then divided the food onto the two plates. She began to eat her lunch, sharing bites with Inny as she carried on a conversation with her grandmother.

"I think I've settled on my initial line of fragrances for the retail shop. I decided to limit the number to five after my visit to the handmade soap store at the upscale mall in Dallas. Their products are fabulous, but the scents assault a customer when she walks in. I want my store to be fresh, inviting, and tempting. Not cloying and not overpowering."

She munched her apple and pictured the property she'd rented with an option to buy on Fourth Street between Spruce and Pinyon. The house needed some work, but it had personality, and when she imagined it with a coat of paint, windows washed, and red geraniums on the porch, she sensed she would love living and working there. A previous owner had begun the conversion of the downstairs into retail space, and Savannah had hired a local schoolteacher, Jim Brand, who supplemented his income by taking handyman jobs, to complete it. Jim had promised to have the retail shop ready to open by Memorial Day.

"The workshop out back was converted from a carriage house," she said, speaking aloud as if her grandmother sat with her, sharing lunch. "It's a great place to work. The window above my workbench has a beautiful view. It's roomy and well ventilated, and the natural light is lovely. A friend has offered to build me shelves as a housewarming gift."

A friend? A special friend?

"No, Grams. Not that kind of friend. He's married. Besides, I don't want that kind of friend. I'm done with men. I learned my lesson."

Now, Savannah . . .

She raised her voice to drown out the one in her head. "Everyone in town calls my house the Golightly place, after the man who built it back in the 1800s. I considered keeping the name for the shop, but it just doesn't feel right. I had intended to call my store Fresh, but believe it or not, Eternity Springs already has a business called Fresh—Sarah Murphy's bakery. She makes the most spectacular cinnamon rolls. Anyway, what do you think of Heavenly Scents, Grams? Or maybe Heavenscents? Heavenscents, featuring Savannah Soap Company hand-crafted products?"

Her grandmother's voice whispered on the wind. *Why, Savannah Sophia, I think that would be right fine.*

Hearing voices in her head wasn't unusual for Savannah. She'd conversed with an imaginary friend, Melody, when she was a child. When she first arrived at Emmanuel, she'd resurrected Melody, fully aware that doing so was a defense mechanism.

Melody's voice had morphed into Grams' in the weeks after her grandmother had passed away. Now, if pressed, Savannah wouldn't swear that Grams' spirit wasn't actually speaking to her from beyond the grave.

Ordinarily they didn't share meals, but then this was a special event. The final event.

"Will I quit hearing you, Grams, once we do this?"

That depends.

"On what? Just how crazy those six years at Emmanuel made me?"

Now, Savannah . . .

Savannah sighed and polished off her half of the sandwich. Eyeing the other plate, she said, "Grams, you still eat like a bird. Shall I help?"

Another time, she would have been embarrassed by her playacting, but not today. She'd been on her way home to have lunch with her grandmother the day her world fell apart. During the awful weeks and months and years that followed, she'd promised herself that someday she would pick up her life where she'd left off. This was the best she could do.

With her meal over, she moved to the next item on the agenda by opening the Mason jar. She sniffed its contents and her eyes watered. "Whoa."

Savannah poured a splash of moonshine into each shot glass. Lifting one of them, she repeated the line her father had always said as he loaded filled jars into the wooden cases he'd built to transport his product to his customers: "Making family proud, one Mason jar at a time."

Saying it made her smile. Her grief for her father had eased in the nine years since his death, but she would always miss him. Despite his faults, the man had loved her.

The liquor burned like fire going down, causing Savannah to shudder. "Grams, I cannot believe you drank this every day and lived to see eighty-five."

All natural ingredients, my dear. And your father had a talent for making it.

Savannah laughed, then secured Inny's leash to the picnic table so that the dog wouldn't wander too close to the edge while Savannah was busy. Picking up the button box, she carried it and the second shot of moonshine toward the overlook, where a large flat rock stretched out over the valley like a plank on a pirate ship. She stood at the protective railing for a long time, her thoughts spinning back through the years, and she mourned.

When the time felt right, she held her glass high. "Here's to you, Grams."

She quoted the Irish blessing that her grandmother had cross-stitched in green thread against a cream linen background and hung in her parlor:

> *"May the road rise to meet you,*
> *May the wind be always at your back,*
> *May the sun shine warm upon your face,*
> *May the rains fall soft upon your fields,*
> *And, until we meet again,*
> *May God hold you in the hollow of his hand."*

She tossed back the drink, swallowed, shuddered, then drew back her arm and sent the empty glass flying. She watched it until it dropped out of sight, listening for the crash of glass against rock, but heard only the wind.

And the sound of her smothered sob.

Not good. Savannah didn't cry. She'd sworn off tears the day she entered Emmanuel, and she'd only suffered a backslide once.

Okay, twice.

Get this done, child. It's time.

"Yes. Okay." She blew out a heavy breath. Closing her eyes, she recited a prayer and swallowed the lump of emotion that had lodged in her throat. Tears welled, overflowing to trail down her cheeks as she removed the lid from the tin and stepped closer to the guardrail.

She wasn't a fan of heights. Gazing out over the valley was fine, but when she leaned forward and looked straight down, her knees went a little weak. The 'shine hadn't helped.

She tested the rail. It seemed sturdy enough. Good. She needed to be able to fling Grams out beyond the rock shelf so that the ashes sailed, soared, and flew on the breeze before falling back to earth. However, she didn't want to join her grandmother.

Maybe this was a bad idea. Maybe she should forget the plan entirely, put the lid back on the tin, take Grams home, and put her on the mantel. Hadn't her grade school friend Annie Hartsford kept her cat's ashes in a shoe box beneath her bed? Hadn't Eloise Rankin left her husband's ashes on a shelf in the garage for almost a year before her children convinced her to put him in the vault? She could—

Savannah Sophia.

"Okay. You're right. It's time." Inside the button tin lay the muslin bag containing the portion of her grandmother's remains that she had saved for this last dispersal in accordance with her grandmother's wishes. Grams had sewn these bags herself, filling them with soaps or salts for sale at retail shops in town. Savannah knew her grandmother would approve of her use of the bags rather than the funeral urn the mortuary had wanted to sell her. Rebecca Rose Aldrich hadn't liked waste.

Savannah removed the bag from the button box and set the tin on the ground. She untied the bag's blue ribbon and watched it flutter in the soft breeze, and in that moment a wave of grief struck her so hard that she swayed, then broke. Tears fell, and she released the sobs she'd held back for so long. She cried for her grandmother, for herself, for the cruel acts committed by "friends" against her family. She wept for the losses she'd endured.

It was a fierce storm, but also a fast one. Cleansed of the dark emotion, she felt a calm, warm sense of peace spread through her and strengthen her. She lifted the open bag up in front of her like an offering at an altar and said, "Rest in peace, Grams. You were my teacher, my nurturer, my family. You were my rock. I will miss you until the day I die."

Leaning over the railing, she shook the bag, waving it back and forth like a flag, and the contents spilled from the bag and sailed away on the breeze. With a bitter-sweet smile upon her face, Savannah watched ashes float and dance and dissolve against the blue springtime sky. "Good-bye, Grams."

Once the bag felt empty, she checked inside it and frowned to see a significant amount of ash clinging to the inner seam. She turned the bag inside out and, holding it by one corner, leaned over the railing once again and shook it hard.

Once. Twice. On the third shake, she lost her grip.

The muslin bag floated to the surface of the rock just beyond her reach.

TWO

❧

"Well, fiddle," Savannah muttered, using her grandmother's most wicked curse, as she scowled at the pouch. She couldn't leave it lying there. It wasn't completely empty. Besides, she wanted it for a keepsake. But did she want it enough to climb out onto the rock?

Great. Just freaking great. At some point the breeze would certainly blow it off the ledge and it would fall to the ground. Where it would lie. And rot.

"Damn." She glanced around for a stick or something else she could use to retrieve it, even as a gust of wind scooted it closer to the edge of the ledge.

Savannah watched the bag and knew she should let it go. It was only a bag. The ashes were ashes, the dust was dust.

She wanted it.

She gripped the railing and swung one leg and then the other over it. Without loosening her hold on the iron rail, she started to sink to her knees, planning to stretch for the bag's blue ribbon tie while keeping herself safely anchored to the ground.

Two things happened simultaneously. When the breeze scooped up the bag and sent it scooting toward the edge of the rock, Savannah reacted instinctively, lunging toward it.

And something clamped around her wrist.

Savannah let out a startled scream. Time seemed to slow to a crawl. Her gaze remained locked on the bag as it skittered toward the drop-off even as the vise around her arm yanked her backward.

She banged into the railing, and pain shot from her hip. Then she felt herself lifted and thrown backward in a fireman's carry. Her breath whooshed out as her diaphragm hit a broad, hard shoulder. For a moment Savannah was too stunned to struggle, too shocked to be afraid, but then a flashback to something that had happened when she was eighteen burst into her mind.

She'd been picking wildflowers in a high meadow above her grandmother's homestead when a big, burly, smelly mountain man emerged from the trees. The ratty jumpsuit he wore identified him as a prisoner, most likely someone who had walked off a road crew. He'd grabbed her and carried her toward the trees, his talk nasty and promising rape.

On that day she'd used her intellect and her knowledge of the mountain to escape before any real harm could be done to her. Now, while she didn't know this mountain, she still had her brain. Plus she'd learned a whole new set of survival skills during those six lost years. She could fight dirty when necessary.

Only a handful of seconds had passed since the stranger had grabbed her up and started toting her away from Lover's Leap, away from the keepsake bag. As she gathered herself to struggle, she felt her captor lean forward. Her body began to slip. Her butt landed hard on top of the picnic bench, and she looked up into a pair of aviator sunglasses.

He stood well over six feet tall in a spread-legged, aggressive stance, wearing faded jeans and an unbuttoned blue-plaid flannel shirt over a tight white T-shirt. Reaching up, he lifted the sunglasses off a straight blade of a nose to reveal piercing blue eyes. But it wasn't his movie-star good looks with those mesmerizing eyes, chiseled cheekbones, and sexy five o'clock shadow that made her mouth go dry.

The gun holstered at his waist managed that.

The moment Zach spied the leggy blonde climbing the barrier meant to block access to the ledge of rock that had given Lover's Leap its name, his heart lodged in his throat. He'd had a jumper in February and one in March. Be damned if he'd allow it to go three for three.

So he'd acted, moving silently forward so as not to startle her, not breathing freely until he'd clamped his hand around her wrist and managed to cart her away from danger's edge.

Once he had her over his shoulder he allowed his temper to flare. Life was precious. More than once he'd watched someone he loved fight for one more day of life in the face of terminal illness. Suicide totally pissed him off. It was the selfish act of a coward.

He toted the woman to the picnic bench, where he set her down a little roughly and demanded, "Give me one reason why I shouldn't haul you off in handcuffs."

Her jaw came up. Brown eyes snapped with temper. "Excuse me?"

With those two words he heard the slow, sexy heat of the Deep South in her voice. He'd always been a sucker for a true southern accent, so his temper flared even hotter imagining it ending in a splat at the bottom of the cliff. What a waste.

With his blood still pumping, his heart continuing to pound from the scare she'd given him moments before, he snarled, "Don't try to give me BS about attempted suicide not being illegal."

"Suicide! Listen, mister—"

"I don't have to charge you with that," he interrupted.

"I can start with reckless endangerment. Add in cruelty to animals, too. You were going to leave the poor dog tied to the picnic table to die of thirst?"

"You think I was going to jump?"

Judging by the scathing note in her tone, she might as well have added the words "you idiot."

Okay, so maybe he'd been wrong.

Nevertheless, climbing over the guardrail made her criminally stupid. It was too easy to imagine a strong gust of wind blowing her off the rock to her death. Dead was dead, no matter if through accidental death or by suicide. Both pissed Zach off.

As he opened his mouth to identify himself, her gaze shifted past him and she gasped. Zach turned to see the peach-colored bag with blue ribbons blow off the rock and sail away into nothing. *Had I not happened along, that could have been her body, not just the bag.* "Guess I can add littering in there, too."

"Gram!" She shoved down off the table and took two steps toward the ledge before Zach caught hold of her arm and held her back.

The woman whirled on him, a touch of panic added to the anger in her eyes. "It's gone. She's gone."

She's gone? Zach recalled his first sight of the woman. She'd been inching her way along the ledge, her arm outstretched toward that bag. "What was in the bag?"

"Not what. Who. I wasn't going to jump, you idiot," she claimed, her molasses tone scathing. "I was spreading my grandmother's ashes and lost hold of the bag."

Not a jumper. Just a fool. "Did you have a permit for that?"

She folded her arms and scowled. "Who are you?"

Zach didn't wear his uniform while fishing on his day off, but he always carried a weapon and his badge. He pulled the shield from his back pocket and flipped the worn leather folder open. "Sheriff Zach Turner. May I see some identification, ma'am?"

She momentarily closed her eyes and her lips formed a silent oath. At her reaction, Zach stifled a grin.

When finally she looked at him, she did so through narrowed eyes. "It's not illegal to spread human ashes in Colorado. You can hire a pilot and plane to do it. I couldn't afford that, so I did this instead."

"We have a local ordinance against that, ma'am. Your driver's license, please?"

She held his stare for a long moment. He could almost see the wheels turning in her mind until suddenly tears welled in her big brown eyes. "It was all I had of her . . . the bag . . . I wanted to keep it. A keepsake. Oh, Grams."

Her obvious sadness stirred every chivalrous atom in his DNA to life, and when the tears overflowed, a ridiculous offer to climb down the sheer cliff and retrieve her bag hovered on his tongue. Zach wore the thrill-seeker label proudly and carried climbing gear in his truck at all times, but descending the sheer rock face from Lover's Leap wasn't done on a whim. He wasn't a man ordinarily manipulated by tears, and he didn't like the idea that it was happening now. His voice gruff, he began, "Listen, lady—"

"Savannah. My name is Savannah."

Ah. He put the clues together. "Savannah Sophia Moore. You're the new girl in town. The soap maker."

A wary look entered her eyes.

"My friends mentioned you," he explained. "You're the talk of Eternity Springs."

"I am?"

"New resident and business owner. It's great for the tax base."

Now that he wasn't busy saving her from suicide or drowning in her eyes, he understood why Nic and the others had been quick to mention her to him. The woman was gorgeous.

Long, thick lashes framed those spectacular brown eyes. Her hair was a just-out-of-bed sexy blond tousle, and her cheekbones were high and her lips full. Then there was that *Sports Illustrated* swimsuit issue build. Seriously gorgeous, seriously hot. A true Georgia peach any man would like to pick.

Once again she cast a sorrowful gaze toward the point. "Sarah Murphy told me about this place. I've hardly encountered any red tape as I've settled into Eternity Springs, so it never occurred to me that I'd need a permit for today's private matter." Wiping away the tears, she added, "My grandmother raised me after my mother died. We were very close. Losing her has broken my heart. I'm afraid I didn't think things through properly."

Now Zach felt like a heel. "Don't worry about the permit. Just promise me you won't disregard warning signs or climb over guardrails or do anything else reckless, and we'll call it a wash."

"Thank you. And you don't have to worry about me, Sheriff. I have absolutely no intention of doing anything to cause you further concern."

He was distracted from the vehement note in her voice by the power of the smile that accompanied the thankyou. It was sunshine giving birth to a rainbow in the aftermath of a violent storm. The beauty of it, of her, took his breath away.

He stared at her, suddenly tongue-tied. All his usual masculine confidence and swagger disappeared beneath a flood of bashfulness. He felt like a high school freshman trying to talk to the senior girl he had a crush on.

He shoved his hands into his pockets but managed to stop himself from rocking back and forth on his heels. Her gaze returned to the point, and she spoke in a wistful tone. "I suppose it would be impossible for me to locate my bag from below."

Zach was more familiar than he'd have liked with the section of the Double R Ranch that lay below Lover's Leap because he had to deal with the bodies of the jumpers. "It would take a miracle, I'm afraid. It's possible to predict where heavy things fall, but something as light as that drawstring bag . . . no telling how far the wind carried it."

Savannah's teeth tugged at her full lower lip as she sighed. "I'm detail-oriented, and I thought I had everything planned out. The bag was a sentimental choice but a poor one. I'll simply have to live with it."

"The land in the valley below belongs to a rancher friend of mine. I'll put out the word for his people to keep an eye out for it."

"Again, thank you for your assistance, Sheriff. I apologize for keeping you from whatever you were doing when you decided I needed rescue."

"Fishing. It's my day off, and I've been fishing a little lake not far from here. Didn't have much luck, I'm afraid."

"That's a shame." She glanced toward the parking area, where an old Ford Taurus was the lone car parked. "I didn't see another vehicle when I arrived."

The Taurus surprised him. He'd have expected something flashier—and more expensive—from a woman with her million-dollar looks. "My truck's back in the trees. I fished the creek before I climbed to the lake."

"I see. Well, don't let me keep you, Sheriff. I'm going to gather up my basket and my dog and return to town. I promise to dispose of all my litter and properly observe all traffic signs on the way. I'll be the poster child for law-abiding citizens of Eternity Springs."

If she wanted to be an Eternity Springs poster child, then the Chamber of Commerce people should tag her for tourist brochures. She was every bit as beautiful as the photo of sailboats on Hummingbird Lake that they currently used. *Jeez, Turner, keep this line of thought up and next thing you know you'll be spouting sonnets.*

"We're always happy to have more law-abiding residents. Welcome to Eternity Springs, Savannah. If there is anything I can do to help you settle in, just let me know. My office is on Cottonwood Street."

"Thank you."

She bent to pick up her dog, and he couldn't think of anything else to say, so he turned to go. He was halfway to his truck before he realized he'd walked off without the gear he'd dropped when he believed he had another jumper on his hands.

Zach felt like an idiot. It wasn't like him to let a woman throw him off stride this way. Honestly, Savannah Moore wasn't that much more gorgeous than Inga, and he'd never gone stupid over the ski instructor.

Had she noticed that he'd walked off without his stuff? How could he retrieve it without looking like a fool? "Good luck with that," he muttered.

He could leave it and return for it later. Were it not his new fly rod . . .

Turning around, he trudged back toward Lover's Leap, completely annoyed with himself and casting about for an excuse he could give. He finally decided that the best excuse was no excuse. He would simply stroll back to where his gear lay and act like he'd intended to walk off without his stuff. Let her think what she would.

But as he approached the point, the sound of her voice had him slowing his steps. As a former undercover cop, he had plenty of experience at eavesdropping, and even though he knew doing so now bordered on stalking, he did it anyway.

". . . moved to Mayberry. I was hoping for Andy Taylor, but instead I get clueless Barney Fife. It's scary to think someone like that is allowed to carry a gun."

Zach stopped abruptly. *Barney Fife? Did that woman just call me Barney Fife?*

"And he was a bit of a perv, spreading his hand all over my butt when he carried me . . ."

A pervert? She's calling me a pervert, too? I was saving her life!

". . . and he kept checking out my chest."

Okay, he pleaded guilty there, but what did she expect when she wore a scoop-neck top that teased him by gaping? And who the hell was she talking to, anyway?

Mouth set in a firm line, he shifted off the path and made his way quietly forward until he could see her and verify that no one had joined her. She must be talking to the dog. Or to herself.

She rolled a yellow tennis ball, and as her dog bounded after it, she continued, "A sheriff. I guess there is something to the whole long-arm-of-the-law thing. I flee to the middle of freaking nowhere, but I can't get away from it. Isn't that just my luck? Some people go their whole lives without having run-ins with the law. Not me. Oh, no. I'm plagued by police. They are the bane of my existence. Every time I turn around, I run into a cop. Or like today, a cop runs into me. Literally."

The dog pounced on the ball, then plopped down on her belly and started chewing at it. Savannah snapped her fingers. "Bring the ball back, Inny."

When the dog ignored her, Zach smirked.

She sighed and strolled over to wrestle the ball away from the mutt. "He should be charged with police brutality. I'm going to have a bruise where his bony shoulder poked my belly."

She rolled the ball again while muttering indistinctly, so the only word he picked up was "manhandler." Zach scowled. That was plenty enough to hear. Ungrateful witch.

The dog started toward the tennis ball but suddenly veered away on a scent. As she dashed into the trees opposite him and Savannah chased after her, Zach saw his chance and hurried to retrieve his rod and tackle box. Five minutes later, he climbed into his truck and twisted the key in the ignition with more force than was necessary.

He was pissed. He didn't expect every woman who crossed his path to like him, but the truth was that most all of them did. Female acquaintances viewed him favorably, and some of his closest friends were women. He'd never had trouble getting dates. He remained on good terms with most of his former lovers. He liked women. Women liked him.

And, dammit, he was a good cop! *Barney Fife, my ass,* he thought.

So what put the pit in the Georgia peach?

He mentally reviewed their exchange, attempting to pinpoint the moment when her mood went cold. As he braked to a stop at the intersection to the main road into town, he figured it out. The woman had bristled when he'd identified himself and asked for her ID.

"Well, well, well," Zach murmured. Savannah Sophia Moore had a secret.

Guess he'd just have to put on his detective hat and discover what it was.

THREE

Savannah spent most of her time in the week follow-ing her unexpected meeting with the sheriff in her work-shop, creating product, ordering supplies, and squeezing every possible bit of buying power from each penny she spent. When Jim Brand presented his under-budget in-voice upon completion of the renovations of the retail space, she'd been hard-pressed not to do handsprings. Overall, start-up costs hadn't been as onerous as she'd anticipated, and as she double-checked the balance in her checkbook, she noted that she had plenty of wiggle room in her budget. The regular pounding of a hammer out in her workshop reminded her that her good fortune was due in no small part to her new Eternity Springs neighbors. They'd all proven quick to offer a helping hand.

At this moment, Colt Rafferty was building the shelves for her workshop. His wife was due to come by any mo-ment with her baby and the balance of their housewarm-ing gift. It felt like Christmas morning to Savannah.

The town of Eternity Springs was an eclectic mix of commercial and residential space with most business properties aligned along one of the four "tree" streets, Cottonwood, Pinyon, Spruce, and Aspen, with most but not all of the houses in town located on the numbered streets, First through Eighth. Apparently zoning had never been a consideration. Since Savannah's place was on Fourth between Spruce and Pinyon, the retail shop she planned needed something eye-catching to lure tourists down the side street.

Impressed by the signage across the street at Vistas, Savannah had asked for the name of the graphic designer responsible for the art gallery's logo. After claiming the design as her own, Sage had offered to do the logos that Savannah needed as a gift. What Savannah hadn't known at the time she accepted her new friend's largesse was that in addition to being the gallery's business owner and manager, Sage was a renowned artist with a studio above her shop.

The generosity overwhelmed Savannah. She'd seen so little of it in recent years, and she didn't quite know how to react. She knew she came across as standoffish and perhaps even unfriendly, and she was working on improving that impression. Maybe in time she could actually make friends with some of these people—as long as they didn't find out about her, of course. People who knew what she was, where she'd been, wouldn't want to count her as a friend. The nice people of Eternity Springs would run her out of town.

She was saved from going down that particular dark path by a knock on the door. Sage stood on the front porch with nine-month-old Colton Alexander strapped into a stroller. The boy was a darling little butterball with red hair and rosy cheeks, and he gnawed happily on the handle of a green plastic toy hammer. Savannah couldn't help but smile at the sight. Her arms ached to lift him out of the stroller.

Determinedly she quashed the maternal ache and lifted her gaze. Spying the sketchbook in Sage's arm, Savannah's pulse accelerated. Despite all the planning and work she'd done to get her business up and running,

Savannah Soap Company and Heavenscents didn't seem real to her yet. She suspected that having logos might change that.

"Welcome," she said, opening the screen door. "Please come on in, you two."

Sage tucked an errant strand of wavy red hair behind her ear, then gestured toward the porch steps. "It's the three of us. Snowdrop is hoping that Inny would like a play date."

"Of course. Inny would love . . ." Savannah's voice trailed off as she got a good look at her neighbor's dog. "Oh, my. What is that dog wearing?"

Sage flashed an unapologetic grin. "It's her Easter dress. And hat, of course."

The ensemble worn by the white ball of fur—a bichon frise—consisted of something that looked like a knit sweater with an attached tutu in pastel pink netting. The hat was a little straw bonnet tied with a ribbon. "Okay, then," Savannah said, amused. "Guess you were hoping for a girl when you had your boy?"

Sage laughed. "No, Snowdrop's outfits predate my marriage. They started as a joke between Colt and me, but now she wouldn't be Snowdrop without her finery. Besides, she's an excellent marketing tool because she draws children along with their parents into the gallery. She's never as happy as when she is sitting in someone's lap being petted. Everybody is relaxed, and I end up selling more."

"Hmm . . ." Savannah cast a considering glance toward Inny. "I'll have to keep that in mind. Maybe I could have a T-shirt made for Inny to wear that says 'Smell me' to advertise my pet shampoo."

Interest lit Sage's eyes. "You make pet shampoo, too?"

"I do. My grandmother loved her pets, and she had one dog that lived to get dirty and stinky. She figured out a recipe that worked to her standards, and she sent it off to the University of Georgia to make sure it was safe."

"You'll have to tell Nic. She'll stock it at the clinic if you'd like. We like to do cross-marketing whenever possible."

"I noticed the VISIT VISTAS sign beneath the portrait of the Callahans' boxer hanging in her vet office."

"Clarence. He's so ugly that he's cute. And he has the sweetest disposition. I can't say the same about Cam's Boston terrier, though. Have you crossed paths with Mortimer yet?"

"No."

"Cam calls him the 'Boston terrorist' for good reason. He—"

Sage broke off abruptly when the baby let out a squeal, waved his arm, and the hammer went flying. "Dada! Dada!"

"Alex!" Sage scolded. "Don't throw your toys."

"My fault." Colt Rafferty opened the back door and stepped into Savannah's kitchen. "He saw me standing on the stoop and he was saying hello."

Savannah watched with a twinge of emotion she refused to name as envy when Colt greeted his wife with a casual kiss, then bent to release the safety strap on the carriage and lift his babbling son into his arms. "Hey, Racer. Have you been a good boy for Mommy this morning?"

"Racer?" Savannah asked, curious.

"His initials are CAR," Sage explained with a sigh.

"Racer Rafferty. He crawls at light speed," Colt added. He nipped playfully at the boy's fingers, then lifted his voice to speak above the giggles. "Your shelves are finished, Savannah. The paint needs the rest of today to dry, but tomorrow you'll be good to go."

"I can't thank you enough, Colt."

"Glad to help. We do that here in Eternity Springs. It's

the most neighborly place I've ever lived." He glanced at his wife. "I need to stop by the Callahans' and talk to Gabe about the rocking chair he wants me to build for one of his sisters-in-law. Want me to take the little man? You know Meg and Cari will want to play with him."

"The Callahan twins are almost four. Alex is their own living, breathing doll," Sage explained to Savannah. "I'll be thrilled if you take him, Colt. I need to do some paperwork this afternoon, and that would make it so much easier."

While the Raffertys spent the next few minutes making child care arrangements, Savannah led Snowdrop to the backyard. Inny barked an excited hello and the two dogs began to scamper. Savannah returned to the front room just as Colt and his son departed.

"We are still trying to find our way when it comes to balancing parenting and work," Sage said, watching them go. "Nic and Gabe make it look so easy—with twins—that I thought Colt and I would have smooth sailing. Boy, was I naive."

"Have you considered putting him into day care?"

"We have a babysitter lined up for him once tourist season starts and I need to spend more time at the gallery. The problem is that the U.S. Chemical Safety and Hazard Investigation Board has called Colt in to consult about last week's plant explosion in Ohio."

"Oh, the one that killed so many people?"

Sage nodded. "It's just horrible. Thirty-three dead, sixty-seven hospitalized. He's leaving tomorrow, and I'll be on full-time mommy duty for at least the next two weeks, which is fine with me—except that I need to spend most of my time in the studio or I won't be ready for my next show."

"I'll be happy to watch this little bit of sugar for you some while Colt is out of town, Sage." A bittersweet memory washed over Savannah as she added, "I do have some experience with toddlers. My nephew lived with me when he was the same age as Alex."

"Really? I'll be thrilled to take you up on it. Thank you." Sage reached out and gave Savannah a quick, friendly hug.

Instinctively Savannah stiffened. She didn't like being touched—a remnant of the Emmanuel years.

Luckily, Sage didn't appear to notice, and Savannah felt a wave of relief. The last thing she wanted to do was to offend her new friend.

"Now," Sage continued, "let me show you what I've come up with for your logos. They're only sketches, mind you, and if they're not what you had in mind, don't hesitate to say so. You won't hurt my feelings."

"I love your work, Sage," Savannah said as the other woman flipped open her sketchbook. "I can't imagine not . . . oh, wow." In front of her were three different conceptualizations of the word *Heavenscents* done in shades of peach and blue. Each of them was wonderful, but Savannah's eyes were immediately drawn to one with a halo hovering over the *t*. "I love them all, but the halo . . . it's perfect. Just perfect."

Sage beamed. "It's my favorite, too. The font gives it a floaty feel, and the halo is fun. It's inviting, and it suits a shop in Eternity Springs."

"It suits me."

"I figured it would. After all, you named your dog Innocent." Sage flipped the page and continued, "I went with a different look for the Savannah Soap Company. Clean and natural, feminine but not frilly."

"Simple. I love it, too, Sage." The artist had taken her vague ideas and created something special and unique. Excitement swelled inside Savannah. After months— actually years—of planning, her dream was about to come true. "Again, I can't thank you enough. These are wonderful, and you are wonderful, and your husband is wonderful. Your baby and dog are wonderful. Eternity Springs is the most wonderful place in the world."

Laughing, Sage said, "Tell me what you really think."

Savannah gave a bashful smile. "A little over the top, hmm?"

"Maybe a little. That's okay, though. We are pretty wonderful, if I say so myself." Sage glanced around the room and added, "Speaking of wonderful, I love the colors you've chosen to represent your business. Peach is so warm and inviting—it looks great on the walls. The complementary shade of blue you've used is the perfect accent color. With the fresh scents . . . I predict that people will come into your shop and linger. And buy."

"Thank you. I'm glad you think so. That's the idea." Savannah couldn't contain her enthusiasm as she outlined her plans for the store. "The entire downstairs will be open to the public. Most of my space will be devoted to the mail order portion of the business, since that's where I'll have most of my sales, but I'm not going to segregate the two aspects. I want retail customers to be aware of the mail order operation."

Sage nodded thoughtfully. "For repeat business. The tourist who purchases your bath soap while on vacation and falls in love with it at home will know it's easy to replenish her stock."

"That's the idea."

"An excellent one. How do you intend to set up your displays?"

"I'm going to keep the look and feel of a residence, with home products displayed inside the home. I'm in the market for Victorian antiques, so if you know of a source . . ."

"I might. Have you been inside Cavanaugh House yet?"

"Is that the big mansion on the grounds of the spa resort?"

"At Angel's Rest, yes."

"I visited yesterday. It's fabulous. The furnishings just in the lobby are enough to make me green with envy."

"They're original to the house. The owner, Celeste Blessing, has heaps more in storage. When she bought the property, the contents of Cavanaugh House were included. She's away at an innkeepers' conference now, but when she returns, you should talk to her. I'll bet she'd be happy to sell you some things for Heavenscents."

"It's a lovely thought, but I'm sure I couldn't afford them."

"Talk to her. You might be surprised. Celeste has a way of working miracles for people. Knowing Celeste, she might commission some business from you, too. Angel's Rest already has a signature line of lotions and soaps, but Celeste does like to stir things up fairly regularly. She may be ready for a change."

The two women discussed that possibility and Savannah's plans for a few more minutes, then Savannah presented Sage with the huge basket of lotions and soaps she'd prepared as a thank-you gift. Sage sifted through the contents, then beamed with delight. "Ooh, a lavender bath melt. That will be my reward for sitting through the Chamber of Commerce planning committee meeting tonight."

"Are they that boring?"

Sage winced. "Oops. You are still planning to attend, aren't you?"

"I was, but now I wonder . . ."

"They're not horrible, I promise, and we really can use some new blood on the committee."

"New blood? For what . . . ritual sacrifice?"

"Don't be silly." Sage crossed to the back door and

called for Snowdrop, and after the dog bounded to her, she affixed the leash to her pet's collar. She scooped up the gift basket, shot Savannah a grin, and added, "Although I'd think twice about bringing your pet chicken along."

Zach strode into the Eternity Springs sheriff's office with a dozen different problems rattling through his brain. Since his last day off a week ago, he'd dealt with one firestorm after another. He had a list of follow-up issues as long as his arm, and while the good citizen in him was glad to see Eternity Springs grow, he couldn't deny that he missed the good old slow days. Spying his dispatcher, a sixty-eight-year-old salty-tongued wonder woman named Ginger Harris, he asked, "Have we heard back from Judge Landry about that warrant?"

"Not yet."

Zach sighed. "I'll call him again."

Ginger held up a stack of yellow slips. "The phone has been ringing off the wall since Jeremy Paulson posted his video of a bear on his backyard trampoline online and it went viral. You have half a dozen interview requests from radio talk shows and cable news. They've made the connection that you won the Governor's Award for heroism, so they're wild to talk to you."

Zach groaned as he hung his hat on the rack beside his desk. "I'm too busy for nonsense like that."

"Mayor Townsend called with a special request that you at least give a couple interviews and mention that Eternity Springs is safe and we don't have bears roaming the streets of the town. He's afraid this publicity will hurt tourism."

Zach propped his elbows on his desk, closed his eyes, and massaged his temples with his fingertips. He knew better than to speak the heresy that from his perspective, less tourism wasn't such a bad thing. More people in town meant more people behaving badly, which meant more work for him. This spring break season was the worst he'd seen since he'd taken the sheriff's job in Colorado. After four years working undercover infiltrating the methamphetamine trade in Oklahoma, he'd wanted— hell, he'd needed—a nice, laid-back, boring job. He'd had it, too, until Celeste Blessing revived Eternity Springs by opening Angel's Rest.

Ginger set a stack of mail on his desk and asked, "Did you get any hits on the fingerprints from the burglary out at the Pulaski place?"

"Turns out they belonged to a houseguest who they had forgotten had visited."

"That's too bad."

"Yep."

"Any other leads?"

"Nope."

"Well, now, that's just splendid. Maybe I should call Jeremy and tell him to bring his video camera to the sheriff's office."

Zach lifted his gaze and scowled at her. "Excuse me? Why in the world would you say that?"

"Jeremy specializes in bear videos, doesn't he? I see one great big angry one sitting in front of me."

Zach bared his teeth and growled at her. Ginger laughed, then asked, "What can I do to help you, Zach?"

"Have we had any resumes arrive that seem promising?"

"I put two into your in-box. They're the best we've received."

The tone of her voice didn't sound promising, but as he searched through his box for the résumés, Zach held out a glimmer of hope that at least one of these applicants would do. When he returned to the office following

his day off a week ago, he'd learned that his deputy—
a navy reservist—had been called to active duty. This,
two weeks after his other deputy took a job in Durango.
Since then he'd averaged only four hours of sleep per
night, and he couldn't keep up the pace much longer.

With the tourist season bearing down upon him—pun
intended—he needed to hire help fast. If they did have
an emergency, he'd be deputizing friends in order to deal
with it, and that was no way to run a law enforcement
office.

He scanned both resumes and remained underwhelmed.
However, his in-box was beginning to resemble Murphy
Mountain, and since Ginger had a point about his grizzly-
bear attitude, he picked up the phone on his desk and
called the first candidate. Martin Varney answered on
the third ring and was happy to participate in a telephone interview with no advance notice.

Zach made notes on a yellow legal pad as he spoke to
Varney. Concentrating on the conversation, he paid
scant attention when the front door opened and Ginger
rose to greet the man who stepped inside. Ten minutes
later, encouraged by what he'd heard, Zach ended the
call by inviting Varney to town for an in-person interview. Only when he hung up the phone did he tune in to
the conversation between Ginger and the stranger. He
frowned when he realized that his dispatcher was cooing.

The man was tall and athletic-looking, with dark hair
and a face that Zach recognized, though it took him a
moment of thought to place him. "Coach Romano?"

Zach followed college sports. Anthony Romano was
an assistant men's basketball coach for the University of
Colorado.

"No, Tony is my brother. I'm Max Romano."

"Max Romano," Zach repeated. "So, you're not the
coach at Western State, either."

"No. That's Lucca."

"You share a strong family resemblance."

"True, but I'm better-looking," Max fired back with the ease of an oft-stated claim. "I don't coach basketball, either. I realize I don't have an appointment, Sheriff Turner, but I'm hoping you have a few moments to spare? Ginger wasn't certain."

In fact, Ginger knew very well that he didn't have the time, but obviously Romano had charmed her. "Is there a problem?"

Following an almost imperceptible moment of hesitation, he answered. "That's what I'm hoping to find out. I'm on a fact-finding mission for our family. We have some questions."

"Questions about what?"

This time Max Romano's hesitation was noticeable. "Could we speak privately?"

Ginger's eyes gleamed with curiosity, but she took the hint and picked up her purse. "I'll make the lunch run now, Sheriff. You want your usual from Fresh?"

"That'll be great, Ginger. Thanks."

As his dispatcher slipped out the door, Zach gestured for Max Romano to take a seat in the chair opposite his desk. "So, what can I do for you?"

Romano sat, rested his elbows on his knees, and leaned forward, meeting Zach's gaze with a serious, intent look. He seemed to choose his words carefully as he said, "I'd like to hear your assessment of what life is like in Eternity Springs."

For this he needs a sheriff? "That sounds like something better suited to the tourist office. You should talk to—"

"You. I'm interested in what you have to say."

"Why me?"

"I prefer to speak to the man who lives in the trenches,

not someone who's trained in talking points." Romano pursed his lips. "Listen, Sheriff, I'll cut to the chase. My family has troubling personal issues, and we think Eternity Springs might help us."

Troubling personal issues? Zach went on guard, though he made sure to keep his expression blank. Personal issues had a way of becoming public issues, which often became his problem.

"You see," Romano continued, "my father died earlier this year, and my mother is devastated. They were married thirty-two years, and her heart is truly broken. It's been suggested to our family that an extended visit to the area might help Mother deal with her grief. Apparently Eternity Springs has developed a . . . reputation for, well, healing broken hearts."

Nothing to concern law enforcement, then. Good. Zach cleared his throat. "Our resident wise woman says this valley has a healing energy."

"Celeste Blessing."

"You've met our Celeste?"

He shook his head. "Not yet. My sister has spoken with her. Apparently Ms. Blessing is quite the ambassador."

"She is," Zach replied. She was an uncannily good judge of character, too, and Zach's concerns eased. "What exactly would you like to know?"

"I'd like you to tell me whatever you think someone moving to Eternity Springs should know. The real story, not the Chamber of Commerce talking points."

Zach didn't have time for this, but his job was partially political in nature, and this man's brother was a minor celebrity in Colorado, so he tempered his annoyance. "And this someone would be your mother?"

"Actually, I have a lot of siblings. It's very possible one or more of us will join our mother here."

"I see. Would this be a seasonal stay—you'd be summer residents?"

"Mother is on an extended Mediterranean cruise with her sister, my aunt Bridget. She wouldn't arrive here until the fall. It's possible some of us might spend the winter here."

"In that case, I'll give you a year-round report. Most important as far as I'm concerned is that we only have one really good restaurant in town—the Yellow Kitchen—and the owner, Ali Timberlake, doesn't like Mexican food, so you're pretty much SOL if you crave enchiladas. Eternity Springs residents consider early March the best time to go on a warm-weather vacation, since that's when winter weighs upon a man. Beyond those two things, I think it's important to know that the pace of life here is slow, and in the winter it crawls. Not everyone is cut out for it."

Romano studied Zach. "You like it here?"

"I do, but then I enjoy winter sports."

"What if you're not a sports enthusiast? Are there any book clubs in town?"

Zach nodded. "We have a book club and a quilt group and church groups. Honestly, people who live here are not any different from people who live elsewhere. We work, we play, we laugh, we love. . . ." Movement outside his office window distracted him momentarily and reminded him of that background check he'd yet to find time to make. Savannah Moore sashayed across the street carrying a brown lunch sack. When she took a seat on his favorite bench beside Angel Creek, another observation just rolled off his tongue. "We lust."

He pulled his gaze back to Romano and found the man smirking. A little embarrassed, Zach brought his chin up. "Eternity Springs is a good place. It's my job to make sure it stays that way. I hope I've been of some help to you, Mr. Romano. Now, if you'll excuse me, I need to get back at it."

"Of course." Romano stood and extended his hand. "I appreciate your time and your insight, Sheriff."

The man's grip was firm and confident, his smile easy and genuine. Yet, as he sauntered out the door, Zach found himself frowning after him. Something about Max Romano made his trouble radar go off. What was it?

His gaze shifted back to the window and locked on the creekside bench where Savannah sat eating a sandwich. Maybe Romano wasn't the source of his unease, after all. Maybe the visitor simply had been caught in the fallout from Savannah Moore.

"Barney freaking Fife," he muttered, the bruise to his ego as annoying as it had been a week ago.

Since Zach had barely had time to breathe since then, he hadn't found time to follow up on his questions about the Georgia peach. He would take care of that right now. He had asked Ginger to begin the process earlier that week, so he dug around for the note she'd left on his desk with sultry Savannah's license plate number. He found the paper beneath a stack of faxes, turned to his computer, and went to work. Within minutes, he had confirmed that she was thirty years old and that Georgia was her previous state of residence.

Then a screen popped up that stopped him. "Well, hell."

He drummed his fingers on his keyboard for a moment as he thought about what to do. Abruptly he deleted the form, then ran a criminal history check through the Colorado Crime Information Center and National Crime Information Center databases.

He got a hit and repeated, "Well, hell."

Next he ran a QR, a query rap sheet. What came back had his stomach taking a nauseated roll. *Son of a bitch. Right under his nose.*

Ginger returned to the office with his lunch to find Zach staring blindly out the window. "What are you looking at, Zach?"

He let out a long, heavy sigh and spoke a single, heartfelt word. "Trouble."

FOUR

The Eternity Springs Chamber of Commerce planning committee met in a conference room on the second floor of the Tourist Information Center, a pleasant two-and-a-half-block walk for Savannah. After an afternoon shower, the clouds had cleared away and sunshine sparkled on the rainwater that dripped from rooftops and splattered into thirsty flower boxes. The town certainly had its flowers on, she observed. In addition to lush hanging baskets and bulging window boxes, huge pots of red geraniums, purple alliums, and yellow lilies lined the street. The cheerful sight made her smile.

Savannah needed a smile. She was nervous. This would be her first appearance at anything halfway official in Eternity Springs, and she wanted to make a good impression. Easier said than done, since the majority of her experience lay at the other end of the spectrum, and her role models for making a good impression were limited.

Reinventing oneself wasn't easy. Especially since the more she got to know the people of Eternity Springs, the more she worried that they'd find out about her past.

Savannah was crossing Second Street when she heard someone call her name. She turned to see perky, petite Sarah Murphy and a redheaded woman she didn't know crossing Spruce Street toward her. She plastered on a smile. "Hello."

"Hi, Savannah," Sarah replied. "Sage told me you might be coming to tonight's meeting. I'm so glad to have another sucker . . ." She flashed a grin and finished, "Um . . . I mean, volunteer, to help. Have you met Cat Davenport?" She gestured toward her companion.

"No, I haven't had the pleasure."

"In that case, let me introduce you to the owner of our weekly newspaper, *Eternity Times*. Cat also helps her husband, Jack, oversee the children's charity that is building the new summer camp up on Murphy Mountain. Cat, Savannah Moore makes the most wonderful soaps and lotions."

"It's so nice to meet you." Cat smiled brightly as she shook Savannah's hand. "Ali Timberlake put your lavender lotion in the ladies' room at her restaurant. It's wonderful."

She noticed the lotion? Savannah was secretly thrilled. "Thank you."

"Cat is a relative newcomer to Eternity Springs, too," Sarah said. Her eyes sparkled with mischief as she added, "Last year she was kidnapped and imprisoned in a luxury estate outside town."

"Oh, no," Savannah said, her eyes widening even as Cat Davenport smirked.

"By her ex-husband," Sarah added. "Whom she remarried in March."

Savannah fumbled for something to say, eventually settling on, "That sounds like quite a story."

"At times I thought it might have a homicide subplot," Cat said dryly. "He was careful to keep his guns away from me, thank goodness."

"I see." Savannah smiled tightly. Where she came from, homicide and guns were not a joking matter.

Talk moved to general subjects as they completed

their walk to the tourist center. There, Savannah made a stop in the ladies' room while Sarah and Cat went on upstairs. When she joined them in the conference room, she saw the tables arranged in a square with the majority of the seats taken. Sarah waved, then indicated she'd saved Savannah a seat next to her.

The mayor sat at the table on her left at the center. Savannah turned to her right and noticed her favorite handyman and high school English and history teacher, Jim Brand. She smiled and waved hello to the handsome older man. He winked back. The mayor picked up his gavel and knocked it on the table just as two newcomers stepped into the room and took seats directly opposite Savannah.

Immediately her spine stiffened.

Having Zach Turner seated directly across from her, light glinting off the sheriff's badge pinned to a khaki uniform shirt, was bad enough, but the woman seated at his right caused a visceral negative reaction within her so strong that nausea churned in Savannah's stomach.

The woman was older—mid- to late sixties, she'd guess. Dressed in sky-blue capri pants and a white blouse, she had cheery blue eyes and a friendly smile. Silver earrings shaped like wings dangled from her ears.

She could have been Francine Vaughn's twin.

The fact that she traveled with a sheriff only made the resemblance more disturbing. Kyle was a cop, not a sheriff, but as far as Savannah was concerned, a badge was a badge.

Or, speaking metaphorically, a baseball bat. A knife to the heart.

Mayor Townsend called the meeting to order. "We have a good turnout tonight. Thank you all for showing up. Celeste, I didn't think you'd be back from your trip for another week."

Francine Vaughn's doppelgänger spoke. "I came home early. I'd been away from Angel's Rest for too long and I'd become a little homesick."

Celeste. Angel's Rest. This must be the famous Celeste Blessing. The woman who, according to everyone Savannah had met here in town, was considered to be the beloved angel of Eternity Springs.

Just like Francine.

Francine had fooled everyone. Especially Grams. Rattled, Savannah reached for the water glass sitting in front of her and missed, bumping it. Water sloshed and splashed onto the table. While Savannah stared stupidly at the mess, Sarah took a tissue from her bag and wiped it up.

She leaned over and whispered, "No need to be nervous, Savannah."

The mayor continued. "Well, we're glad to have you back, Celeste. Town just isn't the same without you."

Oh, wow. They even fawn over her the same way people did Francine.

The mayor continued. "We have a new member of the Chamber I want to recognize. For those of you who haven't met her yet, Savannah Moore is our newest resident and merchant. She is working to open a gift shop in the old Golightly place. She wants to help us clean up our town with her specialty soaps and lotions. Welcome to Eternity Springs and the Chamber of Commerce, Savannah."

"Thank you," she said quietly as those seated around the conference tables broke out in spontaneous applause.

The sheriff kept his hands beneath the table, and so she couldn't tell if he participated or not.

Mayor Townsend continued. "Now, on to business. I promised Zach we'd keep this meeting short, so I plan to rip right through my list."

Savannah made a point to keep her gaze on the mayor and away from the man seated across from her. That didn't stop her from feeling the weight of the sheriff's gaze—make that the sheriff's cold, flat, faintly accusatory glare—upon her. *Just why does he have a stick up his butt toward me, anyway? I haven't so much as crossed paths with him in a week.*

Unless . . . has he checked up on me?

No, why would he do that? She'd given him no reason to do so. Why, she'd been sweet as sugarcane to the man.

"LaNelle, would you like to update us on plans for this year's quilt festival?" the mayor asked.

The owner of the town's needlework shop, LaNelle Harrison, flipped open a manila folder. "Certainly. It's almost hard to believe, and it makes me worry about where we are going to put everyone, but registrations are running twenty-five percent above this time last year."

Jim Brand asked a question, and the discussion veered to hotel space, which effectively derailed the mayor's intention to keep the meeting short.

As beds were counted and the dearth of local B&Bs bemoaned, Savannah attempted to block all thought of Sheriff Turner from her mind and allowed her attention to drift. She'd forgotten to check Inny's water bowl before she'd left. Had she remembered to put the check for her latest essential-oils order in the mail? She needed to be sure to stop by the Trading Post on her way home and buy milk.

Despite her determination to ignore the man, Savannah found herself watching Zach Turner's hands. When he pulled a small black notebook and a silver pen from his pocket and jotted a note, the action struck her as . . . official. Her throat went tight. *Had* he checked up on her? Had her effort to deflect his request to see her ID that day up at Lover's Leap failed?

Every time someone asks me that question, it spells trouble for me. Big trouble. With that, her thoughts went spinning into the past.

Outside the movie theater when she is thirteen, the police officer pulls his notebook and a silver pen from his pocket. "May I see your ID?"

Her heartbeat pounds. Her mouth goes dry. Holy crap, holy crap, holy crap. *"I wasn't trying to sneak in, Officer. I bought a ticket. I promise I did. I thought I put it in my purse. I must have dropped it."*

"The manager says this is the third time he's caught you crashing the gate, and he's pressing charges."

Great. Just great.

Six months later: a policeman motioning her to roll down the driver's-side window as he flips open a notebook. "May I see your ID?"

No, he can't. I'm driving without a license.

Eight months after that while on a delivery run, with the acrid scent of her daddy's moonshine hanging on the air from the half dozen jars lying broken on the floorboards of the wrecked car's backseat: "Step out of the car, please."

Savannah can't imagine having a worse encounter with the law.

Two years later, when the tall, handsome, blond-haired cop warns her that her taillight is cracked, then asks for her cell phone number, she's not concerned. "I don't own a cell phone."

"Your home phone, then."

"I'm afraid I don't have a home phone, either. I don't live here. I commute here to the junior college. I live with my grandmother in a rural area two hours away. We don't have long-distance phone service."

"Now, that's a problem." He flashed a brilliant smile. *"How am I supposed to call you to ask you for a date?"*

A date? Her heart grew wings and took flight. *"My grandmother's next-door neighbor will give me a message. She lets me use her phone."*

She repeated the number, but he didn't write it down. Instead, a grin spread slowly across his face. "You know, life is filled with strange coincidences, isn't it? I know that number. I'm Kyle Vaughn—Francine Vaughn is my mother. You must be Mrs. Aldrich's granddaughter. Got into a little trouble before you moved here, I hear."

Savannah's heart crashed back to earth. She fumbled for words as he slipped his notebook back into his pocket. "I . . . um . . . my family . . ."

He gave her a magnanimous smile. "Don't worry. I understand family obligation. If my dad was a moonshiner, I'm sure I'd have gone into the family business, too. Tell you what. Rather than involve our grandmothers right off the bat, how about I ask you out here and now? Want to go to the movies with me Saturday night?"

In her wildest dreams, she had not guessed that the encounter with Detective Kyle Vaughn would prove to be her undoing.

An elbow to her ribs jerked Savannah back to the present. "Raise your hand," Sarah Murphy urged.

Savannah reacted automatically and raised her hand.

"Thank you, Ms. Moore." Mayor Townsend beamed at her. "It's so kind of you to volunteer, especially when we know you're working your tail off to get your shop up and running. But it's the best way possible to become part of the community."

Volunteer? What did I volunteer for?

She twisted her head to look at Sarah and saw that the other woman was gazing across the table, a smug, satisfied look on her face. Savannah's heart sank. She knew what she'd see before she turned and looked.

Zach Turner wasn't happy.

Zach wanted to strangle Sarah Murphy.

He knew the woman well. He'd been friends with her a long time. They'd even dated for a few months.

He had recognized that wicked glint in her eyes, but by the time he'd figured out that it was directed toward him, he'd been helpless to prevent her interference.

Savannah Moore had been zoned out and staring into space when Sarah jabbed her and told her to volunteer. The woman didn't have a clue that she'd volunteered to work with him. No way would she have done it on purpose. Not with her record.

Why the hell had he asked for volunteers to help with preparations for the planning committee meeting he was hosting, anyway? And not just any old planning committee meeting, either, but one to finalize the curriculum of the Substance Abuse Resistance Education program for schools in the entire state of Colorado.

Of course, he'd asked for help because he didn't have time to even read the sports page these days, and Celeste had silently encouraged him.

Celeste. She and Sarah were partners in crime in this little disaster in the making. He didn't know quite how she managed it, but when Hank Townsend asked if anyone had any special requests, she had leaned against Zach and brushed his arm and before he knew what had happened, he'd raised his hand and stated his case. Then Sarah had done her thing, and now he was stuck.

Damned matchmaking busybodies. He should have moved to Sweden with Inga.

Although maybe this was a blessing in disguise. Hadn't he decided he needed to keep an eye on Ms. Savannah

Moore? This was certainly one way to do it. Who knows, maybe he'd learn something from her, too. Nothing like watching the fox scope out the weaknesses in the henhouse walls to discover what needed to be strengthened.

Zach looked across the table at the soap maker. She looked a little sick, he decided. A little green around the gills. A little brown around the peach pit.

He smiled at her. Nodded.

She closed her eyes.

He felt better.

As Hank Townsend began moving quickly through the other items on his agenda, Zach focused his attention on his other worries and concerns. With a summer schedule like this, he needed to get deputies hired fast. The fax from Denver that had arrived just before he left the office was promising. He'd follow up on that as soon as possible.

The final item on the agenda was a report from Cat Davenport about the summer camp she and her husband, Jack, were in the process of building up on Murphy Mountain. Since the camp would have private-hire security, Zach's interest was primarily personal rather than professional. The Davenports were his friends, and their project—a camp for children who had suffered a significant loss—was a labor of love.

"Unfortunately, negotiating the bureaucracy of regulations is taking longer than we'd anticipated, so we've had to push back our start date again," Cat said. "However, we still want to do a test run inviting local youth as our guests, and we should have the dates for those sessions soon. We'll announce sign-ups in the *Eternity Times*."

"What age group, Cat?" Celeste asked.

"We'll do a day camp for the little kids—first through third grade. Overnight camp will be two separate ses-

Town of Ballston Community Library

sions: fourth through eighth grade, and ninth through twelfth."

Mayor Townsend asked, "When you say guests, do you mean no fees?"

"That's right. No fees. The kids who want to go will be our guinea pigs."

"My grandkids will do back flips. You and Jack are doing a wonderful thing up there on Murphy Mountain." Jim Brand beamed a smile at Cat, then turned to include Sarah. "Let's not forget your husband's part in it, too. The camp wouldn't be a reality if Cam hadn't donated the land for it."

Sarah waved a dismissive hand. "What in the world was he going to do with a whole mountain? He was happy to contribute the land. Besides, it was either sign Jack's contract or shoot him."

Savannah cut Sarah a sharp look. Sarah said, "I speak the truth. It was a close call."

"What is it with you people and guns?"

Sarah laughed and patted Savannah's arm. "Jack interrupted our honeymoon—at an inopportune time, I might add. I will admit Cam eyed his pistol with more relish than warranted."

Because Zach was watching Savannah closely, he saw her flinch at Sarah's touch. Even as he noted the reaction, her lips lifted in a bright, genuine smile.

Zach felt the smile like a punch to the gut. He closed his eyes, swallowed a curse, and sighed. What the hell was the matter with him? Why did he react this way to Savannah Sophia Moore? So she was a babe. So what? She was a babe with a sheet. The worst kind of sheet.

Zach had worked in law enforcement all of his adult life. As a result, he recognized the gray areas in the commission of a crime. He understood extenuating circumstances better than most, primarily because he had witnessed them. Sometimes he had more sympathy for the criminal than he did for the victim. Sometimes the criminal had a damned good excuse for what he or she did.

There was never a good excuse for what this woman had done.

Savannah Sophia Moore, the sexy Georgia peach, was a drug dealer.

FIVE

❧

As the meeting broke up, Savannah's thoughts were spinning. How had she gotten herself into this mess? Volunteering to help Zach Turner? He didn't look any happier than she was about the whole thing.

How could she get out of it? Her stomach certainly felt queasy——was it bad enough to make her throw up?

Look at Celeste Blessing and think of Francine Vaughn. That should do the trick.

It was as if the woman had heard her. Savannah looked up and Celeste was there, standing before her, a wide smile on her face. To Savannah's distress and despite the fact that they'd never exchanged so much as a word, Celeste reached out and hugged her.

"Thank you so much for stepping up to help Zach with the planning meeting," Celeste said. "Volunteering is an excellent way to become part of the fabric of the town."

Oh, jeez. She's from the South, too. She even sounds like Francine!

Her spine stiff, her hands fisted at her sides, Savannah endured the embrace. After what seemed like ten minutes but was in reality only a few seconds, Celeste stepped back. She held Savannah's gaze for a long minute. How weird. A cold, empty place inside her heart suddenly didn't seem so cold and empty.

"You are going to love it here in Eternity Springs," Celeste said. "This little valley has a special energy about it, a healing energy that soothes troubled souls."

Savannah's chin came up. "My soul isn't troubled."

Celeste simply smiled.

The sheriff stepped toward them, a challenge gleaming in his piercing blue eyes. Did he know she was looking for a way to get out of helping him? He leaned down and kissed Celeste on the cheek, then addressed Savannah. "Thanks for offering to help. The SARE meeting begins the day after tomorrow, and I'm really behind the eight ball."

Too bad he wasn't in front of the wrecking ball.

Celeste said, "It's so generous of you to volunteer your time, Savannah."

"I'm happy to do so," she lied.

The look in the sheriff's eyes said she didn't fool him one bit. "How much time can you give me tomorrow?"

Five minutes? "How much time do you need?"

"Whatever I can get. To be honest, due to my workload of late, I've let a lot of things pile up."

She put an extra tablespoon of sugar in her tone as she asked, "Lots of picnickers to harass?"

"You wouldn't believe the litterbugs I have to defend the county against," he replied in a droll tone. "Look, if you want to back out—"

Yes! Except she had more pride than that, and he looked entirely too sure of her as he stood there, all manly and lawly and . . . gorgeous. *Gorgeous? Have I lost my mind?* "I said I'd help. Where and when?"

One corner of his mouth tilted in a knowing smirk. "Reflection Point meeting center. I'll be working there all afternoon tomorrow."

"I have a full morning and a phone appointment at one-thirty. I could probably get there around three."

"Perfect."

In some alternate universe, maybe.

Celeste beamed. "Maybe once things settle down for you, Zach, you can return the favor by helping Savannah get her shop ready to open."

Savannah couldn't prevent her eyes from going wide, and his glimmered with amusement as he replied, "That's a great idea, Celeste."

"I'm glad you think so. Now, I have a million things to catch up on at Angel's Rest, so I'm going to run. Before I go, Savannah, allow me to say welcome to Eternity Springs. I just know that you're going to be so happy here."

Savannah momentarily forgot about the sheriff as she watched her enemy's twin depart the room with waves and farewells. Celeste and the sheriff. This wasn't an alternate universe. This was a nightmare.

Damned if the lawman didn't tip an imaginary hat as he said, "So, I'll see you tomorrow around three."

"I'll be there." Unless she had a convenient appendectomy or something.

Savannah watched Zach Turner walk away and pause in the hallway outside to speak with the mayor. The formfitting stretch of his shirt across his broad shoulders once again reminded her of Kyle Vaughn. Kyle's uniform shirt had been blue, not khaki, and it had brought out the blue in his eyes. Blue eyes hauntingly similar to the sheriff's.

When she dragged her gaze away from him, she saw Sarah watching her, her eyes alight with delight and her lips lifted in a satisfied smile. She dipped her head in the sheriff's direction. "Man candy for the eyes. He's not just pretty to look at, Savannah. Zach is a really great guy."

"Wait a minute." Savannah held up her index finger. "If you are thinking what I think you are thinking, you can just stop it. I'm not interested."

Sarah Murphy clasped her hands to her chest, the very picture of innocence. "I don't know what you're talking about."

"Uh-huh." Savannah folded her arms. "You are as obvious as a weevil in the cake flour, and I'm telling you to let it go."

"Weevil in the cake flour? I love it! That's so southern of you." She put her arms around Savannah and gave her a quick hug. "I need to run. I'm meeting my husband at the Yellow Kitchen for a late dinner. Have fun tomorrow."

Savannah sighed. What was it about these Eternity Springs people? They were always touching her. And they were so darned friendly.

Maybe she should have asked permission to move to New York instead of Colorado. She'd come here to start over, to put her past behind her, and build something new and wonderful and exciting . . . and clean.

And here she was with a county sheriff on her heels and Francine's twin holding court.

Using one of Grams' old expressions, she muttered beneath her breath, "Lord, love a duck."

Savannah still didn't know exactly what that meant, but at this particular moment it felt like the perfect thing to say.

She slept poorly that night, and spent the morning brooding about the afternoon to come. Yet the hours flew by. After finishing her phone appointment with a supplier, she wasted twenty minutes debating what to wear before finally settling on a sundress and sandals. She touched up her makeup, spending a stupid amount of time over her choice of lipstick color, then gave Inny a cuddle and two dog treats.

Savannah drove toward Hummingbird Lake beneath a dark cloud of dread.

The fact that she did so annoyed her. She had nothing to fear from Sheriff Zach Turner. She'd done nothing wrong—well, not since spreading Grams' ashes without a permit, anyway. Actually, she was doing everything right—adding to the tax base with her business, being a good citizen by joining the Chamber of Commerce, being friendly to her neighbors when she frankly wasn't a friendly person. He had no right to harass her. But since when did cops ever care about that?

Once upon a time she'd been friendly and outgoing and oh so naive. Look where that had gotten her. She'd learned her lesson the hard way, so she'd developed a new motto to live by, one adopted from old television reruns: Trust no one.

Maybe she should get the phrase tattooed on her forehead. Under the barrage of seemingly genuine welcomes and offers of friendship since coming to Eternity Springs, she'd let down her guard—and ended up a volunteer. To help the sheriff. With a substance abuse education program.

Oh, the irony.

She wanted to turn her car around, floor the gas pedal, and speed off to . . . where? Another place where her past would eventually catch up to her?

"I'll never outrun it," she said glumly. She'd been a fool to think she could leave the trouble behind. "Once a con, always a con."

She paused and listened hard, hoping to hear Grams' chiding voice. But like every other day since her visit to Lover's Leap, the voice in her head remained stubbornly silent.

Rather than running, she flicked on her turn signal like a good little law-abiding citizen and pulled onto the road leading to Reflection Point.

* * *

Zach worked the morning in town but drove out to his home on the lake for lunch. He'd bought the first chunk of property from the out-of-state owners. Then last fall, when the Raffertys decided that Sage's dreams of a drowning child made lakeside living too stressful for the new mother, they'd dangled precious privacy before Zach by giving him first shot at their home. He'd mortgaged himself to the hilt to buy it, and now he—and the bank—owned all of Reflection Point.

The decision to remodel the buildings on the Reflection Point property into a comfortable house for him and an income-producing property had been sound. As a corporate retreat center, the facility worked great for small meetings, and Zach didn't have to bother with overnight guests, since Angel's Rest took care of that end. His time commitment was minimal. Other than keeping fishing supplies stocked and the retreat building clean and in repair, Zach had little to do to ensure that things ran smoothly.

The reward was substantial. Not only was the weight of his mortgage easier to bear, but except for a half dozen or so weekends a year, his beloved privacy remained intact, too.

He'd been glad to offer the center to the SARE program, but he wished he'd asked someone else to be in charge of putting together the planning packets. He needed help, but he figured the odds were fifty-fifty that the Georgia peach would actually show up.

He wanted to see her, to study her like a bug under a microscope and figure out her secrets.

"I need help," he muttered. The psychological kind.

He grabbed a sandwich at home and spent five relaxing minutes throwing a tennis ball for Ace to fetch. With his dog trailing at his heels, he headed to the meeting center and tackled the yard work while Ace plopped down to guard the door and supervise his owner's work.

Zach mowed and ran the Weed Eater and leaf blower and wondered why he didn't hire a teenager to do this for him. It was stubborn of him, really, to continue to do this himself, but he enjoyed the physical labor. It helped him clear his mind.

It needed clearing after dealing with the Georgia peach.

Sweaty, he ducked into his house for a quick shower, and if he lingered for a moment trying to decide which shirt to wear, he chalked it up to having an overflowing laundry hamper rather than any desire to look nice.

"I wish you would learn to do laundry," he said to Ace, who displayed his lack of interest in the idea by padding to his bed and settling down for a nap.

Back at the meeting center, Zach taped a note on the door instructing Savannah to come on in, then he made his way to the small storage room, where he prepared to make copies on what he guessed might be the only ditto machine still in use in America.

As the first few printed pages rolled out, Zach absently brought a sheet up to his nose and inhaled the scent of the purple ink. He forgot all about Savannah Moore and his SARE to-do list as the fragrance catapulted him back to third grade and math tests. His mom used to wonder why he scored so poorly when he was a whiz at numbers. He'd never confessed that he spent too much time sniffing the paper and too little time doing the work.

The machine, ink, and paper had been one of the treasures stored in the basement at Angel's Rest, and when Celeste offered to donate it to the meeting center, he'd been happy to take it, primarily for nostalgia's sake. The center did have a state-of-the-art copier, but as luck would have it, it was currently out of service until a replacement part arrived, so the ditto machine was coming in handy.

As the machine produced pages for his packets, memories of grade school drifted through his mind: reading groups, dodgeball at recess, cursive writing. Did they still teach handwriting in schools? He wondered if teachers still used that tool with five sticks of chalk to draw equidistant lines on the chalkboard. For that matter, he wondered if they still used chalkboards.

That thought led him to recall his after-school punishment in the fourth grade—writing "I will not fight" on the board one hundred times. It had been a fair price to pay for the joy of pounding on Barry Hill after he'd taunted Zach because "your real mother hated you so much she gave you away." His adoptive parents had agreed with the punishment—then they'd taken him out for pizza, a real treat.

When the last of the purple-inked pages rolled from the machine, he gathered up the stack and exited the room just in time to see Savannah Moore's car pull to a stop in front of the center. Zach drew in a deep, lung-clearing breath. It wouldn't do to have the drug dealer walk into the room and accuse him of being high on the solvents used in spirit duplicators.

He walked through the front door to the porch and gazed out at the old Ford sedan she drove. *Bet that ride is a big step down for a drug dealer.* She switched off the engine and opened her door. His gaze fastened on the bright red polish on toes slipped into heeled red patent leather sandals. Sexy. Thin ankles, long, tanned legs, and a flirty skirt on a yellow sundress. Very sexy.

Zach set his teeth and watched her walk toward him. Very felonious.

He tried to smile, but when her eyes widened, then went narrow, he suspected it came off more like a snarl. But dammit, he'd spent five years of his life working undercover to help disrupt the flow of drugs into schools and parks and lives. He didn't care how hot she was—the woman was drug-dealing scum.

After he'd finally read her rap sheet, he'd made some phone calls to Georgia. He'd yet to hear back from the messages he'd left at the department that had made her arrest, but a cop in the small rural town where she'd been born had remembered her well. He'd been downright chatty relaying information about her youth. Apparently Savannah Moore had been quite the juvenile delinquent before being sent away to live with her grandmother.

The Moore family had been moonshiners, and Savannah had been sixteen when she was arrested for two counts of sale of non-tax-paid whiskey resulting from purchases made by an undercover cop. The cop also recalled shoplifting and check-walking accusations. Of course, those were minor infractions when compared to what had sent her to prison.

She'd served six years for cultivation and trafficking. Sexy Savannah was an ex-con.

Who'd moved to Eternity Springs.

Who'd cozied up to his friends.

Who planned to sell soap.

Soap? Really? Or maybe some other kind of crystals?

As she approached the porch, he greeted her with an inadvertent bite to his tone. "Hello, Ms. Moore."

Her chin came up, and he knew he'd inadvertently put her on the defensive. *Dial it back, Turner. You want to observe and learn, don't you? You won't manage that if you alienate her right off the bat.*

Channeling his old undercover days, he made his smile genuine. "Am I glad to see you."

Her look turned wary. "You are?"

"I sure am. I can't thank you enough for volunteering to help me."

She studied him for a long moment, as if trying to judge his sincerity. "I wasn't exactly sure what you needed help with, so I wasn't sure what to wear. I have old clothes in the car if I need to change."

"No, you're fine." *You're beautiful. Dammit.* "Honestly, I've been so busy with work that I've put off preparations for this meeting until the last minute. There's so much to do, I don't quite know where to start. I have bags that need to be stuffed and vendors who need to be called. I need to test the AV equipment, process last-minute registrations, and clean the bathrooms." He shot her his best sheepish, aw-shucks smile. "I'll do those, of course. They're not bad, but I wouldn't ask you to clean bathrooms."

"That's good to know."

"Why don't I show you around and fill you in on what I'm up against, and we can go from there?" He opened the front door and gestured for her to precede him inside.

She walked to the center of the room. "This is a lovely facility. The view is fabulous."

A wall of windows showed off the sapphire blue of Hummingbird Lake and the snowcapped mountains beyond. "This building started out as a vacation home for a large family from out of state. When I bought the house next door, Celeste suggested converting it to a corporate retreat."

"So this is not a city facility?"

"No. It's private. It's mine. Well, mine and the bank's."

She turned to look at him. "You asked for volunteers to help you make money with your personal business?"

Could she sound more disgusted?

Annoyed, he replied, "No. I asked for help for a nonprofit program I care deeply about. The SARE program isn't paying for the space. In reality, it's costing me money, but this is an excellent program that does a lot of good, and I'm happy to help support it. Let me tell you a little bit about what we do."

He was off and running now, explaining how the privately funded group had been formed a decade earlier with a program similar to the wilderness expeditions of Outward Bound that focused on youth at risk of falling into the drug culture. As he talked, Zach thought, *She was an at-risk youth at one time. She should appreciate SAKE better than most.*

She should be impressed.

She obviously wasn't.

As he further explained about the program, Zach sensed a peculiar tension brewing in the room, that same sort of anticipatory energy that heralded a summer thunderstorm. The kind of tension that made a man feel alive.

He finished his explanation by saying, "I've been a group leader for the past three years, and let me tell you, a week of camping in the Rockies can change the lives of these kids, change them for the better. I've seen it myself."

Savannah lifted both hands, palms out. Her smile was neutral, but her eyes flashed with an emotion he couldn't quite read. Temper, definitely, but something else, too. What was it?

"No argument here," she said. "My bad. I misunderstood. It sounds like a great cause. Now, what can I do to help?"

Zach frowned. He'd expected further argument from her. He'd looked forward to it, in fact. He needed to blow off some steam.

I want to kiss her.

Whoa. Wait just one minute. Have you gone crazy? Your intention was to charm, not be charmed.

He had to get control of his buttons—all his buttons.

Apparently she had the ability to push them without even trying.

Zach cleared his throat and attempted to steer the conversation back to safe grounds. "If you could knock out the bag stuffing, that would be a tremendous help."

"Fine. Lead the way."

He pretended not to notice the insincerity in her smile as he led her into the workroom. A long table piled high with stacks of paper, folders, canvas bags, and tchotchkes stood against one wall. He gestured toward it, saying, "Everything is lined up. I need three folders made for each bag, with pages in the top row going in the red folders, those in middle row put in the yellow folders, and the ones in the bottom row in the blue folders. Each bag gets one of the giveaway items."

Savannah crossed to the table and picked up a mini flashlight on a locking carabiner. "These things come in handy."

"That they do."

"All right, then. I can handle this task. Why don't you go . . . clean the bathrooms?"

He hesitated, then nodded and walked toward the door. At the threshold he paused. He knew he should keep on going, one foot in front of the other, mouth zipped tight. But while he still grasped for button control, the storm broke. He turned around and asked, "You don't like me, do you?"

She shot him a wary look. "I don't know you."

"No, you don't." He folded his arms and leaned casually against the doorjamb, though he felt anything but casual. "So why don't you like me? I haven't done anything to you . . . other than attempt to save your life."

She picked up a carabiner and twirled it around her finger. "I wasn't jumping off Lover's Leap."

"I didn't know that." Giving up casual, he strode

forward. "I risked my life to save yours and you . . . you . . ."

"I what?"

"You called me Barney Fife!"

She went still, then dropped her head and brushed an imaginary speck of something off her skirt. Were her lips twitching? *If she laughs at me out loud, I swear I'm going to blow a gasket.*

Her tongue snaked out and moistened her lips. "When did you hear me say that?"

Zach had to pull his gaze away from her mouth. "You don't know?"

"It's possible I might have used the name more than once."

Zach sucked air past his teeth. She went on the offensive and demanded, "Why have you been spying on me?"

"I haven't been spying on you," he fired back. Though he had run a make on her. Did she suspect that? Was that behind this attitude of hers?

"Obviously you *have* spied on me," she continued. "I wouldn't use a derogatory term like that in public, only in private. I admit I tend to talk to myself, so if you heard me call you Barney Fife, you obviously eavesdropped on a private moment."

She didn't apologize. She didn't explain. Really, little Savannah the drug dealer shouldn't look so superior. Zach felt the urge to cut her down a peg or two. He smiled the smile he'd learned from Cam Murphy, a shark's grin that was all teeth. "If I'd wanted to spy, Ms. Moore, I'd have gone to work for the CIA. Instead, I investigate. I'm an excellent investigator."

She audibly gasped, diverting Zach's attention from her mouth to her breasts. Unfortunately, she caught him staring, and when she spoke again, though she didn't use the words "Go to hell," they came through loud and clear. "In that case, Sheriff Turner, perhaps you should investigate the state of the restrooms rather than my chest. I need to stuff your . . . bags."

Zach couldn't allow her to send him away. Since he'd already been caught staring and because she'd chosen to wear that short, flirty skirt, he allowed his gaze to slowly drift down to her long, shapely, sexy legs and told himself he was being insulting rather than feeding his inconvenient attraction to her.

He also had one more question he wanted to ask. "Why did you come here today?"

"I can leave."

"No, you promised to . . . stuff my bags." He looked her in the eye—not without an annoying bit of regret—and asked, "I'd like to know why you volunteered."

"Because I'm—" She broke off abruptly and sighed, the starch draining from her spine like air from a balloon. "I don't know. I just . . . did. It's Sarah Murphy's fault. She poked me. That woman is a terrier."

Relating to her sentiment, this time Zach was the one who sighed. "She is. So are her friends. Still, you could have come up with an excuse for not showing up."

"I keep my word, Sheriff. And I do not lie." Her gaze was steady, and sincerity rang in her voice.

If Zach hadn't known better, he'd have believed her.

Knowing the time had come for a strategic retreat, he left her alone with her volunteer work while he made quick work of cleaning the restrooms, then went outside to the toolshed. Earlier he had noticed that a couple of nails had worked their way loose on the back porch. Pounding nails struck him as the perfect task to do at this particular moment, so he grabbed his hammer and went to work.

Thwack. Why did she throw him off his game so bad? *You're attracted to her.*

Thwack. Thwack. Okay, fine. So what? It was understandable. She was gorgeous. Sexy. Spirited. He liked a little attitude in his women. And those legs . . .

Savannah Sophia Moore isn't your woman. She will never be your woman. You can never go there. It would go against all your principles.

True. He had to squash this attraction like a bug.

Thwack. Thwack. Thwack.

With the porch nails sufficiently pounded, he reentered the building and commenced his AV equipment check. Once he completed that, he grabbed his cell phone and the folder he'd left on a table in the main room and began making the vendor calls. He was halfway through his list when a noise in the doorway to the office caught his attention and he looked up. Savannah stood in a beam of sunshine, and streaks of burnished fire highlighted the curls in her golden hair. She looked like an angel, he thought, and again, frustratingly, his blood heated.

"I've run short on three of the handouts," Savannah said. "If you'll show me how to work the copy machine, I'll finish up. I've never seen one like it."

Zach slipped his phone in his pocket. "It's a ditto machine, and I suspect it qualifies as an antique. But it works, so I'll use it until it gives up the ghost. Which pages do we need more copies of?"

"These. I'm short six copies of the first two and seven copies of the third."

When she passed over the pages, their hands brushed. The touch was electric, and judging from the slight widening of her eyes, he suspected she felt it, too. She didn't look any happier about it than he did.

That made Zach feel marginally better. It made sense that an ex-con drug dealer would harbor hard feelings toward law enforcement. It seemed only fair that if he was going to suffer, then so should she.

For the first time since he checked her rap sheet, Zach

wondered how someone like her had gotten tangled up in the drug trade. She should be teaching school or baking cookies or, well, making soap. Not growing weed or cooking meth or recruiting members for her drug ring. What circumstances had caused her life to veer off the straight and narrow?

Family influence had to be part of it. Or lack of influence from a family. He'd seen *that* often enough.

He turned his attention to a demonstration of how to use the machine. When she leaned forward to study the paper feed, he caught a whiff of her clean, fresh scent—a blend of lavender and summer rain—and the workroom suddenly felt crowded. One of her own soaps, he surmised. *She'll make a mint.*

He jabbed at the on switch with his thumb.

The ditto machine spat pages. Savannah picked up a sheet stained with fresh purple ink, brought it close to her nose, and inhaled deeply. Her full lips stretched into a sensuous smile. She literally purred. "Oh, wow. This makes me think of third grade."

Zach went hard as Murphy Mountain. The urge to kiss her swamped him, and Zach leaned forward.

A sliver of self-preservation guided words onto his tongue and he drawled, "That's the closest you'll find to cocaine around here, Ms. Moore."

She froze. The paper slipped from her hand. Her gaze flew up to meet his. Grimly she said, "You know."

SIX

Savannah felt sick. "You ran a background check on me."

Knowledge gleamed in his blue eyes along with the too-familiar blend of disapproval and disgust. "I keep an eye on what happens in my town."

Bitterness washed through her. From the moment she'd discovered who had yanked her away from the point at Lover's Leap, she'd known this would happen. Was there some sort of lawman homing beacon embedded in her butt?

The sheriff's lips twisted in a sneer as he added, "I'm putting you on notice that if you're thinking to grow anything other than geraniums in Eternity Springs, you'll be answering to me."

"Oh, for heaven's sake. What is this? The Cartoon Channel? Showdown at the Purple Ink Corral?"

"Try the reality of being on probation. What did you do to warrant unsupervised probation, anyway?"

"What? You think I screwed a cop or something like that? Typical." She pivoted and headed for the door, calling over her shoulder. "Guess what, Barney—traditionally it's the other way around."

She almost could hear his teeth grinding. She was halfway to the outside door when he said, "What's your story, Georgia?"

She stopped and whirled on him. "What do you mean, 'What's my story'? It's all there in the databases, isn't it?"

"The bare facts are there, yes. I know you were convicted of cultivation and distribution of a controlled substance and served six years in a Georgia women's prison. What I don't know is why."

"Why should you think you get to know why? You don't have a right to any information about me beyond what you can look up on your computer. I haven't forfeited all of my rights just because I'm a felon. I think I still have the right of privacy."

If this *were* the Cartoon Channel, she'd see steam coming out of his ears, she decided. He braced his hands on his hips and declared, "I despise drugs. They destroy families. They destroy communities. They destroy lives. I won't let you hurt people I care about. I won't let you hurt this town."

Emotion rolled through her, the familiar combination of rage and pain and helplessness that she'd first felt shortly before her scheduled wedding day. Fierce, hot, and mean, it was a sensation she'd sworn she'd never again experience. *Damn you, Zach Turner.*

She faced him, folded her arms, and in a voice dripping with scorn asked, "What do you think I'm going to do? Peddle weed across from the elementary school? I was in prison for six years, Sheriff Turner. Six years! If you think I'll do anything that might put my freedom at risk, then you're even dumber than the one-bullet wonder."

"The what?"

"You need to bone up on your TV trivia. Sheriff Andy only let his deputy have one bullet for his gun."

"If you don't stop with this Barney Fife business . . ."

"What? You'll arrest me for hitting too close to home?"

With that, she turned her back on him, marched to her car, and slammed the door. It took every ounce of her self-control to refrain from gunning the engine and spinning her wheels on the gravel road as she left, but she wouldn't put it past Zach Turner to dash to his patrol car, chase her down, and arrest her for reckless driving.

Savannah held the wheel in a white-knuckled grip and blinked back tears as she drove sedately back to town. "What a first class jerk," she muttered. "I went out there to help him! Leave it up to Deputy Doofus to be the poster boy for looking a gift horse in the mouth."

Although she wasn't exactly the brightest crayon in the box herself. She had gone out to Reflection Point. Talk about stupid. She'd let peer pressure—literally, Sarah Murphy's elbow—make her do something she absolutely hadn't wanted to do. "This is what you get for trying to fit in. For trying to make friends. For trying to be a friend. Did you learn nothing in six years at Emmanuel? You can't afford to care about anyone other than yourself."

She needed to remember that after Zach spread the word about her past. Of course he'd do just that. Never mind ethics; he had to protect his precious town, didn't he? " 'I won't let you hurt this town,' " she mimicked. "Bastard."

What really put the cherry on top of her humiliation was that he'd been about to kiss her. Yep, right there beside that old-fashioned duplicating machine, he'd been about to lay one on her. She'd seen it in his eyes, the way they'd fastened on her mouth, the way his lids had grown heavy. The air between them had all but crackled with energy.

And, dammit, she'd wanted it. Her mouth had gone dry. Her heart had skipped a beat, and for the first time in forever, she'd yearned. She'd wanted a man's—that man's—mouth on hers. She'd wanted to taste him, to feel his arms around her. She'd wanted to touch and be touched, for the first time in what seemed like forever.

Damn him. Damn him for doing that to me.

By the time she reached the Eternity Springs city limits, she'd managed to fight back the tears and lock away her emotions. At least, that's what she told herself as she unlocked the door to her Victorian and stepped inside, calling, "Inny? Where are you? Mama's home."

The dog came running and yipping a hello. Savannah scooped her up into her arms and squeezed her tight. Too tight, she realized, when the poor baby squealed.

Then Inny was licking her face and Savannah cooed back at her. Thank heaven for pets. They were a true blessing. Unlike humans, they gave unconditional love. They didn't intentionally hurt people.

Inny squeaked again, so Savannah put her down. Her arms immediately felt empty, and a restless energy hummed through her. Now seated at her feet, Inny thumped her skinny little tail, her head tilted to one side as she waited expectantly.

"What?" Savannah asked her. "Are you bored? Do you want to go for a walk? Down to the dog park, perhaps?"

Actually, a walk to the dog park was a good solution for both of them. Inny loved her walks. Hearing the *w*-word almost always caused her to leap with joy. However, the little dog wasn't built for accompanying Savannah on the long, draining run she needed right now, so she decided she'd let Inny play in the dog park while she ran the circumference of the fence until her legs gave out.

It took her only minutes to change, and soon they strode up Spruce Street toward Davenport Park. Savannah plastered a smile on her face and waved at neighbors, doing her best to keep her mind off the events at Reflection Point. For the most part she succeeded, and when she reached the dog park and released Inny to play, she returned Ali Timberlake's greeting with a genuine smile.

Ali was quite a bit older than Savannah, though she didn't look like it. Slim and stylish, Ali had that smart, city-girl look that the rural southern girl inside Savannah would have loved to emulate. How Ali pulled off that look wearing sneakers, athletic shorts, a scoop neck tee, and a sun visor, Savannah couldn't hazard a guess.

"What perfect timing," Ali said. "I stopped by your place earlier but missed you."

Evidently Ali hadn't heard about the Chamber meeting. "I was . . . out . . . for the afternoon."

"I wanted to invite you to join our softball team. We have a lot of fun, and it doesn't require a lot of time." She gestured toward the baseball diamond at the far side of the park. "We practice once a week in May until the weekly games begin in June. Summer is such a busy time for everybody, but we all need a break and this is a fun way to do it. Please say you'll join us? Practice is about to start."

Savannah's gaze drifted across the baseball diamond, and yearning filled her. Once upon a time, fast-pitch softball had been her world, and during those awful years at Emmanuel, the time she'd spent playing ball had saved her sanity. She hadn't picked up a softball since, but oh, how her fingers itched to give it a go.

She spied Nic, Sage, and Cat Davenport, along with a handful of other women she didn't recognize. She didn't see Sarah Murphy, and for that she was glad. She wasn't up to dealing with the matchmaking machinations of the relatively new Mrs. Murphy, and she did want to join the softball players for at least tonight. Once Zach

Turner spilled the beans about her past, they probably wouldn't invite her back.

Savannah glanced toward Inny, who was playing happily with Nic Callahan's boxer. An extended stay at the dog park wouldn't bother her one bit. "I'd love to join you, thank you. Except, I'm afraid I don't have a glove."

"Excellent, and don't worry about a glove. Someone will have an extra." Ali beamed a smile toward Savannah and motioned her toward the baseball diamond.

That was another thing Savannah liked about Ali Timberlake. She gestured. She didn't reach out and touch. She didn't hug each time she said hello and goodbye.

Ali introduced Savannah to the other players whom she had yet to meet. Rose Anderson was the local doctor and Sage Rafferty's sister. Julie Nelson taught third grade, Christy Hartford was a stay-at-home mom, and Megan Smith helped run the Blue Spruce Sandwich Shop.

Practice began amid much laughter and camaraderie. Savannah was dismayed to learn that the official coach and assistant coach of the team were Celeste Blessing and Sarah Murphy and that they were due to arrive in half an hour. "Sarah's mother is in a memory care facility in Gunnison, and she and Celeste went to visit her this afternoon," Nic explained to Savannah.

Oh, joy.

While Savannah debated whether or not to mention that she could pitch—she didn't want to answer a bunch of questions—Rose Anderson said, "Please, Savannah. If you have any athletic skill whatsoever, would you please consider taking my place at shortstop? I'm terrible and I miss balls, and then my sister gives me grief. You would be doing me such a huge favor if you'd let me retreat to the outfield. Oh, please? Oh, please?"

Savannah couldn't help laughing. "Sure, I'll play shortstop."

Rose thanked her, and Savannah took her spot. Nic Callahan occupied the pitcher's mound. Practice consisted of easy pitches, a lot of pop flies, some girly base running, and some plays that had Savannah's chin dropping in admiration. Cat Davenport could run like the wind. Rose was a slugger at bat.

Savannah made a couple of diving plays on line drives that had her new teammates cheering and left her shorts covered in grass stains. On her first time at bat, she hit a home run. She ran the bases and arrived at home, then said to the catcher, "This team has some good players."

"We have our moments," Nic replied. "When Lori Murphy is here, we're actually pretty good. She's played a lot of intramural softball in college and she can throw a pitch."

"She's not home from school yet?"

"No. I'm not sure she's coming home this summer." A shadow chased across Nic's face, then she shook her head and added, "What about you? You can throw a softball. Have you ever tried to pitch?"

Savannah hesitated, then responded, "Yes."

Before she could say any more, Sarah and Celeste arrived. "We saw your home run," Celeste said. "What a great hit!"

"Thank you." Savannah tried to smile at her greatest enemy's clone, but she knew that what she offered was a sickly version. Intellectually, she recognized that Celeste Blessing and Francine Vaughn were two different people. Emotionally, she couldn't see past the haunting kind eyes and familiar easy smile. The bottom line was that Celeste Blessing gave her the heebie-jeebies.

Sarah didn't seem to notice Savannah's awkwardness. "Oh, wow. You are awesome. With you on our team, we're gonna win. I just know it. So, how did it go with Zach today?"

Savannah bit back a sigh. Sarah was a newlywed. She obviously lived and breathed romance. "Let's play baseball, shall we?"

Sarah frowned and looked ready to argue, but Celeste distracted her with a hand to her shoulder. "Sarah, I think you should take the pitcher's mound so you have plenty of opportunity to warm up before the other team shows up for our practice game."

"Practice game?" Savannah asked.

Sarah nodded. "Girls against the guys."

Guys? Her stomach dropped. "Who are the guys?"

"Our husbands and friends. It's a good time. We play by our own set of rules. The guys only get two outs per inning instead of three, and there's a five-run cap per inning. Plus Jack Davenport and Mac Timberlake have to pitch left-handed. They're too good otherwise."

As Sarah jogged out to the pitcher's mound, Savannah ground her teeth. There wasn't a doubt in her mind that Zach Turner would be one of the "friends" who showed up to play. That seemed to be the way her luck was running.

She glanced toward the dog park and debated using Inny as an excuse to leave, but decided against it. She was enjoying herself. Be damned if she'd slink away and let him do his dirty work behind her back. Let him stand behind the plate and call her life like an umpire—a blind umpire. Or a heckler. A blind heckler who umpires.

"Oh, for heaven's sake," she muttered beneath her breath.

"Yes, dear?" Celeste said.

Savannah frowned at the older woman. "Do you have relatives in Georgia, Ms. Blessing?"

"It's possible. I'm from the Carolinas. You recognized my accent?"

"Something like that." Savannah gave her a weak smile, then grabbed the glove and returned to the field of play.

Sarah proved to be a decent pitcher, but as practice continued, Savannah's fingers itched to throw the ball. At ten minutes to the hour, the men began to arrive. Colt Rafferty showed first, his son in a papoose carrier on his back. Gabe Callahan arrived next, sans his twin daughters. "Your summer intern asked if she could babysit," he explained to his wife. "I told her she'd regret it, but she insisted that if she could take a Rottweiler's temperature, she could babysit our twins."

Nic snorted. "And to think she's near the top of her class in vet school."

Cam Murphy and his son, Devin, showed up next and were followed shortly by Mac Timberlake and his sons, Chase and Stephen. That made seven players, enough for a team. Despite her better sense, Savannah's hopes rose that the angels might smile upon her and Zach wouldn't want to play softball with girls. He was a macho sort of guy, after all. Maybe he considered such activity beneath him.

By the third inning, she'd gotten caught up in the game and stopped watching for the sheriff. Her fellow players were a competitive bunch. She liked the way the guys didn't go easy on their women—and the way the women used all the weapons in their arsenal, not only on-target throws but come-hither smiles and suggestive winks . . . and surely Nic Callahan hadn't flashed her breasts at Gabe? Savannah must have imagined that.

She had just made a diving play for a pop fly that Ali had misjudged, stood up to her teammates' cheers, and brushed the dirt off her shirt when she saw Zach arrive. He called a general hello and, with the inning over, loped out to cover second base. Sage batted first and struck out. Savannah batted next, and the way her luck had been running, she hit a line drive just beyond Colt's reach at shortstop; as it rolled toward the fence, she had no choice but to stretch the single into a double.

In the outfield, Mac Timberlake scooped up the ball. Running hard, Savannah judged the throw. She could make it. She simply needed to properly time her slide. She eyed the ball, then focused on the base and threw her legs out in front of her just as the sheriff squared up to catch the ball, blocking second with his body. Her feet caught him at the side of the knees, and he tumbled down on top of her.

Or maybe it was a mountain. He weighed a ton. Had he caught the ball? Had she touched the base? Broken a rib?

He rolled over and his big right hand spread out over her breast. And lingered. They both froze. He gazed down into her eyes, his expression unreadable. Then his gaze fell to her lips and seconds passed like hours. *No,* Savannah thought. *We are not doing this. Not again. Especially not in front of witnesses.*

She lifted her chin, narrowed her gaze, and declared, "Safe."

He scowled. "Don't begin to believe that."

He finally moved his hand and rolled back onto his knees. "I tagged you. You're out."

"I got to the base first."

"No, Peach. You were slow. You're out."

Suddenly furious, she scrambled to her feet. "Safe!"

"Out."

"Safe." She looked to her teammates for help, but their expressions weren't encouraging. Sarah said, "It happened too fast."

Nic shrugged. "Sorry, I had a bad angle."

"Looked like a tie to me," Rose offered.

Savannah pounced. "Tie goes to the runner."

Zach shook his head. "Umpire, can we have a ruling?"

"The runner was out by a feather," Celeste Blessing called. "So sorry, Savannah dear. You'll do better next time."

It was all Savannah could do to refrain from sticking her tongue out at the old bat. She'd bet a hundred dollars that at some point in time Celeste and Francine had hung from the branches of the same family tree—upside down.

Savannah walked off the playing field, but rather than take a seat on the bench, she stood off to the side and stretched her arms, mimicking throwing motions, warming up her muscles. When Colt struck out his sister-in-law for the final out of the inning, Savannah was ready. She approached Sarah, saying, "Let me pitch. I'm good."

Sarah studied her face. "Zach will take a turn at bat now."

"I'm counting on it."

"This game is just for fun."

"Oh, I intend to have fun."

"Savannah . . ."

"I won't hit him. I promise. I'm not just good, Sarah. I'm very good. The man deserves to be put in his place. He's a pig."

"Zach? Our Zach? He's not a pig."

"He used our collision at second base to cop a feel."

"No . . . Zach's not like that. It must have been an accident."

Savannah could have told her otherwise. She had plenty of experience with law enforcement officials who used every opportunity that came their way to take advantage of a woman who had no power to defend herself. "All right. Maybe it was an accident. I still would like to pitch."

"You won't hurt him?"

"Maybe his pride."

Sarah tossed her the ball. "Good luck with that."

The chatter in the dugout slowly died when Savannah strode out to the pitcher's mound.

Cam Murphy called to his wife, "You okay, sweetheart?"

"I'm fine. Our new team member wants to show us her stuff."

That comment gave rise to good-natured whistles and catcalls, and Savannah played her part, smiling and waving and giving her hips a little jiggle.

"You gonna take a few practice pitches?" Nic asked, taking her place behind the plate as catcher.

Savannah glanced at Zach, who stood in the batter's box, swinging the bat one-handed, then nodded at Sage. "A couple."

The first pitch she threw slow and easy, a strike that thumped into Nic's catcher's mitt. The second pitch sailed across home plate similarly to the first. Savannah caught Nic's return pitch, then nodded her readiness toward Celeste, who called, "Batter up."

Zach stepped up to the plate. He took one practice swing, then another, then set his feet, drew back the bat, and awaited the pitch.

Savannah fired the pitch toward the plate. Zach swung and missed it by a mile.

"Whoa, what was that?" Colt exclaimed as Zach stepped out of the batter's box and studied Savannah with a speculative look. Sarah chortled. Cam and Gabe stepped up to the fence, seeking a better view. In the outfield, her teammates whistled and cheered.

Zach stepped back up to the plate. He shot Savannah a challenging grin. She fired one of her own right back.

And then she blew a second pitch past him.

"A ringer," Mac Timberlake marveled. "You've brought in a ringer."

Zach got a piece of the third pitch, then she fooled him completely with an off-speed throw and struck him out. She resisted the urge to pump her fist and instead sent him a smug, victorious smile.

Everyone—except for Zach—cheered. Cam Murphy came up to bat next and started teasing her with challenges. She struck him out in three straight pitches. At that point the structure of the game disintegrated. All the guys wanted a turn at bat.

Savannah thoroughly enjoyed herself. She threw well, proving that muscle memory is a powerful thing. Some of the guys got hits off her, and the more times they faced her, the better they did. The women all wanted a chance at her, too, so Savannah's arm got a good workout. It didn't escape her notice that Zach never lined up for another turn. Neither did he leave. He stood watching her, studying her, and only when someone mentioned babysitters and people began gathering up their things to leave did he step up to the plate and ask, "How's your arm? Do you have it in you to face one more batter?"

"You?"

"Yes. I think I can hit you, but I want to do it fair and square. If you've thrown too many pitches . . ."

No way would she back down on this challenge. Daring him with her smile, she said, "Batter up."

It became a battle, with Zach getting a piece of the ball every time, though not enough of a piece to actually put the ball in play. Finally, on the twelfth pitch, he popped it into the air. Savannah took two steps back and made an easy catch.

The ballplayers, men and women alike, gave her a round of applause.

Colt Rafferty stepped forward. "So, Savannah, fess up. Where did you learn to pitch a softball? Did you play college ball? Are you an Olympian?"

Savannah glanced at Zach. He was watching her like a predator waiting to pounce.

So this was it, then. He was going to out her, spill her beans. All her new friends were here, and he would "protect" them with one grand announcement. She could read it in his eyes.

Well then. Fine. She'd just beat him to the stab to her heart. She straightened her spine, squared her shoulders, lifted her chin, and said, "Not an Olympian, no. I've played softball since I was a child, but I polished my skills while in pris—"

Zach's voice boomed across the ball field, drowning her out. "Priscilla Hoskins. You're from Georgia. I'll bet Priscilla Hoskins was your high school softball coach. Didn't she go on to coach at Georgia Tech? I'm right, aren't I? You learned how to pitch from Priscilla."

Savannah had never heard of a women's softball coach named Priscilla Hoskins. She did, however, recognize a softball when one was lobbed her way. He wasn't going to give her secret away, after all. Not here and now, at least. Why?

What was Zach Turner's game?

SEVEN

The SARE meeting encountered a few bumps the following day. Zach was nursing bruises to both his ego and his ass as a result of his collisions with the Georgia peach. His colleague from Montrose had to leave halfway through the morning meeting due to a family emergency, and Ginger called Zach away from the afternoon meeting to work a single-vehicle accident just south of town. Nevertheless, they managed to get their work completed and plans finalized for the upcoming summer program.

Zach had thought long and hard before declining to serve as a program leader for a week in August. Two new deputies had accepted his job offers, but he couldn't in good conscience leave a rookie department still in the midst of their first tourist season. Too many strange things happened in Eternity Springs during summer. He would miss his week camping with the kids, but maybe if today's interview went well, he could make it up next year. Maybe volunteer for two weeks.

With that positive thought on his mind, Zach heard a laugh in the front office and he glanced up from his paperwork.

Well, well, well. His eleven o'clock interviewee had arrived early. Denver policewoman Gabriella Romano and Ginger were chatting and neither woman noticed him, so he took the opportunity to study his visitor through the window in his office door.

She shared a family resemblance with her brothers, he decided. Her hair was dark, and she was tall for a woman, with a sleek, runway model build. He couldn't see her eyes, but her smile was big and bright. She was a pretty woman. And single.

That fact had given him pause. He'd wanted to add some diversity to his department, but he didn't want to deal with on-the-job romances between his deputies. As far as he was concerned, workplace romantic attachments were off limits. If he hired Gabriella Romano, everyone would need to be clear about that. The last thing his department needed was a sexual harassment lawsuit.

Getting ahead of yourself, Turner. Go in and interview the woman first.

He opened the door to his office and stepped out. Both Ginger and Gabriella looked in his direction. Zach upgraded his opinion of her looks from pretty to gorgeous. Her eyes were a clear, brilliant blue, and in that moment, they studied him like twin blue laser beams.

"Officer Gabriella Romano, I presume?" he asked. "You're early."

Following a moment's hesitation, she stepped toward him, her hand outstretched. "Gabi Romano, Sheriff Turner. Yes, I am early and if that's a problem, I'm happy to leave and come back at eleven if you'd prefer."

"No, not at all," Zach said, accepting her firm handshake. "That was an observation, not a complaint. Welcome to Eternity Springs."

"Thank you. I'm already in love with the town. I drove in after my shift yesterday and spent the night in one of Angel's Rest's creekside cabins. Was up before dawn and caught three trout for my breakfast."

"So you like to fish, do you?"

"Honestly, not so much. I only went so I could call my brothers and give them grief about it."

Zach laughed. "I like your style, Officer Romano. Why don't you come with me to my office and we can talk about the job."

Zach knew within the first five minutes that he wanted to hire her, so he skipped right to the tougher questions. Finally he asked. "Why do you want to leave Denver?"

"My brother told you about my mother's situation, and I admit that's part of it. Frankly, I'm not so sure that my brothers will convince her to come to Eternity Springs. I'll be honest—I'm trying to move beyond a bad breakup, but I'm having a difficult time, since I see the jerk every time I turn around."

Oh, crap. "He's a cop?"

"Worse. A firefighter. I'd sooner date a priest than a cop, and I'm a good Catholic girl." She flashed that smile, then added, "When I talked to Celeste Blessing about Eternity Springs, she sold me on the idea that this is the perfect place to put old ghosts to rest. Then when Max figured out that you had an opening in your department . . ." Gabi shrugged. "It seemed like fate."

He nodded. He'd been a resident of Eternity Springs, and acquainted with Celeste, too long to argue with the notion.

"All right, then," he said. "What questions do you have for me?"

She took a moment and considered her response. "I'd like to know a little more about the department and the people I'd be working with. I hope you won't take it as being nosy, but I'll be honest—I am a straight shooter, I don't prevaricate, and I don't see the benefit of pussyfooting around. If I want to know something, I'll ask it. But . . ." She flashed him a smile. "I won't take it personally if you tell me it's none of my business."

"Fair enough."

"So, tell me about yourself, Zach, your background in law enforcement, your family."

"It's none of your business," he quipped.

She frowned. "Now that's just being mean."

He grinned and gave her a quick recap. "I grew up in Oklahoma. Went to college in Florida on a basketball scholarship."

"You played college basketball? Really? I did, too. Not in Florida. I played for Connecticut."

"They have a great ladies' program."

She nodded. "They do."

"Good family genetics for athletics, obviously."

"We're all sports fiends." Then she gave her head a shake. "And after college? Did you go straight into law enforcement?"

"Yeah. I originally thought I wanted to be an attorney, but when a friend of mine was killed during a convenience store holdup during our freshman year, I changed course. Guy was high on crack and murdered three people for seventy-eight dollars."

"Man, that sucks. Drugs are evil."

"They absolutely are."

"Did your parents mind the switch?"

His mouth lifted in a wry grin. "They weren't thrilled. . . . I was their beloved son, and they worried."

"Do they still worry?"

"If there's such a thing in heaven, then I expect so."

"They're both gone? I'm so sorry."

"Thanks. They were great people and wonderful parents. I miss them."

"I have to say that losing my dad was the hardest thing I've ever gone through, but I'm thankful I have a big family who are my support system. What about you? Big family? Small?"

Zach had begun to feel like he was the job seeker and

she the job giver. "Is that your way of asking if I'm married?"

"No. Celeste already answered that question for me." Her grin was bright and unapologetic. "You don't need to worry, Sheriff. I give you my solemn oath that I have absolutely no romantic interest in you or any of your deputies. If you hire me, you don't need to worry about on-the-job flirtations. Any flirtations at all, for that matter. I've sworn off men." Wincing, she added, "And I'm only into women as friends. My question about family is because I'm looking for some common ground here. I was asking if you had siblings or aunts and uncles. See, I have a huge extended family, with all the blessings and curses that includes. You'll understand me better if you have walked in my shoes, so to speak."

"I was an only child. If I hire you, you'll just have to educate me on the issue."

"Count on it. I won't be able to avoid it." Gabi Romano's grin went serious. "I'd like the job, Sheriff Turner. I'm a good cop, and I'll make you a good deputy."

"Good. I want to offer it to you."

She beamed, and her smile lit up the sheriff's office. Looking over her shoulder, Zach saw Ginger give him a thumbs-up. He sighed, stood, and shut his office door so that they could hammer out terms and agree on a start date in private. When Gabi left the building half an hour later, Ginger gave her a hug on the way out, then made a beeline for Zach's office. She hugged him, too. "Thank you, Zach. She's wonderful. She's a woman! Do you know how thrilled I am at the thought of having a woman around the office? What a happy coincidence that her brother happened to stop by when you were doing a phone interview with your door open right when Gabi decided she needed a fresh start and jus after Celeste had primed her to think kindly about Eternity Springs! Gabi called it fate; I say it's angel dust."

"I won't argue with it," Zach replied. A person couldn't live in Eternity Springs for long without coming to appreciate the special properties of angel dust.

He thought about coincidence and fate, angel dust and Eternity Springs as he drove home later that afternoon. Celeste claimed that the valley had a unique energy that made it a place where special things happened to those who opened themselves to the healing powers of love. Four years ago he would have rolled his eyes at the notion, but he'd since witnessed the phenomenon himself too many times not to give it credence. Call it fate, kismet, or the guiding hand of God, but if a man had faith in a higher power—and Zach did—then he had to take the energy of Eternity Springs into account when making decisions about the people who found their way here.

Not everyone received the benefit of what he and Cam Murphy had dubbed the Eternity Springs "woo-woo." Some visitors and citizens were simply sorry SOBs who would need to breathe the valley air for a hundred years or have a mountain of angel dust fall on them for their stone hearts to melt. Having the job he did, Zach tended to meet those folks more than most.

That train of thought led him to the town's newest resident. Where did Savannah Moore fit into the scheme of things? Was her heart black, or was it simply in need of healing? Had she found her way to this valley by accident, or had she had a push from fate or kismet or the hand of God? What was the woman's story?

Why did she get beneath his skin like no other woman he could remember?

Was it hormones, or was it . . . angel dust?

With these questions uppermost in his mind, Zach

wasn't at all surprised when he negotiated a bend in the road and spied a car pulled off to one side.

Savannah Sophia Moore's old, worn-out Taurus.

Angel dust? "Well, hell."

Savannah was so frustrated that she wanted to scream. Was it not enough that having a gasket replaced at Eternity Springs Auto and Sports Center just this morning had blown her budget to smithereens? Or that the owner had told her that her Taurus was on its last legs? That he'd said her car had a condition they called the "black death"? The black death! He'd told her to Google it, and she had. It wasn't good.

She needed a new car. After pouring all her savings into starting up her business, she couldn't afford one.

And now she had a damned flat tire, and who knew the state of her spare? Savannah had a well-earned aversion to looking into trunks, so she didn't use hers unless she had no choice.

She gave into the urge, kicked the flat tire, and let out a yell that would have made her Rebel ancestors proud.

Sighing heavily, she studied the road. After bailing her car out of the shop, she'd driven down to South Fork to check out a potential packaging supplier. She'd dawdled on the way back, playing tourist and stopping at all the scenic overlooks. The beauty of the mountain vistas simply took her breath away and provided a welcome respite from all the worries and concerns churning through her mind.

What was she going to do about her car?

Had she made the right decision in going upscale with her packaging?

When was Barney Fife going to pull the rug out from under her?

Thinking about Zach Turner caused her to kick the tire again, and then do it once more for good measure.

"Okay, Moore, you have three choices," she muttered to herself. "Call the Auto and Sports Center and have them send someone out to fix this, wait around for a good Samaritan to stop and help, or figure out how to do it yourself."

Since she didn't have the money to have the auto shop fix it, that option wasn't her best bet. The last time she'd let a good Samaritan near her car, she'd ended up in prison, so that didn't appeal much either. "All right, then. You can do this yourself. It doesn't matter that you've never changed a tire before. You are an intelligent woman. You can figure it out."

If she could get up the nerve to open her trunk, that was.

"Oh, stop it. The black death is under the hood, not in the trunk." She hit the trunk release, marched around to the back of her car, and ignored the instinctive tremble in her hand as she opened the compartment. Empty. She released a sigh. "Of course it's empty, idiot."

She stared into the trunk at the donut tire, and her teeth tugged at her lower lip. Years ago, her father had shown her how to do this. "Okay, Dad. I hope you'll be watching over my shoulder now."

She paused, halfway expecting to hear the sound of his voice in her head. Since she hadn't heard Grams' voice after that day up at Lover's Leap, it was certainly time for someone to step in.

Nobody did. Her head remained a silent zone.

She sighed and reached to unscrew the keeper bolt to free the spare tire, then lifted the tire from the trunk. Rolling it around to the front of the car, she leaned it against the left front fender and went back to remove the jack and the lug wrench from the trunk. After she carried them to the front of the car, she frowned. She had thought she knew what to do, but it had been a long time. She needed a set of instructions.

When she'd bought the Taurus from a used-car lot in Atlanta, it hadn't come with instructions. "Use your head, dummy," she muttered. "And your phone. Smartphones make for smart tire changers."

She typed "how to change a tire" into her search engine, read through a step-by-step how-to guide, then watched a three-minute video tutorial. Her memory refreshed, her confidence renewed, she searched the vicinity for something heavy to place against the back tires. She'd knelt beside the car and was beginning to loosen the lug nuts when she heard a vehicle pull in behind her. Glancing up, she spied the grille of a white Range Rover . . . with flashers on top. Her stomach sank.

Maybe it's one of his deputies.

The driver's door opened. She forced herself to lift her gaze from the sheriff's decal on the door.

Of course it's not one of his deputies. When have I ever been lucky?

Zach Turner climbed out of his vehicle, shut the door, and sauntered toward her. "Need some help?"

Yes. "No, thanks. I can do it."

She leaned on the lug wrench. The blasted nut wouldn't budge.

He waited, watching, for a long moment. "Savannah . . ."

"I've got it!" she snapped, frustration giving an added *oomph* to her force upon the wrench.

"No. Actually, you don't. You need to turn it counterclockwise."

Savannah froze. Damn. She knew that. The blasted man had her rattled.

Without acknowledging his comment, she switched directions, but since she'd just spent the last minute or so tightening the nut, she still couldn't manage to move it. She shifted the wrench to another lug nut and twisted counterclockwise viciously.

"You are stubborn, aren't you?"

"I've learned that stubbornness helps a girl survive."

After successfully loosening the other lug nuts, Savannah returned her attention to the first. She still couldn't get it to budge. As a squeal of pure frustration welled up in her throat, she sat back on her heels and glared up at Zach, who stood with his hands shoved into the back pockets of his jeans. His amused grin only stoked her temper hotter.

"Calling calf rope?" he asked.

"Pardon me?"

"Are you done? Ready for me to help now?"

Savannah knew she was being stupid. What good did it possibly do her to refuse his offer of assistance? And yet with every stubborn fiber of her being she wanted to change this tire by herself. She braced herself and then gave one more massive effort, pulling harder . . . harder . . . harder. . . . The nut moved. "Yes!"

She shot him a triumphant smile. "Feel free to go on about your business."

He folded his arms and returned a challenging look. "It's part of my job to assist stranded motorists."

"I'm not stranded," she grumbled beneath her breath. Now he had her so rattled that she had to take a peek at the how-to guide on her phone to double-check her next move. Yes, jacking up the car was next.

Savannah carefully placed the jack under the Taurus' frame, inserted the jack handle, then went to work. This part was even less fun than loosening the lug nuts, but she got the job done. Then she threw Zach Turner another smugly victorious grin.

He smirked back at her.

She refocused her attention on her task and pretended to ignore him. She removed the lug nuts, set them beside her on the ground, and wrestled the flat tire off the axle. was heavy and dirty and smelled like, well, an old tire.

Yuck, she silently said as she allowed it to fall onto the ground.

She lifted the lighter donut tire, fitted it onto the wheel studs, and retrieved a lug nut from the ground. Remembering that the video had suggested that the nuts be tightened in a star pattern, she began at the top, then placed the second, third, and fourth nuts. She reached for the fifth.

She couldn't find it.

Frowning, she looked hard at the rocky ground around her. Where did it go? Had she set the tire on top of it?

"It rolled," the sheriff said, holding the nut in the palm of his hand, offering it but not handing it to her.

Jerk. What was he trying to prove?

Savannah hesitated. She supposed she could go without it. Surely one missing fastener wouldn't hurt. *He'd probably arrest me for unsafe driving, though.*

Biting back a sigh, she rolled to her feet and took the four steps over to within reach of his hand. She nabbed the lug nut, but as she drew her hand back, he grabbed her wrist.

Savannah's gaze flew up to meet his. He was staring at her, his eyes narrowed and intent, almost angry. "Son of a bitch," he muttered.

Then he dragged her against him and kissed her.

His mouth was hot and hard and hungry, and Savannah resisted it . . . for about three seconds. It had been so long since a man's arms had held her. So long since a man's mouth had captured hers. So very, very long since she'd felt the liquid heat of desire zinging through her veins. It felt so good, so delicious, that she surrendered to it.

When he lifted his head a few moments later, those sky blue eyes of his hazy with desire and just a little bit stunned, she put her hand on his head and guided his mouth back down to hers. Just before their lips touched, he repeated, "Son of a bitch."

He backed her up against the Taurus, his tongue stroking her lips, slipping between them, meeting hers. He kissed her deeply, passionately, and tasted of spearmint and danger. This was no first-date kiss, but then, this was no date, was it? This was impulse, greedy and furious. It was as if Zach acted against his own better judgment, against his own will, as if he was helpless against his attraction to her. The possibility of it filled her with a heady feeling of power.

Not that she was actually doing much thinking at the moment. Her blood pounded, her skin tingled, she ached. She needed. While a part of her recognized that she might have just tripped over the line into insanity—after all, she was enthusiastically indulging in a very public display of affection with a sheriff she didn't even like—she was too caught up in the moment to care.

His hand began to move, skimmed across her breast, thrilling her. Her breath hitched, and for an instant he froze.

Zach released her mouth and his arms fell away as he jerked back and stepped away. Her stomach dropped with an instant of loss before good sense prevailed. For a long, humming moment he stared at her with eyes gone dark and edgy, the angles and planes of his face pronounced. *I did get to him,* she thought, pleased.

He got to you, too. And he's the sheriff! He knows about you. It's only a matter of time before he tells everyone in town.

Savannah wasn't nearly as pleased as she'd been a moment before.

Maybe her displeasure showed in her expression, because all of a sudden Zach relaxed. That oh-so-talented mouth of his lifted in a smug, knowing smile. He tipped an imaginary hat and turned to leave. "See you later, Peach."

Only after his Range Rover had disappeared around a curve in the road did she turn back to her tire. That's when she realized that at some point in the proceedings, she'd dropped the stupid lug nut. It took her five minutes to find it, then another five minutes to finish with the tire. Pulling back onto the highway, she headed for Eternity Springs and the comfort of a long, hot bath and a glass of wine.

She never noticed the truck parked on the side road that slipped onto the highway after she passed and followed her stealthily back to town.

EIGHT

Zach strolled into Cam's outdoors store shortly before closing time later that same day looking for distraction. His friend stood at the cash register ringing up a sale to a family of tourists, so Zach eyed the different areas of the store, deciding where to spend his time. He wandered over to the golf section, lifted a putter from the display, and tested its weight. A good merchandiser, Cam had a bucket of balls, an Astroturf putting surface, and an electric ball return machine available for customers to try out the products.

Zach dropped a white golf ball onto the green surface and rolled a putt. He missed the target by six inches, scowled, and tried again. Then again.

"That one is two sixty-nine ninety-five," Cam said.

"That's a stupid amount of money to pay for a golf club."

"I agree, but I sold two of them this week. If you're looking for a putter, you should try this one." Cam removed a club from a golf bag and handed it to Zach. "It's under a hundred dollars and it has a great feel."

Zach used the club to hit another ball. "Nice. I didn't come here to buy a golf club, though. You got time to go by the pub and grab a beer? Or do you have to get home to the ball and chain?"

Cam sputtered a laugh. "Do me a favor. Let me be there when you use that term around Sarah."

"She'd kick my ass."

"Absolutely. Let me take care of my receipts and lock up. We can take the scenic route—I'll need to drop off my deposit at the bank."

While Cam returned to the cash register, Zach sidled up to the table where Cam had his fly-tying tools and supplies set up. Without really thinking about it, Zach tightened a hook into the jaws of the vise and picked up the bobbin. As he wound floss around the hook, his thoughts returned, yet again, to the incident along the highway. "Has Sarah said much about the newcomer from Georgia?"

"The delectable Ms. Moore." Cam eyed Zach with interest. "Sarah bought a soap from her that makes her skin smell like butterscotch ice cream. Makes me want to lick my wife all over."

"I really don't need to hear details about your sex life, Murphy."

"You're jealous. Totally understandable, as is your interest in sexy Savannah."

"Did I say I was interested in her?"

No, you just kissed the hell out of her, numbnuts. On the side of a public roadway. What were you thinking?

"You didn't have to say anything," Cam fired back. "I watched you at the softball game. You're interested."

Zach scowled and wound floss around the hook. "I'm not interested."

"My wife will be crushed. She's decided that the two of you are perfect together."

Perfect together? Zach set down the bobbin. "A perfect disaster, maybe."

"Why do you say that? I've never seen you shy away from a gorgeous woman."

"I'm not shying away from anything." No way was

Zach going to mention the ex-con aspect of Savannah's history. "I just know that she and I wouldn't work."

"Uh-huh," Cam replied in a disbelieving tone. "Sounds to me like you protest a bit too much, but I'm not going to argue. I'm ready for that beer. I need a few more minutes with my receipts, though. You have time to tie a fly."

"I don't need any fishing flies," Zach said, suddenly frustrated with . . . everything. "I am covered in flies. Deerflies are the bane of my existence. They lie in wait for me in my garage."

Taking the change of subject in stride, Cam asked, "Did something die in your garage?"

"No. Jack says it's what I get for living on a lake. We have armed hostilities going on."

Cam grinned. "Armed?"

"Out-and-out war. The flies have teeth, you know, and they bite. I've started biting back."

"That's disgusting, Zachary."

"I don't eat 'em. I get wasp spray and a flyswatter, tie a bandanna around my head, and go Rambo on them. You gotta keep moving fast, or they'll bite the fire out of you." He hesitated a moment, then asked, "Why does Sarah think that?"

"About you and Savannah? I dunno. I can't recall. I'm too distracted by the mental image of you fighting deerflies in your garage."

"It's a battlefield, I'm telling you. The buggers are fast and mean."

"Try any ninja rolls on them?"

Zach pursed his lips. "No, but it's a thought."

"Sarah says that once Savannah is comfortable with someone, she warms up and is generous and fun to be around."

"So is my dog," Zach muttered. "Now that I think about it, ninja rolls might be just the ticket. The flies aren't entirely stupid. They know when you're running out of pookie from the change in spray-can harmonics, and that's when they blitz your position. A roll would shake up the spray, too. Economy of motion." He waited a beat and said, "She's secretive."

"That's part of what makes her intriguing. Why wasp spray and not something made for flies?"

"What's the challenge in that? Besides, there is no trap or bait or spray that will kill them or drive 'em away. I guess you're right about the intriguing part. I've always liked to solve mysteries. The woman has layers. I want to peel them away."

"I'd ask if you mean clothing or psychological layers, but I know you better than that. You'd say both. So if spray doesn't kill them, again I ask: why wasp spray?"

"Zap 'em with it and they'll fly full speed into walls, fall, flop around, then finally go legs up. Bottom line is, I don't want to get involved with her."

Cam shrugged. "Then don't. Tell Yenta the Matchmaker to look for another victim."

"You tell her. She's your wife." Zach fingered a turkey feather on the work table and finally gave voice to the thought that had been rolling around in his brain. "Maybe sleeping with her would get her out of my system."

Even as he said, he realized the idea didn't sit well. It wasn't just sex with Savannah that he wanted. He'd had plenty of sex. This was different. This was weird.

Dangerous.

Cam scowled at him and spoke with a bit of grump in his tone. "Let's try to have a little more white space between the phrases 'your wife' and 'sleeping with her,' all right?"

That managed to get a smile out of Zach. "You really are bothered by the fact that Sarah and I dated, aren't you?"

"No. Okay, maybe a little. And because of that, I

think I'll point out that from my perspective, your being able to sleep with Savannah is far from a sure thing. All those sparks I witnessed at the ball game could be plain old dislike. Maybe your charm isn't as legendary as you like to think."

"Nah." The sparks were real. The kiss this afternoon had proved that.

The woman confused him, probably because even though he knew the facts of her conviction and prison sentence, the circumstances around it remained unknown to him. She'd committed a crime and paid her debt, but until he knew her story, he didn't really know the woman. Layers again.

"You know, Turner, it occurs to me that you've said more about Savannah in the past five minutes than you ever said about your snow bunny. I find that little detail interesting."

Zach found it annoying. He couldn't get the woman out of his mind. "Are you about through? I really would like to get that beer."

"Almost. I just need to get something from the supply room. Give me a minute."

It took him three, and when he returned, he handed Zach a brown paper bag containing something cylindrical. Looking inside, he saw it wasn't the beer he expected. "What's this?"

"I know I don't have a license to sell ammo, but I couldn't resist. It's industrial strength."

Zach read the label on the can of flying insect spray and grinned. "Awesome. Thanks, man."

"Hey, if you're contemplating ninja rolls on deerflies, supplying a little firepower is the least I can do. Especially since I want to be there to see it."

A long, scented bath was first on Savannah's to-do list when she returned home, but she found a note from Celeste Blessing hanging on her workshop door. Celeste requested that Savannah phone her at Angel's Rest at her earliest convenience in order to discuss a potential business relationship. Savannah was tempted to ignore it—for no other reason than the older woman's resemblance to Francine Vaughn. But as a businesswoman, Savannah couldn't afford to miss potential opportunities due to her phobias. Whatever Celeste suggested, she would consider it, study it closely, and do her level best to use business instincts, not emotions, to make decisions.

Savannah put off her bath long enough to make the call, which turned out to be an excellent decision. Celeste wanted a new custom scent for the toiletries used at Angel's Rest, and she'd offered Savannah the opportunity to present samples and a bid to win the business. The bed-and-breakfast business was something Savannah had targeted in her marketing plan, and getting Angel's Rest for Savannah Soap Company products right out of the gate would be huge.

Ideas and possibilities swirled in her mind. She decided to forgo that bath and glass of wine for a quick shower and a diet soda while she retreated to her workshop to experiment with scents. She lectured herself to leave her worries about Zach Turner at the door, and for the next three days, she managed to do exactly that. Most of the time, anyway.

Celeste wanted a signature fragrance that was "light as a cloud, fresh as springtime, soothing to the soul, friendly, and uplifting, with a hint of spice to make it interesting." Creating that scent would require much trial and error.

Savannah spent one entire morning categorizing her essential oils with Celeste's wishes in mind. After that, it was match, mix, toss out; match, mix, toss out; et cetera, et cetera. By the time she left her workshop three days later with a tote bag filled with samples, she was on such a creative high that she could have sprouted wings and flown to Angel's Rest.

As it was, she decided to walk to her meeting instead of taking the Taurus. It was a gorgeous morning and after three days trapped inside her workshop, she needed the exercise. Sunshine warmed the air and cast a glow on dewdrops clinging to flowers and lawns. The scent of baking bread drifted on the air, and Savannah's stomach growled. "I shouldn't have skipped breakfast," she said to Inny, whom Celeste had invited over to play with the dachshund she was fostering for the area rescue group that Cat Davenport ran in her spare time. Privately, Savannah didn't see where the woman found any. Between being a newlywed, building a summer camp, and running the town newspaper, Cat was one of the hardest workers Savannah had ever met. She liked Cat, too. She hoped that over time they could become better friends.

Focused on the presentation, she'd been too excited to eat this morning. A part of her wanted to prove herself to Francine's twin more than anyone else in town. That was the emotional part of the proposition, and it was ridiculous, really. Celeste wasn't Francine. She was no more important than any other woman Savannah had met since moving to town.

Celeste wasn't Grams, either. Savannah's grandmother had been the very definition of a true southern lady. And she'd be proud of Savannah, no matter what. That's what really mattered.

Of course, the money she would make from sales to Angel's Rest *was* important, so part of this need to impress the woman was real. She believed she'd do it with what she brought to show Celeste Blessing today.

She'd settled on four very distinct fragrances to offer Celeste. Savannah honestly believed that these selections were the best she'd ever produced. She strolled through town with a smile on her face and a spring in her step. When she arrived at the intersection of Fourth and Cottonwood, she glanced to her left just long enough to check traffic, her gaze sliding right over the vehicles parked in front of the sheriff's office. She didn't care where Zach Turner was or what he was doing or whose secrets he was spilling. At least that's what she tried to tell herself on the lovely late spring morning.

She crossed the footbridge over Angel Creek and struck a course for the building that once upon a time had served as the carriage house for the Cavanaugh family's Victorian mansion but now housed the spa facility for Angel's Rest Healing Center and Spa. As she walked through the rose garden, the church bells in town began to chime the hour. "Right on time," she murmured, stepping onto the spa facility's porch just as the tenth bell pealed. Taking a moment, she mentally pictured Celeste Blessing, then Francine Vaughn, and she grimaced and shuddered. Savannah figured it was better for her to face her distaste and deal with it now so that she wouldn't react stupidly when she saw Celeste.

She needed to get over this reaction. It was stupid and unfair to Celeste. Everything she'd seen and heard about Celeste Blessing made her out to be a truly wonderful person. Savannah figured she just needed to be around her more often so that when she looked at her she saw Celeste instead of Francine.

She opened the door to the spa and stepped inside. Glancing around, she didn't see Celeste, only a tall, dark-haired woman who was in the process of kicking off her shoes as she took a seat in the pedicure chair. Spying Savannah, she said, "You must be Savannah Moore?"

"Yes."

"I'm Gabi Romano. I've just moved to Eternity Springs. Celeste tells me you're a newcomer, too."

"I am."

"It's nice to meet you, Savannah. Maybe we can help each other settle into town."

Savannah's first reaction was to put on the chill, but then she remembered that she was trying to make an effort there, too. Adding friendly warmth to her voice, she said, "I think that would be nice."

"Me too. Now, Celeste called a few minutes ago and said to tell you she's running late, but for you to relax and enjoy a pedicure on the house." She gestured toward the massage chair beside hers. "The water is warm and ready for you. Erin, the attendant, has gone to the kitchen for more ice, but she'll be right back."

"Oh." Savannah glanced from the chair to her toes. She seldom indulged in pedicures, but did love them, and if it was on the house . . . why not? "Okay, thanks."

As Savannah bent down to unbuckle the straps on her sandals, Gabi Romano's cell phone rang. She checked the number, then said, "Excuse me, Savannah. I should get this. Family." Then, "Hey, big brother. What's up?"

As she listened to her call, Gabi wiggled her toes in the bubbling water of the salon chair's tub. When she abruptly froze, Savannah eyed her with concern. Something was wrong.

"He did what?" Gabi asked, her tone hard and flat. After a good thirty seconds, she made an angry splash at the water with one of her feet. "He said that to Captain Kosarek? That son of a bitch. I swear, Max, next time I see him I'm going to kick those balls he's so proud of up under his eyebrows."

The woman talked tough, but Savannah didn't miss the tears pooling in her eyes as she listened to her big brother's side of the conversation, though she blinked them away before they fell.

Gabi sighed heavily then sat up straight. "No, don't do that, Max. It doesn't matter. Honestly. If my new boss won't judge me for what I do rather than what someone else said I did, then I don't need to be working for him anyway. Really."

Savannah found the massage chair control and switched it on. Pressure against muscles stiff from bending over her workbench for too long felt wonderful. She slid her bare feet into the warm scented water swirling in the bowl. Lavender, Savannah recognized. Nice, but ordinary. Nothing like the heavenly scent for footbaths nestled in her tote.

"I love you, too, Max," Gabi said, relaxing against her own chair. "Thanks for the heads up, and don't worry about me. I'm so done with letting that man dim my shine. So, have you heard anything from Mother?"

As Gabi's conversation moved into family matters, Savannah turned her attention to the display of nail polish hanging on the wall and debated which color she should choose. Moments later, the woman next to her ended her phone call, saying to Savannah, "I apologize for subjecting you to my personal family business. I needed to take the call and I didn't want to get up and track oily water across the floor for Erin to slip in when she returns."

"Not a problem," Savannah replied, offering a friendly smile that shifted to concerned when she spied a pair of big fat tears spill from Gabi Romano's eyes. "Are you okay? Can I do something to help you?"

"Oh, just ignore me. I'm fine." Gabi angrily swiped the tears off her cheeks. "Just an old boyfriend who won't take no for an answer. My brothers are worried and acting watchdog for me. . . . You're not wearing a ring. Are you married?"

"No."

"Then let me give you a piece of advice. Never date a fireman or a cop."

The laugh burst out of Savannah unintended. When

Gabi drew back in surprise, she explained. "Like the saying goes, Been there, done that. Have the knife-through-my-heart scar to prove it."

"Really." Gabi's smile warmed, and her blue eyes gleamed with friendly curiosity. "Do tell."

In that moment, Gabi reminded Savannah of someone, though she couldn't place just who. "You know, not to be cranky, but I'd rather not talk about it."

"Not a problem. I understand." Gabi dipped her right-hand fingers into the manicure bowl. "Ordinarily I'm discreet, too, but when I'm angry like this, everything spews out. It's like I hear his name, so I want to vomit. Better to spew words than bile, I guess. My ex is bile. Vile bile. I think the worst part of it is that he had me totally snowed. I believed the lying bastard. Men don't fool me. Not often. I grew up surrounded by jock-straps in a house full of brothers. I know men. I understand their tricks. With him . . ." She shook her head sadly. "I never saw it coming."

"What did he do?"

"He destroyed me. He's the lowest form of life on earth."

We're kindred spirits. I think I found a sister, Savannah thought. "And he's a cop?"

"A firefighter. Swaggering slime."

A teenager entered the room carrying a pitcher filled with ice. She smiled at Savannah. "Hi, Ms. Moore. I'm Erin Stewart. I'm glad to see that you decided to take Celeste up on her offer. She's really sorry that she's been delayed."

"Not a problem."

"Let me finish up with Gabi and I'll get to you." She filled two glasses with ice and lemon-flavored water and placed them on the table between the two women. To Gabi, she asked, "Have you chosen a color?"

"For my toes I want that orange color on the end."

"A Good Mandarin Is Hard to Find." Erin nodded. "That's pretty."

"And appropriate," Gabi added, before Erin's shoes caught her attention. "Oh my gosh. I want those shoes. Those are the cutest sandals I've ever seen. Where did you get them?"

Conversation turned to shopping, fashion, makeup, and hairstyles while Erin completed Gabi's pedicure and started on Savannah's. It was the most girly-girly half hour Savannah could recall, and she enjoyed herself immensely.

As Erin brushed a topcoat onto Savannah's toes, Gabi said, "Erin, I've changed my mind about that manicure. Do you have time?"

The teen glanced at the clock. "I do for a simple manicure. My next appointment is due in fifteen minutes."

"Perfect. A coat of clear will do me. As much as I love tangerine on my toes, I have to keep my hands looking professional. Especially since I am starting my new job tomorrow. Wouldn't want my new boss to think I come across as flashy."

Savannah suspected Gabi would be flashy no matter what. "Where will you be working, Gabi?"

"The sheriff's office. I'm the newest deputy with the Eternity Springs Sheriff's Department."

NINE

As Savannah's chin dropped, the salon door opened and Celeste Blessing swept inside. "Hello hello! I'm so sorry I'm late."

Caught off guard by both Gabi's revelation and Celeste's appearance, Savannah grimaced. Judging by the other women's reactions, it must have been a particularly vivid expression. *Idiot! You're here to sell something to Celeste Blessing, remember? Must you always shoot yourself in the foot?*

Celeste carried a canvas tote bag sporting the Angel's Rest logo, and she set the bag on the salon's checkout counter. "Oh, Gabriella, I love that color. It's A Good Mandarin Is Hard to Find, isn't it? That's my favorite summer orange."

"I love it, too." Gabi wiggled her toes.

"And that's a luscious red you chose, Savannah. So lovely with your skin tone. I'm afraid I can't wear pretty reds like that. The color just washes me out."

Savannah smiled, but she suspected it looked sickly.

Celeste continued, "So, Gabi, are you all settled in at Nightingale Cottage?"

"I am. I love it so much you might never get rid of me." To Savannah she explained, "I've rented one of the cottages at Angel's Rest for the summer. It's perfect for me. One bedroom with a small living area and kitchenette, which is exactly what I need because I'm not much of a cook. Best of all, it's steps away from Angel Creek, and nothing soothes me like the sound of a babbling brook. If the job works out and my mother decides to move here, too, I'll look at getting something more permanent."

"You're going to love the job," Celeste assured her. "Zach is a great guy, and Ginger Harris says he's a good man to work for."

"I like Zach a lot."

Something in her tone caused Savannah to look at Gabi closely. Was she interested in him? After her never-date-a-cop talk?

Gabi continued. "He's so much like my brother Max that it's scary. I get along with my brothers as a rule, so I think I'll work with Zach just fine."

That didn't sound like a romantic thing. When Savannah realized that the emotion she felt was relief, she grimaced.

Celeste smiled beatifically. "I predict that Eternity Springs will work its magic on your entire family." Turning to Savannah, she said, "Shall we adjourn to the Tranquillity Room? I think it offers the best surroundings for your presentation."

"Whatever you'd like, Celeste. I'm ready."

Nerves fluttered in Savannah's stomach as she picked up her sample bag and followed Celeste to the Tranquillity Room, where every feature and item of decor contributed to an atmosphere of peace and relaxation. Savannah took a moment to study the square-shaped waterfall that fell in thin lines from the ceiling to a fountain in the floor. "Oh, that's nice," she said. "The entire room is simply lovely."

"Thank you. Our favorite landscape architect did the design for me. Gabe Callahan uses water in his designs extensively, and when he suggested this fountain for our Tranquillity Room, I had to have it. There is so much symbolism in water, don't you agree? Cleansing, renewal, rebirth. Plus the sound of falling water brings me peace." Winking, she added, "And makes me want to pee."

That startled a laugh out of Savannah.

"The ladies' room is right through there if you need it." Celeste gestured toward a door. "Now, what do you need for your presentation? If we sat on the sofa, will the coffee table work?"

"That would be perfect." Savannah discreetly wiped her sweaty palms on her slacks as she took a seat on an overstuffed sofa and reached into her tote. "With your purpose in mind, I've developed four unique scents, each with two subsets designed to appeal to males and females. For today's presentation, I have incorporated the scents into shampoo, conditioner, soap, and lotion. Remember that I have a full spa line, so we can incorporate your chosen fragrance into those products, too."

Celeste sat beside Savannah on the sofa and laced her fingers. "This is so exciting!"

"The scents are color-coded. For today's purposes, let's call the blue caps the Sky fragrance, whites the Cloud fragrance, yellows Wildflower, and greens Forest." Savannah pasted on a salesperson's smile and began placing her products in eight rows of four on the coffee table, soap lying on pieces of parchment paper, and clear two-ounce bottles with caps of blue, white, yellow, and light green. Each soap and cap had an M or F drawn upon the top. "Once you choose a fragrance, we can develop colors and packaging that suit each scent and purpose."

"Excellent. Where do we start?"

With her products arranged on the coffee table, Savannah said, "I suggest we begin with the lightest, airiest scent. This is Cloud." She picked up the small bars of white soap and handed them to her customer. "One idea I had is to mold the soap cakes into the shape of an angel's wing.

"Cloud?" Celeste asked, bringing the female sample to her nose for a sniff. "Oh, how lovely." She tested the male version. "Oh, my. This is perfect. It's Michael."

Savannah started to ask her what she meant by Michael, but Celeste had already moved on to the next samples, her concentration focused on the scents. Without looking up, she said, "See the gold notebook beside the lamp? Please use it and take notes for me, Savannah."

No sooner had Savannah picked up a pen than Celeste began to dictate. "Cloud is a winter fragrance. Names are Michael and Zuriel. The color is pearl—and I do love the angel wing idea. Forest will be our autumn scents—Raphael and Tabbris. I'll want them aspen-leaf yellow. Wildflower is spring and a new life, green. Hmm . . . names must symbolize rebirth. Perhaps Gazardiel and—"

"Can you spell that, please?"

Celeste did so, then continued. "Sky is summer blue, Mihael, M-I-H-A-E-L, and Gabriel. Blue, like Zach Turner's eyes, like my eyes."

She turned to Savannah. "These are all lovely. Just what I had hoped for. You've produced exactly what I wanted, dear."

"I'm so glad." Savannah allowed her smile to blossom. "Although I have to admit that I missed exactly which fragrance you preferred."

"Why, all of them, of course."

Savannah blinked. "All of them?"

"I admit it's more than I had planned, but you've done an extraordinary job, Savannah. I couldn't be more pleased. Where did you learn your craft?"

"My grandmother." Savannah's heart was singing. Her soaps and lotions in Angel's Rest! It was all she could do not to dance a jig, but in that moment she'd never missed Grams so keenly.

"Tell me about her, dear."

Savannah swallowed the sudden lump of emotion that had formed in her throat. Then she shared a little about the woman she'd so loved with this woman who so resembled her grandmother's once-upon-a-time best friend. "Her name was Rebecca Rose Aldrich. She was my maternal grandmother, and I called her Grams. My parents lived in Atlanta when I was born, and we'd go visit her every summer. She lived up in the Great Smoky Mountains in northern Georgia. On her mountain, actually. My mother was her only child, but when Mamma married my dad and moved to Tennessee, Grams couldn't bear to leave her home."

"Children grow up and leave. It's the way of life, but that doesn't make it easy."

Savannah paused then, her thoughts spinning, her grief as raw as the moment she'd been told the news that Rebecca Rose Aldrich had passed. "My mother died when I was eight, and my father and brothers and I . . . well . . . we just fell apart. When I was sixteen, I got into trouble. Dad sent me to live with her. Grams turned my life around."

"I'm sure you were a blessing to her, too."

"I tried to be." Her lips gave a quick, sad smile. "I was a sponge, a city girl who knew little about the country. She taught me how to garden, how to sew. How to make soap. That's how she made her living. The nearest town was halfway between two tourist destinations, which made the little general store there a perfect pit stop. Grams sold her lotions and soaps in town."

"So you are following in your grandmother's footsteps. What a lovely tribute to her."

"She was a wonderful person. My rock."

"I imagine she'd be proud to see what you are building here in Eternity Springs."

"Yes, I think she would." Savannah picked up one of the soaps—the Cloud fragrance, which was a derivative of one of her grandmother's original recipes—and a fierce sense of accomplishment swept through her. "It makes me happy to use the gifts she passed on to me to support myself."

"How long ago did you lose her?"

Savannah spoke past the sudden lump in her throat. "Three years. It's been three years now."

"I'm so sorry for your loss, Savannah. You mentioned other family? Your father? Brothers?"

Savannah didn't want to open that particular can of worms, so she simply said, "I'm on my own."

"Well, that's not the case any longer, is it." Celeste reached over and patted her knee. "You have new friends. New people who care about you. And perhaps a budding romance?"

"Romance!" Savannah laughed nervously. "Why would you say that?"

"I enjoy mountain climbing as a sport. I was out climbing the other day and had a good view of the roadway when I saw you wrestling with that flat tire . . . and our sheriff."

Savannah winced and wished she could disappear.

Celeste's blue eyes twinkled. "Zach Turner is a very nice man. He needs someone in his life."

"Well, it won't be me."

"Now, Savannah, what do you have against Zach?"

Other than the fact that he's a lawman? A lawman who knows my secrets? A lawman who kisses like the devil himself? "I don't like his eyes. He has blue eyes. I don't like blue eyes."

"Aha! Is it the color of my eyes that causes you to react so negatively when you see me?"

Embarrassment washed through Savannah, and heat stung her cheeks. She straightened her samples on the table to keep her hands busy. "I'm so sorry about that, Celeste. I'm mortified you noticed."

"You sometimes look at me as if you're sucking a lemon."

Savannah shut her eyes briefly, then opened them. "Please accept my apology. You look like someone I used to know, and I react to that person, not to you."

"I gather this someone didn't treat you well?"

The words flowed out before Savannah could stop them. "She destroyed my life."

"Oh, dear." Celeste leaned toward her, her gaze solemn. "I'll be happy to listen if you'd care to share."

Savannah was tempted. With Zach knowing the truth, it was bound to come out sometime. Wouldn't it be better if she controlled the how and when?

Maybe. But she wasn't quite ready to take that leap right now. "Thank you, but I'm trying to put the past behind me and look forward."

"Yet every time you look at me, you see . . . ?"

Again, despite her decision to zip her lips, the name spilled from her mouth like bile. "Francine Vaughn."

Now why in the world had she done that? It was as if Celeste smiled at her and syllables rolled off her tongue. When Celeste repeated the name thoughtfully, Savannah couldn't stop a shudder.

"I don't believe I've ever met a Francine Vaughn," Celeste said. "Was she a professional acquaintance of yours? A friend?"

"A neighbor who claimed to be a friend."

"Ah. I see. That's why you're wary of making friends in Eternity Springs."

"I'm not wary of making friends," Savannah protested, sitting up straighter. "I've joined the softball team, haven't I? I'm wary of losing friends."

"Why would you say that?"

Because Zach Turner is going to tell everyone that I'm a jailbird.

Celeste picked up a blue-capped shampoo sample, the one she'd named Mihael, and seemed to have decided to change the subject. "This is the scent you are wearing this morning, isn't it?"

"Yes."

"You wear it quite often. I believe you wore it the day I first met you."

"It's my current favorite. I tend to wear a scent for a time, then move on to something else."

"Are you familiar with Mihael?"

"No, ma'am."

"Mihael is known as the angel of loyalty. She leads us to friends who are trustworthy and loyal. I believe it's no coincidence that you wore her scent when you came to Eternity Springs."

Oh, jeez. Angels? Really?

Savannah knew she shouldn't be surprised. All she had to do was look at the woman. Celeste Blessing wore angel earrings and an angel wing necklace. She rode a Honda Gold Wing motorcycle, for heaven's sake. She named her resort Angel's Rest. Why wouldn't the woman believe in angels?

"Allow me to share a piece of advice, Savannah. You can trust the friends you make here. They won't betray you. They won't let you down."

"I'd like to believe that."

"You can believe it. You have found a good place in Eternity Springs. You can have friends here, a home here. A life here. Perhaps even a love here. You've left those who betrayed you back beyond the front rang

Don't let your past blind you to the truth. Eternity Springs is true blue, Zach Turner is true blue."

"He's a sheriff."

"And a pretty good kisser, from what I'm told. So, girlfriend . . ." Celeste grinned wickedly, elbowed her in the side, and teased, "Dish. How was his kiss? On a scale of one to ten?"

Recognizing the baiting as Celeste's way to lighten the mood, Savannah made a zipping gesture over her mouth. "Sorry, I don't kiss and tell."

"Not even to your girlfriends?"

A pang of regret pierced Savannah's heart. "Honestly, Celeste. I don't know. It's been a long time since I've been kissed. Even longer since I had girlfriends."

"Well, you can't say that any longer, can you? From what I saw, Zach kissed you thoroughly, and I know for a fact that you now have at least a half-dozen women you can count as girlfriends."

Yearning washed through Savannah, fierce and hot. She wasn't ready to deal with the whole idea of Zach, but friends . . . oh, how she longed to have friends. Real, true women friends around whom she didn't have to guard every word.

Real, true friends who would stand by her once they learned her deepest secrets.

Celeste's smile was gentle, her touch on Savannah's arm feather light. "Friends are like kisses, blown to us by angels. You're one of us, now, Savannah. Trust that. Trust us.

"Trust yourself."

TEN

Memorial Day weekend and the beginning of the tourist season rushed toward Eternity Springs like snowmelt over Heartache Falls. With the holiday still two weeks away, citizens scurried about to put the finishing touches on the annual postwinter spruce-up. Victorian houses sported fresh coats of paint, sunshine glittered off the surface of newly washed windows, and half barrels filled with bright red geraniums accented sidewalks swept free of the detritus of winter. Zach parked his truck in his customary spot in front of the sheriff's office, gathered up the paperwork he'd taken home to complete the previous evening, and then walked toward the office door, where his diminutive dispatcher stood on tiptoe to pour red syrup into the hummingbird feeder that hung from a bracket outside the office's front window. "Hold on, Ginger. Let me help."

"Thanks."

Zach noted the droplets of water clinging to the petals of the petunias in the window box as he lifted the feeder off the bracket and removed the top. While Ginger filled the feeder, he observed, "Since you're out here watering your posies and feeding the birds, I assume it's been a quiet morning?"

"Your newest deputy is a godsend. She does the work of two people."

Zach smiled with satisfaction. "She's a dynamo, all right."

As Zach reached for the door, it opened and Deputy Dynamo, aka Gabi Romano, rushed outside, her features set in a grim expression. Seeing Zach, she said, "Domestic disturbance."

The pleasure of his easy morning melted away. "The Armstrongs?"

"Yes."

"I'll go with you."

It was the first call in what quickly evolved into an extremely lousy day—a rare occurrence for his little mountain town. They arrived at the Armstrong household to find a bruised and battered Nina cradling a broken arm and her alcoholic husband passed out on the couch. As usual, Nina made excuses for her man, which totally pissed Zach off. While he pleaded with Nina and warned her about the reality of escalating violence, Ginger radioed with a report of a car accident with injuries just north of town, and the news that Deputy Martin Varney had called in sick with a stomach virus and would miss his afternoon shift. Zach left Gabi to deal with the Armstrongs and rushed off to the car wreck.

The worst call of the day had happened just before three and wasn't a call at all, but an accident he witnessed when responding to a car burglary report at the campground up on Mirror Lake. The simple family picnic gone terribly wrong had been the most heartbreaking thing he'd seen in years.

When the god-awful day finally ended and he went home to his dog, Zach sought solace with his fishing pole and the soothing, familiar rhythm of casting his line into Hummingbird Lake. Ordinarily, fishing soothed his soul, but tonight visions of the day haunted him, with peace remaining elusive and his heart as heavy as Murphy Mountain. When he heard the crunch of tires on the gravel road leading to his house, he glanced over his shoulder, glad for the interruption.

He almost dropped his rod. Savannah Moore?

She climbed out of her old beater of a Taurus wearing a belted white shirt over an ankle-length yellow print skirt, a scowl on her face. Ace rose and loped down the drive toward his visitor. After a moment of silent self-debate, Zach returned his attention to the lake. If she'd come here looking for the sheriff rather than the man, his on-duty deputy would have given him a heads-up. But Gabi hadn't radioed him, and Zach couldn't imagine what had brought Savannah out here. He admitted that he liked her spit and vinegar and that any other night he likely would have enjoyed watching her sashay toward him. Tonight, though, he just wasn't in the mood.

When she approached close enough to speak without raising her voice, she said, "Okay, Sheriff. I surrender."

"Is there a warrant out on you?"

"You tell me."

He glanced over his shoulder. She walked down the point with her shoulders squared, her hands clasped in front of her. Add a length of rope around her wrists and she could be a pirate's prisoner about to walk the plank.

For the first time in hours, his heart lightened.

"You haven't told them. Why haven't you told them? I've tried to do it myself, knowing it's bound to happen at any moment, but I just can't make myself say the words. Every day for more than a week I've waited for it. Who will it be? Which one of them will shift their eyes away from mine? Whose smile will go from genuine to plastic? Will Nic Callahan warn me away from her children? Will Sage Rafferty ask me to move my shop? Celeste says you're trustworthy, but what does she know? You're a cop. Why are you doing this to me, Zach?"

Zach. She'd used his name. Finally. He liked that.

"Do you like to fish?" he asked.

"Excuse me?"

"Here." He handed her his fishing rod. "I have another in the shed. You apparently want to talk, and I want to fish. No reason we can't both be happy."

Savannah sputtered as Zach strode back up the point to the storage shed behind his house. When he returned with his second-favorite fishing rod and a quilt—the temperature dropped quickly once the sun went down, and if this conversation turned into a long, drawn-out drama, she'd get cold in that sleeveless outfit of hers—she was casting his lure into the lake.

He tossed the blanket near his tackle box. "Why did you pick tonight to come out here?"

"It was either this or make brownies, and I'm already past my dessert limit for the week. I ate dinner at the Yellow Kitchen last night, and I couldn't resist the tiramisu Ali had made. I don't want to put on my bathing suit and look at my hips and think of you."

A mental image of his hand on Savannah Moore's string-bikini-clad hip flashed through his mind midway through his cast. Zach inadvertently jerked his hand, sending his line flowing off target. The hook caught on a half-submerged log, and Zach scowled. "Why would you . . . oh, never mind. I've had a helluva day, Peach. Let's see if we can't cut to the chase. If I'm reading this situation correctly, you want to know why I haven't shared with our mutual friends the fact that you have a prison record. Am I right?"

"Yes."

"You've been waiting for the hammer to drop."

"Yes."

"It makes you a little crazy."

"Yes!"

"Crazy enough to challenge your personal Darth Vader at his Death Star."

She threw out her arms. "A movie villain? You think this is all a big joke?"

"Better a movie villain than a two-bit TV sitcom co-star," he snapped, then sighed. "What I think, Savannah, is that either you are enormously insensitive or else you didn't hear about what happened up at Mirror Lake today."

She drew back, her expression growing wary. "What happened at Mirror Lake?"

Zach didn't have the first clue why, but he felt compelled to share the events of his day with the felon from Georgia. As he opened his tackle box and chose a new bait for his line, he said, "Doing what I do for a living, I'm no stranger to violence or to tragic circumstances. But when it involves kids . . ." He exhaled a heavy breath. "It's so damned hard."

Following a brief hesitation, she asked, "Children?"

Zach fixed the fly onto the end of his line. "I patrol a loop that circles around Mirror Lake. It's about fifteen miles from here, up above Heartache Falls, and I met a family from Kansas as they set up their campsite three days ago. Nice people. Real nice people. The father sells insurance and the mom teaches fourth grade. They have two kids, eight and six. Tom and Elizabeth. Those kids were having a ball. Today I had just turned in to the campground when I heard screaming. Tom ran out of the trees . . . he had Elizabeth in his arms. Both kids were shrieking at the top of their lungs. They were just terrified. Turns out they'd been playing hide-and-seek in the trees just beyond the campground and they flushed a mountain lion."

"Oh, no."

"Tom ran toward camp. I'll bet he was planning to

take shelter in the family's Suburban because he was yelling about keys. Anyway, he hit a soft spot on the trail too close to the edge of a drop. His feet slipped out from under him. Both children fell into the lake. Tom's head whacked a rock on the way down."

Savannah dropped her chin to her chest and shook her head. "That's horrible."

"Yeah, it was. Neither one of the kids came up, and both parents jumped into the water. I called it in and followed them."

She stared up at him with troubled eyes. "You jumped into the water?"

"Yeah." Zach stood silent for a long moment as memories of those next horrible minutes rolled through him. "The water was ice. Murky, too, this time of year. Mirror Lake is pretty to look at but a bitch to search."

He paused. Blew out a heavy breath. Cast his line into the water once again, but just let it sit and sink. "I've never felt so damned helpless in my life."

"How horrible for you."

"Not as horrible as it was for them. I'm pretty sure I'll hear the mother's screams in my nightmares for a long time to come."

Savannah set her fly rod aside and picked up the quilt. She spread it across the grass, then gestured toward it. "Sit down, Zach. You look pale."

He did as she suggested and lowered himself to the quilt, where he sat with his legs stretched out in front of him, crossed at the ankles, facing west. Leaning back, he propped his weight on his elbows and watched the setting sun. The sky was beautiful, a crown of crimson and gold surrounding blue-shadowed mountains capped with snow.

Savannah took a seat beside him and quoted, "Purple mountain majesties."

"A little glimpse into heaven." Zach found comfort in the notion, and after a few moments of peaceful silence, he continued his tale. "I've never worked a drowning before. I didn't want to do it today. Diving beneath the water, I could hear only the clock ticking in my head, and every second sounded like a death knell."

From the corner of his eyes, he saw her reach out to touch him. Her hand stopped six inches away and she pulled it back. "How terrifying it must have been."

The absence of her touch was tangible.

Zach closed his eyes as he relived the frantic dives, the strain upon his lungs as he pulled back to the surface to fill his lungs with air, the mother's screams and the father's frantic shouts, the gunshot when another camper took down the big cat. "The father found the boy first. He wasn't . . . good. The bounce against the rock had cracked his skull. Those poor parents were torn— needing to help the boy, to find his sister."

"I cannot imagine what they were feeling. What you were feeling."

"I was too cold to feel. I just kept diving. By then my hands were so numb that it almost didn't register what touched me. It was a little round plastic ball. The girl's ponytail holder fastened with two plastic balls, and one of them brushed my knuckle."

He heard Savannah gasp a relieved breath. "You found her."

"Yes, thank God." He barely recalled the rush to the surface, the swim to the bank, hauling her from the water, and beginning CPR. "Elizabeth was limp as a dishrag when I got her to shore. Prettiest sound I ever heard was when she began to cough."

"So you saved her."

"Her brother saved her. That cat was in full attack mode. The wildlife guys will test it, but I wouldn't be surprised if it was rabid. I don't think it got to either child, but I'm not certain."

"How is the boy doing?"

After a long, silent moment, Zach rolled to a seated position. He scooped up a handful of gravel and began tossing the pebbles, one by one, into the water. Savannah sat with her legs tucked primly to the side. The quilt was large and a full three feet separated them. Nevertheless, he could smell that unique citrusy scent she used, and it floated past him on the evening air like a song. He wanted to reach for her and hold her. To be held. Comforted.

Turner, you're an idiot.

"I don't know. Head injuries are tough. We lifeflighted him to a trauma center. Last I heard he's touch and go."

"I'm so sorry, Zach."

"Me too." He threw a marble-sized pebble into Hummingbird Lake, and as twilight faded to night they sat in silence. When the last glimmer of sunlight was extinguished, leaving a spattering of lights from the houses across the lake to cast a silver shadowed illumination over Reflection Point, the burden of Zach's day slowly eased. Talking to Savannah had helped, he realized, but what had made the difference was the quiet understanding she offered with her silence.

Her company eased him. She brought him peace.

I should return the favor.

He thought the idea through for a couple of moments, then said, "Listen, Peach. As far as I'm concerned, your conviction is your private business. If you want to share it with folks around here, fine. If you don't, that's fine, too. Unless you do something stupid that brings your past into relevancy where my job is concerned, no one will hear about it from me."

* * *

No one will hear about it from me.

Savannah wanted to believe that. She wanted to believe him.

Everyone she'd met in town sang Zach Turner's praises. Celeste Blessing said he was trustworthy, and after their meeting at Angel's Rest, Savannah had learned to accept that just because Celeste looked like Francine Vaughn didn't mean she had Francine's black heart.

Just because Zach was in law enforcement didn't mean he was a lying, thieving gutter rat like Kyle.

Zach had saved a life today. Today he'd been a hero to a tourist family from Kansas.

Tonight, by claiming he'd keep her secret, he'd offered her the moon—if only she could accept it.

Trust. She hadn't trusted anyone other than herself in a very long time. Dare she do it now? Could she believe him, considering that he didn't know the whole story?

Tell him. Tell him and see how he reacts. If nothing else, maybe it will provide him a distraction from his crappy day.

Savannah drew a deep, cleansing breath, then exhaled in a rush. "I was engaged to a cop."

Full night had fallen and the moon had yet to rise. Reflection Point lay in shadow, so she sensed rather than saw that he'd turned his stare toward her.

"My dad was a boat mechanic in a little town in Tennessee. He ran the service department of a marine dealer. He met my mother when they were both hiking part of the Appalachian Trail. They got married and had three boys and then me. I was eight when my mother was killed in a car accident. My dad did his best, but money was tight and the boys were in and out of trouble. In and out of jail. My dad turned to an old family tradition to make ends meet."

"Drugs," Zach said.

His assumption was understandable considering what

he knew about her conviction, but annoying nonetheless. "Moonshine. It was the family business, and my brothers helped. I was sixteen when Gary asked me to make a delivery for him because he had a date. Turns out the law was waiting for him. I got arrested."

"So you have a juvie record, too?"

"Not anymore. I served my probation and it was expunged. I'm telling you this part of it because it's the reason I went to live with my grandmother, my mother's mom. My father wasn't a bad man. He was an independent man who didn't like anyone—especially not the government—telling him what to do. My brothers took after Dad, but when I got into trouble . . . they didn't like it. They wanted better for me, so they sent me away."

"That must have been hard."

"No, not really. They didn't abandon me. They came to visit. I loved my grandmother. She gave me a stability that life with the Moore men didn't offer, and when we lost Dad to a heart attack, she nursed me through my grief. She taught me to make soap and to do well in school. She encouraged me to join the softball team. I was offered a softball scholarship, I'll have you know. To Notre Dame."

"You *were* a ringer." He snapped his fingers. "I knew it. So you met this cop when you were in South Bend?"

"No. I never went to Indiana. Two weeks before I was due to leave, my grandmother and I were up on the mountain when she fell and broke her hip. I ran to the nearest house for help. The woman who lived there had recently moved in. I hadn't met her previously. Zach, she looks so much like Celeste Blessing that she could be her sister. Francine Vaughn helped me that day and was so kind. She and Grams became great friends. She had a phone with long-distance service and we didn't. It took a lot of phone calls for me to make arrangements with

Notre Dame to delay my enrollment for a year so I could help my grandmother. Francine was the one who offered to watch Grams on Tuesdays and Thursdays if I wanted to commute to the small junior college two hours away and get a few basic classes out of the way. That's where I met her son, Kyle."

"Kyle the cop?"

"Yes. He was a detective in the local police department. Kyle and I started dating. He was sweet to Grams and nice to me. I fell in love, blew off Notre Dame, and said yes when he asked me to marry him. Three weeks before the wedding, as I left my chemistry class, it happened."

She shut her eyes as memories and old emotions rolled over her. She hadn't let herself think about that awful time in so long. She didn't want to think about it now. But when she sensed Zach moving closer, felt him take her hand, link their fingers, and give her a gentle, encouraging squeeze, she let herself go back.

ELEVEN

Eight Years Ago

The light turned green. Savannah stepped on the gas and pulled into the intersection. From the corner of her eye, she saw the car approach seconds before impact. She screamed as her airbag deployed and the car spun out of control.

It seemed forever before it stopped, though it took only seconds. Savannah grew aware of burning sensations on her face and arms. Breathing hard, she fumbled for the seat-belt release, opened the driver's door, and stumbled out of the car. *Okay. I'm okay.*

"You all right, lady?"

She took it in with a glance. A pickup truck had run the red light and T-boned her car at the passenger-side rear axle. The driver was her father's age, apparently unhurt, but watching her with a worried look on his face. "I'm okay."

"I called 911. They should be—" He broke off abruptly, and Savannah heard the siren. "They're here. That was fast. Good."

A patrol car arrived on the heels of the ambulance. Savannah answered the paramedic's questions, and when the policeman approached her, she responded to *his in turn. "Yes, it's my car. . . . Yes, the contents are mine. . . . Are my textbooks okay? They were in the backseat. Would you please call my fiancé? Officer Kyle Vaughn."*

The patrolman wrote down the name, asked for Kyle's number, then turned her world upside down by repeating a string of all-too-familiar words. "Ms. Moore, you are under arrest. You have the right to remain silent . . ."

After that, things got a little fuzzy. She had only a vague memory of the three hundred thousand dollars in cash and plastic zip-top bags filled with pot. The lawyer from the public defender's office told her about the search warrant for Grams' house and barn.

She vividly recalled Kyle standing in the interrogation room, his expression earnest as he laced his fingers with hers. "I'll stand by you, honey. I'm an excellent detective, I'll figure out who set you up."

And, months later, her fiancé stood in the witness box, one hand raised, the other on the Bible: ". . . nothing but the truth, so help me God."

Francine leaned forward to whisper in her ear. "You stupid, naive girl."

Handsome, clean-cut Kyle used a crisp, white handkerchief to wipe his eyes before he answered the prosecutor. "Yes, sir. I'm so embarrassed and ashamed. She fooled me completely. I saw her loading money and drugs into her car."

Savannah was snapped back to the present when Zach's angry voice demanded, "You are telling me the cop set you up?"

Her emotions were raw, and her throat was tight. The memory of that moment of realization, of the despair washing through her, hit her like a fist, and she pulled her hand away from his.

"You don't believe me," she muttered, scrambling to her feet. Because of course, except for Grams, no one had ever believed her. Not even her brothers. "I've got to go. I shouldn't have . . . good night."

"That's not what I . . . Savannah, stop. Wait."

But she didn't wait. She ran away from Zach, away from her memories, away from the tragedy at Mirror Lake today and the heartache of her past.

She ran home to her little rented house on Fourth Street, where she held Inny and wept. And wept. And wept. Perhaps all those years of not allowing herself to cry made it almost impossible to stop once she got started now. Finally the storm of emotion subsided. Inny wiggled her desire to be put down, and Savannah went in search of a tissue box that wasn't empty. Her gaze fell upon the stack of Angel's Rest brochures Celeste had asked her to display in her shop. "Well, Grams," Savannah said, attempting to deal with her grief in an old, familiar way, "think there's a chance she knows what she's talking about?"

The window curtains fluttered. The scent of ripe peaches drifted on the air. Inny barked, and slowly Savannah smiled.

She awoke the following morning with a tension headache, tear-swollen eyes, and a craving for one of Sarah Murphy's cinnamon rolls. She popped two aspirin, showered, and dressed, and dealt with her puffy eyes with some eyedrops. Inny barked and leaped excitedly upon seeing the leash, and they started out.

At times of great personal crisis, a girl couldn't go wrong with a cinnamon bun.

Her sense of self-preservation had her peeking through the big plate-glass window of Sarah's bakery, Fresh, before she committed to going inside. She spied Cat Davenport seated at a table with Nic Callahan and Celeste. She was happy to speak to them. Maybe a little "girl time" would be just what she needed. Had Zach been inside, she'd have continued on her walk.

She looped Inny's leash around a tree. "I'll just be a minute. If you behave, I'll bring you out a treat, too."

The dog's ears perked up at the word *treat*.

Inside, Savannah ordered her cinnamon roll and coffee, then greeted her friends. "Join us," Celeste said.

"I can't. I have Inny with me."

Nic hooked her thumb toward the window. "She's fine. She's curled up snoozing. We'll keep an eye on her."

Since she had the town veterinarian's permission, Savannah took a seat and removed her cinnamon roll from the white paper bag. Cat eyed the sweet roll greedily. "We had fruit plates. The fruit was good, but that roll . . ."

"It looks heavenly," Celeste agreed.

Nic inhaled the scent of warm yeast bread, cinnamon, and sugar. "I'm gonna need a drool cup. I limit myself to one of Sarah's cinnamon rolls a month, and I had mine last weekend."

Savannah cut the huge roll into four pieces and pushed the plate to the center of the table. "Here. Be bad. Blame me."

"Don't mind if I do." Cat picked up her fork and dug in. She moaned with delight. "I love being bad."

"Well, I need the energy boost from a little sugar," Celeste said, sampling her piece. "With tourist season right around the corner, I'm busy as a beaver on Angel Creek these days. As are you, I expect, Savannah. When is your grand-opening celebration?"

Savannah smiled, wishing she could look at Celeste without seeing Francine. "I'm opening on Memorial Day, but I didn't plan on any sort of celebration."

"No celebration!" Celeste drew back, obviously appalled. She clicked her tongue. "Well now, we can't have that. A new business is opening in Eternity Springs. That's a huge cause for celebration. You must have an open house."

Savannah glanced from Nic to Cat. Both women licked their forks and nodded. "It's a great idea," Nic said. "You need to do it."

Savannah had never even been to an open house. What on earth would she do? "Whom would I invite?"

Cat said, "I'd start with the Chamber of Commerce list. You'll introduce your products to other business owners, who will recommend them, plus you'll sell a bundle."

Savannah took a bite of roll, and as sugary, sinful pleasure exploded on her taste buds she considered it. What if it flopped? That would be the worst! "I don't know. Seems like a lot of work. I already have so much to do. Maybe if I had more time . . ."

"We'll do all the work," Celeste declared. "It's right up our alley, isn't it, girls? Sarah and Ali can handle the food. Cat, you can take care of the invitations, can't you?"

"Sure."

"Oh, that's really thoughtful," Savannah said, wondering how she'd lost control of the conversation—and her business plan, apparently. "I appreciate the thought, but I can't ask you all to—"

"And why not?" Sarah stood beside the table, a coffeepot in her hand. Pouring a refill for Celeste, she said, "We're your friends, aren't we?"

Savannah's heart did a little pitty-pat. "Well, yes, but—"

"I'll bring my lemon pound cake. What night will we have this shindig? I suggest Thursday."

"Thursday!" Savannah said as Sarah responded to Nic's nod by topping off her cup, too. "That's two days away!"

Cat said, "You said you're opening Memorial Day weekend."

"Wednesday night is out because it's Baked Goods

Bingo night at Saint Stephen's." Celeste smiled at Savannah over the top of her coffee cup. "Don't fret, dear. Just dust and make sure you have change and enough inventory to restock after you sell twice as much as you expect."

Ten minutes later, Savannah departed Fresh with a dog biscuit for Inny, a to-do list a mile long, and a new spring in her step. Not only was she on a sugar high, but she was going to have a party. Her first!

And she couldn't think of anything better to keep her focused on moving forward rather than looking back . . . or thinking about Zach.

It was a good plan that didn't quite work out, because when she arrived home she found a note taped to her door. *I do believe you*, it read. There was a name scrawled at the bottom: *Zach*.

She stayed in her workshop most of the day, trying not to think about events at Reflection Point, preparing inventory, and wondering if she was crazy to make so many of the Spring Cleaned bubble bars. To her the scent said springtime in Eternity Springs, so she thought the locals would like them. She spent her evening fielding calls about the open house and trying on almost every outfit in her closet. While jeans and a T-shirt were the ordinary uniform of the day in town, she thought her first party deserved something a little more.

Not that she had that much to choose from. Six years in prison garb had given her a pent-up demand for pretty clothing, but the desire to save enough money to get out of Georgia had limited her spending on nonessentials. Still, she'd shopped smart and she did have a few nice pieces in her closet. After much inner debate she'd settled on skinny jeans with a red cashmere sweater and red peek-a-boo pumps.

By morning she'd changed her mind and decided on a bohemian look with a broomstick-pleated skirt, a

V-necked knit top, and a hand-beaded, fringed leather belt.

By lunchtime she'd switched her choice to a designer sundress she'd bought in a consignment shop in Denver.

She'd just finished dressing in the skinny jeans and sweater when her doorbell rang a full forty-five minutes before the open house was due to begin. Her annoyance disappeared when Sarah Murphy said, "We're here to help with last-minute preparations."

Her husband, Cam, gave Savannah a gratifying wolf whistle and a kiss on the cheek. "Don't you look gorgeous."

His wife elbowed him in the ribs. "Stop flirting with my friend and go get the pound cake out of the car."

"Didn't your son already drop off a pound cake?" Savannah asked as Ali and Mac Timberlake followed the Murphys inside. Devin Murphy had brought boxes of desserts around four o'clock, and Savannah knew a lemon pound cake had been one of them, because she'd snatched a piece.

"I decided we needed extras," Sarah said after Savannah welcomed the newcomers.

Ali added, "I talked to Cat and she said she only received one invitation decline. It's going to be a packed house. I have extra canapés in the warming oven at the restaurant. Mac said he'd go get them when we need them."

Savannah's stomach rolled over with nervousness. *This is going to cost a fortune.* "Sarah, Ali. Thank you so much. About your bill . . ."

"What bill?" Ali asked. "This open house is on the house."

"But—"

"Don't argue," Sarah added. "We coerced you into having this party. I can pop for a few cupcakes. Consider the refreshments a welcome gift from me and Ali.

After all, Sage did your design work as a gift. That made us look bad."

"You guys are wonderful."

"We know." Sarah flashed an impish smile and changed the subject. "Before everybody gets here . . . I've got gossip about Zach."

Oh, dear. Savannah's smile dimmed, and when the doorbell signaled another early arrival, she was glad for the distraction.

"Actually, not so much about Zach as about his new deputy. Have you guys met her?"

Savannah opened the door to the subject currently under discussion. "It's Gabi Romano," she said, raising her voice so that Sarah would take care with her words.

It proved to be a wasted effort, because Sarah turned and went full gossip on Gabi. "Gabi Romano! I was just talking about you. I've been dying to meet you. Sage and Nic and I are fangirls of Coach Romano. He was the object of our sexual fantasies—"

"Sarah!" Cam protested, scowling, as he walked through the room carrying a pound cake.

"Let me finish." She turned back to Gabi, gave an impish wink, and added, "Until we met the loves of our lives. We were Colorado fans, of course, so we knew about Anthony. Gabe was the one who told us he had a twin who also coached basketball. We all felt so terrible for him when that team bus accident happened.

"Now tell us what it was like growing up with male gods. Two of them. Actually, I heard a rumor that you have a third brother who's no slouch, either."

Gabi snorted. "Don't even get me started. I'm the only girl in my family, and growing up was like living in a gym—sweaty jocks everywhere you turned, literally and figuratively. Not to mention all the panties that ended up in my lingerie drawer. Panties that weren't mine, mind you, but somehow ended up in the family wash.

Women have been throwing their underwear at the Romano men for a long time."

"Gotta admire that quality in a man," Cam said.

Gabi wrinkled her nose. "It makes me question the intelligence of a legion of females."

"A legion?" Cam asked. "Really?"

"I can understand it," Nic said. "The coaches Romano are hawt."

"Stop it," Gabe interjected. "You're giving me a complex. Didn't we come early to help Savannah? Shouldn't we get started?"

Savannah went along with the teasing. "That's okay. I don't mind hearing stories about Gabi's sexy brothers."

Gabi's mouth twisted in a grin Savannah couldn't quite read. "I could shock you, believe me. Better it wait for another time, I think. So, what can I do to help?"

Before Savannah knew it, Heavenscents was overflowing with people, conversation, and laughter. Jack Davenport kept champagne glasses filled from bottles he'd furnished from his wine cellar, while Mac Timberlake played waiter, passing around hors d'oeuvres. Nic Callahan and Sage Rafferty conducted a sales competition, though Celeste's efforts put them both to shame. Savannah spent so much time answering questions and accepting praise that Sarah shooed her away from the cash register and took control of the financial end of the evening.

It was the most exciting evening Savannah could recall. At one point she looked around and saw Sarah and Ali and Celeste laughing, and she marveled that these women had helped her simply because they were good people and they wanted to do it. It made her feel—

She broke off the thought when Gabi pulled her aside. "Congratulations, Savannah. You're a hit."

"I know." She couldn't hold back her excitement. "Thank you so much for coming. Tonight has been just . . . wow. I don't have words. It's more than the money—though that part is wonderful, too—but all this . . . them . . ." She waved a hand toward her helpers. "They've welcomed me. They've made me one of them. I've never belonged like this before."

"I'm glad for you, and I'm glad I could come. You don't know how badly I wish I didn't have to go to work now. I'd love nothing more than to sneak back to Nightingale Cottage with a bottle of Jack's champagne and put one of these bath bombs I bought to good use."

"Which ones did you buy?"

"I bought the Serenity Sampler, Bubbling Peace, Silver Strike Salts, and Lavender Mountain Melt. I figure that might last me a week."

Savannah laughed. "From your mouth to my banker's ears."

After Gabi left, Savannah enjoyed a nice conversation with Jim Brand and his wife, Marsha, about the likely history of the antique bookcase on loan from Angel's Rest that she used to display her line of lotions. Despite being engrossed in the conversation, something—some inexplicable change in the room's atmosphere—caused her to glance over her shoulder.

Zach Turner had just walked into Heavenscents' open house.

TWELVE

Zach couldn't get Savannah Moore off his mind.

From the moment she'd fled from him and Reflection Point two nights ago, she'd haunted him. After nearly a decade in law enforcement he knew that 98 percent of the time you could count on a guilty person to claim innocence. He could count on one hand the number of times he wondered if the perp might actually be telling the truth.

Crazy at it sounded, he believed Savannah's story. Was it good intuition or old-fashioned horniness?

Well, horniness certainly was a factor, but either way, he guessed, it didn't matter. The fact remained that he *did* believe her and he wanted to get to know her better. A lot better. The woman appealed to him like no woman had in a very long time.

She was like a scrappy little terrier, a survivor who didn't take crap from anyone. He felt sorry for her, and he suspected she'd hate it if she knew it. Betrayed by a lover. Framed by the man for a crime she didn't commit? He'd like five minutes alone in a room with the son of a bitch.

A son-of-a-bitch cop. That really burned him. Dirty cops held top billing on his shit list.

Kyle Vaughn. *Detective Kyle Vaughn*, Zach had discovered. He'd testified against her at her trial. The sorry bag of crap. Zach didn't know where this thing he had with Savannah would go, but having a dirtbag ex in the same profession as his own certainly wouldn't help matters. She obviously held his job against him. *Barney Fife my ass.*

Zach intended to find out more about her case—he'd requested transcripts of the trial, for one thing—but first he thought he'd take the opportunity to investigate this business venture of hers . . . and score a glass or two of that fancy champagne Jack Davenport was passing around. When Gabi arrived at the sheriff's office nearly late for her shift and babbling about Savannah's success, he headed for Heavenscents.

He wanted to see Savannah in her glory. Hell, he wanted to see Savannah, period.

She was talking to the Brands when he walked in, and he enjoyed an unobserved moment of watching her. She looked gorgeous in a clingy red sweater and high-heeled shoes. She looked happy, too, and the light in her countenance put a smile on his face.

"Well, well, well," Jack Davenport said, offering him a glass of champagne. "I recognize that look. So, you have a thing for our sexy soap maker?"

Zach shrugged. "Let's just say I'm considering having a thing."

"Can't say I'm surprised after watching you at softball that night. I was a little afraid that you'd have to arrest yourself for violating the burn ban."

"What are you talking about?"

"The two of you sent enough sparks flying around that I thought you might set the field on fire. So . . . what gives?"

Remembering the collision on the field, Zach gave a

crooked grin. Maybe she sensed the men's interest, because at that moment Savannah glanced over her shoulder and met his gaze. He lifted his champagne to her in a silent toast. She frowned and returned to her conversation.

"She's not sure she likes me."

"Woman has some sense."

"Ass."

Jack sipped his champagne. "She has spirit, too. That always makes a woman more interesting."

"I agree."

"I think you should go for it—if only because it would put an end to the matchmaking schemes of my wife and her friends."

"That would be a good thing. I swear this town gets more like a reality TV show every day." Zach was distracted by the sight of Ali Timberlake entering the room carrying a platter of chicken kabobs. "Those look good. I haven't had dinner yet."

"You should see if she's got any of the crab cakes left. They're spectacular."

Zach filled a plate—including crab cakes—then spent a few minutes looking around Savannah's shop. He liked what she'd done with this Victorian. Her displays were inviting, and she'd arranged them in such a way as to display a lot of stuff without having the place feel stuffy. But honestly, ten dollars for a ball of soap?

Judging by the way she appeared to be racking up the sales, she must know what she was doing. Gabi had admitted to spending over a hundred dollars tonight. Of course, his new deputy was a badass girly girl, but still, a hundred bucks?

He visited with his friends and fellow citizens, keeping one eye on the clock and the other on the prize. It didn't escape his notice that she kept track of where he was, too. Every time he moved closer, she scooted away.

Zach bided his time, and as the crowd thinned, he decided he'd given her enough line and time to run. He picked up two glasses of champagne, then sidled over to her. Seeing her notice him and go tense, Zach made a judgment about which compliment she'd prefer hearing most. "The place looks great, Peach."

It took her a moment, but she visibly relaxed and actually smiled at him as she accepted the glass of champagne he offered. "Thanks."

"I like how you've named your products with an Eternity Springs theme."

"Since my primary market for the retail shop is the tourist trade, I thought it would be fun."

"Looks like you've sold a lot to locals tonight, too."

Her smile brightened with satisfaction. "I have. I completely sold out of Spring Cleaned bubble bars."

"As sheriff, I appreciate that Eternity Springs can boast of a clean citizenry." She rewarded him with a laugh, and Zach continued, "Also as sheriff, I like to support local businesses, so why don't you help me pick out something to buy?"

"I can do that. How about something for Ace?"

"Dog bubble bath?"

"I was thinking about a shampoo."

"That'll work."

Savannah led him to a display called "Suds for Spot," and as she described the differences in the three dog shampoos she offered, Zach's attention wandered. Something on the shelf next to the dog stuff smelled great. "I'll take the green stuff," Zach told her, then gestured toward the shelf. "What is this scent?"

"Isn't it wonderful?" She picked up a cellophane bag filled with crystals and untied the ribbon bow that fastened it closed. She passed it to him to get a better whiff. "It's something new I put together, and it's quickly becoming my favorite scent. It's a combination of oakmoss, bergamot, and . . ." A rosy blush stained her cheeks as she added, "Peaches."

"Peaches. No wonder I like it." He inhaled the spicy, appealing fragrance, then read the label. It was a takeoff on the name of the mountain pass leading into town, Sinner's Prayer Pass. "Sinners Make a Pass Bubble Beads."

He had a swift, intense mental picture of a naked Savannah Moore climbing into a bubble bath in a Victorian slipper tub. His voice was a little raspy as he said, "I'll take this, too."

Savannah clarified, "It's bubble bath, Zach."

"Yeah." His vision shifted to a naked Savannah sinking into his hot tub at home and crooking her finger at him. "Actually, I'll take half a dozen bags."

Savannah gave him a quick once-over. Her voice sounded a little tight as she said, "I have that scent in soap if you'd rather."

A naked Savannah in his shower. "Yeah. I'll definitely take some soap, too."

"Too?"

"Too." When his fantasy moved to his bed, he distractedly asked, "Does it come in massage oil?"

She closed her eyes and moistened her lips. "No. No. I don't have a line of massage oils."

"Maybe that's something you should consider."

"I . . . uh . . . can I check you out?"

As soon as she spoke the words, she winced, and he knew she hadn't meant it as a double entendre. Because she looked so miserable, Zach took pity on her and swallowed the suggestive remark that popped into his mind. "Great. I'll pay cash."

Five minutes later, Zach exited Heavenscents wondering just how the hell he'd just spent $105.62 on soap. After his comments to his deputy earlier, if Savannah told Gabi, he'd never hear the end of it.

At the threshold he paused and glanced back over his shoulder. She watched him with a curious combination of yearning and regret. Zach sniffed at the soap and considered.

When the last of her guests departed and only her girl-friends remained, Savannah gave them all enthusiastic hugs, gushing thanks, and huge gift baskets filled with lotions and soaps.

"It was a lot of fun," Sarah said.

Nic nodded. "I had a blast."

"Me too," Ali added. "The party gave me an excuse to try out a couple of new recipes. The crab cakes were a hit."

The women gathered up their things and departed, and when the door shut behind them, Savannah took a moment to gaze around her shop. She hugged herself and twirled around with a huge smile on her face. "Ah, Grams, did you see this? They love our soap. I wish you'd been here to share tonight."

She waited, hoping that the message she'd read in the flutter of curtains and scent of peaches meant her Grams was back. She listened, hoping to hear the words *I was here, Savannah Sophia*. But the voice in her head remained stubbornly silent.

"Well," she murmured, "I still feel your love in my heart and that's what's most important."

But because she did feel lonely she went looking for her dog . . . and found more than she'd bargained for. Inny was in the backyard where Savannah had put her before the party, but she wasn't alone. Zach Turner sat in the porch swing with Inny draped across his lap.

Savannah treated herself to a moment of drinking in the sight of him. Lamplight shining through the back windows cast him in a warm, honeyed glow. The man was so darned delicious to look at—in a totally masculine sort of way with his thick, dark hair, sculpted cheekbones, and squared jaw sporting a five o'clock shadow. He sat sprawled on the swing, his big hand stroking little Inny's coat. Those glacier blue eyes of his watched her with an intensity that started her blood humming.

"You came back," she said, sounding a little breathless to her own ears.

"I never left."

"Why not? Is my dog okay?"

"I didn't want to leave, and your dog is fine. Come sit with me."

"I shouldn't." But she wanted to. Oh, how she wanted to.

"Why not? It's a beautiful night. Your dishes are done. I looked."

Because you're dangerous. "I need to make a night deposit at the bank."

"I'll walk you over in a little while." He patted the empty space beside him. "Swing with me, Savannah."

Temptation resonated in his voice, and Savannah couldn't help herself. She crossed to the swing and sat beside him. Inny's ears perked, but she didn't so much as lift her head from Zach's lap.

The dog knew when she had it good.

The porch swing was one of Savannah's favorite spots in town. She sat there and drank her morning coffee and sometimes a glass of wine before bed at night. Ordinarily, sitting in the porch swing relaxed her. Tonight, though, she wasn't relaxed. Tonight excitement hummed in her blood like her daddy's moonshine.

"What a gorgeous night," Zach said, staring up at the

star-filled sky. Then his gaze shifted and roamed over her with frank male appreciation. "Gorgeous night. Gorgeous woman."

Deliberately he looked at her, his intention in his eyes. Savannah shivered as he reached out and tucked her hair behind her ear, then skimmed his hand along her jaw to cup her cheek. "You left Reflection Point before I had the chance to say good night, Savannah."

His mouth closed over hers and he proceeded to give her the sweetest, slowest, sultriest kiss she'd ever enjoyed. She melted against him in response.

He tasted dangerous and delicious and powerfully male, and as the kiss went on and on and on, a thick languor stole over her. She thought she might have purred. She knew he growled low in his throat. Savannah lost herself in the sensual pleasure of the moment, only vaguely aware that at some point Zach had shooed Inny down from the swing. He pulled Savannah onto his lap, her bottom set squarely between his rock-hard thighs.

"Now it's time to say hello." He deepened the kiss, his tongue seeking, then taking. She inhaled his masculine scent, and even as her hands slid up and across the broad expanse of his shoulders, a little part of her brain wondered how she could re-create the fragrance. *I'd make a mint.*

She bubbled along in a current of sensation like a leaf drifting in a mountain stream. She wished this could go on forever. She needed this man's mouth on hers.

She needed more.

He gave her more.

His hand cupped her breast, his thumb flicking across the hard peak of her nipple and sending a bolt of desire shooting through her. His mouth left hers and went nibbling across her jaw, instinctively homing in on the sensitive spot on her neck that had her whimpering in response.

Zach gasped out, "Why don't we take this inside before I have to arrest myself?"

The rueful laugh bubbled up inside her and spilled out onto the gentle night. "Good try, Turner, but no. I'm not that kind of girl."

He groaned once more, then sighed. "You sure?"

No. "Yes. It would be stupid. You're a cop. I'm an ex-con."

"I'll let you use my handcuffs. On me."

A fantasy image of the sheriff of Eternity Springs naked and spread-eagled on her bed, his wrists cuffed to her iron bedstead, flashed into her brain. He removed them from his belt and dangled them before her eyes. Temptation, like the apple from the tree.

In self-defense, she scrambled off his lap and sat on the far end of the swing. "I should be insulted. We've never even been on a date."

"Want to go to dinner tomorrow night?"

She closed her eyes. *Yes.* "No. It's a bad idea, Zach. Any minute now I'm going to be horrified by what just happened."

"Why? We're two single adults."

"Like I said. You're a cop."

"Sheriff. And what does that have to do with . . . wait." He scowled at her. "Wait just one damned minute. You're not comparing me to your ex, are you?"

Of course she compared him to Kyle. That man had fooled her completely, hadn't he? Experience had proved that she had no sort of judgment where men were concerned, hadn't it?

Yes, everything she knew about Zach pointed toward him being a stand-up guy. *But like they say, Been there, done that, got the orange prison jumpsuit to prove it.*

Dodging the question, she said, "Look, I'm not myself tonight. I'm still on a post-party high."

His scowl darkened. "You're not claiming that I took advantage of you."

I wish. She shook her head. "Absolutely not. You should know I value truth more than just about anyone you'll ever meet."

"That's understandable considering what happened to you."

The unstated support of her version of the tale warmed her like brandy on a cold winter night. It also made her vulnerable. She couldn't go there with this man. She was finally getting on with her life, and he would be a complication. A delicious complication, true, but . . . "Look, Zach. It's been a very busy day and I honestly don't know what I'm feeling tonight. I think it's best for both of us that you leave now."

"Here's your soap; what's your hurry?"

"Don't be difficult. Please?"

"All right." He sighed dramatically and stood, but the gleam in his eyes showed her he had no hard feelings. "Want me to drop off your deposit for you?"

Savannah opened her mouth to say no and surprised herself. "Yes, thank you. That would be very nice. Wait here and I'll get you the bag."

"So you do trust me."

"With my money, yes."

"That's a start." He laughed and grabbed her hand and pulled her to her feet. He bent and gave her another thorough, knee-melting kiss. "Good night, Peach."

Once she handed him her money bag, Sheriff Zach Turner picked up his bag of soap and headed around the side of her house with a wave and a parting comment guaranteed to haunt her through the night: "Guess I'll just go home alone and take a bubble bath."

* * *

Memorial Day weekend kicked off the Eternity Springs summer season with a bang—literally. The Wounded Wings One Hundred charity bike race, which wound through the mountains above Eternity Springs on a hundred-mile-long route, started on a pistol shot. The streets bustled with people, and in shops and other businesses all over town cash registers dinged and beeped and rang up a satisfying number of sales.

The bike race kept Zach busy, but not so much that he didn't spare a thought or twelve about a certain shop-keeper.

He'd spent a restless night following the open house. Sexual frustration and mental puzzles clamoring to be studied didn't make for comfortable sleep. After devoting considerable thought and a good bit of fantasy to the events of the evening, he'd concluded that Savannah likely did look at him through eyes clouded by her experience with a dirty cop, and that he needed to do something to change that.

He wasn't that guy. He wasn't like any of the men who had let her down throughout her life, and she needed to know that. He decided to make convincing her of that a personal challenge.

After his bike race duties ended, he strolled his patrol route through town and supported local business by stepping into the Taste of Texas Creamery and ordering two cones. Five minutes later, having increased his pace so that the ice cream didn't melt, he slipped into Heavenscents just as a pair of tourists took their leave.

Savannah stood at her register ringing up a customer. Otherwise, the shop appeared empty. *Perfect timing.* Gallantly he held the door open for her departing customers, then offered her the cone. "Can I tempt you?"

She gave him a droll look but accepted the ice cream. "I'm a sucker for sweets."

"Feel free to call me sugar, honey." He waggled his brows in a teasing leer.

She rolled her eyes, but that couldn't hide the amusement twinkling inside them as she took a long lick of the ice cream cone. "It's peach."

"I was thinking about you. What else could I have chosen?" He stared her straight in the eyes and took a long, slow lick of his ice cream. Her cheeks flushed, and satisfaction washed through him. His purpose accomplished, he backed off. "How has business been today?"

"Slow until the cyclists made their way out of town. Then I got so busy I couldn't keep up. It slowed down again once they were due back and people began collecting near the finish line."

"Bet you sold a lot of soap to cyclists' spouses. A shower is one of the first things I want when I finish a long ride."

"You ride a bike?"

"I love mountain biking, though I'm not into races like we had today. I like to ride the back roads and explore. It's great exercise, a wonderful way to see out-of-the-way places." He paused, considered asking her to go on a ride with him, but decided against it. It was too soon. He had a plan and he needed to stick to it. "Well, enjoy your ice cream."

He hadn't intended to kiss her, but she had a little dollop of peach at the corner of her mouth that needed to be licked. So he did it. Then followed that with a quick press of his mouth against hers. "I'll see you around."

He whistled as he exited Heavenscents, leaving Savannah standing with a stupefied look on her face. "My work here is done."

For today, anyway.

The following day he didn't stop by her shop, but he

did send her flowers. The day after that he dropped by with a bone for Inny. Savannah appeared genuinely impressed by that effort.

Like most Eternity Springs merchants during tourist season, she worked ten hours a day, seven days a week, closing only Sunday mornings. As much as Zach would have loved to spirit her away for a scenic alpine picnic on his day off, he knew that June was not the time to do it.

June was a good time to give her some pampering, however, so he arranged to have the masseuse from the spa at Angel's Rest take her mobile table to Heavenscents at the close of a workday. At the end of the hour scheduled for her massage, Zach showed up with a bottle of port and a tin of chocolate-covered blueberries. He found Savannah sprawled bonelessly in her outdoor swing wearing a white spa robe and a languid smile.

"Hello, beautiful."

"I'm not stupid, Zach Turner. I know you have an ulterior motive for being so nice to me. Massages and dog bones and flowers—you're not fooling anyone."

"An ulterior motive?"

"You want to get beneath my spa robe."

"Well, of course I do, but I've made no effort to hide the fact." He sat beside her. "This is something you need to understand about me, Peach. I'm a straight shooter, too. Unless I'm on the job and you're under interrogation, I won't lie to you."

She wrinkled her nose in disbelief. "You're a man."

Zach hated to upset her relaxed state, but she'd served the opportunity on a platter, and he couldn't pass it up. "I'm not Kyle Vaughn."

At the name, she sat up. She clutched her robe at the neckline, set her mouth, and narrowed her eyes. "You read up on me."

"I sure did. I read the trial transcripts. Guy was a real ass."

She studied him, meeting and holding his gaze for a long minute. "You really do believe me, don't you."

"Crazy, isn't it? I never believe the claims of innocence of—"

"Convicts?" she drawled in that slow molasses accent of hers that he found so arousing.

He rolled his tongue around his mouth. "Law enforcement clients."

She snorted a little laugh. "I can't make up my mind about you, Sheriff. You confuse me."

"Just don't confuse me with the d bag."

Savannah tilted her head and studied him. "Sarah said you've dated more women than any other guy in town. Ski instructors, summer residents . . ." Her brows dipped in a frown as she added, "Her and Nic and even Ali. And Ali was married!"

Showing interest. Excellent. "Now, that's not true, Savannah. Ali and I didn't date. We just flirted a little, and this was during the time that she was separated from Mac. She'll tell you I was good for her. I'm a nice guy. Give it a little time and you'll figure that out."

"A little time," she repeated before giving her head a baffled shake. "Why? We have nothing in common. We're as different as can be. Why me, Zach? Because I'm handy? I'm handy and you're horny?"

"That's insulting to both of us."

"Then explain it to me." She punctuated her demand by waving her hand.

Zach could see that she seriously had doubts about him. The woman was gun-shy, and he needed to put her at ease. Otherwise, they'd never move forward . . . and he very much wanted to move forward.

So he used the most powerful weapon in his arsenal—

the truth. "Honestly, I would if I could, but I don't know that I understand it myself. Not totally. You intrigue me, Savannah. You challenge me. That's a turn-on for me. I like climbing mountains. I like backcountry skiing. I like trying to get beneath your skin—not to mention your spa robe."

Her eyes narrowed. "So this is sport to you. A game."

"Maybe. I admit that's part of it. At the risk of sounding egotistical, I haven't had to work for a woman in a long time. You are work, Savannah Sophia Moore." He ignored her wrinkled nose and sniff of disgust and pressed on. "I'm not afraid of work and I'm not afraid of challenges. I'm not afraid of relationships, either. Maybe that's where you and I are headed."

"A relationship?" she asked, horrified.

The squeak in her voice made him smile. "Maybe. Or maybe we'll settle on a friendship."

"Maybe we'll want nothing to do with each other."

"Maybe you'll break my heart. Or . . ." He kissed the back of her hand. "Maybe we'll fall in love."

She leaped out of the swing as if her butt was on fire. "Love? Fall in love? Now you are being insane. You're a cop. I'm a convict."

"So?"

"So that's like . . . I don't know what that's like. Oil and water."

"I admit, it's a long shot. Still, don't you think it'll be fun figuring out the answer?"

Zach rose and stepped toward her. Savannah, of course, backed away, until she bumped up against the house. "You smell like summertime and champagne. Kiss me, Peach."

She placed her palm against his chest. "I am not having sex with you tonight."

"A good-night kiss. That's all I'm asking for. Trust me, Savannah." Silvered moonlight illuminated her face, and the yearning in her expression broke his heart. "You can trust me, Savannah."

Her hand slid up his chest and around his neck. Silently she offered him her lips.

For now, that was enough.

THIRTEEN

"The man confounds me," Savannah told Gabi, who sat beside her in a salon chair in the Angel's Rest spa. "It's been three weeks. He sends gifts. He calls me. He drops by the shop to visit. He tells his friends that he's 'seeing' me, but he hasn't asked me out."

"Really? How do you know that?"

"Sage told me. Is this some sort of weird mountain dating ritual? Not to go on dates?"

Gabi laughed. "Not that I know of. I agree it's weird that he's never asked you out. It's not like he's trying to work up the nerve. From everything I've seen, Zach Turner doesn't do timid."

Savannah eyed the red polish on Gabi's toes and second-guessed her own choice of a pink shade. "Well, he did ask me out once, but that was at the open house."

"You turned him down?" When Savannah nodded, Gabi continued. "Well, there's your answer. He's waiting for you to make the next move."

"Excuse me? Are you saying he's waiting for *me* to ask *him* out?"

"Knowing my boss, that's a good guess. Zach is a proud man."

"He's a pest." Savannah indulged in a minor sulk. "And the whole thing is complicated."

"Why, because you have a jerk in your past?"

Savannah startled. Had Zach spread her personal business around? Before she could ask, Gabi continued.

"You don't own the market on a-holes, Savannah. A lot of us have scars from that particular battle."

"Maybe so, but some wounds take longer to heal. Some wounds never heal."

"Sure they do . . . as long as you don't let them fester. You need to let yourself see where this thing with Zach takes you. Don't stress and don't overanalyze. It causes wrinkles."

Was Gabi right? The idea did make a weird sort of sense. The behavior was annoying, so of course it would be something he'd do. She nodded toward Gabi's feet and changed the subject. "What color is that?"

"Wine for Me, Baby."

"It's pretty. It complements your olive complexion." Savannah glanced up as the nail technician exited the back room carrying a stack of towels. "It probably would look garish on me. I'm too pale."

"You are peaches and cream. I'm jealous. So back to the matter at hand. You should ask Zach out, Savannah. Make a picnic and have him take you up to Heartache Falls or something." Gabi held up one foot, then the other, so that Molly could slip her sandals on. "Make your peach cobbler."

"Your boss isn't the only pest in town," Savannah said glumly. "Don't you need to go give somebody a parking ticket or something?"

"Meow." Gabi shot her an unabashed grin.

A few minutes later, after Gabi had left the salon, her words lingered in Savannah's mind as Molly gave her a pedicure. And while she shopped for groceries at the Trading Post. And when she opened the shop at ten and ate her lunch at twelve-thirty and sold an eighty-seven-dollar gift basket to a tourist from Arizona at three.

Gabi's suggestion trumpeted through her mind like a brass band when she was out on the front porch watering her geraniums and Zach drove by in his sheriff's Range Rover. Two days later, she gave in, as much to still the voice in her head as for any other reason. At least that's what she tried to tell herself.

At two o'clock on a Wednesday afternoon, Savannah made a phone call to Celeste, then hung the BACK IN TEN MINUTES sign on Heavenscents' front door. She marched over to the sheriff's office, greeted Ginger with a tight smile, and asked if she could speak to Zach for just a minute.

"Sure, honey," Ginger replied. "Go on back."

Savannah hesitated outside his office door, her heart pounding, her mouth dry as sand. He sat scowling at his computer screen and looked so handsome doing it that she almost chickened out. *Curse the man. Why does he have to be so darned agreeable?*

Summoning her nerve, annoyed that she needed to do so, Savannah rapped on his door. Zach glanced up, and surprise briefly widened his eyes before he offered a warm smile. "Hello, Peach."

Without a preamble or a greeting or even a smile, she blurted, "Do you want to go on a picnic with me Sunday afternoon?"

He didn't hesitate an instant. "I'd love to go on a picnic with you Sunday afternoon."

Holy soap flakes, he said yes. Now what? "Okay, then. Pick me up at one. I'll bring the food. Can you choose the spot?"

"Absolutely."

"Okay, then." She spun on her heel and exited the office. She had just reached the corner when she heard him call her name. She stopped, exhaled abruptly. *He's going to cancel.* Bracing herself for the humiliation of rejection, she turned around. "Yes?"

"Shall we bring the dogs along?"

The rest of the week, Zach alternated between smugness and nervousness. The nervousness really pissed him off. His plan had worked, hadn't it? She'd marched into his office and asked him out. He'd worn her down, just like he'd planned. So then why was he antsy about this? Women didn't make him nervous. Not since high school, anyway.

Savannah Moore made him nervous.

"That's what you get for being smug, you idiot," he muttered to himself as he loaded Ace into his Jeep at ten minutes to one on Sunday.

And yet he had every right to be smug, didn't he? His strategy to subtly seduce was working like a charm. The woman was skittish as a new colt where men were concerned, for good reason. Still—and he'd never admit this to another soul—he'd been shocked when she burst into his office, her eyes looking a little angry and wild, and belligerently asked him on a picnic.

When she answered his knock on her front door, the fake smile on her face and dread in her eyes restored his good humor for some reason. "You look like someone just drop-kicked little Inny. I'm not the Big Bad Wolf, you know."

"No. You're the Big Bad Sheriff." She sighed heavily. "And this is a really bad idea."

Well, hell. "Are you trying to chicken out?"

Her chin came up. "No. I do what I say I'm going to do. Our picnic lunch is ready and Inny is ready and I'm—"

"Beautiful." She wore faded jeans and a pale pink camp shirt that shouldn't have been sexy but was. "So what's on the menu?"

"Fried chicken, potato salad, coleslaw, and peach cobbler for dessert. Zach, I haven't been on a date since Kyle. I'm not ready for this."

"It's a picnic, Savannah. I'm not taking you back to my place to have hot, raunchy sex." *Damn the bad luck.* "There is nothing for you to be 'ready' for other than maybe to catch a trout."

"Fishing? You're taking me fishing?"

"Do you have something against fishing?"

After a moment's hesitation, she said, "I don't know. I've never been fishing before."

He gaped at her. "Now, that's just sad. We will definitely take care of that this afternoon. I'm taking you up to this place I know on Murphy Mountain. It's a beautiful picnic spot, and the fishing is great. You can give it a try, and if you don't like it, we can hike over to Heartache Falls or just sit and talk."

"Fishing sounds fun. I do like to hike, too."

Zach followed the path of her gaze and noted she wore sneakers. "You might want to bring along some boots, just in case. Want help with the food?"

"Sure. The basket is on my kitchen table. Let me get my boots and Inny's leash and we're ready to go."

Zach's dog, Ace, gave a happy yip when Savannah put Inny in the backseat with him. The two dogs had played together twice before at the dog park and had become great friends.

They stopped by Cam Murphy's sporting goods store and bought a fishing license for her. Zach kept the conversation general and light as he took the scenic back road up the mountain and she slowly relaxed. *Like gentling a horse,* he thought.

When he turned off the road and onto a rutted trail, she cut him a glance. "You sure you know where you're going?"

"Trust me." He flashed a wide grin and added, "It is

rough through here. You might want to grab the hold strap."

She held on to it for dear life, her brow furrowed in concern until the moment the path curved and the Jeep burst onto the meadow. "Oh," she breathed, a smile of pleasure brightening her face. "How lovely. The view is absolutely breathtaking."

"Best view of Sinner's Prayer Pass around. Cam would like to build a house up here, but Sarah says it's not practical with them both having businesses in town."

"He owns this land?"

"Yep. He owns all of Murphy Mountain except for the section he sold to Jack's charitable foundation for the camp they're building."

"Cat mentioned something about it, but I haven't heard the details. It's for troubled kids?"

"Children whose lives have been touched by tragedy. They had hoped to open in June, but licensing red tape held them up. I think they're set now for some time in August. They're going to have a couple of test run sessions for local kids first."

He drove to the center of the meadow and stopped the Jeep beside the creek. "Here's our lunch spot. So, what would you like to do first? Eat? Hike? Fish?"

"You said we can hike to Heartache Falls from here?"

"Yes. Takes about half an hour."

"Is it too difficult for the dogs?"

"No, but we'll need to keep them on their leads. If we run across wildlife, it's better that we keep control."

In the process of lacing up a hiking boot, Savannah glanced up warily. "Wildlife? Are we talking mountain lions and bears?"

"It's possible, but chipmunks are much more likely. I've seen how Inny guards her backyard against the evil chipmunk interlopers."

"Yes, she is the ruler of her domain."

Zach kept a loaded pack in his Jeep for hikes, so he grabbed it and Ace's lead, and once Savannah was ready, they headed into the sun-dappled forest. To Zach's ears, a heavily wooded mountain had its own unique sound, a muted sense of life that, though quiet, was never still. A forest's city street was the crash of a falling pinecone onto a pile of brittle windswept leaves, the chatter of birds above, and the bubble of a brook almost always out of sight. Fir trees dominated the landscape on this part of the mountain and perfumed the air with a scent Zach always associated with Christmas. He said as much to Savannah.

"I'm still traumatized by the year my parents decided we needed an artificial tree instead of a real one," he added. "I thought there was just something wrong about dragging your Christmas tree out of the attic instead of traipsing to the Boy Scouts' tree lot to pick out the perfect one. That only lasted a year, though. Dad and I whined about it enough that the next year, Mom compromised. Dad and I got our real tree, but when it came time to take it down and put the decorations away, we did the work and Mom shopped the after-Christmas sales."

Rather wistfully, Savannah said, "We used to steal our Christmas trees."

Zach swung his head around and arched a brow at her. Savannah chuckled. "It's true. I'm not a drug trafficker, but I'll cop to being a Christmas tree thief. It was a family tradition, and I admit it was one I just loved. My dad and brothers and I would pick one out every summer as we hiked up to the stills. When we finally settled on one, I'd tie a red hair ribbon around it, and then the Sunday after Thanksgiving, no matter what the weather was like, we'd pile into Daddy's truck and go get it."

"Tell me you're not carrying a red hair ribbon today."

"I haven't owned a hair ribbon in years."

"Good. Don't make me arrest you come December, Peach."

"Well . . ." she drawled in that slow molasses voice as she made a show of studying the nearest Douglas fir. He scowled at her, and this time her laughter pealed out like church bells. "Don't worry. After she caught me shoplifting toothpaste at the local Walmart, Grams made me swear I'd never steal anything ever again."

"You stole toothpaste?"

"Let's just say I learned early on in life how to stretch the grocery budget. What about you, Zach? Did you ever shoplift or were you always a Boy Scout?"

"I didn't shoplift and I am an Eagle Scout, but I did steal a car one time."

She halted abruptly, her eyes bugging, and now it was Zach's turn to laugh. "Undercover cops get to do all sorts of criminal things in order to protect their cover."

"That is so not fair."

Zach gave Ace's leash a tug, and the whippet abandoned his intent sniffing at the base of a fallen log and returned to the trail. Like a pesky younger sister, Inny followed right at Ace's heels.

Their conversation lagged as the trail took them on a rocky incline that required concentration. Twice Zach reached back to give her a hand up, and the second time he didn't release her, but laced her fingers with his. "You mentioned brothers. How many brothers do you have?"

"Three."

"Older? Younger? Any sisters?"

"Older brothers, no sisters. You?"

"None of either. I'm adopted. My parents were beginning the process for a second child when my grandmother had a stroke, Mom became her primary caretaker, and they decided she had her hands full. I always wished I had a brother."

"Is your grandmother still alive?"

He shook his head. "I lost all three before I turned twenty-three. Nana had another stroke, my mom died from breast cancer, and my dad . . . they said it was a heart attack, but I think losing Mom broke it."

Savannah's eyes went soft and caring. "Oh, Zach. That's terrible. I'm so sorry. That must have been very difficult for you."

"It was hard. My heart was broken, too. I loved them very much. Being on my own at that age was tough. Took me a little while to adjust. I almost flunked out of school." Now why the hell had he told her that? He didn't talk about that. He wasn't one to delve into his past.

"Did you ever try to find your biological parents?" she asked, then winced. "I'm sorry. That's nosy of me. It's none of my business."

"No, it's okay," he replied, and continued his blabbermouth ways. "And the answer is no, I never have. Never wanted to. I had great parents. I guess I didn't think it'd be right to go digging around in the past looking for replacements. That said, I always wished I had a brother."

She pulled her hand from his. "Sometimes brothers are more of a pain than they're worth."

"Tell me about yours."

Savannah took another ten paces before replying. "One of my brothers left home when I was still in high school. One went to jail for drugs and the last I heard was still there. The other married and had a kid."

"Niece or nephew?"

Her smile was bittersweet. "A nephew. Tommy. But can we talk about something else, please? We should be talking about the weather or the hot springs at Angel's Rest or the Fourth of July fireworks over Hummingbird

Lake. This is our first date. We should be talking about the scenery and making small talk!"

"Small talk is okay. Making out is better." With that, he pulled her into his arms and lowered his mouth to hers. His kiss was hot, passionate, and carnal, and as Savannah melted into his arms, her words from moments earlier whispered through his mind like a summer breeze through an aspen grove. *So you're alone.*

I have been. Maybe not anymore.

She means something to me.

Shaken, he ended the kiss. Taking a step away from her, he filled his lungs with air, then exhaled a heavy breath. "It's our first date."

She shook her head as if clearing away cobwebs. "That's what I said."

Zach drank in the sight of her. Sunlight beaming through the trees caught strands of red in her hair, turning it a burnished gold. Her big brown doe eyes and graceful manner of movement made her suited to the forest. She wasn't a deer, however. She was a mountain lion. "I think you might well be the strongest woman I've ever met, Savannah."

Now she closed her eyes. "Why did you say that?"

I don't know. "Because it's true."

"I certainly don't feel strong right now. You make me feel weak."

"I'm an excellent kisser, so while I appreciate the sentiment, that's not the sort of weakness I'm talking about. Here, let me show you."

Taking her hand once again, they stepped into the clearing that offered an unobstructed view of Heartache Falls. They stood at almost the halfway point between the top of the falls and the pool at its base. It was a long, narrow ribbon of water, swollen with snowmelt, that roared over the rocks and crashed some sixty feet below.

Zach and Savannah stood close enough that mist drifted over them, dampening their skin.

"It's beautiful," Savannah said.

Now he knew why he'd said she was strong. "It's energy and music and life flowing over bedrock that stands firm. That's you, Peach."

She gave him a searching gaze as color stained her cheeks. "That's poetic. And flattering. You continually surprise me, Sheriff Turner."

"I think that's probably a good thing." Then he leaned down and kissed her again. She melted against him again.

Zach concluded that their first date was off to a darned good start.

Back at the meadow, they ate lunch, and after Zach finished rhapsodizing about Savannah's southern cooking, they threw tennis balls for their dogs until the pups pooped out and plopped down on the quilt for a nap. Zach wouldn't have minded joining them, but Savannah was ready to fish. When he carried his tackle box and two rods to the bank of the stream, excitement gleamed in her eyes and ignited his own.

This was the first time he'd ever taught someone how to fish, and he found Savannah's enthusiasm entertaining and, well, arousing. Of course, he found most everything about her arousing these days. When she landed her first fish—a nice-sized rainbow—and bounced up and down and then shimmied with unadulterated joy, he felt like he'd given her the moon.

He also wanted to drag her to the ground and have his way with her, but he'd hate to have to arrest himself for public indecency.

It was a fun afternoon. She scoreboarded him where fishing was concerned, catching three to his one. As they were getting ready to leave, loading up the Jeep with dogs and fresh trout for dinner, he said, "That wasn't so hard, was it?"

"Fishing?"

"Going on a date with me."

She waited a full thirty seconds before replying. "I enjoyed today, Zach. Thank you."

"Want to give it another go?"

"Are you asking me out on a date?"

"Absolutely. It's my turn." She rewarded him with a faint smile, and Zach shifted gears, then reached for her hand. "I'm working every day until the Fourth. I have to work the parade and afternoon picnic, but I'm off that night. How about joining me for fireworks on Reflection Point?"

She cleared her throat. "Fireworks?"

Oh, yeah. "Eternity Springs' fireworks show is over Hummingbird Lake. The best view around is from my hot tub."

"Fireworks. A hot tub."

"I'll grill some steaks, open a good bottle of wine. It'll be nice. Relaxing." *Romantic. Maybe not-so-subtle seduction.*

She turned to him with wary, troubled eyes. "I enjoy being with you, Zach. I'd like a Fourth of July second date. But I'll be honest. This whole thing between us . . . it scares me. It's happening too fast."

Too fast? Compared to what? Cold molasses?

Okay, maybe not seduction after all. Dammit.

"Don't be scared, Savannah. There's no need for that. I'm not a jerk and I'm not out to hurt you. You can trust me."

Bitterness colored her tone. "No, Zach. I can't. I can date you. I can make out with you. Maybe one of these days I'll even sleep with you. But I will never trust you or any man ever again. You need to understand that."

"That's a little melodramatic, don't you think?"

"Try spending six years in prison for a crime you didn't commit because someone you loved betrayed you, then see what strikes you as melodramatic. Okay?"

Zach pursed his lips, knowing that now was not the time to further pursue this line of discussion. Instead he nodded. "I hear you. So, we're on for the Fourth and fireworks? Do you prefer T-bones or rib eyes? Cabernet or Merlot?"

She smiled. "You pick."

At least she trusted him with that.

"I'll bring homemade peach ice cream."

Now who was trying to seduce whom?

FOURTEEN

The summer days breezed by. Savannah stayed thrillingly busy at Heavenscents—so busy, in fact, that she hired two part-time employees to help in the retail shop and another to assist with shipping online sales. She used the time the extra help gave her to replenish her inventory and order her supplies. At the end of June, her sales were running 40 percent higher than her projections—40 percent!—and she treated herself to an online shopping spree with expedited delivery.

She bought a new sundress and shoes to wear for her Fourth of July date.

She'd seen Zach occasionally in the days since their picnic—though he made sure he was seldom gone from her thoughts. He continued to send gifts, make phone calls, and duck in to say hello whenever his foot patrol took him past Heavenscents. It hadn't helped that one of his new hires had missed three days of work with the flu, forcing Zach and his other deputies to work extra shifts. When Gabi told her that, Savannah had shut her door an hour early and baked a peach cobbler, which she delivered warm to the sheriff's office.

She'd thought that Zach was going to break down and cry.

Each day, with its wink and wave and "Hiya, Peach,"

brought Savannah closer to a momentous decision until finally, during her lunch break on July 2, she made one more Internet purchase and chose overnight delivery.

No way was she going to buy condoms in Eternity Springs.

It had taken a fair amount of soul-searching for her to admit to herself that she might have a need for them, but Savannah didn't lie, not even to herself. Especially when what she really, really wanted to do was lie to herself.

She had the hots for the sheriff. Another law enforcement officer. What in heaven's name was wrong with her? She obviously had some sort of mental issue.

No, her issue was definitely physical.

In her defense, Zach Turner in full magnetism mode was difficult for any woman to resist. Hadn't she seen that in the way even the older women in town preened and blushed when he turned on the charm? He had a boyish grin, an athlete's build, and a wicked glint in those devastating blue eyes that could turn a woman to mush. Yet those attributes were only part of what made him so appealing to her. What had breached her defenses was learning that he had no family, either.

Savannah's heart had ached for him when he told her about losing his loved ones. The information had created a common bond between them, whether they acknowledged it or not. Despite her father's failings, she had loved him and she'd grieved for him when he died. Her brothers had been worthless, as always, but she'd had her grandmother to help her through the loss of her dad. Kyle, too, had been a help—at least on the surface. Zach had had no one. He still had no one. The two of them were a match made in . . . well, not heaven. The thoughts on her mind were definitely earthy.

The morning of the Fourth dawned gray and damp, but by the time the parade started at ten, the clouds had

burned off and the sun shone brightly. Like the majority
of the businesses in town, Savannah kept the shop open
for the holiday, though she did close down for an hour
while the parade was taking place. Despite the curtailed
schedule, she had the best sales day ever, and as she
readied herself for her date after work, excitement siz-
zled in her veins. "I'm a success, Grams," she said as she
gazed at her reflection in the mirror. She gave her hair
one more stroke with the brush. "I'm going to make this
business work."

She paused, listening hard, and when she didn't hear
her grandmother's voice echoing through her mind, she
added, "And there's a good possibility that I'm going to
have sex tonight. With a totally hot guy. Who tonight
will be Zach, just Zach, and not Sheriff Zach."

Her doorbell rang. She shut her eyes and drew a deep,
bracing breath. Pasting on a smile, she went to open her
door.

Zach's easy grin died as he got a look at her. His lips
pursed and he gave a soundless whistle as he gave her a
thorough and blatantly masculine once-over. "You look
gorgeous. You sparkle like sunlight on Hummingbird
Lake."

Her smile went from nervous to genuine, and she resisted the urge to twirl. "Thank you. I'm happy. Heavenscents had its best day ever."

"Congratulations. Maybe I'll break out a bottle of
champagne and some caviar."

"Really? I've never tasted caviar."

"Oh, honey. We can fix that tonight."

Wonder what other "nevers" he could fix . . .

Zach told her about his workday during the short
drive out to his house, thoroughly entertaining her with
a story about a fox in a construction site Porta-John.
Savannah remained surprisingly relaxed, and when he
excused himself to clean up, since he'd picked her up on

the way home from work, she grabbed a tennis ball from a bucket near the back door and went outside to coax Ace into a game of catch. It didn't take much coaxing. Inny liked to play catch. Ace *loved* it.

Zach exited the house twenty minutes later wearing worn blue jeans and a white oxford shirt and carrying a tray holding two flutes filled with bubbling champagne and a plate of bread crusts with a small bowl of black caviar surrounded by ice. She gestured toward the plate. "Is this a staple of yours, Zach?"

"Caviar? Not hardly. I can handle steak just fine, but I ordered hors d'oeuvres from the Yellow Kitchen." He set down the tray and handed her one of the glasses. Lifting his, he toasted, "To record-breaking sales days."

The champagne bubbled on her tongue, and when he offered her a toast topped with a dollop of caviar, she added, "And new experiences."

She tasted the caviar. It had the consistency of butter and melted in her mouth. "Oh, that's good. It's not salty at all."

"Ali said good caviar is supposed to taste like a fresh ocean breeze."

"It's wonderful. So is the champagne."

He named the label, then asked, "Are you hungry?"

Oh, yes.

"I can put the steaks on now, or we could wait a little while to eat."

Dinner. He means dinner, stupid. "Either way is fine with me."

"Then let's walk out to the point. I have a new addition I want to show off."

They strolled hand in hand toward the tip of Reflection Point. Drawing closer, Savannah spied the addition he'd mentioned. He'd placed a lovely, two-person wooden lawn swing at the end of the point. "You do like your swings, don't you?"

"It's a recent acquisition. Something about sittin' in a swing with a luscious Georgia peach makes me content as a dog with two tails."

He led her to the swing and sat beside her, close to her, and gave the swing a push with his long legs. "Tell me your favorite Fourth of July memory."

After a moment's consideration, she talked about her family. "I told you I have a nephew. He's my middle brother's son. Gary is four years older than me. He got his girlfriend pregnant in high school and they got married, but that was a disaster. She ran off and left Tommy behind. By that time, I was living with my grandmother, my dad was sick, and Gary asked us to babysit for a week while he delivered a car for someone to California. He had some trouble—it was a big mess and not entirely his fault—but he didn't come back for six weeks."

"He dumped his kid on you for six weeks? And you were just a kid yourself?"

"I enjoyed it. Tommy was such a sweetheart and so affectionate. When you asked about my favorite Fourth of July, that's the memory that popped into my mind. It was the first time he'd seen fireworks, and he oohed and aahed and squealed and screamed. It was so much fun. Once the show was over, he hugged my neck and told me he loved me." Her smile turned bittersweet as she added, "His dad showed up to get him three days later."

"Where are your brother and Tommy now?"

"I didn't hear much from them after I went to jail. When I got out . . ." She shrugged. "They'd moved away."

He laced his fingers with hers, then brought her hand up to his mouth and kissed it. "I'm sorry, Peach."

"Water under the bridge." She forced a smile onto her face and said, "Tell me about your favorite Fourth of July."

He told her a funny story about a greased watermelon

scramble at the city swimming pool in the town where he'd grown up. Then, when they finished their champagne, he suggested it was time to grill the steaks.

He served her a wonderful meal with a lovely wine, and Savannah's mood mellowed. As night began to fall, Zach removed a pair of what looked like headphones from a cabinet, slipped them over his dog's ears, then motioned for Ace to get into his crate. Zach offered Savannah a sheepish explanation as the whippet followed his master's command. "Ace hates fireworks and thunderstorms . . . any loud sound. These Mutt Muffs work pretty good."

"You bought earmuffs for your dog," she said, her heart going mushy.

He looked her in the eyes and said, "I take care of those I care about."

It was as if he'd made a promise to her. Savannah blinked back sudden, silly tears as he took a quilt from the closet and tucked it beneath one arm. Again he took her hand as they walked back out to the end of the point. Savannah peered across the lake toward the park where the townspeople gathered to watch the show, but it was now too dark to see how big a crowd had gathered. Zach spread the quilt atop a thick patch of grass and they sat down just as the first *whee boom* signaled the start. From across the water, she heard the cheering of the crowd. Happy and excited, she leaned back on her elbows and smiled up at the spectacle lighting the sky. She did indeed love fireworks shows.

Being here was surreal. She couldn't believe that she was actually here in Colorado, at peaceful Reflection Point, sitting beside a broad-shouldered hunk of a man who smelled faintly of the sandalwood soap she made. During her years in prison, she'd yearned to sit outside in the dark and watch the stars. Yearned to be free. Every Fourth of July she'd spent behind bars, she'd imagined herself somewhere watching fireworks burst upon an infinite sky.

She'd never imagined herself doing so while she sat next to a date.

She hadn't thought kindly about men in those days. When exactly had that changed? Why had that changed? Turning to Zach, she drank in his profile, highlighted by the bursts of color streaming from the canvas of the night sky. He lay stretched back on the blanket, relaxed and propped up on one elbow as he watched the show above.

The summer breeze skittered across the lake and drew light fingers through his hair. Savannah itched to repeat the motion, yet her hand fisted with a slight and sudden measure of hesitation.

Go ahead. Touch him. Make the first move. Everything is perfect. You don't need to hold back. He's been good to you. He hasn't pushed or demanded. He's different.

He isn't like Kyle.

Except for the badge.

"Now, that's cool," Zach murmured absently as a particularly large firework split into falling cascades of orange and teal. "The committee really went all out this year."

Unaware of her perusal, he kept his attention on the sky. Pleased that she had the opportunity to simply watch him, Savannah realized how much she'd come to enjoy his presence in her life. She waited for the inevitable rush of fear and mistrust to dash this warm, pleasant feeling to bits, but instead she felt an ache that she had not experienced in a very long time.

She wanted him.

As if on cue, another loud bang rent the air, replacing her musings with a huge starburst that reflected its splendor upon the mirror of Hummingbird Lake's flat, still surface. Savannah watched the colors fade, her heart pounding and her body yearning as she was swept up in the romance of the moment. Perhaps she should harness this energy before it diminished, rather than be left with regret for yet another experience missed, another instance of life passing her by.

Beneath the backdrop of a vibrant display of fire and brilliance, she decided it was time to let go of some of the baggage.

So he *did* have a badge. So she *did* have a record. Tonight, here and now, they were simply two people who'd been alone for a good part of their lives. Two people who enjoyed each other's company. Two people who were attracted to each other, despite everything that should keep them apart.

"I never expected anything like this." And she hadn't. Never in a million years.

He turned just then, his smile filled with genuine pleasure. His eyes held a depth of something Savannah couldn't exactly name when they fell upon her. Whatever it was, the mysterious emotion called to her. He wanted her, too. The past wasn't important. Tonight she'd simply focus on the here and now.

"Savannah."

She loved the way he said her name. The husky sound drew her like a siren's song.

"You're not watching the fireworks anymore."

Her throat grew slightly dry. "Perhaps I want to make my own."

At that, his eyes glittered with an almost hypnotic lure. He tipped her chin toward him and the warmth of his hand traveled up to cup her cheek. "I bet you can. We can." Yet he didn't move to take her in his arms. He remained on his side of the blanket as the festive sounds crackled above them. "If you're sure . . ."

"I am sure. I'm ready." Reaching up, she set her hand

upon his and laced their fingers. It felt so good, she realized. His grip was strong and confident. He'd waited for her to make this move, wanted her to reach for him.

Finally giving herself over to what she craved, she whispered, "I'm ready for you. I want you."

He inched closer. His mouth dipped to capture hers with sweet insistence. "I want you, too. I've been ready for a while now." Pressing her back on the blanket, his lips traveled a possessive path down her neck to the soft hollow of her collarbone. "I need to be with you, Savannah."

Working up her nerve, she stiffened a little. "I have to tell you that it's been a while . . . for me. For this." She swallowed, and dropped her voice to a murmur. "I don't have a lot of experience." Feeling small and incredibly vulnerable, Savannah waited for his reaction as he leaned up to face her. Her unspoken statement coursed between them: *What if I am a disappointment?*

With the fireworks still erupting over his shoulders, Zach merely smiled and kissed her again. Gently. On the cheek. "Honey, I only care about your experience with me."

At that, Savannah felt a tug somewhere in the vicinity of her chest that she dared not dwell on. Without thought, she placed a hand on the back of his neck and pulled him down. Kissing him hard, she savored every taste, every moment. Soon his breathing quickened and his mouth grew hot and demanding. He let her lead, but kept the pace strong. Whispering against her seeking lips, he told her, "You don't know what you do to me."

"I think I do," she replied. "Because I feel it, too."

Longing burned low within Savannah, and while the action was familiar, the feelings were not. She returned his passion with a zeal that surprised her. Her initial misgivings soon faded into echoes, dwarfed by the continued sparkle and boom above them and the physical pull of desire. There was no better time, no better place.

No better man.

She tugged at his shirt, pulling it from the waistband of his jeans. Slipping her hands beneath the soft fabric, she reveled in his growl of delight as she treated herself to an exploration. Her senses reeled, elevated by Zach's familiar scent and his touch. They'd kissed before, even made out . . . but this was different. This was a prelude to something more.

She didn't hold back this time, didn't stiffen, didn't discourage him. This time she instigated, and it felt wonderful. As her eyes met his gaze, the lust pooled in the pit of her stomach and rippled down into a need she couldn't define.

Never had she been this brazen before, so wantonly bold! It both shocked and exhilarated her, and soon any insecurity vanished like the smoking remains of a fading firework.

"You are perfect," he whispered, nipping at the whorl of her ear, then her neck. His mouth soon found hers again as his hands pulled at the straps of her sundress until her lacy bra was exposed. Drawing in a swift, appreciative breath, he traced the seam with the tip of his fingers and released the clasp to bare her fully.

"Zach," she said, letting her eyes close briefly, wanting to capture the moment in her mind forever. Yet she couldn't stop watching him. The look on his face . . . it was intense. And personal in a way she'd never experienced with—

No. You will not bring his memory into this moment.

Zach didn't want just sex. He wanted her. His awe and appreciation was for her. This moment meant something to him. *She* meant something to him.

Maybe neither would be able to define what that

something was, but Savannah knew that she couldn't ignore it. It was too powerful, and it brought a mist to her eyes that she blinked back hard.

"What?" he asked softly. "Are you all right?"

Covering, she offered him a wobbly smile. "It's been a while, like I said. I'm a bit rusty."

As if mesmerized, Zach drew a path down, drawing a circle around her hardened nipple with a feather touch. "You're perfect. I've imagined this."

When he bent to taste her, Savannah gasped and her back arched in automatic response. "I've imagined it, too," she choked out as she ran her hands across his shoulders, up into his thick hair.

Holding his head as he suckled her, she whimpered mindless pleas and tilted her hips instinctively toward the erection that pressed against her thigh. Heat quickly coiled through her, promoting her body to react.

Yet Zach took his time, savoring her skin and softness as if she were a fine wine. He murmured words of praise and enjoyment. For this one moment in time, Savannah Sophia Moore felt like the only woman in the world.

"So beautiful," he whispered, raising his head to meet her gaze. Something raw burned in his blue eyes. He reached beneath her skirt . . . then suddenly he froze. Grimacing, he mouthed the word "Damn."

Savannah went stiff. "What?"

"I hate to break the mood, but I didn't plan for this. I'm not exactly, uh, prepared. We'll have to go back up to the house."

After a beat, she got his drift. *Condoms. He's talking about condoms.* She shook her head. "It's okay. Let's stay out here. I . . . um . . . I'm prepared. They're in my purse."

He gaped at her, and Savannah felt her cheeks flush with embarrassment. "Hey, I'm a responsible woman. I didn't want you to see them. I mean, until there was an . . . um . . . need. I wasn't sure myself that I . . . that we . . ."

"Savannah," he said, admiration in his tone.

She shrugged and confessed, "I ordered them online. Hope they're the right kind."

"Peach, I don't care if they're bright pink with smiley faces."

Her purse sat just beyond her reach. He left her long enough to retrieve it and hand it to her. She practically ripped the zipper opening it, then handed over the prize.

With a halfway smothered laugh, he asked, "You brought the whole box?"

She winced, and then started to laugh at his incredulous expression. With a helpless shrug, she told him, "I . . . well, yeah, I did."

"There's a throwdown for you." He tumbled her back upon the quilt. Nuzzling her breast, he twirled his tongue around her nipple. "I hope I can live up to the challenge."

"I'm not worried."

He paused in the act of tugging down the zipper of her dress. "I'm glad, honey. You don't need to be worried about anything."

Again he said it like a promise, and to her surprise, Savannah believed him. She emptied her mind of everything beyond the moment as he practically ripped off her dress. His eyes immediately feasted on her pink thong panties.

"Those are amazing. Another online purchase?" He caressed the elastic, sliding a finger beneath and yanking them down without much ceremony.

"The gift shop at Angel's Rest. Celeste says she gets lots of honeymooners as guests."

"She's a wise woman, our Celeste." He tossed the panties over his shoulder, and then bent to kiss her neck, finding that one special spot that he loved to tease with his tongue. "Maybe I'll go shopping at the gift shop. You need them for every day of the week. Different colors."

"Why bother?" she gasped, and gripped his flexing shoulders. "You enjoyed them for a nanosecond before tearing them off."

"Yeah, but that nanosecond was worth the wait."

"Speaking of waiting . . ." She brazenly reached for the top button of his fly. The male moan of pleasure against her neck when her fingers touched him spurred her to work him free and caress him fully.

"Ah . . ." he said on a shudder, then pulled back just long enough to rid himself of the rest of his clothing. Returning to her side naked and fully aroused, he pressed her down onto the blanket. The weight of him felt warm and right as he kissed her mouth and then the base of her throat, working his way down to her breasts. Whispered words of encouragement fell naturally between them as the magic built.

They discovered each other's bodies with careful urgency, every touch illuminated by the torrent of color rippling against a backdrop of stars. As if knowing what her body craved, Zach slipped his hand down and stroked her warm, slick skin. The sensation was incredible, and she found herself nearly sobbing as the pressure built. Over and over, Zach coaxed with soft persistence until the first wave of pleasure crashed over her and rolled through to her toes.

Before Savannah could recover, he left her briefly to slide on the condom. In an instant, and with one long, languid motion, Zach embedded himself into her. He stretched her, filled her, and she gasped with the pleasure of it. It had been so long. It had never been like this before.

Savannah purred and Zach grabbed her hips, pulling her tight against him. Creating a soulful rhythm, he demanded, "Again. This time . . . with me."

She could only whimper a faint response, unsure of the possibility. Yet the stirring beckoned again, low and deep within her. He kissed her forehead, her eyes, her nose, treasuring every part of her despite the quickened tempo of his thrusts.

A multitude of fireworks soon traveled up to burst into a fiery display of color and spark amidst the night sky. The sounds boomed, one upon another, stronger and faster. As the expected and climactic ending of a fireworks show exploded above her, Savannah couldn't separate what occurred above and upon the earth.

Her body clenched around Zach's, and as he called out her name in a hoarse cry, Savannah shattered and saw fireworks that had nothing to do with those painting the sky.

Zach collapsed atop her, his weight heavy as one of the mountains that ringed the valley. When she gasped for a breath, he immediately rolled off onto his side, came up onto his elbow, and settled his open mouth against hers in a kiss like none other. Strong and deep and thrillingly possessive, it further weakened Savannah from blood to bone.

"That was spectacular," he said huskily. "Thank you."

Then he kissed her once more, this time sweetly.

Sudden, unexpected tears flooded Savannah's eyes. She blinked them away. "Thank you. I've never . . . not like that. It's never happened that way to me before."

"Well, then." He gently touched her cheek and gave her a sated, satisfied smile. "I'm glad that was mine."

He lay on his back and pulled her close, one arm around her waist, the other pillowing his head. She rested her head on his bare chest, where a dusting of hair tickled her nose. Staring up at a star-filled sky, Savannah observed, "Guess the fireworks are over."

"It's just intermission." His hand skimmed down and gave her rump a playful little pinch. "After all, you brought a whole box."

FIFTEEN

Zach drifted toward wakefulness through a hazy cloud of sensation. He felt good, real good. Warm and relaxed and—oh, yeah. Savannah. He had the Georgia peach herself clinging to him like a vine. A very soft, sweet, sexy vine. He turned his head and nuzzled her neck. She smelled like heaven. It was a similar but different scent from the one that had drawn him the night of her open house. She'd added a little something extra to this recipe, and man oh man, did it do it for him.

Everything about her did it for him.

She'd been shy in bed to begin with, her inexperience endearing. On top of all his other sins, the rat bastard who betrayed her obviously had been a selfish lover. Just as soon as tourist season was over and he had more than two minutes to spare, Zach was going to do some snooping around where he was concerned.

Unable to resist the temptation, he skimmed his hand over the soft, naked curve of her hip. She stirred. He opened his eyes, found the clock, and considered. It would have to be quick—he didn't have time to give her more—and this early in their relationship he didn't want Savannah feeling used.

She stretched like a cat against him. "Mmm. What time is it?"

"Quarter after eight."

"We slept late."

"We were up late."

She rolled toward him and his morning erection brushed her belly. Her eyes still closed, she smiled. "Do you never stop?"

"Not when I have a gorgeous Georgia peach in my bed, no. Unfortunately, I don't have more than five minutes to spare. I have to be at work at nine."

Now her eyes flew open wide, her smile went impishly wicked, and she rolled on top of him. "Why don't you show me your quick draw, Sheriff?"

She didn't have to ask him twice.

Zach threw himself into the task and she rewarded him with a scream three minutes and forty-five seconds later. He felt like a king when he rose from the bed and padded naked toward the shower. "Ordinarily I'd invite you to join me, but . . . one more like that and I'd probably have a heart attack in my shower. I'd keel over on top of you, you'd hit your head on the tile, and it just wouldn't be good. You're better off using the shower in the other bathroom."

"Don't fret yourself, Turner," she fired back smugly. "I'm done with you. For this morning, anyway."

At his bathroom door, he hesitated and met her gaze. "So, in all seriousness, Savannah. Can I count on that? Is this more than a hookup? Are we in a relationship now?"

She pulled the sheet up over her naked chest. "Go take your shower, Sheriff. I'll make coffee and then we'll talk, okay?"

Zach nodded, but he cursed himself as he switched on the hot water. What was wrong with him? What happened to his patience? Had he totally forgotten how to deal with a skittish filly? He should never have asked that question. Never! His strategy of patiently waiting for her to come to him had worked superbly, and he'd enjoyed every minute of it. Why press her now?

Idiot. Impatient fool. Why couldn't you keep your big mouth shut?

Because he wanted more from her than a one-night stand. Because he was falling for Savannah Sophia Moore, and he wanted her to fall for him right back.

Grabbing a towel from the bathroom linen closet, he wiped himself dry with brisk, efficient, frustrated motions. Minutes later, dressed and ready, he eyed the clock once again. He had fifteen minutes to get to the office. He could be a little late. He was the boss, after all. However, he liked to set a good example for his deputies.

Besides that, Gabi knew he'd had a date with Savannah last night. If he came in late this morning, she'd give him hell.

Savannah handed him a steaming mug of coffee when he walked into the kitchen. She smelled of his everyday soap, and she wore one of his T-shirts and a pair of his gym shorts. "Your dress . . ." he said, wincing.

"We left it down on the point. Under the circumstances, I didn't want to run the risk of a fisherman calling in a report and you having to arrest me for public nudity. I didn't think you'd mind sharing your clothes."

"Peach, you're welcome to anything you desire around here, anytime." He sipped his coffee and forced himself not to add, *Including me.*

She drank from her own cup of coffee, drew a deep breath, then said, "Zach, last night was special, and I thank you for that. You treated me with respect and showed me passion like I've never known before. You are a wonderful lover and a great guy . . . even if you do carry a badge. I hope we can do this again sometime."

Opening the refrigerator door, he bit back the question, *Tonight?*

"But if you're looking for more from me, if you want

a relationship, you need to understand that I'm not ready for that. I may never be ready for that. The last relationship I was in cost me six years of my life."

"Dammit, Savannah." He slammed the door. "I'm not Kyle Vaughn."

"I know that, Zach." She set down her cup. "What you need to understand is that the problem isn't with you. It's with me."

"Oh, I'm pretty sure I'm aware of that," he snapped back, then immediately regretted it. Frustrated with himself as much as with her, he shoved his fingers through his hair and closed his eyes. "I'm sorry. I don't mean to be a jerk. If you're not ready for more, you're not ready, I understand that. Truly, I do."

"Thank you."

"I guess I'll just have to be satisfied with spectacular sex."

"How kind of you to sacrifice that way," she said, her drawl pronounced.

"I am a prince of a guy." He drained his coffee, then set the cup in the sink. Taking her hands in his, he stared down into her eyes. "I understand that you're scared, honey. I understand that you have good reason to be so. But there is something I want you to understand. You are important to me. I care about you. I think I might be falling in love with you."

"Love!" Her eyes went wide with alarm, and she actually took a step backward. She stared at him in shocked silence for a long, excruciating minute.

Why had he said that? Because his nerves were raw and he was tired of trying to prove himself?

Finally she whispered a question. "Why did you say that?"

"Because it's true. You need to know that I'll tell you the truth. I'm an honest man, Savannah. You can trust me. I don't need you to love me right now . . . that will come or it won't. Time will tell. But what I do want . . . what I do need . . . is for you to trust me."

Her mouth flattened. "I came to you last night, didn't I? Believe me, buster, that took a level of trust."

"I know it did. It blew me away. You blew me away."

"Then why now? Why all this . . . this . . . information?"

"Like they say, information is power."

"Power for whom?"

"For us both. I admit I don't like it when you compare me to your ex." She opened her mouth, but he held up his hand to ward off her protest. "I do like being open and honest with you. Truth is a powerful thing. You know that better than anyone, I expect. Now, I've got to go or I'll be late and my deputies will make assumptions I'd just as soon not have to deal with."

He leaned down and gave her a quick, hard kiss, then opened the drawer beside her and removed a key ring with a set of house keys. He handed it to her, then headed for the door. "Lock up when you leave, would you? And why don't you just keep that set of keys. I'll call you later. I'll miss you today."

"But . . . but . . ."

Grinning, he walked away from her and whistled for his dog. Ace came running, and when Zach opened the door to his sheriff's Range Rover, he bounded up inside.

Zach started the truck and put it into gear as Savannah came out onto the porch and stood gaping after him. He tapped his horn twice, then turned out of his drive onto the road.

A glance into his review mirror showed that she hadn't moved from his front porch, and Zach's grin widened into a smile. "There's a difference between truth and strategy, Ace. An intelligent leader will utilize both."

* * *

Savannah didn't see Zach again for almost a week. A group of hikers had a confrontation and guns had been fired, wounding two. The shooter ran off into the national forest, and the Eternity Springs Sheriff's Department had joined an alphabet of other agencies in the search for a man who had eluded capture for going on five days. Local folks concluded that since Zach hadn't tracked the man by now, the fellow might well have gone to ground—literally. "I'm betting he sneaked into one of the abandoned mines around here," Sarah observed as she sliced peaches at Savannah's kitchen table. "We lose someone every summer."

Ali Timberlake nodded, frowning at the consistency of the cobbler dough she was mixing together at Savannah's direction. "These weren't hardened criminals, either, but teenage boys swigging at the liquor bottle and fighting over girls. I am so glad my boys have finally outgrown the infinitely stupid years. They are not quite through the marginally stupid years, but so far so good."

"People can get in trouble at any age," Savannah said, placing her sugar canister next to the bowl of sliced fresh peaches. Ali and Sarah had come begging for the secrets of Savannah's cobbler, and she was teaching by having them do the work. "Believe me. I know."

She must have revealed something in her tone, because Ali and Sarah shared a look, then Sarah asked, "That sounds like a story. You have something to share with the class, Savannah?"

She considered it. "Well, I could tell you about the time I got into trouble at ten, or the one when I was twelve, or about the doozy of a pickle I got myself into last week."

"Last week?" Ali and Sarah declared simultaneously.

"I'll bet it involves Zach," Ali added.

Sarah nodded briskly. "You had sex with him, didn't

you? I'll bet he's really good at it. Am I right? I bet I'm right. His kisses can curl a girl's toes."

"That's true." Ali nodded.

"Wait a minute. Zach has kissed both of you?"

"We told you that. Haven't we told you that?"

Now that Sarah mentioned it, yes, they had, but Savannah hadn't felt nearly so possessive as she did now. "Did you guys . . . uh . . ."

Sarah's oh-so-innocent look morphed into a grin. "No. Zach and I made great friends, and we were content to keep it that way."

Ali said, "Mac and I were separated but not divorced. Zach's attention was good for my ego, but it was innocent. So, what sort of trouble are you in, Savannah? Zach-related trouble, which could be wonderful, or non-Zach-related trouble, which is maybe not so great?"

Unaccountably, she experienced the strangest urge to tell them about her time in prison. For a long moment the words hung on the tip of her tongue. That shocked her, and she wondered just where she'd left her brain. Life was good at the moment. Why would she want to screw it up?

Truth is powerful, Zach had said.

Maybe he was right. She wrinkled her nose. However, she could darn sure start out slow. "I don't want to talk about Zach, but maybe I'll share my speck of trouble with the regulators."

"Regulators?"

"It involved moonshine. I was a kid. Let's get the cobbler in the oven, then I'll spill the beans."

"Awesome!" Sarah said. "What's next?"

"My secret ingredient. The secret to my peach cobbler is—"

The ringing of her office telephone interrupted her, and though it was after hours, she didn't want to ignore it. Besides, she had fun teasing Sarah this way.

Walking into the room she used as her office, Savannah picked up the receiver. "Savannah Soap Company? May I help you?"

A male voice said, "I'd like to speak with Ms. Savannah Moore, please?"

"This is she."

"Oh. Very good. Ms. Moore, I'm happy to have reached you. My name is Alan Powell. I'm an attorney in practice in Atlanta."

An attorney from Georgia. Her stomach sank to her toes. *I haven't done anything wrong. Nothing. I'm innocent!* "We ship to all fifty states, Mr. Powell. Which of our items do you wish to order?"

"I'm not calling about a soap order, Ms. Moore."

Can't blame me for trying. "I'm not interested in franchising my business at this time."

"That's not the reason for my call, either. I'm calling about your nephew."

Tommy? Surprised, Savannah shifted her phone from one ear to the other. "Excuse me? What did you say?"

"Thomas James Moore, age fourteen. The only child of your brother Gary Moore and his wife, Jane, now deceased."

"Jane is dead?"

"We have confirmed that information, yes. Jane Moore died of a drug overdose in Peoria, Illinois, ten years ago."

Not long after she abandoned Gary and Tommy, Savannah realized. "Is Tommy okay?"

"Your nephew is currently in a temporary foster home under the direction of Social Services. Ms. Moore, your brother Gary is being held in jail without bond on numerous alcohol-related charges. He hit a pedestrian while driving drunk."

Oh, no.

"Luckily, the injured woman survived, so at least he's

not facing manslaughter charges. I've been appointed his public defense attorney and I'm good, but I will be honest. Barring a miracle, he's going to jail. That leaves his son in dire circumstances. Ms. Moore, TJ needs your help."

TJ? Thomas James. Tommy.

"Will you take him?"

Savannah grabbed for the edge of her desk to support her suddenly weak knees and in doing so, accidentally sent a metal staple gun skimming across the surface. It crashed against a flower vase, which teetered and then fell. Glass shattered against the wood floor, the sound bringing Sarah and Ali to check on Savannah, concerned looks etched across their faces.

Savannah only vaguely noticed them. Her mind was spinning. Gary had visited her one time while she was in jail, and he'd been an absolute ass. He'd said that he and TJ were moving to Atlanta, and he believed everything Kyle had said. He'd told her to her face that she was a worthless human being and that he was washing his hands of her. After her release, she'd sucked up her nerve and attempted to pay him a visit, but he'd refused to let her in the front door and denied her the opportunity to see Tommy.

"Ms. Moore? Are you still there?"

"I . . . uh . . ."

Ali placed a hand on Savannah's forearm. "Honey, you okay?"

"She's white as a sheet," Sarah said, stooping to pick up the larger shards of broken glass with her hands.

"Mr., um . . . what was your name again?"

"Powell. Alan Powell. I know this is an unexpected phone call, but I'm concerned about the boy."

"But I couldn't possibly do that. They wouldn't let me. I'm a . . . a . . ." She remained aware enough to re-member that she wasn't alone, and she couldn't think of another term for "convicted criminal" that Sarah and Ali wouldn't pick up on. "Do you know where I lived before I moved to Colorado, Mr. Powell?"

"I do. Your record doesn't rule you out as a guardian for TJ. You are his family. You are all he has."

"What about Jane's parents? Are they dead, too?"

From the corner of her eyes, she saw Sarah and Ali share another worried look. In her ear, she heard the lawyer respond. "TJ's maternal grandparents are unwilling to accept responsibility for him. They have . . . issues . . . where their daughter is concerned. They refused to take him once before when your brother spent time incarcerated—"

Gary has been to jail before, too? And he was such a jerk to me?

"—and based on conversations with them now, Social Services and I agree that even if we convinced them to step in, they wouldn't provide a healthy environment for TJ."

"But they—"

"They call him a delinquent, Ms. Moore. They have nothing good to say about either of his parents, either. TJ is understandably bitter, but I honestly believe that all the boy needs is some kindness and attention and he'll be just fine." He paused a moment, then added, "I understand that you had some troubles as a teen and that your grandmother stepped in to help."

Savannah closed her eyes. Blasted attorneys. The good ones always knew just what to say, didn't they? This guy was especially good. Gary had gotten lucky with his public defender. Her own lawyer had been a tool.

She didn't have a choice. She'd lost that the moment he'd mentioned Grams.

Actually, she'd had no choice the moment Alan Powell had said *TJ needs your help.*

Clearing her throat, she asked, "You're not asking me to return to Georgia for this, are you?"

"No. TJ would come to live with you."

"Does TJ want to come live with me?" At that, Sarah's and Ali's eyes rounded in surprise.

"TJ wants to live with his father."

She waited a beat for him to continue, but the line remained quiet. *Great. Just great.*

Savannah let out a long sigh. "All right. What do I need to do?"

She made arrangements with the lawyer, then ended the call. She stood for a long moment with her back to her friends, trying to absorb how her life had just changed. She was nervous and scared and filled with dread.

But beneath the darkness of spirit, excitement sparked to life.

Family. She had family coming to visit.

SIXTEEN

"It's about time," Zach muttered as the feds finally packed up the last of their equipment and departed the sheriff's office.

Gabi smiled pleasantly as she told them good-bye, then she shut the door behind them, turned, and gave a fist pump. "I thought they'd never leave."

Seated behind her dispatcher's desk, Ginger nodded. "I think Perkins hung around trying to work up the nerve to ask you out."

"As if." She sniffed with disdain. "Did you see how much noise he made in the woods? City boy. The only reason the perp evaded us as long as he did was because Perkins tramped through the forest with as much subtlety as an eighteen-wheeler."

"Not to argue," Zach said, preparing to do just that. "Is it fair for you to call him a city boy? I thought you grew up in Denver."

"I went hunting with my dad. That gives me forest trail cred."

Zach grinned and glanced at the clock. Almost lunchtime. "I think I'll grab something to eat. You all hold down the fort until I get back, and if we get a call that involves any jurisdiction other than this one, tell them they have the wrong number."

He picked up his hat and stepped outside into the summer sunshine, pretending not to hear his dispatcher's knowing comment: "Tell Savannah we said hello."

Strolling toward Pinyon Street, Zach dragged a hand over his two-day beard and wondered what Savannah would think of his new look. He'd chosen not to shave and worn flannel rather than his uniform shirt just to annoy the stick-up-his-butt, spit-and-polish, citified pretty boy who thought rural meant stupid. Freddy the Fed hadn't liked it one bit when the network news reporters chose to interview Zach over him. Ordinarily Zach shunned such attention, but after having spent three days in the incompetent's company, the infantile revenge had been just the ticket and put him in a right fine mood. As did the fact that he now had time to put soap on his grocery list.

"Hey, Zach," called LaNelle Harrison as he walked past her on the street. "Saw you on CNN this morning. Congratulations on the arrest."

"Thanks, LaNelle. Just doing my job." And ever so glad to have his town back to himself. He whistled as he turned the corner onto Fourth and caught sight of Heavenscents up the block.

He stepped up his pace. Savannah sometimes shut the store down for lunch. Wonder what his chances were of talking her into having her sandwich in bed? Maybe if she really liked the scruffy look, he could convince her. Maybe she'd seen the interviews and would consider his fifteen minutes of fame a turn-on.

He bounded up the porch steps and entered the shop. The pleasing scents wrapped around him like a soft blanket on a cool night and he experienced a sense of coming home.

Then Savannah shocked him. Entering the room from the back of the shop, she took one look at him, burst into tears, and threw herself into his arms. "Zach!"

Whoa. She must have really been worried about me. "It's okay, Peach. I'm okay. It was just a small exchange of gunfire."

"Oh, Zach. You'll never believe what has happened. I'm going to have a teenager!"

"Excuse me?"

"My nephew. My family. He'll be here in three days and he's going to live with me. Permanently."

Permanently? But what about my sandwich in bed?

"How am I going to do this?" Her eyes were big brown pools of worry. "I don't know anything about being a mother. He probably doesn't even want a mother. I don't think he's ever had one. Not before Dad died, anyway. Dad wouldn't let Gary's girlfriend move into the house unless they were married, and Gary wasn't going down that road again. He really got burned the first time. I know how that feels. We Moores just aren't lucky in love."

Well, then. So much for CNN and scruffy. "I'm a little bit out of the loop. I've been busy. Want to start at the beginning?"

He didn't like hearing the note of petulance in his voice, but the facts had hit him like a two-by-four to the head. A kid? Now? Just when they were finding their way into a relationship?

She pulled away and shook her head. "Oh, what am I thinking? I'm sorry, Zach. That was rude of me. You've had a hard few days yourself. I'm so glad you weren't hurt in the gunfight."

"It wasn't exactly a gunfight," he muttered.

"Look at you." She reached up and cupped his cheek. "Mr. Cable News Outdoorsman Hottie. I had five phone calls within three minutes of the interview. You're the talk of the town. Sarah said women are going to be mailing you their panties."

"She what?" Now Zach was embarrassed. Mollified,

but embarrassed. "Forget about me. I want to hear about your nephew. Start at the beginning."

She did, and as she talked, stress ramped back up in her voice. Hearing the story, Zach couldn't blame her. The responsibility she was taking on was overwhelming.

It was also something he'd need to think about. The idea of falling for a woman was one thing. Falling for a woman with a kid was something else. Not that the idea of children bothered him. He wanted a family someday. Someday soon, to be honest. But to be fair to himself, to Savannah, and to the boy, TJ, he needed to move forward with care.

So maybe he wouldn't try to talk her into a nooner after all. *Damn the bad luck.*

A customer entered the shop, interrupting Savannah's story. She asked Zach, "Have you had lunch?"

"No."

"I can offer you a chicken salad sandwich if you'd like to wait until I'm through with this customer and close up."

"Sounds great."

"Go on into the kitchen and make yourself at home."

He did and decided to peruse her refrigerator. Spying the chicken salad, he made sandwiches for them both, then fixed himself a glass of iced tea. Savannah made delicious, traditional southern sweet tea that hit the spot. Inny came in through the doggie door to say hello, which made Zach miss Ace. He hadn't seen much of his dog in the past week. Maybe after lunch he'd make a run out to the house and bring Ace to the office for the afternoon.

Events of the past week were on his mind when Savannah entered the kitchen a few minutes later. He wanted to hear more about her nephew, but first he had something he wanted to get off his mind. "There's something I need to say to you, Savannah."

Wariness washed through her expression, so he quickly pressed on. "I'm sorry I disappeared on you after the Fourth. That's not what I intended when I brought you home."

"I'm sure you didn't intend for a felon to go crazy in the forest, either." She approached him, rose on her tiptoes, and planted a quick kiss on his mouth. "Thank you for the sentiment, but it's unnecessary."

"Good." Zach took advantage of her nearness and wrapped his arms around her. There was nothing quick about the kiss he gave her.

Or about the nooner he ended up getting after all.

He asked her out to dinner before they both returned to work, but it was quilt group night, and as the newest Patchwork Angel, she didn't want to miss one of the few meetings held during the summer season. Instead, they made a date for the following night, which also was Zach's first day off since the Fourth.

He spent the next morning catching up on neglected chores and taking Ace on a long walk around the lake. That afternoon he accepted an invitation from Jack Davenport to join him and Cam Murphy up at Jack's estate, Eagle's Way, to watch a Rockies game. For the first time in a very long time, he looked forward to his day off being almost over with.

He took Savannah to dinner at the Yellow Kitchen, and they had a delicious, romantic candlelit meal. He didn't miss the thumbs-up Ali gave her when she went to the ladies' room or the smile Savannah flashed in return, and it pleased him. Savannah had made friends with his friends in Eternity Springs. One of these days she'd learn she could trust them with the truth about her background, but that was an argument for another time. First she had to navigate the turbulent waters of the next few weeks.

The subject of her nephew had not come up over dinner, but as they waited for dessert to be served, he asked, "Do you want to talk about TJ?"

She took a sip from her water glass. "Actually, I'd just as soon not. I'm as ready as I'll ever be, and I can use the distraction. Not that you're merely a distraction," she hastened to add. "That sounds insulting."

"Hey, I'm happy to be a distraction."

"In that case, I have a big favor to ask. Is there any chance that you could go with me to the airport tomorrow?"

Zach didn't hesitate. "Of course. I'll be happy to go. One of the perks of being the boss is getting to jerk around my subordinates' schedules."

"Thank you."

Relief filled Savannah's eyes, and the smile she gave him was so bright he thought he might need blinders. He sat gazing at her until Ali approached their table carrying their dessert order. "One piece of double chocolate cake and two forks."

"Yum," Savannah said. "I've heard wonderful things about your double chocolate cake."

"From Sarah, I expect," Ali said with a laugh. "It's a recipe I found, but she bakes it for me. She does have a magical touch. You two enjoy."

Savannah took a bite of cake, and, watching her, Zach was lost. He'd been mesmerized by her smile; the way she ate chocolate cake totally seduced him. She licked her fork. She purred with pleasure. She smacked her lips and swooned.

He went as hard as that piece of petrified wood he'd found up on Murphy Mountain during his first summer in Eternity Springs.

She invited him in when he took her home, thank the good Lord above. The moment the door closed behind them, he pressed her up against the wall and took her mouth in a sizzling kiss. It proved to be the start of one of the most erotic nights of his life, and by the time he finally drifted off to sleep, he'd decided that *distraction* was one of his favorite words in the English language.

He was pleasantly tired as they headed out of Eternity Springs the next morning, bound first for a quick stop at the Gunnison police department, where Zach needed to deliver a file to a detective, and then afterward for the airport. Yet with every mile they traveled, Zach could see his formerly-relaxed-by-distraction lover grow more and more tense. Concerned about her, he reached out and patted Savannah's knee. "It'll be okay."

The smile she gave him in response was wan. "I'm scared half to death."

Zach braked gently as he rounded a curve to discover a herd of seven bighorn sheep crossing the road some fifty yards in front of them.

"How cool is that?" Savannah murmured. "This is something I never saw in Georgia or Tennessee."

"I never saw it in Oklahoma, either." Zach waited until the sheep had cleared the road and they could continue on their way, then he brought the conversation back to the subject at hand. "I won't try to tell you that parenting TJ won't be a challenge, but I will say that I have no doubt at all that you will rise to meet it. That's what you do."

"It's not something I want to do," she replied with a bit of a pout in her voice. "Why do I have to have more challenges? Haven't I had my fair share?"

"My dad always used to say that fair is where you show your pigs in October."

"How am I possibly going to care for a fourteen-year-old boy?"

"With care and compassion and grace. Maybe get him a dog." He took her hand and held it casually. "I've watched you in your shop. You have good instincts with people."

"My instincts are telling me I'm clueless when it comes to teenage boys." She hesitated a moment before adding, "The lawyer asked TJ to call and talk to me. He wouldn't do it."

That wasn't a good sign.

Zach had seen kids whose parents were in jail. It could go either way—or right down the middle. It wasn't a given that he'd be a problem. So what if his maternal grandparents called him a delinquent? Their idea of a delinquent could be a kid who plays video games.

"He was such a sweet little boy. Maybe he's just shy. I can deal with shy."

"Maybe he's just angry about being disrupted again. Sounds like the kid has had a few curve balls thrown his way. And as for shy . . . you can deal with shy. You dealt with me, didn't you?"

That got a laugh out of her, just as he had hoped. He went for further distraction when he added, "And may I say once again how much I enjoyed how you dealt with me last night?"

That got the blush he'd expected, too. Her smug look had him adding, "Not to mention this morning."

"You're trying to distract me," she said. "Thank you."

"I've decided that distracting you is my greatest pleasure—in every sense of the word."

"In that case, talk to me about something else."

"All right. What would you like to talk about?"

"I don't know. Maybe . . . Celeste? I spoke with her quite a bit at quilt group the other night. She is a most interesting person. She likes you a lot."

"I like her, too. There is something about southern women. My mother would have really liked Celeste."

They discussed Celeste Blessing, his mother, and Savannah's grandmother until they passed the Gunnison city limit sign. At that point, Savannah grew quiet. Zach decided to let the conversation lag. She needed this time to gather her forces. For that matter, he did, too.

He had thought long and hard about dating Savannah in the wake of her new circumstances, and he'd decided to have a positive attitude about it. He cared enough about her to be open to the possibilities. His presence during this time of adjustment would be helpful to Savannah and maybe to the boy, too. He'd decided to make a sincere effort to help TJ Moore to adjust. After all, his undercover work in Oklahoma had given him some experience with substance abusers, and he knew tales to tell that TJ might relate to. The boy would need a positive male influence in his life. Zach had always wanted to make his job matter. Now he had the opportunity to do it in his personal life, too.

If Celeste Blessing had been riding in this car this morning, she would likely say that God had put him in this place, with this woman, at this time for the purpose of helping TJ Moore and his aunt Savannah form their family. She might well be right.

They pulled into a parking place in front of the airport terminal. Zach shifted into park and switched off the ignition. He blew out a breath, then said, "I'm ready. Are you ready?"

"As ready as I'll ever be, I guess."

He gave her hand a comforting squeeze, then kissed her cheek. "All right, then, Peach. Let's go welcome young Thomas James Moore to Colorado and his new family."

Savannah swallowed hard but nodded. "We will welcome him to Eternity Springs. It's a wonderful town, the perfect place for broken hearts to heal."

TJ gritted his teeth and, concealed by the jacket he'd draped across his lap, dug his fingernails into his jean-clad thighs. This was the first trip he'd ever made by airplane. Flying itself was okay. The takeoffs and landings scared the crap out of him.

Not that he'd let F-wad Fisherman in the seat next to him see it. He'd gone total incommunicado with the a-hole somewhere over Kansas after Mr. Fish made a pissy comment about his earrings. TJ had his reasons for getting his ears pierced, and he didn't owe anyone an explanation.

A *ding ding* sounded in the airplane, followed by a man's voice saying, "Flight attendants, please prepare for landing."

Oh God oh God oh God oh God. He couldn't stop himself from looking out the window. Mountains all around. In his mind's eye, he saw the plane go splat against a rock cliff.

The plane descended. Nausea churned in his stomach. *I will not barf. I will not barf. I will not barf.*

Wheels touched. Bounced up. Touched again. There was a big whooshing sound, which he knew—at least since landing to change planes in Denver—meant the pilot had applied the brakes. *I hope they work. I hope the runway is long enough.*

Then he remembered that Savannah Moore would be waiting to meet the plane. Maybe he'd be better off in the long run if the plane did crash.

As the airplane's tires rolled toward the gate, a familiar rage rolled through TJ. He mentally cursed his father with every vile, vulgar epithet he'd ever heard.

He'd been down this road before.

The first time Dad got sent away, the kindly, criminally incompetent Social Services people sent him to live with foster parents, the beautiful Susan and movie-star-handsome Alexander Rowe.

Or, as TJ now thought of them upon the rare occasions he didn't try to block them from his mind, the pervs.

Thinking of them made him want the plane to crash.

But he'd survived, and Dad had come home, and life had been good for TJ. He'd been doing okay in school. He'd made the middle-school basketball team.

Then his father got laid off, went back on the booze, and back to jail.

And I lose my home.

The plane rolled to a gentle stop, and the pilot came on the intercom and said, "Welcome to Gunnison–Crested Butte Regional Airport."

At that, the nausea in TJ's stomach did another roll. Next to him, F-wad Fisherman rose and rummaged in the overhead compartment for the round tube that TJ figured held his fishing pole. TJ remained seated. He didn't even unbuckle his seat belt. He'd almost rather face another takeoff than drag his ass off the plane.

Then he was the last one left. The flight attendant stood in the aisle, watching him expectantly. "Son, is everything okay?"

I'm not your son!

He gave no verbal response, but sullenly stood and grabbed his backpack from the overhead bin. The flight attendant gave him a fake smile, then stepped back into her little galley area to give him space to walk by her. Then he was walking up that long hallway thing toward the terminal. His aunt was supposed to be waiting for him at the baggage claim.

Aunt Jailbird. Sister of Uncle Jailbird, Uncle Ran Away, and DUI Dad. For all TJ knew, she'd been best friends with OD Dead Mom.

Did he have great genes or what?

TJ followed the signs toward baggage claim, his spine growing stiffer with every step. If, deep inside himself, the naive kid he used to be nurtured a seed of hope that this time might be different, he refused to recognize it. Approaching the security exit, TJ donned his defenses like a suit of armor. He'd spent years building them, and going through puberty had helped with that. Now when people looked at him, they didn't see a skinny little kid with blond hair and brown eyes and a dopey grin. They saw a tall guy with a spiked multicolor Mohawk, seven earrings, a nose ring, and a tongue stud. They didn't see the young, vulnerable kid; they saw the don't-f-with-me teen. He'd survived Alex Rowe. He'd survived the night the uniforms knocked on the door to arrest Dad. He'd survived the effing airplane ride.

He would survive Savannah Moore and the middle-of-nowhere town where she lived. Eternity Springs. What sort of stupid name was that? Sounded like the name of a freakin' cemetery.

He saw her through the glass wall that divided the baggage claim from the terminal, and a brief memory flashed through his mind. *You want me to push you higher? Really, Tommy?*

Really, Auntie. I do! Push me high! High to the moon!

Hold on tight, then, but don't worry. I'm your auntie Savannah. I will never let you fall.

"Get ready to put your money where your mouth is, lady."

SEVENTEEN

Savannah saw the boy behind the glass window that separated the secured area of the airport from the baggage claim. Her gaze skidded away from the bright orange and lime spikes of his hair and the glint of metal from piercings in places that made her wince. That boy dressed in black clothing adorned with silver chains was tall for fourteen. That boy wasn't her Tommy.

When he stepped toward the exit, her stomach sank. Not her Tommy, but undoubtedly TJ. The hope that she had nurtured for an easy transition evaporated. Were those shadows around his eyes real or was he wearing eye makeup?

This was a boy in full rebellion.

"Uh-oh," Zach murmured. "Maybe it isn't him."

"It's him." Savannah offered the boy a smile and tried really hard to get it to reach her eyes. She doubted she succeeded.

He carried a canvas backpack slung across one shoulder and a chip the size of Colorado balanced on the other. He crossed the space with a loose-limbed, insouciant stroll, and the look in his brown eyes was flat. Savannah knew she should probably move to meet him halfway, but her feet remained rooted to the spot.

Until Zach's hand at the back of her waist gave her a little shove. "Go," he said softly.

She stumbled forward a step, then drew a bracing breath and shook off her unease. "TJ?"

"Yeah."

"I'm your aunt Savannah. I'm so glad to see you again." Her instincts told her to hug him, but when she opened her arms and stepped forward, he stepped back.

He pulled his backpack into his arms, holding it between them in an obvious effort to ward off any embrace. "I checked a duffel bag."

Feeling helpless, Savannah kept her smile pasted on as she glanced toward the baggage carousel. A light flashed, a buzzer sounded, and the conveyor began to move. "What color is it? We'll help you look for it. Oh, and TJ? Let me introduce you to my friend, Zach Turner."

Zach offered a casual, friendly smile as he extended his hand for a handshake. "Welcome to Colorado."

"Whatever." TJ ignored Zach's hand and stepped toward the carousel.

Savannah turned a despairing look toward Zach, who gave her a reassuring wink and mouthed, "Patience, Peach."

She dug deep for it when TJ rather rudely ignored Zach's offer to help him carry his gear. She kept hold of it by a string when her nephew veered into the men's room without so much as an "excuse me." But when they walked out into the parking lot and Savannah gestured toward the Range Rover with the sheriff's badge on the door, explaining that they were riding with Zach, the boy stopped abruptly and snapped an obscenity, and Savannah had enough.

"That's it. Stop it right now," she declared, bracing her hands on her hips and scowling at the boy. Though only fourteen, he was almost as tall as she, so this was close to being an eye-to-eye standoff. Without shifting her gaze away from TJ, she asked, "Zach, would you please excuse us for a few moments?"

"Sure. I'll go check the score of the Rockies game."

She waited until he'd moved beyond earshot, then said, "This is not how I wanted to begin, TJ, but begin we will. I am sorry that your life has been upended. Believe me, I understand how difficult that is. However, you need to get a couple of things straight from the start. You don't have to love me. You don't have to even like me. What I will demand is that you respect me. That includes acting respectful toward my friends. Zach is my friend, a dear friend."

While Savannah spoke, TJ's expression grew set and sullen. "He's a cop," TJ spat, his tone filled with disdain.

Compassion fluttered through Savannah. Cops had arrested his father, hadn't they? "Look, it was hard for me to get past that myself. But he is a good man and can be a good friend to you if you give him a chance."

"Like I'd want a cop for a friend," he scoffed.

"Actually, he's a sheriff, and there are times in life a friendly law enforcement officer can come in very handy." Savannah's gaze drifted toward the man sitting behind the wheel of his truck. Very handy.

"Yeah, right."

"Look, you and I have a lot to talk about. We need to establish a common ground of what each of us expects and requires from this relationship we're entering into, but the conversation can wait until we're home in Eternity Springs." She folded her arms and added, "In the meantime, I expect you to be respectful to Sheriff Turner. Got it?"

She took his shrug to be an affirmative answer, decided they'd work on "yes, ma'am" and "no, ma'am" pretty quickly, and headed for the truck. TJ shuffled slowly behind her, so she and Zach had a moment alone. "You okay?" he asked.

"What was it you said earlier about my being able to meet challenges?"

"I didn't say anything about it being easy."

The back passenger door opened, and TJ threw his duffel and backpack inside, then climbed in. He didn't say a word, but in the wake of the comments he had made earlier, Savannah considered that a good thing.

They stopped at a Mexican restaurant for lunch before heading back. Savannah didn't have much of an appetite and only picked at her taco salad. Both males seemed to inhale their meals. Nobody wasted much effort with conversation.

She and Zach made small talk during the first portion of the return trip to Eternity Springs, but once they made the turn onto the two-lane road that would take them over Sinner's Prayer Pass, Zach gave her a reassuring wink, then glanced into the rearview mirror and asked, "Do you like to fish, TJ?"

It took him a good thirty seconds, but TJ finally responded, "I guess."

"Angel Creek is a stone's throw away from Savannah's house, and fishermen pull some nice trout out of there. Our friend Cam can get you fixed up with gear and a license."

Savannah watched her nephew in the vanity mirror mounted on the visor and noted interest that the boy tried to hide but couldn't. *Good instincts, Zach.* Following his lead, she brought up other outdoor activities that Eternity Springs and the surrounding environs had to offer. Zach picked up where she left off, and they basically tag-teamed TJ like tourist office employees. He acted disinterested, but Savannah could see through that look.

She knew that look very well. She'd seen it in the mirror a million times. TJ was interested in the possibilities that awaited him here in Colorado, but he wasn't going to get his hopes up over anything. He'd been burned before. Until he stood at the banks of Angel Creek with a rod in his hand and fish on his line, he wouldn't believe he could go fishing. Same for camping, zip-lining, snow-mobiling, and skiing. However, she and Zach had successfully planted the seeds, and the boy would think about it.

One they'd exhausted the activities travelogue, Zach struck up a conversation with Savannah designed to pique TJ's interest in the people of the town. He spoke about Celeste and Nic Callahan, and when he talked about Jack Davenport he made sure to drop those three little letters guaranteed to catch a boy's interest: CIA. He mentioned Colt's summer baseball league team, but it wasn't until he mentioned basketball that TJ abandoned all pretense of disinterest. "Basketball camp? With Coach Romano? Which one? There are two of them."

Finally, he speaks, Savannah thought.

"Both Anthony and Lucca Romano will be here," Zach said. "They are my deputy sheriff's brothers. The basketball camp is a fund-raiser for the summer camp the Davenports are opening later this year. It'll be some-time in August, right, Savannah?"

"It's actually over Labor Day weekend. Gabi said it was the only time both her brothers could arrange time off together. Apparently basketball recruiting season has become a year-round thing, just like football."

"I've played some one-on-one with Gabi Romano. I'm no slouch on the hardwood, but she can whip my butt. She helped me with my hook shot, though. She wants to get me into shape for a pickup game with her brothers."

"I suppose this camp is just for high-school-age kids?" TJ asked.

"Yes, it's for varsity-level players."

Crestfallen, TJ slumped back in his seat. Savannah twisted around and studied her nephew, sensing that she'd been handed a golden opportunity. Gabi had already offered to help Savannah with TJ in any way she could. It appeared she'd just been handed a bargaining chip. "Gabi Romano has become a special friend of mine, TJ. I expect we could arrange a private lesson or two with the Romano brothers if that's something you'd be interested in."

He went still, then narrowed his eyes. "What's the catch?"

She couldn't help but grin. Of course there would be a catch. For Moores, there was always a catch. "You have to give me, give us, a chance. I know this has been a terrible time for you and I understand why you arrived here with a chip on your shoulder, but life will be so much better for both of us if you'll try to make a life here, try to make a home with me."

Temper flared in his eyes. "Screw that. My life and my home are in Georgia. I'm going back there real soon."

"You'd rather be in the system there than living with family here?" Zach asked.

"I'd rather be on my own at home. They had no business making me leave. I can take care of myself. I was doing just fine at home on my own. I didn't need supervision. I've been getting myself to school—and making good grades, by the way—for months now. I kept groceries in the house and cooked and did laundry. I even mowed the lawn. I sure as hell didn't need to go into foster care. I didn't deserve that. If not for a busybody cop, I'd still be home and we'd all be happy. It's not like you want me here anyway. I got forced on you."

"That's not true," Savannah said. "I could have said no."

"At least you had a choice. Everyone else gets to make choices. I should, too."

Anger rolled off the boy in waves and Savannah decided now was not the time to argue with him, or even to try to reason with him. "Well, if you decide you want to put down your chip and pick up a basketball, let me know."

She turned back to Zach and asked, "Have you been into Vistas recently? Sage has acquired a new artist. He lives near Durango and he paints wildlife. She has one painting he's done of an elk up on Sinner's Prayer Pass that takes your breath away."

With that, talk returned to generic topics and TJ didn't participate, but instead sat behind them fuming. When they finally reached the Eternity Springs city limits sign, Savannah wanted to cheer. Once Zach pulled up in front of the house, she asked him, "Would you like to come in for a few minutes? Let me show TJ where to put his things, then I'd like to speak with you."

"Tell you what. Let me drop off my wheels at the office, then I'll stop back. I rode my bike in this morning."

"You bought a new bicycle, didn't you? Cam had a bet on how long you'd resist it."

Zach grinned that devilish smile of his. "I heard. I waited one day past the date he'd bet on." He glanced over her shoulder, then deliberately leaned down and kissed her softly on her mouth. "See you in twenty."

Zach drove away and Savannah turned to see TJ scowling after him. *So, Zach was staking his claim with that kiss, was he?*

Of course he had been. Savannah sighed, then muttered with disgust, "Boys."

TJ's insides were churning. Not like he was gonna be sick, but like he was gonna puke, roaring like he was gonna explode. He imagined flames shooting out of his mouth, laser beams zapping from his eyes, and steam blowing out of his ears. Not like a cartoon character, though. Like a monster. TJzilla. He wanted to grow a thousand feet tall and stomp all over Eternity effing Springs.

Instead, he stood silent and unmoving, waiting for his drunk dad's druggie sister to tell him where to put his stuff.

She gave him a fake smile, then proceeded to tell him that the first floor of her house was a shop. "We can use the kitchen and downstairs bathroom, but since we share it with the shop, we need to be sure to keep everything very clean. I prefer you shower only upstairs."

He almost told her, *That's okay, I don't shower,* but the idea of not showering grossed even him out.

"I closed the shop today so that we could have a chance to get you settled in. Ordinarily we're open nine to eight Monday through Saturday and one to six on Sunday through Labor Day. After that, we'll go to winter hours and most of the business will be by mail order. It's a little weird living above the store, but you'll get accustomed to it. Follow me and I'll show you your room."

She led him up the stairs and down a short hallway. "I thought I'd let you choose. I have a regular bedroom here that is two doors away from the bathroom, or you could use the attic room. It has heat and a bed, but it's less convenient. On the other hand, it's more private and bigger, and you could do what you want to—within reason—with the space. The choice is up to you."

He knew without looking that he wanted the attic. The farther away from her, the better.

It was an awesome space, and for a few minutes he forgot to be pissed. Because the house had a high pitched roof and a lot of dormer windows, the attic room had nooks and crannies that made it interesting. It'd be cool to live up here. "This'll do."

"Okay, then. I have a friend, Celeste Blessing, who has

a treasure trove of furniture and other items that she's offered for you to choose from to decorate your space."

"Whatever."

She stared at him like a cockroach in the kitchen. He tried to give her his don't-give-a-shit smile, but he was afraid he couldn't pull it off, so he went with sauntering over to the bed and throwing his duffel and backpack on top of it. "Where's the pisser?"

After a long moment's pause, she replied, "Consider this fair warning. I'm going to give you today, TJ. No matter how hard you try to hide it, I know this must be a very difficult day for you. Frankly, it has been for me. So I'm going to give both of us today. The *bathroom*"— she emphasized the word— "is the first door to the left at the bottom of the attic stairs. Supper is at six."

She left him then—just in time, thank God, because he felt the tears welling up inside him and he'd rather die than let her see him cry. But the minute he was alone, he sprawled across the bed and bawled like a baby until at some point he fell asleep.

He slept until four o'clock, and when he woke up, he did need to use the crapper. Glancing in the mirror as he washed his hands, he scowled at puffy, red eyes. This sucked.

He went snooping for eyedrops in the drawers and cabinet. When he saw tampons, fingernail polish, and powder-scent antiperspirant instead of shaving lotion and nose hair clippers, he experienced a pang in his chest all over again. He blew out a breath and found anger to replace the pain. Then his gaze fell on an un-opened package of eyedrops. Five minutes later, he was sneaking down the staircase hoping to escape the house without his aunt's notice.

He heard her talking to someone and he stopped to eavesdrop.

". . . his hair. He's not going to fit in and make friends

looking like that. I don't know much about kids, but I do know if I say anything it will backfire."

Another woman said, "I don't envy you, Savannah. At least with Alex, I get fourteen years to get ready to have a fourteen-year-old. You didn't even have a week."

TJ silently mocked the woman. *You didn't even have a week. Try being on it from my side, lady.*

Downstairs, he turned away from the voices and made his way through the shop to the front door, where a rectangular sign reading OPEN faced him. He unlocked the door, and as he went out, he flipped the sign around so that OPEN faced the street rather than the word CLOSED.

"Serves her right for talking about me behind my back," he declared.

At the end of the walk, he looked both ways. One direction appeared to be just as boring as the other. He headed west, then turned north on a wide street named Spruce, noting that her house was on Fourth so that he could find his way . . . not home. Never home. Back to his aunt's house.

He shoved his hands in his pockets as he strolled up the street. His fingers found the money the lawyer had given him for his trip, so when he passed a sandwich shop, he went inside and ordered a soft drink. He couldn't help but notice that the girl behind the counter had a nose ring.

He wondered if hers was real or fake like his.

He wandered into a gift shop, where the clerk pointed out the NO FOOD OR DRINK sign on the front door. He considered "accidentally" dropping his cup on his way outside, but he still had half of it left. As he walked past the barber shop, he noticed the barber's disapproving stare, so he grinned and gave his spikes a pat. Good thing he knew how to use the clippers himself and didn't have to count on anyone else to cut his hair.

TJ didn't want to have to count on anyone else for anything.

He finished his drink as he reached the intersection of Spruce and Sixth. He spied a trash can and took two steps toward it before he remembered himself and tossed his paper cup onto the sidewalk.

Across the street on his right was a school. To the left, a park—Davenport Park, according to the sign. Telling himself he wasn't one bit curious about the school, he entered the park.

The playground teemed with rug rats and moms with strollers, plus a few families he pegged as tourists. Seemed to be a lot of tourists on the streets, and in a moment of honesty he could understand why. The weather was great; about a million times better than it was in Atlanta this time of year. The place was pretty to look at, too, and all those activities the sheriff talked about? They sounded like a blast.

It made him think of the times he'd gotten to visit his great-grandmother up in the Great Smoky Mountains.

Just then a little kid let out a yell on the playground, catching TJ's attention, and he noticed a couple of kids half his age who had haircuts like his. A six-year-old couldn't shave his own head. That meant his parents had to be in on the style. Really? No way would his dad have let him wear his hair this way.

Isn't that why you went for the style? To piss him off, since he couldn't do anything about it?

Thinking about his father depressed him, so he turned and walked away from the playground. Passing an empty baseball diamond, he heard the familiar *thump, thump, thump* of a basketball bouncing on a cement court. He veered toward the sound, rounded some bleachers, and spied a guy near his age shooting baskets by himself.

TJ blurted out the question without thinking about it. "Hey, wanna play horse?"

The guy turned. "Sure."

Not a guy. A girl. Well, okay. TJ didn't have anything against girls.

"My name is Mandy West. What's yours?"

"TJ."

"You want to warm up first, TJ?"

He shrugged. "Okay."

She tossed him the ball and started talking. Mandy was thirteen years old, in seventh grade. She had one brother and one sister and her parents were divorced. Her mother called her father a deadbeat dad because he hadn't sent child support since he moved in with his girl-friend in February. "We're poor now and Mom has to work more and we don't get new sneakers for school this year because the ones we have are still okay. I'm mad at my dad for being deadbeat, but I still miss him, you know?"

TJ absolutely did know.

He won the first game of horse, and she challenged him to two out of three. She only stopped talking when they were actually taking their shots. After blabbing about herself, she started asking questions about him. She thought he was a tourist. He didn't tell her other-wise at first, simply saying that he was from Atlanta and had just arrived in town that day.

"How long are you going to be here?"

After a moment's pause, he replied, "I'm not sure."

"Are you staying at a place in town?"

"Yes." He didn't elaborate at first, but then he decided it was stupid to put it off. "I'm not exactly a tourist. I'm staying with my aunt for a while."

"Who is your aunt?"

"Savannah Moore."

Mandy's face brightened. "Ms. Moore from Heavenscents? That's cool. She's really nice. She doesn't mind me coming in just to smell stuff even though I can't buy anything, and when I wanted to buy my mom something for her birthday from Heavenscents, Ms. Moore gave me a big discount so I could buy a bubble bath bar. Mom loved it."

Bubble bath? That's what all that stuff is? He'd noticed the smell in the shop, but he'd been in a hurry to make his escape, so he hadn't looked around.

The second game lasted a little longer than the first, mainly because Mandy started talking about kids in the seventh grade and wouldn't shut up. She told him stories about a dozen people before she finally wound down. After she missed a shot for her S, she turned to him and asked, "Can I ask you a question, TJ?"

Could I possibly stop you?

"When you have a ring in your nose, does it hurt to sneeze?"

He couldn't help it—he started to laugh. It was the first time he'd laughed since his father got arrested.

His laughter died when he heard someone call his name. Zach Turner stood at the edge of the court, his arms folded, his mouth set in a fearsome scowl.

EIGHTEEN

After two weeks of "motherhood," Savannah was ready to pull her hair out. How could one teenage boy create so much havoc? If he was this big a pain at fourteen, imagine how he'd be at sixteen.

Of course, she admitted, she was part of the problem at times. From the first day when she discovered he'd left the house, assumed he'd run away, and called the sheriff's office for help, to today when, in a hormonal snit, she'd yelled at him for leaving the seat up in the bathroom, she had done her share of making matters worse. She was supposed to be the grown-up in this relationship, but sometimes she'd acted ten years old to his fourteen. Getting her feelings hurt because he didn't like her ginger cookies was just plain stupid, and so what if the one time she'd seen him engaged and open was while talking about basketball with Gabi Romano? She should be glad for every non-juvenile-delinquent moment she got! Instead, she snapped at him, he stormed out, and then she spent the rest of the day fretting.

The phone rang, and she picked it up without checking caller ID. "Heavenscents."

"Hello, dear," Celeste said. "Have I called at a bad time?"

"Not at all. Business has been slow today. I admit it

worries me a little bit. August is supposed to be the height of tourist season."

"You'll have days like this going forward. The key is to remember that the sun always rises on a new day."

That rather cryptic comment caused Savannah a modicum of concern. Why did she think Celeste might be talking about something other than walk-in customers?

She knew, of course, and she couldn't hold back a sigh as she asked, "What has he done now?"

"TJ is such a troubled boy. My heart truly breaks for him."

"Celeste, what did he do?"

"He is quite inventive, you realize. Has a bright, creative mind. He simply must learn how to channel all that creativity—without a can of spray paint."

Oh dear.

"Some graffiti artists are true artists. Coming from the city like TJ does, it's not surprising that he turns to that outlet for some of his anger."

Anger? I'll show him anger. "Where is he?"

"He's at Angel's Rest, dear. He decided to decorate Cougar's Lair cottage. I'm afraid that my spa manager spied him in the act and called the sheriff's office. Zach is here."

Savannah closed her eyes. "I'll be right there."

Zach was pissed enough to chew the bark off a Ponderosa pine. The little dipstick had gone too far this time. It wasn't simply the fact that TJ had defaced Angel's Rest. *What* he'd painted was beyond inappropriate. Savannah was gonna blow a gasket.

He stared at the cottage wall and considered the state of his own gaskets. In all his years in law enforcement, he'd never been tempted to use the power of his office as payback . . . until today. Cam Murphy and Mac Timberlake had already been by to take a gander. He figured

Callahan and Rafferty weren't far behind. At least Davenport was out of town. Zach would be hearing about this all winter long.

A male figure sat in the image of the claw-foot bathtub now painted across the long side of the dark red, Victorian style cottage. You couldn't tell by the face that the guy was meant to be him, but the badge painted on the naked chest made it clear. Soap bubbles floated on the air all around him, and a cartoon speech balloon read, "Hey, Peach, want me to soap your fuzz?"

Zach turned a fierce, narrow-eyed glare on the unrepentant little hoodlum as the Angel's Rest caretaker arrived with the supplies Zach had requested. "These are my last two gallons of the red, Sheriff," the man said. "Should be enough to paint the wall unless those neon colors bleed through."

"Thanks."

"It's been over a year since I painted this cabin. Could be that a fresh coat on this wall will stick out like a sore thumb."

"If that's the case, TJ will repaint the entire cottage. He'll also replace the paint he uses today."

TJ smartly chose to keep quiet as the caretaker unloaded a paint tray, roller, paintbrush, and rags from the back of the utility vehicle. Only after the man drove off did TJ quip, "Just call me Tom Sawyer."

Zach had plenty of things he'd like to call the kid; Tom Sawyer wasn't one of them. "Pain in the ass" was near the top of the list. Not only had TJ caused an unending amount of trouble, but Zach hadn't gotten laid since TJ Moore had blown into town.

"Have you painted anything before? Do you need instruction?"

"I can handle it."

Zach folded his arms. "Then get to work."

"Are you going to stand around and watch me?"

"Depends. Would you rather I leave?"

"Yes."

Zach smiled pleasantly. "In that case, I'll stay."

TJ's reaction had Zach recalling his mother's caution: *Careful, son. You don't want your eyeballs to get stuck in the back of your head.*

The memory lightened his mood somewhat as he watched the boy stir the paint, then pour it into the tray. When he spied Savannah's Taurus approaching, he was able to offer her a genuine smile. She exited the car like the queen of the Amazons ready to go to war. The sight of her struck Zach with an arrow of wanting, and his voice was husky when he said, "Hello, beautiful."

She cut him a look that said, *I don't have time for that.* He'd grown quite familiar with that look during the past three weeks. "Thomas James," she snapped. "What in the world . . . oh my."

She gawked at the graffiti, then her cheeks went red as hummingbird syrup. "Why?"

TJ lifted his chin. "I didn't figure it was private, since you talked bubble baths in front of me."

"We didn't know you were there!"

The boy was referring to the previous evening, when Zach had stopped by as Savannah closed up Heavenscents and tried to talk her into spending the evening out at Reflection Point. He'd been teasing her, teasing them both, when TJ walked out of the kitchen, which both had believed to be empty.

"You eavesdropped on a private conversation," she continued. "You should have made your presence known."

"I was too embarrassed."

"So you decided to embarrass me back."

Zach didn't believe the boy had been embarrassed. He didn't have room for embarrassment because of all the anger he nursed. Zach couldn't remember a time he'd ever seen a boy with so much fury inside him. Thinking about it drained more of Zach's own anger.

Then the boy went and stepped over a line he should have stayed well away from.

"Oh, lighten up, Auntie Drug Dealer. If I'd wanted to embarrass you, I'd have painted you wearing an orange jumpsuit in your prison cell."

Savannah gasped. Zach's temper blew. "You little jackass. You do not talk to your aunt this way."

"Why not?" TJ slammed the paintbrush to the ground. "Why shouldn't I say it? It's the truth. She's an ex-con who went to prison for drug dealing. That's pretty embarrassing if you ask me, and I should know. I'm an expert on embarrassment. My whole family is an embarrassment. My uncle's in jail, my dad's in jail, my aunt was in jail. Do I have good genes or what? But hey, I guess I shouldn't complain. It could be worse. I could be in foster care again." Then, so softly Zach wasn't sure he heard it, the boy added, "With the pervs."

Zach's radar went onto high alert. *The pervs?*

The boy's jaw went hard and his hands fisted at his side. He started blinking. Blinking. Blinking.

TJ Moore was crying.

Savannah saw the tears swell in her nephew's eyes, processed the words he'd just said, and her fury evaporated. She didn't know what to say to him, what to do. She sent a beseeching look toward Zach, but he was staring at TJ, a troubled look on his face.

TJ jerked his gaze away from Zach and Savannah, grabbed up a roller, and almost shoved it into the paint. He painted a wide swath of red across the center of the image he'd created and in that instant, Savannah knew what to do. She picked up a brush, dipped it in paint, and began attacking soap bubbles. A moment later Zach grabbed another roller and joined them.

Her gaze remaining on the wall before her, Savannah asked, "Did you ever hear the story about the time your father saved the life of a woman on his paper route?"

TJ cut her a sharp look and she spied the surprise in his eyes.

"Mrs. Pimlott. She was in her late seventies, but she still drove. She had a big old Cadillac. Dad used to call it a land yacht. Anyway, it was Saturday afternoon and we'd had a lot of rain the previous few days. Mrs. Pimlott was on her way to church when she found her way blocked by some orange safety cones. Instead of stopping, she maneuvered around the cones and drove right into a creek that had overflowed its banks. That's when Gary saw her."

Savannah paused and dipped her brush into the paint can. Though TJ didn't say a word, she could tell that he was paying close attention. "The water was up to her neck, and afterward she told everyone that she'd been certain she was about to die. She wasn't strong enough to open the door.

"Gary rushed right into the water. He managed to get the door open and helped her out of the car. Even then they weren't safe because the water was really churning. You know that scar he has just above his left knee? That's where the tree branch hit him."

"I thought he got that scar in a bar fight."

"Nope. He got it saving Mrs. Pimlott's life. He waited with her until an emergency crew showed up and helped them out of the creek. He was seventeen, I believe. Maybe sixteen. He acted selflessly and courageously, and we were all so proud of him."

Savannah didn't say any more, allowing TJ time to consider the story.

While filling his roller with paint, Zach suggested, "Tell him the story you told me about your dad and the guy in the grocery store."

It was another story that showed TJ's family in a positive manner, and Savannah repeated it with pleasure. Of her brothers, she'd been closest to Gary. She knew he loved his son, had seen how he'd grieved when TJ's mother left them. The fact that he'd believed Kyle instead of her was a wound on her heart still today.

With three people working, the image fell quickly beneath a cover of crimson. Savannah said no more, but she continued to watch TJ closely, so as the last soap bubble disappeared beneath his roller, she didn't miss the tears that spilled from his eyes and trailed down his cheeks. For a moment, she debated how to react. Instinct told her to take him in her arms and hold him, but experience—the lack of experience—kept her rooted in place.

"I miss my dad," TJ said.

Her heart twisted. "I know you do, Teej."

"Why did he have to be so stupid? He knew the consequences. He knew they'd throw his ass in jail if he got another DUI. He knew I'd be alone!"

Savannah had asked herself that question, and she didn't have an answer. Fumbling for a response, she met Zach's sympathetic gaze. He said, "Alcoholism is a disease, son. In my job, I've seen over and over how it grabs hold of a person's will and strangles the life out of it."

"He should have gotten help. He didn't even try. I heard his lawyer tell him he needed to go into a program. He wouldn't. And they warned him what would happen to me. He just didn't care."

"He let you down," Zach said.

"Big time!"

TJ wiped his nose with his sleeve, and Savannah squelched the automatic urge to tell him to find a tissue.

"I'm so pissed at him . . . he didn't even say good-bye to me. The day they came and got him, all he had to say were excuses."

Savannah said, "But you still miss him."

"Yeah, I do. He's my dad."

She totally understood.

"I didn't get to see him. I was supposed to get to see him the day before I left, but there was some screwup at the jail and it didn't happen. The lawyer said he'd get Dad to call me, but I don't know how that's supposed to happen with me here. Dad may not even know where I am. I don't have a cell phone and he won't call you, Aunt Savannah."

It was the first time he'd actually addressed her as "Aunt Savannah," and despite the circumstances under which he used it, she felt a rush of pleasure.

"See, this is where having a friend in law enforcement can help," Zach said. "I can make a phone call happen . . . if I want to make it happen, that is."

Savannah could easily read the warring emotions on TJ's face. He didn't want to ask for any help from Zach, but the sneaky smart sheriff had dangled something the boy desired. She took pity on him and asked, "What would make you want to make it happen, Zach?"

TJ watched him suspiciously.

Zach allowed the moment to stretch out before saying, "Nothing. I'm happy to help make it happen for you, TJ."

"What's the catch?"

"No catch."

Distrust clouded TJ's expression. "You'd do that after I . . ." He gestured toward the cottage wall. "Why?"

"You should be able to speak with your dad. I think being able to talk to one's parents is up near the top of any kid's list of important things. If my parents were still alive, I'd want to talk to them. I'd give just about anything for that."

TJ seemed to consider this carefully. "You're not going to try to bribe me into acting . . . different?"

"Nope."

"You're not going to make me bow and scrape and apologize?"

"Oh, I expect an apology, and we will deal with that. You need to apologize to your aunt, and to me, and to Celeste, too. But the issue with your dad is a separate matter. I'll make some calls and we'll figure out a way for you to talk to him. That is a no-strings-attached offer."

Savannah's gaze shifted between man and boy. Zach was good. He had found just the right approach to get through to the boy.

Her mind was spinning, haunted by his use of the word *pervs*. Was this simply a case of exaggeration, or could her nephew have been abused in a foster home? She needed to find out the answer, but how? Asking him outright wouldn't work. If she'd learned anything about TJ during the past three weeks, it was that they still had a ways to go before he'd talk to her about anything of importance.

Yet she would need to get him to talk to someone. Who? A doctor? Maybe the school counselor? She assumed the school did have a counselor, but she honestly didn't know. The question had never been an issue with her. She'd have to get to work on that.

In the meantime, she had an idea. "I have an offer to make that does come with strings, TJ."

His scowl couldn't hide the apprehension her comment had caused.

"I'll make a deal with you. If you don't give me any more trouble, if you'll help around the house and the shop and behave respectfully to me, to my friends, and to yourself for the rest of the summer, during fall break I'll take you to see your father."

TJ's eyes widened. Zach's mouth gaped. "You'll go back to Georgia?"

"Yes, I will. For a visit. If TJ makes an effort to get along and works with me instead of against me."

Zach leveled a look on TJ. "You should probably understand that going back to Georgia would be a huge deal for your aunt. She's told me dozens of times that she'd never go back. That she would do that for you, after . . . everything"—this time Zach was the one who gestured toward the wall—"that's an offer you need to appreciate."

Savannah wouldn't deny Zach's claim, but she thought enough had been said. She set down her paintbrush and picked up a rag. Wiping paint from her fingers, she asked, "So, what will it be, Teej? Do we have a deal?"

She didn't miss the leap of excitement in his brown eyes. *Oh, Gary. Do you know how much your son loves you?*

"Yes, ma'am." He wiped his hand on his jeans, then stuck out his hand for a handshake. "We have a deal."

Ma'am. Smiling, she took a risk. Stepping forward, she wrapped him in her arms for a hug instead.

NINETEEN

For Zach, Boy Scout summer camp had been the highlight of every summer during his youth. That's where he first enjoyed the activities he continued to love today. Hiking, fishing, orienteering. And, during the later years, sex.

The Girl Scout camp had been right next door.

Yet, despite all the fun he'd had, he'd never been as excited about a week of summer camp as he was about this one. In twenty minutes, TJ would board a school bus to take the short trip up to Jack Davenport's camp on Murphy Mountain. It was the local kids' week for fishing, hiking, and orienteering.

Zach got to stay home and have sex.

To say that TJ's presence in Savannah's household had put a crimp in his style was the understatement of the century. It impressed him that she tried to do the responsible thing in front of her nephew, but still . . .

"Man, I love summer camp," he said to no one in particular at the sheriff's office. Gabi and Ginger shared an amused look, then Gabi observed, "As grumpy as you've been lately, I've decided that I love summer camp, too—despite the fact that my boss asked me to give up my days off to accommodate his love life."

"Now, hold on a moment. I didn't ask you to give up your days, I asked you to switch. And I never said anything about my love life."

Ginger snorted. "Like we all can't tell that you are pawing at the barn door to get to your heifer in heat."

"Heifer in heat?" Gabi chortled a laugh. "I can't wait to share that one with Savannah."

This friendship between his deputy and his lover made life awkward at times. However, Zach was in too good a mood to allow workplace teasing to bother him today. He glanced at the clock. Half an hour until the bus's scheduled departure.

"I think I'll do one more foot patrol before I call it a day." He'd feel better about things if he actually watched TJ get on the bus and saw it drive out of town. "Buzz me if anything needs my attention . . . until ten o'clock. After that, Gabriella is in charge."

"Ah, words that are music to my ears," she said. "I have such plans for this little burg. Ginger, as soon as he leaves, let's get to work on that town beautification idea we discussed."

Against his better judgment, Zach asked, "Town beautification?"

"I noticed that the budget has three thousand dollars in surplus funds for that line item. We thought we'd use it for pedicures for local residents."

"Very funny." He strode toward the door, lifted his hat from the hat rack, and offered up a parting shot. "You girls be good."

"Bet you don't say that to Savannah," Gabi called after him.

Zach grinned all the way to the school parking lot.

There he saw Savannah dressed in that yellow sundress of hers, the one that was his favorite, and—whoa, was that TJ? What had happened to his hair? It was . . .

brown. And trimmed. Couldn't even tell he'd had a Mohawk. Plus he only had one earring in one of his ears.

Savannah stood with Sarah Murphy, Ali Timberlake, and Cat Davenport. He joined them, indulged in the urge to give Savannah a quick buss on the mouth, then asked, "So who is that kid standing in for TJ?"

"Crazy, isn't it?"

"What brought it on?"

"I'm not sure. He came downstairs like this, didn't say a word, and with one of those mule-headed looks told me not to ask."

"Where did he get those normal clothes?"

"Sarah brought them over. She said they were some of Devin's things that he'd outgrown."

"That was nice."

"It was a lie. She and Gabi got together and bought a few things and washed them a half-dozen times. They even authenticated the shirt with a chocolate stain."

"Your girlfriends scare me, Peach," he said, meeting Sarah's smirking gaze.

"I see nothing wrong with that sentiment," Cat said.

Zach decided to bring the conversation back around to the boy. "Whatever the reason, we can be thankful for it. He looks good."

"I think he has a crush on Gabi," Savannah said.

"Oh-h-h. Yes. That makes sense. She told me she'd been shooting basketballs with him and Mandy West."

If Savannah hadn't been in his life and he hadn't been Gabi's boss, he probably would have had a crush on her, too.

Cat said, "Looks like our camp director is ready to load the kids up."

Zach observed the excitement on the faces of the town's children. "You and Jack are doing a wonderful thing here, Cat. Most of these kids' parents couldn't afford summer camp."

"We are just as excited as the kids—excited and nervous. We're happy to have these sessions for the local kids to give us time to work out the wrinkles. We want everything to go smoothly, but I know we'll have our challenges."

"According to Devin, not for lack of preparation," Sarah said, speaking of her son. "Devin said that training for the Wounded Wings One Hundred bike race had nothing on what Jack put the counselors through during their training sessions."

Cat shrugged. "Jack went a little overboard. It's his background. Says you can never be too prepared."

"True," Zach said. Whatever work Jack Davenport had done for the government, he no longer did it. He and Cat had dedicated their efforts to the charitable foundation, Lauren's Gifts, established in the name of their deceased daughter. Zach was glad to see the Davenports so happy after the bumpy road they'd traveled.

The children began filing onto the bus, and Cat said, "Okay, then. I'd better head on up there. I promised Jack I'd beat the bus so that we're together when our first campers arrive."

"Good luck," Sarah and Savannah both said. Zach watched TJ break off a conversation with Aiden Marshall. The scowl on both boys' faces gave the sheriff a bit of a pause, and he hoped there wasn't anything going on there. Aiden was the son of one of the partners in the local bank. He was a good-looking kid, a talented athlete, and Mr. Popular at school. He was always respectful to Zach, but something about the boy made Zach's radar go on alert.

He didn't seem like the sort of kid who would make friends with TJ.

But then, it didn't exactly look like they were friends, did it?

Mandy certainly looked a little concerned. Now, there was a sweetheart. Mandy was dyslexic and as a result had struggled in school both academically and socially. But she was as nice as could be, cute as a button, a blessing to her struggling mom, and a darn good basketball player. He hoped TJ would continue to treat her with friendship and respect.

Aiden let out a laugh and gave TJ a good-natured slap on the back. TJ grinned, and Zach thought, *Well, good*.

TJ stepped up into the bus, pausing on the stairs to give a quick, backward glance toward Savannah. She smiled and waved. Zach resisted the urge to give a fist pump.

The bus pulled out at 10:05. "You did make arrangements for Heavenscents, right? You still have the rest of the day off?"

"No." Disappointment washed over him like a cold rain before he noted the teasing light in her eyes. "I have the rest of today and tomorrow morning off."

Zach grabbed her hand. "Bye, Sarah."

Grinning impishly, Sarah waved her fingers. "Ta-ta."

Zach cursed himself for having walked to the park rather than driven, and he all but dragged Savannah out of the park. He didn't realize he was close to breaking into a jog when she let out a little laugh, pulled her hand from his, and said, "Whoa there, big boy. If I trip and twist my ankle, that will compromise both of our styles."

"Sorry. I'm just a little anxious." His gaze fell upon the creekside cabins at Angel's Rest, and for a moment he considered checking in, but his better sense prevailed. What he needed was privacy with his woman, not to become the lead item on the Eternity Springs gossip hit parade.

"I think I'm just afraid that my radio will go off before . . . well, before."

She returned to his side and slipped her arm through his. "If I weren't a good citizen, I'd see that the battery in your radio somehow got lost."

"Sounds great, but then I'd have to arrest you."

"Would you use your handcuffs? I kinda miss those days."

His jaw gaped. "Savannah Sophia Moore. Did you just make a joke about jail?"

Laughter bubbled from her. "I'm happy, Zach. This was such a great morning with TJ. Didn't he look great? No nose ring, and he's down to one piercing—although I'm pretty sure those others were all fake. And now I don't have to work and I can spend some time with you. My heart is singing."

"Give me half an hour and the rest of you will be crooning harmonies." He took hold of her hand and brought it up, pressing a kiss against her knuckles.

The look she gave him then was downright wicked.

He made it to Reflection Point in record time. What followed once he got her into his house, into his bed, rocked his world. Somewhere between the first fast, furious coupling and the second one, which was slow and sensual, a certain knowledge whispered through his mind that he wasn't prepared for. One that actually frightened him a little bit. It almost had him reaching for the phone to cancel today's events.

But then Savannah put her mouth on him and sensation drove all thought from his mind. It didn't return until it was too late. He could hear the *whop whop whop* of the helicopter approaching Reflection Point.

He sprang out of bed. "Quick, Peach, we need to hit the shower and get dressed. I lost track of time and Logan will be here in minutes."

"Who will be here?" she asked, sitting up, clutching the sheet to her breast. "What's going on?"

Zach walked into the bathroom and turned on the hot water. "I intended to ask you, but then I got distracted by . . . you. You're not afraid of flying, are you?"

"Flying!"

Zach stepped into the shower and called, "Helicopter. Since our time is limited, I didn't want to waste time traveling. Logan McClure will take us over the mountains instead of around and get there quick."

She stepped into the bathroom, all naked and glowing and gorgeous, distracting Zach all over again. He stared at her, felt himself stir back to life.

Savannah reached into the shower and shut off the hot water. "Zach Turner, what in the world are you talking about?"

Cold water blasted him back to attention. "Our date. I made plans for a special surprise. I'm taking you up to Silver Eden Lodge." He switched the hot water back on. "Logan will pick us up in the morning and bring us home before work. Okay?"

She gaped at him. "Silver Eden Lodge? Isn't that the one that's so exclusive? It only has, like, ten rooms, and movie stars and royalty go there?"

"Yeah." He stepped out of the shower and nudged her in.

"But . . . but . . . jeez, Zach. It'll cost a fortune."

He grabbed a towel and dried off with quick, brisk motions. "While I'd love to impress you with my ability to pay a stupid amount for a luxurious getaway, the truth is the owner was a good friend of my dad's. He's the one who helped me land the Eternity Springs job, and I get a special rate."

"But . . . but . . . I can't go. I don't have any clothes. And what about the dogs?"

He flashed a wicked grin and tossed his towel over his shoulder. "The lodge provides a robe. You're not going to need much else. Nic is going to swing by both our places later, pick up the dogs, and board them at the clinic."

"Zach!"

"I have everything covered, Peach. Trust me." With that parting shot, he exited the bathroom, dressed, grabbed the overnighter he'd prepared earlier, and went out to meet the helicopter.

Zach had discovered that the owner of the town's grocery store had a pilot's license when he volunteered to assist during a missing-person search. He'd called upon Logan in a professional capacity a number of times since then. The man had a nice little side business going, ferrying corporate folks from the airport to the conference center. This was the first time Zach had hired him personally.

"I appreciate your taking the time to do this," Zach told him as the men shook hands.

"Glad to help. Your conference retreat business has paid my mortgage for the past couple of months. Are you two ready to leave?"

"Almost." Zach glanced back toward the house, hoping he was right. Savannah never had responded to his question about flying.

Just as he made the decision to go in and check on her, Savannah exited his house carrying her purse and a tote bag she'd left at his house before TJ entered their world. She gave him a look that was part excitement, part trepidation, and part bewilderment before greeting Logan and letting him help her up into the helicopter.

The flight took thirty-five minutes. For the first five of them, Savannah held his hand in a white-knuckled grip. Then she relaxed and began to enjoy herself, especially when Logan flew them past Heartache Falls for a bird's-eye view of the magnificence of nature, complete with rainbows in the waterfall's mist.

They landed at Silver Eden Lodge, and by the time they'd exited the helicopter, a golf cart driven by a young man dressed in black slacks and a white shirt sporting the lodge's logo was there to meet them.

"Welcome to Silver Eden," he said, raising his voice to be heard over the helicopter as it lifted off for the return trip to Eternity Springs. "My name is Robert, and I'll be your personal assistant while you're here."

Savannah's smile was as bright as sunshine on snow.

The resort looked different from most of the luxury hotels nestled in the Colorado Rockies. Rather than traditional log cabins or Swiss chalets, Silver Eden's architecture was modern with clean lines, lots of glass, and lots of water, with infinity pools and sophisticated fountains everywhere you turned.

"It's the prettiest place I've ever been," Savannah said.

"Gabe Callahan was the landscape architect on the project."

"I love it."

Their escort took them to an expansive third-floor suite that included cheery fires burning in fireplaces in both the sitting area and the bedroom. Frameless French doors opened onto a private balcony, where steam rose from the outdoor hot tub with a million-dollar view.

Robert pointed out the suite's amenities, then added, "You'll find the appointments you requested on the desk. If you wish to make any adjustments to the schedule, just let me know. Your lunch will be up in . . ." He checked his watch. "Ten minutes. I'll leave you to settle in. If I can be of any assistance, please pick up the phone."

Zach shut the door behind Robert, then turned to look at Savannah. She made a slow circle in the center of the room, her mouth a little agape as she studied the room. "I can't believe this. Zach, why didn't you say anything?"

"I wanted to surprise you. It's been a tough few weeks, and I thought it'd be nice for us both to do something special. Who knows when we'll have the opportunity to be alone together again."

Tears sparkled in those big brown eyes of hers, and she gave him a tremulous smile. "No one has ever gone to so much trouble for me, Zach Turner. I'm a little overwhelmed."

Me too. That little voice was back whispering the words he still wasn't ready to acknowledge. "No need to be overwhelmed. The idea is to enjoy ourselves. That's all this is about."

She walked toward the desk and picked up the schedule. "Room service luncheon . . . three-hour spa appointment?"

"Don't tell Celeste. I'll catch hell for going to the competition."

"Dinner at . . ." Her voice trailed off, and she looked up in alarm. "Ali told me about this restaurant. Zach, we can't go there. It's fancy. My dress is too casual and you'd need a coat and tie."

"Stop worrying. We're all set. The boutique put some things in the closet for you to choose from. It's part of the surprise and the only job you have is to enjoy yourself."

"This is just unreal," she murmured. "I don't know whether to giggle, bawl, jump with joy, or throw you onto the bed and have my way with you."

"I vote for number four." A knock sounded on the door. Lunch had arrived. "Damn. What timing. Save that thought."

While room service set out their meal, Savannah disappeared into the bedroom to check out the contents of the closet. The gasp of delight he heard from her made him grin.

Once the waiter departed, leaving them alone once more, Zach walked to the bedroom door. "Soup's on, Savannah."

She turned away from the closet. "There are no prices on these dresses."

"That's because you don't need to know them. Just pick out your favorite and wear it for me for dinner tonight. Now, as far as what you wear for lunch goes, I'm partial to that hot pink bra you have on."

"I'm not eating lunch in my underwear."

"Spoilsport. I ordered scallops." Her favorite seafood, he knew.

A wicked gleam entered her eyes. "I might . . . just might . . . flash you."

"This was the best idea I've ever had."

Over lunch, they caught up on local issues they hadn't had a chance to discuss since TJ arrived. An unspoken agreement between them kept her nephew out of the discussion, but they did spend some time talking about the Davenports' camp. Savannah said, "I've never seen so many children so excited for anything besides Christmas."

"My office got a call asking if we'd have Jack Davenport Day like we had Cam Murphy Day last year," Zach replied.

"Did you tell Jack?" Savannah asked, laughing.

"No. I told Cam he's been replaced, and he called up Jack and complained. Said it was his mountain, after all." Zach waited a beat, then asked, "So, the scallops were delicious, weren't they? Maybe the best you've ever had?"

Savannah narrowed her eyes and set down her fork. "You have a one-track mind, Sheriff Turner."

"It's been a long dry spell."

"Since nine o'clock this morning?"

He shrugged. "That appetizer had oysters in it."

She smirked, then licked her fingers. Slowly. One by one. "If I'm going to go to the trouble to unbutton my shirt, I might as well get something for it."

"You want dessert, Sugar?"

"Yes. Yes, I do believe I do." She set her napkin on the table, stood, then turned away from him and walked, not toward the bedroom, but toward the balcony, dropping her clothes as she went. She stood for a long moment wearing only that lacy pink bra and matching thong and—Zach swallowed hard—her heeled sandals.

He didn't remember throwing down his napkin, rising, or stripping off his own clothes, but by the time she shimmied out of her underwear and shoes and sank into the frothing water of the hot tub, he was naked.

As he pulled himself from the water half an hour later, Zach had decided that hot tub sex was just about his favorite thing in the universe.

They had time for a walk in the garden before Savannah's appointment at the spa. Zach went for a run, then enjoyed his own massage. They met back at their room for a nap—another one of God's gifts to mankind—and then, at Savannah's request, Zach left her alone to get ready for their dinner date.

In the suite's second bathroom, Zach showered and dressed in his freshly pressed gray suit, a white shirt, and the blue tie Gabi had given him for his birthday. As he tied the knot, he wondered if Savannah would notice that the pattern was made of intertwined handcuffs.

At five minutes to seven, he knocked on the door to their room before using his key to enter. The French doors between the sitting room and bedroom were closed. "Peach? Are you ready?"

"I'll be right there."

A moment later, the French doors opened and Zach

all but swallowed his tongue. She wore that luscious blond hair of hers piled atop her head in artful disarray, a pair of soft curls trailing loose to frame her exquisite face. Her dark red lipstick matched her strapless dress. His gaze drank in the sweetheart neckline that revealed a mouthwatering amount of cleavage, the silky fabric clinging to her form before flaring at the waist into a flirty, filmy, gratifyingly short skirt.

She'd finished it off with red three-inch heels.

"You take my breath away, Savannah."

"I feel like Cinderella."

"You look like a fantasy rather than a fairy tale. I will be the envy of every man in the resort tonight." He crossed to her and offered her his arm. "May I escort you to dinner, beautiful lady?"

"Absolutely, PC."

"PC?"

"Prince Charming."

Zach couldn't help but laugh. "From Barney Fife to Prince Charming, hmm? So what did it? The helicopter? The dress? The hot tub sex?"

"No . . . I think it's the handcuffs on the tie."

"You noticed."

She arched an imperial brow. "Ex-cons always notice handcuffs, Sheriff."

Zach's heart went *kathunk kathunk*. She was so beautiful, so spirited, so damned sexy. Once again, a certain knowledge fluttered in his mind, but still he resisted.

Dinner proved to be a feast for the senses, from the shadowed intimacy of the atmosphere to the sublime flavors of food and wine and the sultry piano music they danced to between dinner and dessert. Back in their room, Zach made love to Savannah with an intensity that was new to him, one that came from his soul. They drifted off to sleep locked in each other's arms, and when Zach awoke to a golden dawn the following morning, that knowledge he'd spent the previous day avoiding echoed through his mind like a clarion.

He lay propped up on his elbow, his head resting in his hand, watching her. When finally she stirred, when those big brown eyes opened and those kiss-swollen lips stretched in a soft, welcoming smile, he gave voice to the truth he could no longer deny. "Savannah Sophia Moore, I love you."

TWENTY

Savannah bolted upright in bed, her heart pounding with alarm, fear riding her blood as his words washed over her. *No, please, no.* She couldn't. Not again. Her heart couldn't bear it. *Couldn't I have the fairy tale for just a little while longer?*

"No, Zach. Don't say that. You can't say that."

The soft look in his eyes sharpened just a little. "I did say that."

"That wasn't the deal. You're a guy."

"I'm glad you noticed," he snapped, then his voice gentled. "Savannah, I said it because I mean it. Let's talk this through. I know you've had a bad experience in the past, but you should—"

"No . . . please." She was breathing fast. She could feel fissures splitting her heart into pieces. She couldn't go there. Didn't he see? What they already had was perfect. Couldn't she just have the perfect without the strings? Strings strangle a person. "Guys are supposed to want no-strings, just-for-fun sex. That's the deal."

"What deal?" Zach's gentle warmth now completely disappeared. Temper crackled in his movements as he flung back the covers and climbed from bed. "I don't recall making any deal. Especially about sex."

"We've been dating. That was the deal."

His mouth twisted. "We're lovers, Savannah. 'Dating' is for high school."

High school? Savannah's anger flared at that, and she seized upon it. Anger was much better than fear. So she was inexperienced compared to his vast number of bedpost notches, like the ski instructor Sarah had mentioned or the pharmaceutical sales rep from Colorado Springs whom Ali said he'd been seeing last year. *And let's not forget half of my friends,* she thought. "I know you've had lots of women."

He reached for his shorts with a shrug. "I have. But I've only been with you since we met, so my past pertains to this discussion how?"

"Well . . ." Savannah's thoughts were raw, panicked, confused, and disjointed. He didn't tell all the women he slept with that he . . . that he . . . loved them. Did he? "I'm supposed to be another notch in your bedpost."

A muscle twitched in his jaw. "That's insulting to us both."

She felt tears welling up, and she panicked even more. She was losing control. She had to stay in control, otherwise she would never survive. "See, this is why I told you before that this is wrong. It just can't be. We're too different. We never should have started this. I can't . . . I just can't."

His eyes went to blue ice. "Can't what? Love me back?"

Don't say that!

He started to reach for her but stopped. His arm fell back to his side and he questioned quietly, "Did I ask for that, Savannah? Did I ask for anything?"

"You ask for everything!" She threw out her arms. "You want me to trust you, to forget all the lessons I've learned. Oh, you don't say it aloud, but you're drip, drip, drip. Mr. Nice Guy. Mr. Everybody's Friend and Problem Solver. Mr. Haven't Been Laid in Years? I'll

Take Care of That for You. You wear a woman down, and this is no different."

In the process of pulling on his pants, Zach froze. "I can't believe you just said that."

"It's true, isn't it? You're like a nun with a penis. You're a do-gooder. You're generous and kind and a dream date, a dream lover."

"Well, pardon me for such horrific behavior," he sarcastically drawled.

"You're the sheriff, for heaven's sake!" And through the crazy haze of her emotions, she realized just how true that was. Barney Fife? He'd never been Barney Fife. He'd always been Andy. Andy Taylor, Zach Turner. The perfect sheriff in the perfect little town. Well, they didn't have an ex-con soap maker in Mayberry. *I don't belong in that world. Not with Sheriff Andy, anyway.* "You're the town cop!"

Zach tightened his belt with a jerk. "Yes, I am. But I'm not Kyle effing Vaughn! Dammit, Savannah. That's what this is all about, isn't it? You need psychological help. You cannot equate every man who enters your life with the one asshole who betrayed you."

Now her tears spilled as Zach continued, "You know what? I'm tired of that. I don't deserve that. I've treated you with nothing but respect, but that doesn't matter, does it? It's not enough for you. Well, guess what. I'm done. I might have fallen in love with you, Savannah, but I don't need this. You can hunker down and be afraid and be alone. That should make you perfectly happy."

"Zach . . . I . . ." Her voice trailed off. She wanted to protest, to apologize, to beg for his forgiveness. But if she did, they'd be right back where they'd started. Nothing had changed here, had it? She didn't want to fall in love again. She couldn't do it. He was right. She was afraid and it was easier to be alone.

"Nothing to say? Well, fine. Like I said, I'm done. Forget what I said about loving you, Savannah. That's what I'm going to do. Logan will pick us up at nine-fifteen. I'm through with this. I'm through with you."

He didn't slam the door behind him when he left. Somehow, the quiet *snick* sounded louder than a bang.

Zach didn't speak to Savannah on the return flight to Eternity Springs. If Logan picked up on the tension humming in the air between them, he wisely kept it to himself. Upon their arrival at Reflection Point, Zach tossed her the keys to his truck. "Leave it parked wherever you like. I'll pick it up later."

He ignored the tight look of pain on her face and marched into his house without a look back. He showered, shaved, and dressed in his full uniform, something he seldom did but that seemed both right and necessary today.

Zach was furious with Savannah. Some of the things she'd said would sting for a long time. Bedpost notches. A nun with a penis? Really? It made him want to put his fist through a wall.

He was angry at Savannah, but even more pissed at himself. What in the world had possessed him? No sooner had he come to a potentially life-altering realization than he felt the need to share it without thinking the possible consequences through. How stupid was that?

Pretty damned stupid. He should have kept his big mouth shut. If he'd taken two minutes to think about it, he'd have known how she would react. Savannah had done a fair job of hiding it, but he knew that her heart had been grievously wounded. It needed time to heal, and he'd rushed her. He'd known it even as he allowed the words to roll off his tongue.

Still, a nun with a penis?

He grabbed the keys to his motorcycle and headed in

to work. When he spied a car with California license plates run a stop sign, he was in just a cranky enough mood to stop the driver and write a ticket.

Ginger greeted him with a smile that died after she got one good look at his face. He gave her and his deputies a gruff "Good morning" before striding into his office and shutting the door. He didn't miss the look his dispatcher exchanged with his deputies, but he chose to ignore it.

He managed to bury himself in paperwork, and as the morning waned, his mood eased. Nothing like compiling crime stats for the state to get a man's mind off his troubles. He worked through lunch and had just finished up a phone call with the Colorado Springs district attorney's office when a knock sounded on his door. Glancing up, he was surprised to see Jack Davenport.

This can't be good, he thought as he waved Jack in and gestured for him to take a seat. "Do we have a problem?" he asked without preamble.

"Possibly. Something happened up at the camp I figured you should know about. I brought TJ Moore and Aiden Marshall home today."

Well, hell. "What happened?"

"That's part of the trouble. I'm not exactly sure. What I do know is that between the archery session and horseback lessons, the two had a dustup. I don't know who started swinging first or why. Neither boy is talking."

"Was anyone hurt?"

"TJ has the beginnings of a shiner. Aiden has a busted lip and a swollen nose."

Zach sat back in his chair and considered. He wasn't completely surprised. "So, this isn't something the sheriff's office needs to become involved in?"

"I thought you'd want to know because of Savannah. She wasn't very happy when we showed up at Heavenscents."

"I don't imagine that she was." He hesitated a moment, then asked, "Did you tell her you were coming to me?"

"I told the boys. I thought it might help prevent them from bringing the trouble off the mountain into town—at least for a little while."

"I'll bet they loved that."

"Like I said, I couldn't get either kid to talk, but the animosity was thick enough to cut with a knife. I don't think it's over, and I suspect that at some point in time you'll be dealing with them."

"Do you have a guess on who the instigator was?"

Jack glanced at his wristwatch, then stood. "I'm afraid I'd pick TJ, though it's just a guess. Before they got into it, Aiden seemed to be having fun, but TJ was a little moody. Now, I'd better get back up the hill. I'm scheduled to lead a hike in half an hour."

Zach found himself wishing the fistfight had occurred last night rather than this morning. The Davenports would have called Savannah and their wonderful evening would have been interrupted, but this morning's disaster wouldn't have happened, either.

He shook Jack's hand, thanked him for the heads-up, and wished him smooth sailing for the rest of the camp. Alone again in his office, he assumed his favored thinking position by propping his feet up on his credenza as he gazed out the window.

What now? He probably should develop a strategy for going forward. To do that he needed to figure out what he wanted. To figure out what he wanted, he needed to be firm about what he felt.

Bottom line: was he in love with Savannah Moore or not? Was the emotion real or the result of sensory overload from a spectacular romantic rendezvous? His gut instinct told him it was real, but he'd never been in love before. Maybe he was wrong. Maybe time would prove him wrong.

Everything considered, he decided he'd be wise to give it a few days, maybe a few weeks, to be certain of what he was feeling—and frankly, to get over the sting of this morning's fight. *Nun with a penis, my ass.* He could use the time he wasn't spending with her to make those calls to Georgia he'd been wanting to make. He didn't have to wait until after tourist season. His free time was his free time. He could spend it working if he wanted.

Then he could make a run at her again.

Because, if time proved that he was truly in love with Savannah Moore, then he wouldn't let her fear stop him. If he wanted her, he'd win her. Of that he had no doubt.

Mr. Nice Guy wasn't above playing dirty.

In Eternity Springs, August was the height of the tourist season, as people from all over the heat-baked Southwest flooded to the Colorado Rockies for weather relief and recreation. As a result, Heavenscents serviced customers from open to close, and Savannah stayed so busy that she was able to put Zach Turner out of her mind.

Sorta.

She missed him. She hadn't spoken to him since she left Reflection Point that difficult morning almost two weeks ago. She'd seen him twice at various town events, but he'd made certain to stay far away from her. She told herself she was glad about it. It made life easier, didn't it?

Easier, but not nearly so fun and exciting and thrilling.

Maybe not even easier when it came to dealing with TJ.

The boy might possibly be the death of her.

The day Jack brought him home from camp, the hair dye, earrings, and attitude returned. Around home, TJ continued to meet the terms of their agreement with regard to taking a return trip to Georgia, but he'd reverted to the sullen, angry boy he'd been upon his arrival in Eternity Springs.

Savannah hadn't managed to get one word out of him about the events that led to his being sent home from camp. While he hadn't gone back to his hoodlum ways, neither was he making any attempt to make friends. He wasn't shooting baskets with Mandy anymore. When he wasn't working for her, according to her friends, he was spending his time by himself fishing along Angel Creek.

The shop door opened, shaking Savannah from her reverie. Gabi Romano stepped inside, glanced around, then asked, "You alone?"

"Actually, I am. First time all day."

"Good." She folded her arms and scowled. "Then tell me what the heck you've done to my boss."

Savannah blinked. "Um . . . I don't know what you mean."

"Oh, don't give me that BS."

"I haven't talked to him in two weeks."

"My point exactly. And now we only get rare glimpses of the easygoing, friendly guy I went to work for, because he's hidden in a fog of sulky funk."

Sulky funk? Zach?

"What happened to you two? One minute you're lovebirds and the next he's scheduling himself for double shifts so that Martin can go home to visit his dad who has been ill."

"Martin's dad is ill? I hope it's nothing serious."

"West Nile virus. He's recovering. Talk to me, girlfriend. Did you dump my b—" Gabi hesitated, a strange look flashing across her face before she finished. "Boss?"

Savannah's instincts went on high alert, and a surge of possessiveness washed through her. "Why do you ask? Do you want to date him? I guess that's the next natural step. He's worked his way through the rest of the women in town."

"That's ridiculous." Gabi drew back, frowning. "Of course I don't want to date him. I'm your friend. I'm his friend. I care about you both and I'm worried about you both."

Savannah glanced toward the door, which remained frustratingly closed. Where were her customers when she needed them? "Look, there is nothing at all to worry about. From what I understand, Zach is accustomed to having a revolving door where women are concerned. He'll be just fine. I'll be fine, too. I *am* fine. We had a fun few weeks together, but that's all it could ever have been. I'm not looking for a relationship."

"Why not?" Gabi asked. "This is one of the good guys, Savannah. And he cares about you. Everyone can see that."

Savannah hesitated, debating how to respond. She valued Gabi's friendship and didn't want to alienate her, but Gabi had a militant look in her eyes.

She's on Zach's side, Savannah realized, her heart twisting. Of all her new friends, Gabi was the one to whom she was closest, and the only one whose friendship with Zach didn't predate a friendship with her. *They'll all take his side. I'll lose all of my new friends because I indulged in a romance with the beloved town sheriff.*

Serves you right for breaking his heart, her conscience chided.

"I didn't break his heart," Savannah defensively declared. "We were together for a few weeks. It was sexy and fun. Love doesn't happen that quickly. Not true love, anyway. It takes time to truly get to know someone. It takes years, not weeks, and even then he can fool you."

"Oh," Gabi said, knowledge dawning in her eyes. "I

get it now. You're scared. It's not what Zach feels that is the problem. The problem is what he made you feel. You're in love with him."

"No, I'm not! That's ridiculous. Did you not hear a word I said?"

"Sure. Even more important, I heard what you didn't say. Listen, Savannah, I think—"

Gabi broke off when the radio she wore attached to her belt emitted a beeping noise and Ginger Harris's terse voice repeated a number that meant nothing to Savannah but had Gabi pivoting on her heel and heading for the door, saying, "I gotta go."

Within seconds, Savannah heard a sound that was rare in Eternity Springs—an emergency siren. She gasped in a breath and everything inside her went tense. Zach.

Savannah covered her mouth and prayed, *Please, Lord. Don't let anything have happened to Zach.*

The accident scene was horrific.

Twisted metal, shattered glass. Blood smeared across the pavement. The stench of burned human flesh permeated the air.

With the first rush of dealing with the emergency behind him, Zach allowed himself a moment of emotion as he bent and scooped a child's stuffed bear off the pavement. He tried to brush the gravel off the animal's face, but it stuck to the fluids that had soaked into the fur. "Some days I truly hate this job."

"I think I'll hear that little girl's screams until the day I die," Gabi responded.

Zach let out a long sigh as his gaze settled on the black body bag. "It was all I could do not to join her. This is the hardest accident scene I've had to work in a very long time."

"She was a friend of yours."

"Yes. She always had a kind word and a cup of coffee for me when I stopped in. She did a lot for this town."

Gabi looked toward the northbound roadblock where curious onlookers had begun to gather. "With the fire, I doubt anyone will be able to identify the car, but we had a couple of cars go through before we set up the road-block. We need to make next-of-kin notification soon."

"I'm not sure who that is, to be honest."

"Who would know?"

"Sarah Murphy is my best guess." He rubbed the back of his neck and added, "Those women love their quilt group. This is going to break their hearts."

He shook his head, flinging off the moment, and re-turned his attention to his job. He gave Gabi a list of items to oversee. "I'm headed to the clinic to take offi-cial statements. I'll stop by Sarah's and see what I can find out about LaNelle's family on my way."

"Zach?" The leader of the volunteer fire department climbed up onto the road from the shallow ravine where LaNelle Harrison's car had come to rest. "We are good to go down here if you want to call in the tow truck."

"Thanks, Henry. You guys did a great job. As dry as it's been, I was afraid the fire would get away from us." That would have been tragedy on top of tragedy.

Zach's gaze drifted over the scene once again. "Gabi, just for my peace of mind, take an extra set of photos before we start the cleanup, would you please? I want everything. Skid marks, the entire debris field. The inter-section from every direction." Grimly he added, "Make sure you include the missing stop sign. That's how we make our case for negligent homicide."

"Will do, boss."

A quarter of an hour later, Zach knocked on the glass of the front door of Sarah Murphy's bakery, Fresh. It was after two, so the shop was closed, though he knew she'd be inside making preparations for the following day. She exited her kitchen smiling, but the moment she saw him, she stopped in her tracks and her smile died. He saw her lips form her husband's name before her hand flew up to cover her mouth.

He held up his own hand and shook his head to reassure her. "Cam is fine. It's not about Cam or one of the kids."

She wiped her hands on her red gingham apron and unlocked the door. "I heard sirens earlier."

"Yes. A car accident. It's LaNelle, Sarah."

"Oh, no." Tears flooded her eyes. "She's hurt?"

"It's worse than that. She didn't make it, honey."

"No." Her chin trembled. "She's . . . dead? LaNelle?"

"Yes."

"She was in a car wreck?"

"Yes."

Sarah let out a little sob, then broke.

Zach took her in his arms and held her while she cried, mentally kicking himself for not calling Cam to give him a heads-up. *Better late than never*, he decided. "Let's call Cam, honey."

She pulled away from him. "What happened?"

"I'm on my way to the clinic to take statements now. The people in the other car were tourists. I came to tell you because I knew you were friends and also because I need to notify her family. I don't know them."

"She has a sister in California. Bakersfield, I think it is. Her name is Lucy."

Zach had a friend in the department in Bakersfield. "Do you know her last name?"

Sarah thought for a moment, then her tears flowed anew. "No. I don't remember."

"That's okay. You've given me a starting point and that's what I needed."

"I know LaNelle has her number in her cell phone."

Zach didn't want to tell Sarah that if LaNelle had had

her phone with her, it hadn't survived the fire. "Good. Now let's give your husband a call."

"Yes. And Nic. And Celeste. All the Patchwork Angels. Is it okay if I tell everyone?"

"Give me half an hour, okay?" He pulled two napkins from the dispenser on the counter behind her and wiped the tears from her face. "Call Cam."

"Okay." Sarah picked her phone up from the counter and placed the call. While it connected, she said, "I'm okay, Zach. You go on and do your work. I'm . . . Cam? Oh, Cam. Can you come home? Zach is here and he brought terrible news about LaNelle."

Once Cam said he was headed home, Zach left the bakery. He'd just climbed back into his Range Rover when Sarah came rushing out. "I remembered her sister's name. It's Carrington. Lucy Carrington from Bakersfield."

"Thanks, honey."

On the way to the hospital, Zach contacted his friend in California and arranged to have the next-of-kin notification made personally. Then he tackled the next gut-wrenching event of his day, which was interviewing the driver of the car that had barreled through the intersection and broadsided LaNelle Harrison's car—a sixteen-year-old new driver from Texas who would live with the consequences of today's accident on her conscience for the rest of her life.

Both she and her father, who had been the occupant of the front passenger seat, had suffered cuts and abrasions from the deployment of airbags. The teen's mother and nine-year-old sister, seated in the back and wearing seat belts, had escaped physical injury. However, the father's attempt to rescue LaNelle from the burning car while the mother tended to the freely bleeding cut on her older daughter's head had the nine-year-old screaming hysterically when Zach and Gabi arrived on the scene.

It was a hell of an afternoon and a bitch of an evening. Once he finished with the interviews at the medical clinic, he had to deal with city hall. LaNelle had been a particular friend of Mayor Hank Townsend's wife, and when Zach arrived back at the office to write up his report, Hank had been waiting for him, wanting details.

Once he had the details, he wanted blood. "How long has that stop sign been missing?" he demanded.

"It was there the day before yesterday, Hank. I rode that route myself."

"So it was missing a whole day and no one reported it stolen?"

"I don't know that, Hank. I haven't had a chance to talk to Ginger."

"Any idea who stole it?"

"Kids, I'd imagine."

Hank Townsend harrumphed and grumbled, "Probably that hippie kid from Georgia."

Zach grimaced. Admittedly, the same concern had been hovering in the back of his head, but he wouldn't abide by baseless speculation. Not within his hearing, anyway. "Hank, please keep those sort of thoughts to yourself. We have absolutely no evidence that TJ is involved in any way. For all we know, Celeste Blessing decided to take the stop sign home and polish it."

"Now, that's just stupid."

"So is blaming a kid for this because you don't like the color of his hair. He's had a rough go of it. This sort of talk could hurt him in town."

"Oh, all right." Hank dragged a knuckle across his eyes, wiping away the wetness that collected there. "But I want you to find who did this, Zach. LaNelle deserves that. That poor girl who hit her deserves it, too."

"I'll do my best, Hank."

He thought of his promise as he drove home that night. This wasn't going to be easy. In a bigger town, he'd have had security cameras to monitor. He could have canvassed the area for witnesses. But at that intersection just outside Eternity Springs, any eyewitnesses other than those directly involved likely walked on four legs and had antlers on their heads.

He tried to wipe the day's events from his mind as he took Ace and went on a long evening run. Afterward, he showered and fell into bed, exhausted. Sleep, however, eluded him.

Even worse than most nights during the past two weeks, thoughts of Savannah grabbed hold of him and wouldn't let him go.

He hoped like hell that the stop sign theft wasn't TJ's doing. Time and some good old-fashioned strong-arming by the sheriff would tell.

TWENTY-ONE

Savannah flipped her OPEN sign to CLOSED, then shut and locked the door to Heavenscents. The memorial service for LaNelle was due to begin in twenty minutes.

It had been a sad three days. Having attended only two meetings of the quilt group, Savannah had not known the other woman well. She had liked her, though. LaNelle had had a plainspoken manner and an inherent kindness that had reminded Savannah of Grams. Her death had hit Sarah especially hard, and Savannah had been glad to hear that Sarah and Cam's daughter, Lori, was coming home for the service.

She arrived to find Saint Stephen's overflowing with people. Mac Timberlake saw her and approached. "Ali saved a spot for you with the other quilters, Savannah. They are up at the front."

"Thanks, Mac."

She joined her friends. Sarah introduced Lori, a beautiful young woman with her father's height and eyes and her mother's smile. "It's a pleasure to meet you, Lori, though I'm sorry it's under circumstances like these."

"Me too. My mom sent me a basket of your soaps. I like them a lot."

"Thanks."

Savannah was distracted by the sight of Zach, who

escorted Celeste to the pew reserved for the members of LaNelle's quilting group, the Patchwork Angels. Their eyes met, and he nodded, but she couldn't read his expression. Then Zach smiled warmly at Lori Murphy and greeted her with a kiss to her cheek. Savannah tore her gaze away to find Sage eyeing her with a quizzical look. She was glad when the swell of organ music signaled the beginning of the service, and when beside her Nic began to cry, Savannah linked her arm with her friend's, silently offering support.

It was a nice service, and afterward the mourners gathered at Angel's Rest for an informal reception. As it wound down, members of the quilting group congregated upstairs in the attic workroom, where, with LaNelle's instructive assistance, the Patchwork Angels had stitched their quilts and bonded in friendship.

"I thought it appropriate that we take time today to stitch and celebrate. While it's true we lost our dear friend LaNelle too soon, we can take comfort in the fact that she's in a place where her shears will never get dull."

"Oh, Celeste." Sarah clapped her hands to her head. "I know this sounds terrible, but I've heard all the uplifting sentiments I can bear today."

"Jeez, Mom. Put a muzzle on her, why don't you," Lori said, then added to Celeste, "You say whatever you like, Celeste. You always know what to say, and it always helps. Honestly, sometimes what you said saved my sanity."

Sarah's head came up, and Savannah recognized worry in her eyes as she looked at her daughter. Celeste smiled and reached out and patted Lori's arm. "Your mother has a point. I'm feeling sentimental today, and that's when I tend to get a bit . . . well . . ."

"Preachy?" Nic and Sage said simultaneously.

Everyone laughed, and the sound was a welcome

change. "Not preachy, I think. Philosophical. Which brings to mind a quote from Seneca that I consider particularly appropriate for today: 'The day which we fear as our last is but the birthday of eternity.' I think we should celebrate LaNelle's birthday."

Sarah groaned, but the sound was somewhat lighter. Not for the first time, Savannah recognized that Celeste had a golden touch with words—which suited her, since gold was obviously her favorite color.

"And of course, I'd be remiss not to mention Socrates, who said, 'Death may be the greatest of all human blessings.' "

Ali looked at Sarah. "You should know by now that there's no stopping her."

"I know," she replied with a sigh.

"And of course, I simply cannot fail to mention Bob Dylan: 'Some people feel the rain, others just get wet.' "

Savannah shared a confused look with her friends. Finally, Lori asked, "What does that have to do with death or LaNelle?"

"Nothing. I just think it's fun." Celeste smiled beatifically when Sarah burst into laughter. "Now, let's stitch for a bit, shall we?"

They picked up their needles, scissors, and rulers and went to work. Eventually the women who had known LaNelle the best began to share stories about their friend, and, in doing so, offered one another comfort.

At the end of the evening, Savannah and Sage walked home together. It was a beautiful summer evening, cool and clear with a slight breeze perfumed by the flowers that lined the streets. Savannah felt better than she had in days. Well, actually, two weeks. "That was nice. It was almost as if . . . well . . ."

"Broken hearts healed a little?" Sage asked.

"Well, yes."

"That's Celeste's specialty. And speaking of such

things . . ." Sage's eyes sparkled. "Did you happen to notice who didn't fully participate in the champagne toast to end the evening?"

Savannah nodded. "Actually, I did."

"I think somebody might be expecting."

"I wondered about that myself."

"For a minute there, I thought we might get an announcement." Sage glanced up at the starry sky and sighed, "If it's true . . . oh, Savannah . . . joy will fill my heart to overflowing. Racer is going to need playmates his own age."

Savannah grinned. "You're calling him Racer, too?"

"Did I do that?" Sage winced. "Curse that husband of mine."

"Well, I hope there's something to it." They crossed the footbridge over Angel Creek and Savannah added, "It feels fitting to me. Death and life. I've had enough death for a while. I'd really enjoy some life."

Sage gave her a sidelong glance. "Then why did you dump Zach?"

"I didn't dump Zach!" Savannah stopped abruptly. She hadn't dumped him. She'd just . . . rejected his love. "Why is everyone saying that? Did he say something?"

"Zach hasn't said squat to anyone as far as I know. That's what we've speculated. He seems to be kinda cranky."

"That's because he's trying to find who's responsible for the death of our friend," Savannah fired back. Immediately she regretted it. "I'm sorry. I don't mean to be Debbie Downer. I just don't want to talk about Zach."

Sage slipped her arm through hers. "Okay. Just let me say one thing. He is a good man."

"He's definitely a man." She deliberately changed the subject. If one more person told her how good Zach was, she would scream. *I know he's good. He's Sheriff Andy.* "I didn't have a chance to talk to Colt today, and

I wanted to thank him for sticking up for TJ at the pub last night."

"Heard about that, did you?"

"First thing this morning."

"I heard Gabi Romano has knocked on the door of half the residences in town asking questions. The sooner they can find who stole that sign, the better for everyone."

They'd reached the intersection of Cottonwood and Fourth, and they waited for a pickup to pass before stepping out into the street. "I asked TJ if he knew anything about it," she confessed. "Not that I thought he did it. Despite his attitude, TJ is a smart kid."

She reconsidered that observation when she entered her kitchen a few minutes later to find the bread, peanut butter, jelly, and chips spread across the countertop, and the slow cooker filled with beef stew she'd made early that morning untouched.

"The least he could do is clean up after himself," she muttered before walking to the base of the stairs. In a loud voice filled with frustration she called, "TJ Moore, you come down here right now!"

The call came in while Zach met with his deputies to go over the day's events. Ginger knocked on his office door and said, "Sheriff, I think you should take this."

"All right." He picked up the receiver and punched the button of the line that was blinking. "Sheriff Turner here."

The voice was little more than a whisper, disguised— a towel over the receiver, if he had his guess—but he could tell it was a young person. Boy or girl, he wasn't certain.

The two short sentences sent his stomach plunging. The line disconnected before he could ask any questions. "Ginger! I need the caller ID on that number."

"I'm on it, boss."

Zach considered his next move. Ordinarily he'd follow up a call like this one by knocking on the suspect's door and asking to have a look around. Under these particular circumstances, he'd better do everything by the book.

Ace wandered over to rub against Zach's legs, and he absently petted his buddy as he thought through his choices. LaNelle had been a good woman. She deserved justice.

He picked up his phone and placed a call. "Judge? Zach Turner here. I need a search warrant."

TJ lay sprawled across his bed, his mind spinning, his stomach rolling with nausea. He never should have eaten that peanut butter sandwich, but years ago when his great-grandmother made him peanut butter sandwiches, it had always made him feel better.

Tonight the sandwich sat in his gut like a rock.

He was so screwed.

Maybe he should steal Aunt Savannah's money and run away. She hadn't gone to the bank that day, and between her wallet and the cash bag, she probably had three hundred dollars he could snatch. He could steal her car while he was at it. He knew how to drive, since he'd been driving his dad home from bars for years. Although the crappy old Ford probably wouldn't get him over Sinner's Prayer Pass.

You could tell her the truth.

"Just shoot me now," he muttered.

Savannah stabbed a carrot with her fork. The stew tasted very good, but she'd lost her appetite after she'd lost her temper with TJ. So he'd made a mess in the kitchen. Big deal. *He's fourteen. That's what fourteen-year-olds do. It's no reason to go total shrew.*

She'd taken out her own bad mood on him, and that shamed her.

Savannah set down her fork, carried her plate to the sink, and rinsed it. Then she did something she'd done only rarely since TJ had come to live with her. She climbed the stairs to the attic room and knocked on his door. "TJ, may I come in?"

Twenty seconds ticked by before he said, "It's your house. Do what you want."

If that was the way it was going to be, she thought, maybe she should forget the apology. For tonight, anyway. She could go back downstairs and take a long, hot bath and try to relax.

But no. That wouldn't be right.

She stepped into the room to see him lying on his bed fully dressed, his back to her. She moistened her lips, then said, "Teej, I want to apologize to you. I'm so sorry I yelled at you. I had a long day and I was sad and I think . . . well . . . it's totally stupid, but my feelings were hurt because you didn't eat the stew I made for supper."

He rolled over and gave her a look that said, *You're crazy.* "You didn't leave a note. I didn't think I was supposed to eat it. I thought it was funeral food. I was hungry, so I ate a sandwich."

"Funeral food?"

"Yeah, you know. People make stuff and take it. Everybody knows that." He looked at her with disgust.

"Oh. I took mine over this morning. Green bean casserole."

He shrugged, and she added, "I'm an idiot. Forgive me?"

"It's no big deal. I'm used to being yelled at. Dad liked to yell."

Savannah nodded and took a seat in the lawn chair he'd purchased at a yard sale. "I remember that about Gary. He had that great big baritone voice. He used to scare me, but I liked it that he didn't hold a grudge. He'd yell, but then it was over. Next thing I knew, he'd be hugging me."

"Yeah." TJ sat up. "Dad likes to hug, too."

"Have you told him what's going on here?"

His expression went wary. "What do you mean?"

"Have you told him what happened between you and Aiden Marshall?" When TJ didn't respond, she elaborated. "I thought that maybe he could give you some guidance on how to deal with the problem."

Defensively he asked, "Did I say there's a problem?"

"Every day."

He folded his arms but said no more. Savannah continued, "I knew a boy like Aiden when I was growing up. The rich, handsome athlete whom the other kids fawn over. He got a football scholarship to college, but later I heard he flunked out. I wasn't surprised. He was a jerk who cheated his way through high school."

"Aiden is an ass."

It was obvious from his expression that TJ intended to say no more on the matter, but Savannah was encouraged. This was a start. "Are you still hungry? There's plenty of stew, and Mrs. Murphy sent some of her raspberry pinwheel cookies home with me."

"I'm really not hungry, Aunt Savannah."

Baby steps, she told herself. "Well, if you change your mind, come on downstairs."

In the kitchen, she stored the leftovers and loaded her plate into the dishwasher. She'd just placed the slow cooker into the sink to clean when she heard a knock on her door. She glanced at the clock. It was after nine. Who would stop by here that late?

Grabbing a tea towel, she dried her hands as she walked to the door. A familiar form stood in the glow of her porch light. Savannah's breath caught. Zach!

She couldn't help but smile. Had he been as miserable

as she'd been these last few weeks? Was he ready to try again—on her terms?

Just what are your terms? Do you even care? What does it even matter? He's back!

Hope lifted her heart and her smile was wide as she opened the door. "Hello, Zach. I'm so glad . . ."

Her sentence trailed off and her smile faded. He wasn't smiling. His expression looked grim. He wasn't alone, either. Gabi stood behind him, her expression as dark as his. Martin Varney was with them. Three of them? Why? Apprehension washed through her. "What is it?"

"Is TJ home?" Zach asked.

"Yes. He's up in his room."

"Would you call him, please?"

He didn't come in. He was wearing his uniform. His badge. His gun. His lawman's stare. Fear washed through her. "What is this about?"

"I need you to call your nephew."

"Why? Why are you here?"

Zach entered Heavenscents and handed Savannah a sheet of paper. He was cold. He was detached. He'd been her lover . . . and now he was like an iceberg. "Gabi, go up and get TJ. Savannah, I need you to step outside. That is a warrant to search the premises."

She glanced at the document, saw words that made no sense. A sick, helpless feeling rolled through her. "A warrant! What . . . why . . . ?"

Zach gave Martin a pointed look. He stepped forward and took Savannah by the elbow. "Ms. Moore, please."

Panic had begun to set in, and Savannah reached out to touch Zach. He jerked away. *Oh, God.* Savannah planted her feet. "Zach Turner, talk to me!"

He wouldn't talk to her. He wouldn't even look at her. Instead, he stood turned away, his jaw set, his hands braced on his hips until TJ came downstairs, followed by Gabi. Savannah found TJ's bewildered expression re-assuring. "What's going on?" he asked her.

Zach said, "You need to step out onto the porch now."

In that instant, Savannah's fear turned to rage. His wasn't the voice of her lover or even a friend. This was the cop who had rifled through her trunk in the wake of the car accident. It was the detective who'd fired questions at her in that uncomfortable little interrogation room. It was the prison guard who'd made sexual remarks as he slammed the cell door behind her.

She shot an accusatory look toward Gabi, then lifted her chin. "Come on, Teej. The sheriff is ordering us from our own home."

With the palm of her hand, she shoved open the screen door. Just as she stepped out onto the porch, she heard Zach say, "Savannah, wait."

He strode to Heavenscents' checkout counter and lifted the portable phone from its base. Crossing the room, he looked her directly in the eyes for the first time since his arrival and handed her the phone. Concern clouded his blue eyes. "Call Mac."

Anger drained away and fear returned. Mac. He wouldn't tell her to call a lawyer unless he thought she needed one.

Outside, she took hold of TJ's hand and guided him off the porch and halfway down the front walk. Speaking softly so that Martin Varney couldn't overhear, she said, "Tell me the truth, TJ. Do you know what they are looking for?"

He shook his head as if clueless. "No."

"You have no idea?"

"No! Who is Mac? Why did he say for you to call him?"

"Mac Timberlake is my friend Ali's husband. He's a lawyer."

"A lawyer!" TJ's eyes rounded with fear. "Why do you need a lawyer? What did you do? Oh, shit. You'll go to jail, too, and I won't have anywhere to go. They'll try to send me to foster care. I won't go. I'll run away."

"TJ!" She grabbed him by the shoulders. "I didn't do anything. Not then and not now. That's the truth. But you had better be straight with me, too."

His gaze slid away from hers. "I didn't do anything they need a search warrant for."

Something was there, she thought. But she didn't have time. She needed to make the call to Mac.

Ali answered the phone. Savannah said, "Ali, it's Savannah. I don't know what's going on, but Zach showed up here a few minutes ago with a search warrant. He told me to call Mac."

"What?"

"I don't know, Ali. Please, can I talk to Mac?"

"I'll put him on the phone."

Her voice trembled a little as she outlined the situation for Mac. He replied, "I'll be right there. Don't you or TJ say anything. If they ask you any questions at all, tell them I instructed you not to answer and that I'm on my way."

"Thanks, Mac."

She no sooner hung up the phone than Zach stepped out onto the porch. "Did you call Mac?"

"He's on his way."

Zach nodded, then said something to Varney. The deputy went out to the sheriff's truck and retrieved a small black case and a camera bag. Both men disappeared inside.

"They found something," TJ said.

"Yes." It was in that moment that Savannah acknowledged the fear that had grown inside her from the instant she'd recognized that Zach hadn't come to patch things up between them. "They found the stolen stop sign, didn't they?"

TJ's chin dropped, then he shut his eyes. "Oh, crap."

Oh crap. Oh crap. Oh crap. What do I do now? How the hell had he gotten himself into a fix like this?

He tried to think, to consider what choices he had, but that was all but impossible to do because his aunt had taken hold of his arm and started squeezing it and her eyes were looking a little wild. "You lied to me not five minutes ago."

He couldn't concentrate.

Oh, crap. Oh, crap. Oh, crap.

"TJ, talk to me. You have to talk to me."

He heard the door open and Gabi came out onto the porch. Savannah said, "No. Don't say a word. Say nothing until Mac gets here."

Then, to his horror, his aunt started to cry. She dragged him into her arms and hugged him hard and whispered in his ear. "I love you, Teej. It'll be okay. Somehow we'll make it okay."

He wiggled away from her and did the only thing he could think to do. "Don't cry, Aunt Savannah. I didn't do it. I didn't take the stop sign. I'm innocent."

TWENTY-TWO

I'm innocent.

Savannah froze, then dragged him three steps to the left, to where the porch light illuminated his face. *Dear Lord. This is history repeating itself.* She studied his expression and realized she believed him. Then it was as if someone had flipped a switch and turned her into a mama grizzly bear.

"Okay, then. I promise you this. No matter what I have to do, you will not pay for something you didn't do." She wouldn't let that happen. She would not let him down.

Mac arrived and went inside to speak with Zach. Returning a few minutes later, he confirmed her suspicions. "They found a stop sign in your kitchen."

"My kitchen! That's not possible. I would have seen it."

"Behind the refrigerator. They're dusting it for prints now."

"They won't find mine," TJ told him, defiance ringing in his tone. "I didn't touch it. I don't know anything about it. They can't pin this on me."

"I told Zach I'm taking you to my office to talk, then we'll come to his office for an official interview. Let's not discuss anything until we're behind closed doors."

It was a short two-block walk to Mac's law office. Savannah spent part of the time trying to figure out how that sign had ended up behind her refrigerator. Mostly, however, she tried to fight back her panic.

She had minimal success. When Mac escorted them into his office and asked them to take a seat, she managed to remain sitting for less than a minute before she was up and pacing the room.

Mac asked her for a dollar as a retainer, then focused on TJ. "Okay, son. The most important thing for you to understand now is that you must tell me the truth. If a client lies to me, nine times out of ten it comes back to bite us in the butt. I cannot stress the importance of this too much. Do you understand?"

"Yes, sir."

"Now, tell me what you know about the stop sign."

"That won't take very long. I don't know anything. Honest."

"Okay, then. Savannah, what about you?"

She understood that Mac had to ask the question, but it still annoyed her. She had some really bad memories of being questioned by lawyers. "I don't know how it got into my home."

"Then let's try to figure out when it could have happened. The sign went missing, what, five days ago? When has your house been empty during that time?"

"Sunday morning was about it. I closed the shop today, but TJ was working in the workshop."

"Um, actually, I wasn't there the whole time," he confessed.

Savannah frowned at him as Mac asked, "Where did you go?"

"I went walking around for a while."

Now Savannah sensed he wasn't being entirely truthful. *Dammit, TJ. You're going to make things worse for yourself.*

"When? For how long? Who might have seen you?"

"I left about five. Was gone a couple hours." He gave Savannah a sidelong look and said, "I got all the orders done that needed to go out tomorrow. I'll work extra to make up for the time off." To Mac, he said, "I don't know if anyone saw me or not."

"I'm sure someone noticed you. Town was quiet today, with all the businesses closed for LaNelle's service. I'll bet someone saw you if you were walking up and down the streets."

"I wasn't outside the whole time. I, uh, went into the church. I didn't talk to anyone."

"You went to LaNelle's memorial service?" Mac clarified.

"No. I went into Sacred Heart."

"The Catholic church?" Savannah said. "Why did you go into the Catholic church?"

"It's quiet. It's peaceful. They have the whole light-a-candle-and-pray thing going on. I like that. I lit a candle. And I put money in the box for it, too."

Mac gave him a measured look, then backtracked a bit. "Did you lock up before you left Heavenscents?"

"Yes."

"What about on Sunday?" Mac asked Savannah. "Did you lock up then?"

"I did."

"Was the door locked while you were in the workshop, TJ?"

"No. No, it wasn't. I went in the house to take a . . . to go to the bathroom, and I didn't lock the door when I went back out." He looked at Savannah. "That must have been when it happened."

"What about your dog? Where was she?"

"Inny was in the backyard."

"She wouldn't have barked," Savannah added. "She doesn't bark."

"It's true." TJ nodded. "She's worthless as a watch-dog."

"Okay, then. We can establish opportunity. Now, let's work on motive. Who would want to frame you for the theft, TJ?"

He didn't say anything, so Savannah said it for him. "Aiden Marshall."

That familiar mulish look returned to TJ's face, and Savannah decided she'd had enough. "You have to tell the story now, TJ. You have no choice. What happened between the two of you up at Jack Davenport's camp?"

TJ slumped back in his chair and Savannah wanted to scream. But just as she opened her mouth to scold him some more, Mac cut her off at the knees. "Aiden Marshall didn't put that stop sign in your kitchen, Savannah. His family left on vacation Saturday morning. They're in Europe."

She gripped the back of the chair she'd sat in briefly. "Not Aiden? Then who could it be? Who else has a grudge against you, Teej?"

"I dunno. Honestly, I don't have a clue who might have done this."

"Okay, then. Well, we'll just have to hope that Zach can identify whatever fingerprints they found on the sign."

"That could be a problem, Savannah. They were dusting the sign when I went in to speak with Zach. They weren't through, but he said it looked like it had been wiped."

She exhaled a heavy breath. "So. We have no other suspects?"

Mac spoke to TJ. "Son, you need to open up now. Sure would be helpful to have another name or five to give the sheriff."

"But I don't have one to give. Honestly. If Aiden Marshall and his brother aren't around, I am clueless about who would have done this."

"He's a scapegoat," Savannah said. "When bad things happen, the new kid with the funky hair and the nose ring is the guy to blame. Everyone will believe it. Zach will believe it. He's the sheriff, and he knows TJ vandalized a cabin at Angel's Rest. He'll have a genuine juvenile delinquent in hand and he won't look any further."

The longer she talked, the more worked up she got and the faster she paced Mac's office. Mac had to call her name twice before she actually listened to his attempt to calm her. "Honey, Zach isn't going to railroad TJ. He's a good cop. He'll do a thorough investigation and—"

"We'll be screwed. I've been through this before. I know what will happen." She met TJ's gaze and said, "Maybe we should run. Just pick up and start over someplace else. I won't have you going to jail for a crime you didn't commit."

"Jeez, Aunt Savannah."

"Savannah, calm down. That's not going to happen."

She whirled on the attorney. "It's exactly what could happen. I know. It happened to me. I have a news flash for you, Mac. I'm an ex-convict." She babbled out the details of what had happened to her, finishing with, "I went to prison for something I didn't do. I didn't want anyone to know, but now everyone will know. We might as well leave. My business will be ruined. My friends will be gone. We'll just go somewhere and start over. You can't tell, Mac, because of attorney-client privilege. TJ, come on. Let's go."

"We know about your prison record, Savannah. We've known for weeks. It doesn't matter to us."

Her world froze. *We know. We've known for weeks.*

Savannah's heart began to pound. "We? Us? Who is us, Mac?"

"All of your friends."

All of my friends. For weeks. How?

Then anger flashed. Betrayal stabbed her. "Zach told you."

"No. Celeste. She overheard a conversation at Angel's Rest the day TJ painted the cabin. Since the maintenance man overheard it, too, and he loves to flap his tongue, she wanted your friends to be ready to defend you if necessary. She said it was obviously something you were sensitive about."

Savannah's mind whirled. They'd known. Her friends had known and they hadn't said anything. They'd known and hadn't treated her any differently. "What does this mean?"

"It means that you don't need to run away frightened. You have friends, Savannah. Your friends will help you and TJ through this mess. I believe him when he says he didn't steal the stop sign. I believe that someone else is trying to set him up for it. Zach is a good sheriff. He won't railroad anyone and especially not your nephew when there is sufficient evidence to suspect he's been framed. You need to trust us, honey."

Now she sank down into the office chair and buried her face in her hands. Trusting her friends meant trusting Zach.

Zach hadn't told them. Hadn't betrayed her secret. Not Zach. Of course not Zach. He'd given her his word. Sheriff Andy didn't break his word.

Trust.

Zach was the sheriff. Zach was her lover. He'd told her that he loved her, and she'd run scared. He's hurt and angry at her, but he wouldn't take that out on TJ. Zach wasn't like that.

Trust.

They said the charge would be negligent homicide.

Homicide.

Trust.

Once before, she'd trusted a man who told her he loved her. She'd been a fool. But it wasn't just about her this time. Could she risk her nephew?

Zach is a good man. That's the bottom line.

No, she realized, trust was the bottom line. Did she trust him? *Could* she trust him? Her old fears . . . her memories . . . it might not be fair to Zach, but right now Zach wasn't her priority.

This wasn't about her. Not this time. This was about TJ. She had to protect her nephew. She couldn't let her heart rule her mind. "Will Zach arrest TJ tonight? Put him in jail tonight?"

"No. He's just going to question him. Probably the same set of questions we just covered here."

"What if he tries to trick him? That's what they did to me. The detective lied to me, and I found out later that it's perfectly legal for them to do it."

"Zach won't lie to TJ, and TJ isn't going to lie to Zach. I'll be with TJ the entire time, and I won't let him say anything that could possibly damage his case. I'm an excellent attorney, Savannah. Like I said, you need to trust us."

"Okay." *I'll act like I trust them, anyway. But we need to leave all our options open. Like Grams always used to say, fool me once, shame on you; fool me twice, shame on me.*

Savannah had no intention of being anybody's fool ever again.

Zach wanted a beer. He wanted his bed. Today had been one helluva day, and he didn't expect it to end anytime soon.

The door to the sheriff's office opened and Mac, Savannah, and TJ walked inside. Savannah was as white

as the snowcap on Murphy Mountain. Mac looked
like . . . a lawyer.

TJ looked scared to death. No defiance now, but no
guilt, either. Pale as a ghost. A young, frightened boy. *If
he's guilty, Savannah will . . .*

No. Zach didn't want to go down that road. It would
destroy her.

He couldn't think about that now. He couldn't think
about her. He had to be the cop. The guy with the badge.
Everything she hated.

Zach rose to meet them. "We're going to do this by
the book. Ms. Moore, Deputy Romano will take your
statement at her desk." He gestured toward the small
room that served as the department's interrogation
room. "If you gentlemen will join me in here."

Savannah looked like she might protest and demand
to sit in on his interview with TJ. Mac said, "It's better
this way, Savannah. Trust me."

Well, that won't get him anywhere, Zach thought.

He was surprised and slightly irked when she nodded
and took a seat at Gabi's desk. *Sure, trust Mac.*

Get hold of yourself, Turner. Do the job.

Zach shut the door to the interview room, took a seat,
and went to work. He attempted to establish the boy's
whereabouts during the period during which the sign
went missing until its discovery earlier this evening. Mac
had prepared the boy well, because he gave quick, clear,
concise answers.

Nothing the boy said surprised him. The probability
that he was being framed had occurred to Zach from the
moment he received the phone call. It wasn't until he
asked whom TJ suspected of framing him and the boy
hesitated a long moment that Zach sensed he was about
to be surprised.

TJ dragged his hands up and down his face. Zach
darted a look at Mac, who shrugged. TJ sighed loud and

long. "I'm in such deep shit. I haven't told my aunt about this yet. I was going to, but then she yelled about the peanut butter and . . . I don't know, I was still working up the nerve. I just found out today. That's why I went to church. I had to pray. I needed answers. Oh, man, my life is ruined."

Zach leaned forward. "What happened, TJ?"

"Wait a minute," Mac said. "If this involves a criminal act—"

"No," TJ said. "Just stupid. Really, really stupid." He looked at Zach, a world of misery in eyes wet with tears. "She's pregnant."

Zach and Mac both sat back. Quietly Zach asked, "Who?"

"Linda Treemont."

Aiden Marshall's girlfriend, Zach knew.

Once he got started, the story poured out. Mandy had a crush on Aiden, and everybody knew it. He'd been mean to her about it, but Mandy was too innocent to realize he was making fun of her instead of giving her real compliments. On the first day of camp, Aiden and Linda had had a fight, and to retaliate, Aiden took Mandy off into the woods and started making out with her. Linda saw it, TJ missed the whole thing because he'd gone hiking with Jack and the rest of the group.

"He was just using her," TJ said. "Mandy didn't know. She . . ." He winced. "You know how she is. She wants to fit in so badly that she . . . well, he took advantage.

"Linda was pissed. That night, she got me to leave camp with her and . . . well . . ." TJ had his eyes closed as he confessed, "We had sex."

Mac looked at Zach. "How old is this girl?"

"Seventeen," he replied flatly. "Maybe eighteen."

"That's statutory rape."

"I didn't rape her!" TJ cried.

"Not you, son. Look, was that the only time you had sex with her?"

"Yes, sir. She told Aiden about it first thing the next morning. That's why he and I fought. I haven't talked to her since then . . . except for when she told me she was pregnant." He paused, then added, "She just used me to get back at him and I knew it and I let it happen anyway. Stupid. So stupid."

"How do you think that might tie in with the stop sign?"

"Well, I don't know who else she told. Maybe one of Aiden's friends thought he'd get me in more trouble. Who knows. His friends are all jerks."

Zach asked a couple more questions, then wrapped up the interview. Gabi had finished with Savannah, and the moment TJ was free to go, she ushered him out of the sheriff's office. She never once spoke directly to Zach, a fact that stuck in his craw more than just a little.

"What a mess," Mac observed once his clients had departed and Gabi left to make her eleven o'clock foot patrol. Giving Zach a sidelong glance, he asked, "You don't think TJ stole that sign, do you?"

"No. I don't think he's the father of Linda Treemont's kid, either. If she's even pregnant. That girl has been a schemer and a game player for as long as I've been in Eternity Springs. I know that she's been sleeping with the Marshall boy for months. I chased them off Reflection Point one night."

"I told Savannah you wouldn't be fooled. She was a basket case earlier. She thought for sure that history was going to repeat itself and TJ would get convicted of a crime he didn't commit. She even talked about running off."

Zach went still. "Oh?"

"She blurted out her history. Said she'd do anything to make sure that TJ didn't end up railroaded into jail. I calmed her down, but the woman certainly has issues with the law. You have your work cut out with her, Zach."

"Don't I know it."

"If you still want her, that is."

"Would she run, do you think?"

"I don't know. Maybe. If she has something to stick around for, maybe not."

Zach brooded about it as he typed up his report. *Running off.* He sulked about it as he finally climbed into his truck to head home for the night. *Leaving.* As he turned down Fourth Street and drove past her house, he decided he was pissed about it. Especially after he glanced into the driveway and spied the open garage door. The Taurus's trunk stood open. "Son of a bitch!"

He steered the truck over the curb, shoved the gearshift into park, and viciously switched off the ignition. He slammed the door behind him as he marched up her drive and took up a position leaning against the Taurus. Two filled-with-fuming minutes later, Savannah exited her back door, carrying a suitcase. Seeing Zach, she abruptly stopped. The suitcase slipped from her hand and thudded to the ground.

"Going somewhere?" he drawled.

After a moment her chin came up. "We weren't given instructions that we had to stay in town."

"No, you weren't." He arched away from the car and took two menacing steps toward her. "You certainly weren't under arrest. It's a free country. You can leave Eternity Springs anytime you damn well please. Nothing is keeping you here, is it? You can make soap anywhere, sell it over the Internet from anywhere. You're free as a freakin' bird. No reason at all you shouldn't fly off to somewhere new in the middle of the night."

She closed her eyes. "Zach, I—"

"You what, Savannah? Are a coward? A faithless

friend? But that's not all of it, is it? It's not the bottom line, the marrow of who you are. You, Savannah Moore, are a victim, aren't you?"

He heard her quickly indrawn breath and knew he'd scored a hit.

"It's understandable. You got a raw deal, it's true, so you learned how to be a victim. Now you're an expert at it, a pro. Well, good for you. Everybody should be an expert at something. You enjoy yourself."

He walked back up the driveway half a dozen steps, then stopped and snapped his fingers. "Oh, I'm sorry. I'm afraid I have something to tell you that goes against your narrative. But as the head law enforcement officer in this town, I'd be remiss if I failed to tell you that your nephew is not a suspect in the theft of the stop sign or vulnerable to a homicide charge. The other bit of news I have isn't actually duty, but something I was doing in my spare time, so I think I can keep the details to myself. I don't think it's necessary to tell you about the progress I've made toward proving Kyle Vaughn and his mother ran those drugs, not you. So long, Savannah. Have a nice victimhood."

If she said anything in response, he didn't hear it over the hard crunch of his boots against her gravel drive or the screech of his tires as he pulled away from Heaven-scents.

TWENTY-THREE

❦

Have a nice victimhood.

After Zach sped off in a spray of gravel and tailpipe exhaust, Savannah sank down on her back stoop and tried to process the words he'd fired at her like bullets. Twice she glanced down at her chest to make sure she wasn't bleeding. It felt like she'd taken a direct hit to her heart.

She didn't know how long she'd sat out there alone when the back door opened and TJ came outside. "Aunt Savannah? Uh . . . do you want me to put Inny's bed in the car?"

Long seconds ticked by before she said, "I think . . . I think we can wait until the morning to leave, don't you? I'm tired. So, so tired."

"I think that's a good idea. I have to admit, the idea of driving over Sinner's Prayer Pass in the dark didn't make me happy." He hesitated a moment, then asked, "Are you okay, Aunt Savannah?"

"I'm fine."

"I heard what Sheriff Turner said. Want to talk about . . . things? He was right about some of it, but some of what he said was just damned wrong."

"Don't curse," she said by rote. "I appreciate the offer,

but I'm not in the mood to talk about Zach. Go on to bed, Teej. We'll talk in the morning."

"Okay. G'night, Aunt Savannah. Thanks for standing up for me tonight."

"I love you, TJ."

He spoke so softly, she almost didn't hear him. "I love you, too."

Have a nice victimhood.

Dammit, she'd already been having second thoughts about going. Even as she'd carried the suitcase out to her car, she'd been thinking about how foolish she was being. How emotional.

She'd been thinking about trusting Zach.

Have a nice victimhood.

Abruptly she shoved to her feet. She went inside and quickly changed into running clothes and sneakers, knowing that numbness was her only hope of banishing his accusation from her mind. She ignored Inny's excitement at seeing her don her shoes and left the dog shut inside as she took off. She ran west to Spruce Street, then north to Eighth and east over to Cottonwood, where she turned south. She ran hard, trying not to think, vaguely aware that tears flowed down her cheeks.

At the footbridge over the creek to Angel's Rest, she heard herself sob. She stopped to catch her breath and marshal her defenses. Drawn by the soothing sound of rushing water, she moved to the center of the bridge, sank down, and with her legs folded crosswise, buried her head in her hands and sobbed.

And sobbed.

And sobbed.

Just when the arms came around to hold her, when the gentle hand pressed her head against the soft bosom, when the musical voice began to murmur, "Hush, child. There, there. It's okay. Everything will be okay. Hush, child," Savannah couldn't say.

It was as if Grams had come down from heaven to offer her comfort when she needed it the most. "Oh, Grams. He is so angry at me. I hurt him."

"Yes, you did," Celeste Blessing said.

"I didn't mean to hurt him. I was scared. I *am* scared. Why am I so scared? He told me to have a nice victimhood."

"Ouch."

"Is he right? Is that how I act? Who I am?"

"Do you honestly wish to know the answer?"

"Yes!"

"It will require some honest self-evaluation. Are you ready to look deep inside yourself, Savannah?"

"No," she responded glumly. Honestly.

"You must open your heart and your mind to heal, my dear."

"I'm scared."

"Actually, you are strong, very strong, and you have come a long way. But you must open yourself to the truth if you are to heal that broken heart of yours."

"The truth hurts," Savannah replied, recalling her reaction to Zach's accusations.

"Yes, but the pain from lies scars a soul, especially those lies told to oneself." A hand softly stroked her head. "Why are you afraid, Savannah?"

"It's easier than being courageous."

"Now *there* is a truth. And yet you have shown much courage in your actions, have you not? You took control of your life. Now your challenge is to take responsibility for it."

"What do you mean?"

"Being convicted of a crime you did not commit is a terrible injustice and one not to be minimized. That said, blaming others for the bad things that happen to you empowers the victim mentality, which damages vital parts of your life—ambitions, achievements, and the big one, relationships. From this day forward, you must seize control of that energy. Resolve to stop the blame game and take responsibility for your life. Try it for just one day to begin with. The difference, you'll discover, is really remarkable. You will feel so much better about yourself."

"I don't feel bad about myself. Not anymore, anyway."

When she'd first been released from jail, it had been a different story. She'd been a self-pity queen. She'd thought the whole world was against her, and she'd spent hours and hours thinking about how wrong things had gone and how people who professed to love her had let her down. *You still spend hours thinking about how you can get revenge.*

"Well, maybe I still have some work to do in that regard."

"Recognizing that fact is an excellent step. Because the sooner you take responsibility for your life, the sooner you'll feel gratitude for all the joys that fill it, and thus the sooner you'll feel fortified for the most difficult task that awaits you."

Love, Savannah thought.

"Forgiveness."

"What?" Savannah pulled away. She twisted around to look incredulously at her companion—not Grams, as she'd pretended, but rather Celeste.

"Forgiveness. In order for your poor, wounded heart to heal, you must find forgiveness within it."

"You want me to forgive who, the Vaughns?"

"Precisely. You are bound to them by your resentment. Isn't it true that your thoughts return to them and the harm they did you over and over again? That activity inflicts enormous suffering on your psyche, Savannah. Forgiveness is the only way to sever that bond and free yourself."

"You must have opened another bottle or twelve of champagne after I left, Celeste. You're obviously not thinking clearly."

"Look past your defenses, dear, and you will see that I am right. Think about how wonderful being free can be. Think about what a gift a whole heart would be to those who love you. TJ needs that gift from you. So does Zach."

Savannah rubbed her eyes, now filled with new tears. "I blew it with Zach. He's done with me."

Celeste's laughter bubbled like the creek beneath them. "Oh, honey. You're smarter than that. Zach's heart is wounded, true, but you know what it needs to heal."

The familiar fear fluttered inside Savannah, and for the first time she gave it voice. "I'm afraid to love him, Celeste."

"All right, then. You're afraid. That's perfectly understandable, considering. But let me ask you this. If you let yourself love him, what's the worst thing that could happen?"

Savannah opened her mouth . . . and couldn't think of what to say. It wasn't about letting herself do anything. She did love him!

When a full minute had passed, Celeste patted her knee. "You think about that, sunshine. You think about that long and hard, then either throw yourself off this bridge or take your life by the horns and live it."

Throw myself off the bridge? "Celeste, the water is maybe two feet deep."

"And it's cold. Cold enough to shock some sense into you if you're still thinking silly. Good night, Savannah. Sweet dreams, and God bless." She gave Savannah's knee one last pat, then rose gracefully to her feet and left the bridge.

"Good night, Celeste." Savannah leaned back on her elbows and lifted her face toward the sky. Against the inky blackness of the moonless night, a million stars shone. One in particular twinkled.

"Good night to you, too, Grams."

Following a restless, mostly sleepless night, Zach left Reflection Point that morning with one task on his docket—to solve the mystery of the stop-sign-behind-the-fridge before the hotheads of Eternity Springs did something stupid. He didn't know how the news had gotten out, but the fact that it had was small-town ordinary. He'd already fielded three calls, and he wanted to put this whole disaster behind him.

He needed to quit thinking about Savannah Moore before he blew out an artery. He was still incredibly pissed, which was why he opened the door of the Mocha Moose, where he knew Linda Treemont worked the morning shift, with a little more force than was necessary.

At least his timing was good. The coffee shop appeared to be empty. "Good morning, Sheriff. Do you want your regular?"

"No. I'm here on official business. Where is Christina?"

Linda set down the paper cup she'd picked up to fill for him with the house bold brew. "She has a doctor's appointment this morning."

"Oh? Is she pregnant, too?"

Her mouth dropped open in shock, and while he had her off balance, he asked, "Is TJ Moore really the father? You know, false paternity claims can get you in a lot of trouble. So can being eighteen and having sex with a fourteen-year-old boy."

She blinked rapidly. Once. Twice. "I don't . . . I never . . . oh, damn. I'm not pregnant."

"Why did you tell TJ otherwise?"

She picked up a dishrag and began nervously wiping the counter. Judging that she was casting about for an excuse, he pressed, "Was it Aiden's idea or yours? You're still going out with Aiden, right? Aiden is pissed because you and TJ hooked up, so he told you to lie to the Moore kid."

Linda's shoulders slumped. "He said I had to prove myself."

That little ass. He folded his arms and studied her. "What else did he ask you to do, Linda? Steal a stop sign? Or did he steal it and ask you to ditch it inside of Heavenscents?"

"What?" Her brow wrinkled in confusion. "I don't know . . . whoa. Did you find the missing stop sign? At Heavenscents?"

"You need to answer my questions before asking ones of your own, Linda."

"I don't know anything about the stop sign. Honestly, Sheriff Turner. I'm telling the truth about that. Aiden didn't say a word about it before he left. I don't think he had anything to do with that, either."

Damn, he thought. He believed her. Zach swallowed a sigh and reached into his back pocket for his wallet. "Go ahead and get me my usual, Linda."

The relief on her face was clear, but Zach wasn't ready to let her off the hook completely. He inhaled the rich aroma of his coffee, took a sip of the flavorful brew, then said, "What you did to TJ was cruel, Linda. You should be ashamed. You also should give some thought to what kind of guy would ask you to do such a thing. Character is important. You should look for it in those you surround yourself with, and work on improving your own."

He exited the coffee shop and waved absently to Gabe

Callahan, who was walking his dog on the opposite side of the street. His mind chewed on the stop sign problem as he began the walk to his office. He'd honestly thought he'd had it figured out, that Aiden had stolen it and Linda had stashed it.

"Back to square one," he muttered.

Stop sign stealing happened everywhere, and most people considered it a relatively harmless prank. Nine times out of ten, kids were the culprits and the most serious consequence was that taxpayers had to foot the bill for a replacement. This time was different. This time the consequences involved the loss of a life.

Zach knew his town, knew the kids in his town. He'd learn the identity of the thief—or, more likely, thieves— sooner or later.

He also knew he needed to talk to TJ again ASAP and let him know he was off the pregnancy hook. Another time he would have walked straight to Heavenscents and taken care of it. Today, though, he didn't want to go near Savannah's house. *If she's even still there.* For all he knew, she'd finished packing up her car and run last night anyway. After all, she didn't trust him, did she? She probably thought he'd lied to her.

In order to avoid her place, he turned down Fifth Street. Halfway down the block, his gaze skimmed over a house, then his steps slowed. He knew his town. He knew the kids in his town.

His gaze jerked back and fastened on the house. *Hmm . . .*

It shared a back fence with Savannah's place. Wouldn't be hard at all to sneak the sign into the back door. Part of the problem that had niggled his brain was how did whoever sneak the sign down the streets. *Hmm . . .*

He walked up to the house and knocked on the front door. A minute later, a teen answered it. "Hello, Sheriff Turner."

"Hello, Mandy. I'd like to talk to you about the stop sign."

She burst into tears.

As Savannah hung up the phone, she realized her hand was shaking. *Thank God.*

She sucked in a breath, then smiled at her customers, a woman and her teenage daughter from Kansas. "May I help you? Answer any questions?"

"We're fine, thank you."

"Okay, then. If you'll excuse me for a moment, I need to check on something in the workshop. I'll be right back."

She hurried through the kitchen and almost ran to the back. "TJ, Ginger Harris just called. They want us at the sheriff's office. She said they have good news."

TJ all but melted with relief. He stepped away from the box he was filling with an order from the pet supply line—quickly becoming one of her bestsellers—and said, "Let's go."

"I have customers. I'll hurry them on their way as quickly as possible."

"Okay," he said, rushing past her. "I'll meet you there."

He took off running, and Savannah stared after him, a little peeved. She'd intended for him to wait for her.

Back in the shop, she waited with outward serenity and inward impatience for her customers to make their selections. It proved to be a sixty-five-dollar sale, so when she thanked them and handed them their bags, her smile was genuine.

It faltered when a new group of shoppers entered Heavenscents as the others made their way out. Twenty minutes later, they finally left, Savannah flipped the door lock and turned the OPEN sign to CLOSED, then dashed out the back door. Arriving at the sheriff's office, she was surprised to discover that TJ and Zach had gone for a walk.

Gabi invited—no, instructed—her to sit down. "I have information about the stop sign to share with you, but before I do it, I need your word that you will keep it quiet until this office gives you permission to share. Do I have it?"

"Yes." The coldness in her friend's tone didn't surprise Savannah, but it did bother her. Gabi was loyal to Zach. Very loyal. Almost too loyal. It was weird.

"Mandy West saw Aiden Marshall and his brother throw the stop sign on the side of the road the morning of the accident. She picked it up and was going to use it as a decoration for her bedroom because she's nuts about Aiden, poor thing. After the wreck, she got scared and didn't know what to do. She took it to your house to ask for TJ's advice, and when something happened that hurt her feelings, she hid it in the kitchen and called in an anonymous tip. Zach will deal with the Marshall brothers upon their return at the end of the week. In the meantime, as I mentioned, you must keep this information confidential."

"I don't understand. I thought the Marshall family was out of town."

"They left later that morning. The boys were out causing trouble early."

Savannah was shocked. Mandy West had tried to place the blame on TJ? "Why did Mandy do it? They're friends."

"That's something we're going to let TJ explain to you. So that's the story." Gabi folded her arms, lifted her chin, and added, "Now, aren't you glad you didn't run off last night after all?"

"Zach told you."

"No, actually, TJ mentioned it. Dammit, Savannah, I

am so pissed at you! It's one thing for you to be afraid of being in love. I get that. But running out on your friends? You couldn't call me? Why?" She pointed to her badge. "Because of this?"

"Gabi, you don't understand. I wasn't thinking clearly."

"That's totally obvious. You couldn't trust us to do our jobs? This after Zach has busted his ass to prove your innocence?"

Savannah recalled the words Zach had thrown at her last night. *I don't think it's necessary to tell you about the progress I've made toward proving Kyle Vaughn and his mother ran those drugs, not you.* "I don't understand. What has he done?"

"Only called in every marker he had with both the feds and with people in Georgia. He went to bat for you, Savannah. He put his reputation on the line for you. He believed in you. And what do you do? You're ready to run out on him at the first sign of trouble. You should be ashamed. That's not how you treat people you care about. People you love and who love you. Well, guess what. I think I've changed my mind about you. You don't deserve Zach. You don't—"

"That's enough, Gabriella," Zach snapped.

Savannah twisted around to see the sheriff, tall and handsome and cold as a winter wind, standing with his hand on TJ's shoulder. TJ looked both happy and pained, as if the weight of the world had lifted from his shoulders at the same time as he wanted to melt in embarrassment.

Savannah stood, her heart pounding, her mouth suddenly dry as burnt toast. "Zach, can we talk? Privately?"

If possible, his expression grew harder. "In my office."

He led the way into his office and gestured for her to take a seat. He shut the door, then took his seat behind his desk. Silence dragged out for a long moment. "You wanted to talk?"

"Yes." She started out with the easy one. "Thank you for what you did for TJ. I appreciate it more than you'll ever know."

"I did my job."

Short. Clipped. Still angry. She knew she deserved that.

She went on to the next subject, this one more difficult. "May I ask about something that isn't your job? Will you tell me about Georgia?"

A muscle twitched in his jaw. "Gabi made it sound like more than it is. I made a few calls. Asked a couple people I know to take a look at the case. They found someone who was willing to talk, and we used what they learned to convince Georgia to reopen your case."

Reopen my case? "I don't understand. They can't revoke my probation, can they?"

"They're working to overturn your sentence, Savannah. They followed the money and ran a sting. Got Kyle Vaughn to talk to an undercover. We have on tape that he and his mother used you as a mule without your knowledge. Francine would load up your car, and while you were in class, Kyle and his cohorts would make the transfer. Nobody likes a dirty cop, so they are moving quickly on what we found. They're pounding the last nails into the coffins now. You should expect arrests within the next couple of weeks."

"Arrests?" She couldn't believe it, so she wanted him to say it flat out. "Whom are they going to arrest?"

"Kyle and Francine Vaughn. After that, you'll need to work with a Georgia attorney to get your conviction overturned, but you won't have trouble finding someone good. Don't hire a shark, though. You'll have a settlement coming your way, so the scum lawyers will be circling. Talk to Mac. He'll help you figure all that out. In the meantime, you should sit back and let Georgia do its thing."

She sat back and attempted to take it all in. They had believed her. Zach had believed in her. Somebody had been on her side.

She couldn't believe it. "It's that easy? Just like"—she snapped her fingers—"that?"

"Once someone looked at your case without wearing blinders issued by Detective Vaughn, it was pretty straightforward."

"You did this for me. You believed me."

He looked at her stonily.

"Zach, I—" She reached a hand across the desk toward him. "I'm so sorry. I've been so stupid. I . . ." She hesitated, working up her nerve.

He stared down at her hand, then shook his head. "Look, Savannah, I don't have the energy for this. It's been a long week and I'm whipped. A woman I liked and respected is dead because of stupid teenage drama that could have been avoided. So I'm not in the mood for any more adult drama. I've had my fill. So let's just go on about our business, okay? We had something, we ended something. It's done. But in the meantime, TJ has something to tell you, so take him home and listen to him."

Her pulse had begun to race. She felt him slipping away and it frightened the truth from her. "Zach, I love you."

He looked at her and gave a snort of disgust. "Sure you do. Now. Because I proved myself. It's all about that, isn't it? You couldn't take me and all of this"—he waved his hand around his office—"at face value. I had to prove it. Prove I wasn't like that dickwad in your past. Prove that I'd stand by you—unlike your brother. Over and over and over. Well, I'm done proving myself.

I managed just fine before you. I'll be peachy keen after you, too."

"But I was wrong. I know that. I love you."

"It's too little, too late, Savannah. You should have trusted me. You should have loved me for who I am, not what I do."

"But I do love you for who you are, Zach! I trust you."

"Oh, really? Well, guess what? We've had a bit of a sea change around here. I don't believe you. I don't trust you. Now, if you'll excuse me, I have work to do." He stood and exited the office, leaving her shaken and trembling and brokenhearted.

Savannah sat frozen, devastated and uncertain, staring blindly through her tears at Zach's empty chair. At some point TJ entered the office and said, "Jeez, Aunt Savannah. What did you do to make Zach so angry? He didn't do anything wrong. He's a good guy. He really helped me."

"I know that, Teej."

"I, um, need to talk to you about something. It's nothing bad. Just stupid. I'm not in trouble or anything."

"Yes, he mentioned that. Can it wait? I'm a little . . . distracted."

"Absolutely! No rush. No rush at all. I'm going to go talk to Mandy if that's okay with you."

"Sure."

The boy hesitated, then stepped toward her. He bent over and pressed a kiss against her cheek. "Everything will be okay. Don't worry. Thanks for being there for me."

TJ left, but Savannah still didn't move, remaining lost in her thoughts and sunk into her misery. Eventually she noticed that Zach's chair no longer sat empty. Gabi was watching her with pity in her eyes. "You told him you loved him, didn't you?"

"Yes."

"Your timing sucks, girlfriend."

Savannah's tears spilled. "I blew it. I am so stupid. Gabi, it wasn't because of what he did, I promise. I had a long talk with Celeste last night and she helped me see what was in my heart. I spent this morning practicing how to tell him. But I'm too late. I don't know how to fix it. I've lost him and it's all my fault. I really screwed up."

"What you've lost is your good sense. He's angry, Savannah. His feelings are hurt. You shot him down, and guys never take that well, especially not men like Zach. His pride has been wounded. That's almost more serious than wounding his heart."

"I know."

"But that doesn't mean you've lost him. It means you're going to have to work to get him back."

At Gabi's words, a little flame of hope flickered to life inside Savannah. "Do you really think it's possible?"

"Yeah, I do. People don't fall in and out of love that easy. You know that. He's mad right now, but he'll calm down. What you need is a plan for how to heal his wounded pride."

"Okay." Savannah nodded. "That sounds good. What will it be?"

"Honestly, I haven't a clue. I think we need help from people who have known Zach Turner longer than you and I."

"What? You want to call a town meeting?"

"In a manner of speaking, yes."

Savannah's throat went tight with emotion. "Thank you, Gabi. Your friendship means . . ." Choked up, she blinked back tears. "Everything."

"Oh, just calm down. I'm sure there will be a point when you have to do something like this for me. No one is perfect, Savannah. You gotta remember that. You just have to trust people who care about you."

Gabi picked up the phone on Zach's desk and punched in a number Savannah recognized. "Sarah? Gabi Romano here. Savannah did something stupid and now she needs our help. Can you call a meeting? We need the Eternity Springs matchmakers to do their thing."

TWENTY-FOUR

"We could try an intervention," Celeste suggested as she sank into the largest of the hot springs pools at Angel's Rest three days later. To Savannah, she added, "We have quite a bit of experience at that."

Sarah kicked off her flip-flops, then sat on the edge of the pool and dangled her feet in the water. "Interventions are a specialty of ours."

Nic frowned thoughtfully. "We've never done an intervention with a guy before. I'm afraid it could backfire."

"Mac wouldn't like it," Ali said, scooting over to make room for Sage.

"Colt wouldn't, either." Sage waved at Gabi, who had just ended her shift and ducked into the dressing room to change out of her uniform into her swimsuit.

"I think we should return to our original strategy," Sarah said. "Oh, this water feels good. My feet are killing me."

"What original strategy?" Savannah asked.

Nic explained. "We chatted you up to him every time we saw him."

"We were Eternity Springs water torture," Sage added with a laugh.

Savannah said, "I appreciate the thought, but I don't think y'all understand just how angry he is."

"She's right," Gabi said as she joined them. "The man is one great big impossibly bad mood. I've tried three times to bring up Savannah's name, and he cuts me off with that laser look of his. The last time I tried it, he handed me a stack of old paperwork to file. Took me four hours. I don't dare mention her again. Trust me, Zach is PO'd. She needs something big to get through to him."

"A grand gesture," Celeste said. "Hmm. That could be fun."

Nic said, "Grand gestures are very romantic. Gabe won my heart with a grand gesture. He decorated a nursery for the twins."

"Gabe already had your heart before he did that," Sarah protested. "Though it did break through your anger. You were pretty angry at him."

"He deserved it. He'd been a total jerk."

"Zach isn't being a jerk," Savannah defended. "He's hurt."

"Yes, he is," Nic said. "That's why he's not thinking clearly. We have to help him clear his mind by reminding him what is important."

Celeste and Sage nodded. Celeste said, "Okay, then. A grand gesture. Ideas?"

"I can't top Zach. He chartered a helicopter and flew me to one of the most exclusive resorts in Colorado for a night of wild sex."

Following a moment of shocked silence, Sage, Sarah, and Nic shared a look of surprise. "He did?" Sarah asked. "We didn't know about that. How did we miss that little detail?"

"I don't want to hear about wild sex," Gabi said. "I'm single with no prospects. It'll make me jealous."

Celeste waved a dismissive hand. "Let us get Savannah and Zach settled and we'll go to work on you."

"A grand gesture," Sage mulled aloud. "Remember how Jack proposed to Cat? He took her hang gliding over a field strewn with yellow roses that spelled out 'Marry Me.'"

Nic said, "And Mac bought the yurt from Bear and went all Arabian Nights sheikh on Ali."

"Well, I'm doomed," Savannah said. "That's all out of my league."

"We just need to think." Sarah kicked the water absently. "Zach is a sports fiend. Maybe something sports-related?"

"I think it needs to be something public," Gabi said. "I think you need to make yourself a fool for love, Savannah."

"Now, there's an idea," Sage agreed. "Something to do with peaches, maybe?"

Nic rested her head back and looked up at the stars. "He loves your peach cobbler. Baking is always a good way to get to a man. Right, Sarah?"

The owner of the most successful bakery in three counties nodded. Celeste said, "You could do a broad theme around peaches. Peach cobbler, peach ice cream, peach jam in Sarah's pinwheel cookies."

"Peach lingerie," Nic suggested.

"Peach massage oil," Sage added.

"I like the thought, but I don't think I could get him close enough to notice scents." Savannah's thoughts were glum. "I'm sure lingerie is out of the question."

Gabi said, "I think it needs to be something public that involves risk on Savannah's part. Not physical risk. Emotional risk. And you'd better be prepared for him to give as good as he got from you."

"Yes," Nic agreed. "You could break the ice with something like that, then follow up with peaches."

"Would you be up for that?" Sarah asked.

Savannah didn't hesitate. "Yes. I love him. I want a life with him. I'll do whatever it takes to earn his forgiveness. If the icebreaker doesn't work and the peach follow-up isn't practical, well, I'll just do something else. I'm not above groveling in the street."

"That's the attitude, girlfriend." Sage sank lower into the pool until her shoulders were completely submerged. "Now we just have to figure out the icebreaker."

Long minutes dragged in relative silence. Savannah considered and rejected a flurry of ideas that ranged from staging a one-woman picket line in front of the sheriff's office to writing him love letters on signs all around town.

Then Celeste said, "Groveling in the streets, hmm? The annual arts festival is coming up. I have this friend. I think she might be able to provide our solution."

Celeste outlined her idea. It was silly and hokey and made Savannah cringe to think about. But at the same time, she could see it appealing to Zach.

"Well, dear?" Celeste asked. "What do you think?"

"I don't know. I sort of like it. What do you guys think? Is it bold enough? Humiliating enough? Do y'all think it could work?"

The Eternity Springs matchmakers looked at one another and nodded. Then Nic said, "Honestly, Savannah, I think he'd come around no matter what. Zach loves you. He'd forgive you eventually. This will just help eventually come around a little faster."

Savannah sucked in a breath, then let it out in a rush. "Okay, let's do it. The arts festival starts when?"

"Ten days from tomorrow."

"Good. That will give me plenty of time to order the perfect peach-colored bra."

*   *   *

Ordinarily Zach greeted the end of tourist season with mixed feelings. He looked forward to the slow time of year and the opportunity it gave him to spend time doing those outdoor activities he loved, but he missed the constant change that the influx of visitors to Eternity Springs introduced into his days. He especially had conflicting emotions where the summer arts festival was concerned.

It was the final event of the summer season, and of all the special events the town hosted, he enjoyed the arts festival the most. He loved seeing the artists' and craftspeople's creative products. Every year he bought something, whether it was a painting or a photograph or even children's toys he gave to the Callahan twins. He also particularly enjoyed the people the event attracted. Creative people were interesting. No one could deny the talent of those who created breathtaking Colorado landscapes or rocking chairs that made a man want to sit all day long. But the minds that thought of making jewelry out of potatoes or sculpting a fish entirely from beer tabs were downright fascinating.

And yet Zach had some crummy memories of the Eternity Springs summer arts festival, memories that were the source of those conflicting emotions.

His shoulder still ached on cold days as a result of the gunshot wound he'd received while disarming a crazed father out to murder the photographer who'd taken pornographic photos of his son.

Today as the festival kicked off, he almost wished he'd have a law-enforcement emergency to deal with. Rumor had it that he had a surprise waiting for him. Considering just who had been spreading the rumor—his nosy, busybody, way-too-interested-in-his-business friends—he figured the surprise must have something to do with Ms. Savannah Sophia Moore.

"Talk about conflicts," he muttered as he exited the

office, headed for Spruce, where festival booths lined the street. As he would do at least twice a day during the three-day festival, he would start at the top of Spruce and work his way south to the booths in the park area at the south end of town, where Angel Creek took a bend across the valley before flowing into Hummingbird Lake. He'd schmooze with the vendors and shoppers and make sure that everyone knew that the law was watching.

Even if his thoughts continued to return to a certain Georgia peach.

Once his rage at her had abated, he had debated what—if anything—he should do about the woman. Trust was a vital component in any relationship. Love without trust was a difficult road to travel. Was he willing to gamble that the two of them could survive the dips and bumps of the trip? Sometime over the summer, he'd come to realize that it was time to stop being alone. He wanted a home and a family. *Go figure.* But for him, marriage meant forever. Kids meant forever. He wouldn't go into a marriage if he thought it wouldn't last.

How could he and Savannah last if they didn't trust? One thing the events earlier this month had taught him was that trust was a two-way road. Never mind what she thought. He didn't know if he could trust that she wouldn't cut and run at the first sign of trouble.

And yet he loved her. That certainty still existed when the anger faded away.

And she had claimed to love him, too. He hadn't forgotten that, either. Once the red had cleared from his eyes, he'd replayed that moment in his mind. The claim had been so awkwardly stated that he realized she'd meant what she'd said.

He'd also decided that the ball was in her court. The

next move, if there was going to be a next move, was going to have to be Savannah's.

He suspected that might happen today. Gabi had gone out of her way to make sure that Zach did his festival stroll first thing. In the past week, Nic, Sarah, Sage, and Celeste had all managed to look him up and say something about peaches. He figured the only reason Ali and Cat hadn't added their two cents was that they were both out of town. He actually was surprised they hadn't called or emailed him or sent up smoke signals or something.

So as he arrived at Spruce and began his white tent stroll, he did so with an anticipatory spring in his step. All the talk of peaches . . . his best guess was that he'd find a peach booth. How she'd connect that with him, he didn't have a clue.

He strolled up to Sarah's Fresh tent. When she saw him, her eyes twinkled and she grinned. "Have you bought your tickets yet, Sheriff?"

The food and drink booths accepted tickets for their offerings instead of cash. "What, you're not giving me the sheriff discount?"

"No freebies for you this year, Zach."

"Now, go along and don't block the way of paying customers."

Huh. That wasn't like Sarah at all.

The next local booth he passed was the Vistas Gallery booth. He wanted to linger there. Sage always had beautiful things in her arts festival booth. However, when he took his time studying a painting of Hummingbird Lake, the woman gave him the bum's rush. "You're scaring off customers, Zach. Go along about your business. Be sure to buy some tickets, too."

Tickets again. Okay.

He got similar treatment at Nic's pet adoption tent, so he wasn't too surprised when Celeste walked up beside him and slipped her arm through his. "Allow me to walk you to the ticket booth, Zachary."

No sense fighting it. "I give up. Lead on, my lady."

Cam Murphy manned the ticket booth. Upon seeing Zach, he snickered. "How many you want, Turner?"

Zach reached for his pocket. "Give me twenty dollars' worth."

"Well, that won't get you squat. You need to cough up a hundred, my friend."

Zach blinked. "A hundred? How many muffins do you think I'm gonna eat?"

Cam Murphy's grin was downright wicked. "It's not the quantity, it's the quality. You don't want the A tickets. You want the S tickets."

Warily he asked, "What's the difference?"

"S tickets are only good at one booth. Only one person can buy them."

Hmm. "S for Savannah?"

"Or sheriff. I'm not sure which. I don't think it matters." He handed Zach a peach-colored piece of paper. "Here are the rules."

Zach read the bullet points. S tickets were only good at booth number 17. S tickets were only available for purchase by Sheriff Zach Turner. S ticket sales will be matched dollar for dollar by Heavenscents, and all monies collected will be earmarked for registration fees for children of law enforcement personnel who have lost their lives in the line of duty to attend the Davenports' summer camp.

Okay, that's bold. "What's going on at booth seventeen?"

"Pay your money and find out, bro. Throw down a C note for starters, but honestly, I expect you'll be back for more."

"It's a setup."

"Oh, yeah. You've been dealing with these women

longer than any of the rest of us and you just figured that out? But it's a setup for charity."

He glanced over his shoulder at the booth behind him, number 12. He peered down the street but couldn't see 17. "Okay. You win."

"No. The winner would be you, my friend. If you're smart enough to see it."

Zach took his tickets—all two of them—and continued down Spruce, vaguely aware that a grin tugged at his mouth, and totally aware that he'd picked up an entourage. Booth 16 displayed a Heavenscents sign. Mandy West stood at the entrance offering samples of lavender-scented lotion, and TJ sat on a stool beside a gray metal cash box. Savannah wasn't in the Heavenscents booth.

She manned booth 17.

He took one look at her and gawked. His gaze took in the booth, read the sign, and he gaped. Savannah sat on a stool wearing a formfitting scoop-necked black-and-white-striped top and matching short shorts.

She sat inside what appeared to be a . . . well . . . a jail cell. Above her hung a bucket. To the side of the cell, a six-by-eight-foot banner had a target at the center. Words above the target proclaimed, I AM A PRISONER OF MY OWN INSECURITIES, DOOMED TO A LIFE OF LONELINESS UNLESS SHERIFF TURNER CHOOSES TO ACCEPT THE KEY I OFFER AND SETS ME FREE.

A strangled sound emerged from Zach's throat. He'd seen a variation of this game before, most often used as a fund-raiser for schools. Usually a school official—the principal or a popular coach—sat beneath a pail of water. Kids bought tickets to throw a ball at a target that when hit dumped the water onto the principal. Kids loved it.

Zach was having trouble tracking. "What is this?"

"My grand romantic gesture."

This was a grand romantic gesture? "Jack took Cat hang gliding above a field of yellow roses that wrote out words."

She pursed her lips in a petulant pout. "So I heard. I'm not a bazillionaire."

His lips twitched. "I took you to Silver Eden Lodge."

"Yeah, well. Circumstances are different."

TJ sidled up. "Do you have a ticket, Sheriff Turner?"

Zach held up the two peach-colored stubs. TJ took one of them and handed him two yellow tennis balls. He held one in his left hand, tossed the second up and down with his right.

"I'm a little dense this morning. Why this?"

"Well, of everything we thought of, this seemed like the best idea."

His stare trailed over the setup. He couldn't believe she actually brought a prison cell into this nonsense. "That doesn't answer my question. Why this water game?"

"The dunking pool was too expensive to rent."

"And the goal here is for me to . . . dump water on you?"

"Cold water. We added ice. We thought you'd like that."

The woman was bat-crap crazy. "Why?"

"Because I hurt you and made you angry and I'm so very, very sorry and you deserve retribution."

"Retribution."

"We thought it needed to be public."

He still didn't get it. "What are you trying to prove here, Savannah?"

"That I trust you. That I love you. That you can trust me."

Sometimes a woman's mind was simply too foreign to understand. What was his job here today? "So you trust me not to dump ice water on your head?"

"Oh no. You need to do that. That's the retribution I'm offering here in public, in front of our friends and neighbors and strangers. I'm making a very public statement that I have been a total idiot. I recognize that a basic human desire in an incident such as this is one of payback. But at your heart, you are the nicest guy I've ever known. You're too nice to pay me back the way I deserve."

"Yeah," he sneered. "After all, I'm a nun with a penis."

Savannah winced. "I'm sorry about that."

Cam Murphy said, "Whoa. Hold on." He handed Zach another ticket. "My treat, man."

"So dousing you with ice water is supposed to satisfy my need for retribution for your cruel words and offensive actions?"

"It's supposed to be a start. We hope once you've drenched me a few times, the ice will be broken, so to speak, and you'll be more willing to listen to the serious, completely heartfelt apology I want to give to you. In private."

"And the person who planned this with you?"

She shrugged. "My friends. Our friends. Well, the female part of the couples, anyway."

"I never would have guessed."

Now, finally, Zach allowed the faintest of grins to spread across his face. He tossed the tennis ball once, twice, three times. "Okay, Ms. Moore. This is for the nun comment."

A pitcher for his high school baseball team, Zach hit the bull's-eye on the first throw. A bell rang. A rope pulled. A gallon of water rushed down on Savannah Sophia Moore's pretty head. She sucked in a breath. "Ooooh, it's cold!"

By filling her lungs, she'd lifted her breasts and the wet, clinging white stripes on her shirt clearly revealed a peach-colored bra supporting a bounty crowned in tight dusky nipples.

Though Zach couldn't drag his eyes off Savannah, in the periphery of his vision, he saw TJ refilling the bucket from a hose. When the boy picked up a sack of ice, Zach's instinct was to tell him to leave it. But then he thought about the nun comment again and he let the ice go into the pail.

Damn, he'd missed her.

He threw the second tennis ball—another bull's-eye. That was for unnecessary weeks of loneliness.

TJ reset the game. "Add the rest of the bag of ice," Zach instructed. Savannah opened her mouth as if she were about to protest, but abruptly shut it, unafraid to take her medicine, silly as this whole thing was.

And yet, crazy as it sounded, this worked for him. A little innocent payback was soothing his ruffled feathers. A little peek at that pucker had put forgiveness right there at the top of his to-do list.

Once the game was reset and she sat shivering in her seat, looking beautiful and fresh and clean, though cold, Zach tossed the last ball from one hand to the other and debated. "Tell me again what you are hoping to prove."

She clasped her fingers in her lap, her expression open, her eyes beseeching. "I love you, Zach Turner. I trust you. I hope you will consider reconciliation with me, but even if that's not what you want, I'll understand. Fair warning, though, I'll still probably try to change your mind."

Zach looked from Savannah back to the tennis ball, then back to Savannah. "So, one more shot. Do I take it?"

"I'll give you as many shots as you want. I'm not going anywhere, Zach Turner. Never again. I'm staying put. You can trust me on that."

He tossed the ball once, twice, three times. Then he

moved toward the "jail," opened the door, and stepped inside. Savannah slipped off her stool and stood in front of him. "Zach?"

"I cannot believe you did something this silly."

"Did it work?"

"I think it's safe to say that the ice has been broken, yes." He slipped his hand around her neck, pulled her against him, and fitted his mouth to hers. The kiss was long and slow and sweet, offering apologies and making promises. It was a kiss filled with healing, smack dab in the middle of the street in—where else?—Eternity Springs. Zach was just about ready to end the kiss and suggest they retire to somewhere more private when a gush of ice-cold water fell upon them. "Yikes!"

He jerked away from her, shook ice off his shirt, and turned to see the culprit. Culprits, plural, with smug, delighted grins on their faces. "The matchmaking coven," he muttered. And their husbands. "Aren't y'all funny."

Cam Murphy gave the rope attached to the bucket a little shake, making sure the last drops of water fell. "Hey, we're just trying to keep you from having to arrest yourself. Public displays of affection can lead to indecent exposure charges, you know."

Savannah laughed. "I need to go home and change and then . . . Zach, would you have time to talk?"

"How about lunch? Around one?"

"Perfect."

"If you can steal an hour, I'll take you out to Reflection Point. We'd have more privacy."

"I'll look forward to it."

He gave her a quick kiss, then turned to leave. He scooped up his last fifty-dollar tennis ball and decided he'd tuck it away somewhere. Never know when a man might need a little . . . retribution.

* * *

Wrapped in an Angel's Rest beach towel Celeste had contributed to the cause, Savannah floated home. This had gone better than she'd dared to hope.

She'd been prepared for him to walk right by the booth and ignore her, no matter that her friends agreed that doing so would make him a stooge. She wouldn't have been surprised if he'd thrown one ball and walked away or gone back for more tickets and drenched her over and over and over again.

She had not dreamed that he'd throw two balls and then give her a kiss. Not just any kiss, either, but a curl-your-toes, we'll-be-okay, I-forgive-you sort of kiss.

At least that's the way it had felt to her. She wouldn't be confident that she'd read him right until they had a chance to talk.

She glanced at the clock visible through the window at the Mocha Moose as she hurried past. She had forty-five minutes. Plenty of time to shower and shampoo and slather herself in that special fragrance he loved so much. She'd wear her other new set of peach lingerie and her new sundress—peach-colored, of course.

Rather than unlock the shop, she went around to the back of the house and entered through the kitchen. She went straight to the bathroom, where she ran water in the tub and tossed in a bath melt.

She began humming the gazebo song from *The Sound of Music,* the one in which Maria and Captain Von Trapp declare their love, as she entered her bedroom, pulling the wet T-shirt over her head.

"Well now," came a voice from out of her nightmares. "Isn't it nice that you're so anxious for me."

TWENTY-FIVE

❦

Savannah's blood ran cold. "Kyle?"

He was tall, gym-rat built, and he wore his blond hair longer than he had years before. His blue eyes glowed with a malevolent light. His mouth spread in an evil smile. How had she ever thought him handsome?

"What? Don't tell me you don't recognize me. It's only been what . . . seven years? Eight? You always were a stupid bitch, though. Hillbilly trailer trash and too dumb to know it."

"What are you doing here, Kyle?"

"Well, now. That's an interesting question. I came here to take care of one—no, two troublesome details, but I caught part of your little performance earlier. Gave me another idea altogether. Don't stop with the T-shirt, sugar. Take off that pretty little bra."

"You need to leave, Kyle."

"Oh, I'll leave. After I've gotten what I came for." He reached behind him, pulled out a gun. "You really should have left well enough alone, Savannah. You shouldn't have sicced the law on us. Since we had to run, we figured we might as well detour a shade off our escape route and make sure you understood what a big mistake you'd made. Now, let's see those tits."

* * *

Rather than waste half an hour walking back to his office and changing into a dry shirt, Zach bought a T-shirt from a vendor and changed between two booths. He then made his rounds in half the time he ordinarily would have taken. No stopping and shopping for him this year. He had places to go and, with any luck, a person to do.

He wanted to talk to Savannah. He needed to talk to Savannah. However, he needed to be with Savannah, too. In his experience, make-up sex was one of life's greatest gifts—and he'd never had make-up sex with a woman he loved.

"Don't get ahead of yourself, Turner," he murmured as he turned to start down the last row of booths set up in Angel Creek Park. Despite his hurry, a display at the front of one tent caught his eye. "This is interesting. Is it a sculpture? A wall hanging?"

"It's wearable art if a person so chooses, but it can be mounted for display on a wall, or we do sell a table display unit to hold it."

The item was made from skeleton keys that had been soldered together, but the shape . . . wearable art? "I hope this doesn't come across as insulting, because I really find this piece fascinating, but . . . what exactly is it?"

The grandmotherly artist smiled. "Why, a chastity belt, of course."

"Of course," Zach replied. Just like he'd said. Interesting people.

He'd reached the second-to-last booth when Logan McClure called his name. "Hey, Zach. Aren't you the talk of the town today."

"Heard about booth seventeen, did you?"

"I did. It was funny. I was just leaving the first-aid tent

when you walked up with your tennis balls. Celeste came to stand beside me and we exchanged hellos. I didn't pay much attention to her because I was watching you and Savannah."

"I'm so glad we were able to provide the morning's entertainment."

"I certainly laughed. Anyway, that's not the strange part. Celeste started asking me questions about you and Savannah, and I thought it was weird since she knows you two better than I do. I looked at her again . . . and she wasn't Celeste Blessing. But I swear, she looked so much like her that she could have been Celeste's twin."

"Really. Was she wearing angel earrings?"

"Nope. Nor white and gold clothes. That should have been my first tip-off." They reached an intersection of booths, and Logan indicated he was going left. "I'm headed this way," Zach said, pointing right.

"I'll see you around, then. Have a nice lunch, Sheriff Romeo."

"Bite me, Mr. McClure."

Zach strolled on, waving to the mayor, nodding to the lemonade vendor, then stopping to buy a cup since he was thirsty. That caused him to consider what he had at home for lunch. He had offered Savannah lunch. He should have food. He didn't have any food in either his fridge or his pantry. *I'll pick up something from a vendor and . . .*

Abruptly the words Logan McClure had said filtered back through his mind. *She could have been Celeste Blessing's twin.*

He stopped abruptly. Celeste Blessing's twin.

Weeks ago Savannah had told him about Francine Vaughn. *She's Celeste Blessing's doppelgänger.*

The Vaughns had been arrested last week. Had they made bail? He hadn't heard.

Logan had talked to Celeste Blessing's twin.

"Oh, hell." Zach dropped his lemonade and began to run.

Savannah's heart pounded and her mind raced. *Okay. Don't panic. Think. This is your home, your territory. Kyle Vaughn will not defeat you again.*

She needed to stall for time. Zach would arrive here soon. He'd be early. He wouldn't wait until one. He'd kissed her. He'd said he'd take her to Reflection Point for lunch. He'd be wanting make-up sex.

He'll be early. Buy some time, Savannah. Do what you have to do to survive.

She slipped her bra straps off her shoulders and bared her breasts. *It's no big deal. It's not like he hasn't seen them before.*

"Well now, sugar," Kyle said, leering. "I'd forgotten what a nice rack you had. So tell me, did you get yourself a girlfriend while you were in the slammer? Bet you had plenty of ladies wantin' to suck on those pretty tits."

She eyed his gun. Had he come here to kill her? She knew he was a liar, a thief, and a drug dealer, but had he ever killed anyone before? Would he hesitate or would it be easy for him? What should she say? What should she do?

"Now take off those cute little shorts," he demanded.

"My bathtub is going to overflow, Kyle. This is an old house and if it overflows it will leak down the side of the house. Someone might notice. Will you let me go turn it off?"

While he thought about it, she mentally inventoried her cabinets. Surely she could find something to use as a weapon. Hair spray. Tweezers. Didn't she have a pair of scissors in the drawer?

"Don't concern yourself with the bathtub, Savannah.

Look on the good side: you won't need to worry about a water bill. Now, take off those shorts."

Fine. More to distract him with. She dropped her shorts.

He let out a wolf whistle. "Baby, baby. I don't recall you wearing thongs. I think I'd remember that."

Her stomach rolled. He'd come here to kill her, that was obvious. The voice in her head asked, *Okay, then, what are you going to do to stop him, Savannah Sophia?*

Grams, you're back!

Darling, I'm always with you. Now, answer the question, love. What are you going to do to stop this villain?

I don't know!

Sure you do. You'll do something. Anything.

It's a risk. A huge risk. He's got a gun.

And if he kills you, you'll have died taking action.

Taking action. Savannah liked that. Taking action meant not being a victim. Have a nice victimhood, Zach had said.

I don't think so. Not again. Never again.

That's the spirit, Savannah Sophia.

Of course, won't it be just my luck to die right when I've found Zach?

Fiddlesticks. Maybe you won't die. Maybe you'll defeat the villain. After all, you're not a victim anymore.

No, I'm not. I'm Zach Turner's woman.

And she wouldn't be afraid.

Savannah used the weapons she had at her disposal—her voice, her body, her intellect. She arched her back, stuck out her boobs, and asked, "Did you come here to screw me or shoot me, Kyle?"

His gaze dropping to her breasts, he said, "Both."

"You know what I learned in prison? Danger is a turn-on. I'm pretty turned on. My panties are wet. Wanna see?"

His voice tight, he said, "Show me."

It wasn't much of a plan, but it was all she had and as much as she'd have liked to wait for Zach, she sensed she was running out of time. She went into full strip-tease mode, shooting a hip, letting her thumbs play with the elastic, slowly . . . ever so slowly . . . pulling her panties down.

She suppressed the shudder of revulsion. She was a warrior woman, using the weapons at hand, and they were working. He was distracted. He wasn't on guard. Why would he be? He'd known the old Savannah. The innocent, foolish, starry-eyed girl. He hadn't known Zach Turner's woman.

She slipped off the panties, but kept hold of them. She swung them around in a slow circle, once, twice. On the third time, she intended to throw them in his face and lunge at him. She'd knock him to the floor and rip the gun out of his hand and if she had to use it, then so be it. She was Savannah Sophia Moore and she could do this.

It might have worked, too, had everything not gone to hell.

Zach called for backup. He knew he might be over-reacting, but he called for backup anyway. Gabi was on the north side of town. She would be only minutes behind him. Martin was in a department vehicle descending Sinner's Prayer Pass. His other deputy was on the highway north of town. "I'll get them there fast, Zach," Ginger assured him.

Good. If this was a mistake, then he could call them off before they arrived.

Only he didn't think this was a mistake. Every instinct in his body was screaming.

Savannah was in trouble.

He arrived at the house and shifted into hunter mode,

breathing deeply to calm his breath even as he moved forward on silent feet.

He tested the lock on the kitchen door, and the knob turned easily. Crap. Savannah was one of the few people in Eternity Springs who kept her house locked even when she was inside.

Quietly he slipped inside. He listened hard. He heard something . . . water running? The bathtub?

She was taking a bath. He relaxed a little. Maybe she'd been thinking about make-up sex, too, and had simply forgotten to lock up.

Or maybe not. Something didn't feel right. There was a tension in the house that wasn't normal.

Aware of the sometimes squeaky hinges, he opened the swinging door that separated the kitchen from the rest of the house. That's when he heard the voices.

The panties began their third rotation when the sound came from downstairs. TJ yelled, "Savannah? The credit card machine has quit working. Savannah?"

Kyle jerked his gaze away from her and turned toward the door. Time slowed to freeze-frames. Zach in the hall, his gun up. His eyes met hers. *He can't see Kyle's gun.*

"No!" she screamed, throwing herself at Kyle, at his gun, the gun pointed at Zach, just as his finger moved on the trigger.

The bullet ripped into her. Pain stabbed her. Savannah fell even as another shot exploded and gore and blood splattered against her skin. Kyle's body toppled and Savannah knew he was dead, knew Zach had killed him. *It's over. It's over.*

"Peach!" He was there, kneeling over her, those gorgeous blue eyes of his fierce. Worried. "It's okay. Help is on the way. It'll be okay."

He reached for her, and . . . then it wasn't okay.

Freeze-frames again. His body jerks. His eyes widen.

Blood. Zach's blood. *Oh, dear God.* He falls on top of her.

Over his shoulder, a wild-eyed devil stands holding a gun.

Not Celeste. Francine.

TWENTY-SIX

She awoke to the murmur of soft voices and the sight of an angel seated beside her bed. Not Francine. Celeste.

I'm either in heaven or a hospital. Where's Zach? Then she remembered. Zach!

This could be hell.

Her mouth was dry and she tried to say his name, but it emerged as a croak. Celeste looked up from her magazine. A motorcycle magazine. "Savannah, you're awake."

Celeste reached for the white foam cup with a straw on the bedside table and put it up to Savannah's mouth. She sipped and would have thought that the water felt and tasted wonderful had she not had but one thought in her mind. "Zach?"

"He's alive. He's in surgery."

Alive. Thank you, God. Savannah drifted back to sleep.

The next time she awoke, Sage was sitting in the chair beside her bed, reading a novel. Savannah asked, "Zach?"

Sage smiled at her. "Hello, sleepyhead. Welcome back. Zach is in ICU, Savannah. It's serious, but I will tell you that he survived surgery and we have every reason to hope."

Savannah studied her friend's face. Before she'd moved to Eternity Springs and become an artist, Sage had been a doctor. She knew what she was talking about. "Promise?"

"I promise, honey. The next twenty-four hours are key."

Tears flooded Savannah's eyes and she shut them. She said a fervent, silent prayer, sipped the water Sage offered, then said, "I need to see him."

"I know you do. We'll make that happen just as soon as we possibly can. You have my word on it. In the meantime, you need to do your part. You rest and get your strength up and we'll get you in to see Zach."

Good. Okay. "Teej?"

"TJ is fine. He's here. He rode in with Cam and Sarah. You are at the hospital in Gunnison. You are going to be fine, by the way. The bullet went in and out. Nicked a bone and did some muscle damage, but you'll heal."

"Kyle?"

Sage's face went hard. "He's dead. The woman is, too. She had a shoot-out with Gabi."

"She killed Francine?" Savannah asked, wanting to be certain she understood.

"Yes."

"Gabi's okay?"

Sage hesitated. "Physically she's fine. She's understandably upset."

"Warrior woman," Savannah murmured, then drifted back to sleep.

The next time she woke, she thought something was wrong with her eyes. She was seeing double. Two identical, tall, handsome strangers stood at the foot of her bed. Both looked tired and wore identical worried expressions as they gazed not at Savannah but at the figure seated in the bedside chair.

"You need to get some rest, Gabs," one of them said.

"You'll make yourself sick," the other added. "That won't do anyone any good. Max will be landing soon. He'll be pissed if he gets here and sees you looking like a hag."

"I don't look like a hag," Gabi said. "I'm fine."

"You should go to the hotel and take a shower and a nap."

"I will just as soon as they tell us that Zach is out of the woods."

"But—"

"No, Lucca. Save your breath. I'm not leaving the hospital until I know that our brother is going to survive."

Savannah's eyes flew open. She croaked. "Your brother? Survive?"

Holy crap, I hurt.

It'd be easier to sink back into the haze, Zach knew. Awareness meant agony—but something else mattered. Something . . . someone. Savannah.

In his mind's eye, he saw her fall. Felt the warm, wet stickiness of her blood. Savannah! His eyelids weighed a ton. Sound. Make a sound. Say her name. "S-s-s-s . . ."

"He's hissing again," Cam Murphy said.

"That's a good sign," Gabi Romano added. "Right? Don't you think that's a good sign?"

He put all his energy into saying, "Pe-a-ch."

"What did he say?" Cam asked.

"He said 'Peach,' " a woman's voice said in a beautiful southern drawl. "He said my name."

Zach opened his eyes and saw her leaning over him, whole and healthy and full of life and full of love. She wore an angel's wing necklace around her neck, and it brushed his cheek as she leaned over and kissed his forehead. "Thank God. You're back. I love you, Zach. You're going to be okay. We're all going to be okay."

He saw tears pool in her big brown doe eyes and realized with only a twinge of embarrassment that his own eyes were wet, too. He managed a smile as his heart overflowed, then he drifted back to sleep. In peace.

"I'm telling you, there is bad juju around the summer arts festival. It needs to be cancelled," Sarah Murphy said five days later.

"Now, Sarah . . ."

"Don't 'Now Sarah' me, Zach Turner. You've been shot twice—twice!—at our summer arts festival. You lost your spleen, for heaven's sake. What will it be next time? A kidney? Your liver? That's bad karma, and I think changes must be made."

Zach glanced at Savannah, seated beside him here in the hospital cafeteria, the remains of the lunch that their friends had brought with them from their favorite local restaurant scattered around them. "She's turned into such a diva."

"You scared her."

"You both scared me. I don't want to go through anything like that ever again." Sarah lifted her chin and added, "It's not healthy for me."

"Or me either," Cat Davenport said.

"Or me," Nic Callahan concurred.

"Or me," Sage Rafferty declared.

"Or me." Ali Timberlake folded her arms.

Each of their husbands nodded their agreement. When Celeste Blessing failed to chime in, the other visitors looked at her. "I wasn't scared. I knew they'd both make it. And, speaking of angel wings, I think we should get on with our presentation before the nurses come looking for Zach."

"She's right," Sarah added. "Besides, I ate too many enchiladas, and I need to walk around."

They cleared the tables and tossed the paper goods in

the trash as Celeste took her place in the center of the room. "Cam, would you wheel Zach over here so that everyone can see?"

"I can walk," he grumbled.

"No!" a dozen voices said at once.

"Nurse Ratchet will have our asses," Cam added as he hurried to do Celeste's bidding.

She took a small silver box from her bag and smiled at Zach. "My dear, dear Zach. As you know, I award the official Angel's Rest blazon to those who have embraced love's healing grace. The friends who have gathered with you today to witness this presentation each overcame great wounds of heart to earn their wings. One might argue that you've been blessed to avoid such emotional heartache.

"However, I contend that sometimes, wounds exist that remain hidden even from ourselves. If you look deeply, you may recognize such injuries within yourself. They may be different, more subtle, but just as real."

Zach leaned toward Savannah, who had taken a seat beside him, and spoke from the corner of his mouth. "What is she talking about?"

"Hush," his beloved scolded. "Pay attention."

Celeste continued, "Zach, I award you these wings today in recognition of the innate strength of character you possess that has allowed you to overcome these life-long trials and to acknowledge that love's healing grace isn't limited to emotional wounds. Is there any doubt that love compelled you and assisted you in your fight for survival?"

"No," he answered honestly. "Not at all."

Celeste opened the box and removed the angel's wing pendant hanging from a heavy, masculine silver chain. She bent and fastened it around Zach's neck, murmuring in his ear, "Feel the weight of this award in the coming hours, my friend. Draw strength from the knowledge of the joys that life has to give . . . if only you'll open your heart to it."

She kissed him on the cheek, then swept from the cafeteria. Zach sat in his wheelchair pleased, a bit embarrassed, and more than a little confused as, couple by couple, his friends from Eternity Springs offered their congratulations and wishes of good luck as they followed Celeste from the cafeteria.

"Okay, that was weird," Zach said once he and Savannah were alone. "Why do I get the feeling that something else is going on here? What's up, Savannah? Did the doctors find something unexpected when they were digging around inside me? Am I dying, after all?"

"No. That's not it at all." She wheeled his chair around and began to push him back to his room. "However, once again, your instincts are spot on. There are some people waiting for you back in your room."

"People?"

"It's a good thing, honey," Savannah said as they approached his door.

"What people?"

She sucked in a deep breath, then said, "Your blood type is AB negative, which is quite uncommon. Have you stopped to wonder where they got all of that rare red stuff that they pumped into your body?"

His hospital room door opened to reveal an obviously nervous Gabi Romano. Savannah squeezed Zach's shoulder and guided him on into his room where three men stood in front of the window. Zach recognized them all. Max Romano had come to his office. Anthony and Lucca Romano were college basketball coaches of some renown. Lucca Romano had been on the news quite a bit last year when he'd been involved in a tragic team bus incident that had taken the lives of two of his players.

Zach braced himself against the expected pain and

stood. "Deputy Romano, why are your brothers congregated in my hospital room?"

Gabi clasped her hands in front of her, drew a deep breath, and said, "Because our blood runs in your veins, Zach."

"Oh." He smiled and extended his hand. "You donated blood for me. Thank you."

"Yes, we did, and you are welcome," Max Romano said. "But that's not why we are here. Zach, we are your birth family. You are our brother."

Savannah watched his face grow pale. She stepped forward, saying, "Why don't we all sit down."

Zach resisted returning to his bed—the hardheaded idiot—so she shot the Romano men a glare. Once they took seats in the three additional chairs that had mysteriously appeared in Zach's room during lunch, Gabi sank into the bedside chair. And Zach chose to sit on the end of the bed, probably because that kept him higher than the others, Savannah thought.

Leaning against the door, Savannah glanced from one Romano man to the next. *Wow. They do look alike. Even Gabi.* She and Zach had the same eyes. How had she missed the family resemblance in the past?

Zach's gaze, too, shifted from one to the other. Finally, his voice tight, he said, "Somebody explain."

The guys all looked at Gabi. She shook her head, blinking back tears. Lucca went and sat beside her on the bed, his expression tender. Understandably, Gabi had been a bit shaky ever since the shooting.

Max leaned forward, rested his elbows on his knees, and began. "It's not an uncommon story, but it's one we only learned about in March when our father died. I saw Mother add something to Dad's casket right before they closed it. After the funeral, I asked her sister, our aunt Bridget, what it was. She'd had too much wine and she spilled the beans. It was a baby's footprint. The baby Mother had given away.

"Our parents were teenage sweethearts from opposite sides of the tracks. Her parents were wealthy, her father an Irishman who owned a string of filling stations in Philly. Dad's family were recent Italian immigrants doing whatever they could to get by. Mom was fifteen when she got pregnant. Her parents sent her away to have the baby and give it . . . give you . . . up for adoption. After Mom returned to Philly, she continued to see Dad on the sly. She never told him about you."

Zach's gaze sought Savannah's. He patted the bed next to him, and when she sat, he took her hand.

"On Mom's eighteenth birthday, they ran off and got married."

"And had four more kids," Zach said, and Savannah wondered if he heard the bitterness in his voice.

Gabi spoke up, her tone anxious and entreating. "Aunt Bridget said Mom has always mourned you, that every year on your birthday, she'd call Bridget sobbing for Giovanni. That's what she named you. Giovanni Liam, the Italian and the Irish. All our names are that way. She said Dad wouldn't have forgiven her, and that's why she kept the secret. She was only fifteen, Zach."

Zach's thumb stroked over Savannah's hand. She gently leaned against him, careful not to jostle him, silently offering comfort. Zach looked at Max. "This was the reason for your visit earlier this year? You came to check me out? Did I pass muster?"

"It wasn't like that," Max said, looking a little guilty. They all looked a little guilty. "It's all about Mom. She hasn't been the same since Dad died. It was unexpected. A heart attack. Mom has been . . . lost. She dropped thirty pounds she couldn't afford to lose. She stopped leaving the house. Aunt Bridget browbeat her into going away—a sisters' trip to Europe that they'd promised each other for years. They're due back next week."

Zach looked at Gabi. "Does she know about the shooting?"

Gabi shook her head. "That's news better imparted in person."

"So how did you track me down? I went through all my parents' papers after they died. I didn't see anything about my birth parents."

The Romano men shared a glance. Lucca said, "This person who helped us could get in a lot of trouble if you wanted to push it."

"I won't."

"A priest at Mom's local parish helped facilitate the placement and adoption," Max continued. "He knew where you were. Apparently, when Mom got pregnant with the twins, she talked to him about telling Dad and trying to bring you home. But he told Mom you were happy in a good place with a family who loved you. She decided it wasn't right to disrupt your life."

"So this priest has kept tabs on me all these years?"

"No. But he cares about our family and he gave us the Turners' name. We tracked you down."

Anthony said, "You have to understand that our mother's grief is . . . well, it's beyond what is normal. We are truly afraid it will kill her. Aunt Bridget says the trip hasn't helped as we'd hoped. We are hoping that you might be the medicine she needs."

"But we're not going to force it, Zach," Gabi assured him. "If you don't want to be part of our family, then no harm, no foul. Mom will never know a thing about it."

"Despite the fact that our sister took a life to save yours," Anthony added.

Gabi snapped, "Tony!"

He shrugged but met Zach's arched brow stare with a challenging gaze of his own. Gabi added, "The two have nothing to do with one another. It's my job. I'm good at it."

"She is," Zach said. "One of the best deputies I've ever had, though, apparently not the most honest."

"I never lied to you, Zach," Gabi said, her voice fierce.

"You didn't tell the whole truth."

She lifted her chin. "I saved your sorry butt, though, didn't I?"

Zach offered her a warm smile. "So I understand, Deputy. So I understand."

The room fell silent as Zach took some time to think. Throughout, his thumb continued to stroke Savannah's hand. They had never had that talk that had been due the day of the shooting. She didn't think it mattered anymore. Everything that needed to be said had been said with those three oh-so-important words.

"You've been quiet, Peach."

"I'm listening to you think out loud."

His lips flirted with a smile. "What am I saying?"

"That despite it all, the most important thing is that you've been offered a gift—a family. Whether you choose to accept it, though, is your call. Only you can make the choice."

She had no doubt about what he would decide. She'd told Gabi as much when Gabi had confessed the whole story in Savannah's hospital room. And yet Zach deserved the opportunity to make the decision. Savannah had demanded as much during one of those horrible, touch-and-go days when Gabi had been a mess and wanted to summon her mother back from Europe to be at her eldest son's side "while she still can."

Savannah forgave Gabi that comment due to extenuating circumstances, but she'd banished her from the hospital until she rid herself of every last negative thought. Irish and Italian. No wonder Gabi's emotions ran the gamut!

"You all need to understand that I had parents. Great parents. I loved them very much. And I have a family—brothers and sisters of my heart—in my friends in Eternity Springs."

"You are a lucky man," Lucca said.

"Believe me, I know that. Because I also have two extraordinary women in my life whom I love. Savannah, soon to be my wife, who threw herself in front of a bullet for me, and—"

Savannah jerked up straight. "What? Excuse me? Did I miss something here? I don't recall receiving or accepting a marriage proposal."

Zach just grinned and continued, "And Gabriella, my calm, cool, collected sister, who had my back when it counted."

Calm, cool, collected Gabriella burst into tears.

The Romano men—all four of them—smiled. Zach said, "So how do you want to do this? Do you want me to go to her? Do you want to bring her to me? I don't want the shock to kill her. Can she handle this?"

"Mom needs to come to Eternity Springs," Gabi said through her tears. "It's special. What we heard about it at first . . . it's true. Actually . . ." She gave Zach a bravely sassy smile. "Eternity Springs will probably heal her heart all on its own. She doesn't need you."

Zach rolled his eyes in mock disgust and met his brothers' gazes. "Sisters."

God's paintbrush set the mountains aglow with wide swaths of gold, orange, and crimson as autumn settled on Eternity Springs. The promise of snow was in the air as Zach pulled his Range Rover to a stop at the parking area for Lover's Leap.

"I don't think this is a good idea," Savannah told him. "It's a rough trail. What if you slip and fall?"

"No one is going to slip and fall, Peach. We have each other to lean on, don't we?"

She let out a huff. "You are impossible. It's too soon."

"If we wait another week, it'll be too late. The snows are coming. I need to see the season off from up here. It will fortify me for what's ahead. Now, come along with me, Savannah, and quit your fretting. I'm the one who gets to be nervous. I'm the one meeting my mother this afternoon."

Savannah took his hand and squeezed it. "It'll be okay, Zach. No matter what."

"I know. I'm nervous, but excited, too. I've thought about it a lot. I don't resent her or her decisions. I think it all happened the way it was meant to happen. I had a great childhood. Mom always said I was hers and Dad's greatest joy. Mrs. Romano did that for them. For us."

"Mrs. Romano?"

He shrugged. "She may be my mother, but she's not my mom. I didn't even ask what her name is."

"Maggie," Savannah said.

"Oh." Zach drew in a deep breath, then sighed. "It's a little overwhelming. To go from having no family to having a mother, the Three Stooges, and Gabi."

Savannah laughed. "Three stooges, huh? Now there's a brotherly sentiment."

He grinned and changed the subject. "Let's go. I didn't drive up here to sit in the car and talk. Although, if you wanted to sit in the car and neck, I could be persuaded."

"Now there's a shocker. No necking, Turner. I know you, and you wouldn't want to stop at necking. But you're not going any further until you've been cleared by your doctor."

"Spoilsport." He leaned over and kissed her, then climbed out of the Range Rover.

She wrestled the picnic basket away from him and fretted every minute of the hike up to the point, watching him like a hawk. The man was pushing himself too hard during this recovery. He simply didn't use good sense. This picnic he'd insisted on was a prime example. By the time the picnic bench came into view, she was a nervous wreck.

There's not a limit on nervous. We can both be nervous.

She suspected he'd brought her up here to ask her to marry him.

The confounded man had never said another word about the subject since leaving the hospital. Sex, yes. He'd been complaining about the lack of that for a week now. But he hadn't said one word about a wedding.

He sat on top of the picnic bench and Savannah searched his face for signs of pain before taking a seat beside him. "You are such a worrywart," he told her.

"Yeah, well, I've earned the right," she grumbled. "I lived through three days of hell not knowing if you were going to live at all, Zach Turner."

He laced his fingers with hers and brought her hand up and kissed it. "We're both recovering, though, aren't we?"

She sighed. "Yes. Are you hungry? Do you want your sandwich?"

"Sit with me awhile first, Savannah. Let's just be here, together, for a little while."

"That sounds lovely."

And it was. She didn't know how long they sat without talking, simply staring out at the breathtaking vista beyond. Ten minutes? Twenty? However long, it was soothing. A comforting, healing stretch of time.

Eventually Zach said, "I bought a plane ticket this morning."

A plane ticket? Not tickets, plural? Like for a honeymoon? "Oh? Where are you going?"

"To Atlanta. With you and TJ."

"What? No, you're not. We leave next week. You can't make that trip. We've already talked about this ad nauseam. Why, the trip home from Gunnison almost put you back in the hospital. No. Absolutely not. I won't have it."

"I went to the clinic yesterday. Rose cleared me for the trip."

"But—"

"I'll be fine. It's a plane ride and a car ride. I'll be sitting on my ass most of the time. I don't want you making that trip without me. It'd be worse for my health to stay at home. We'd do a role-reversal thing and I'd worry myself sick, and then what would you do? Besides, I want to see TJ in his new digs and meet his dad."

Savannah knew that what really worried him was the possibility that Gary would be an ass. "Zach, I've talked to Gary. It's . . . better. Not great, but okay. A little awkward, but that's understandable. We have some bridges to build."

"Which is why I want to be there."

Truth be told, Savannah wanted him there, too. "Rose really said you'd be okay?"

"She really did."

Savannah blew out a long breath. "Okay, I admit it. I'll be very glad to have you with me. Seeing Gary again . . . and I'm so worried for TJ. What if my brother screws up again? TJ will be devastated."

"Well, yeah. On the other hand, if that happens this time around, we'll be there for him and he'll know it. But I have a feeling it's going to go well, honey. I talked to the authorities who oversee that treatment program. It's had amazing success. Your brother has worked hard to get where he is. Despite his faults, he wants to be a father to his son. He and TJ deserve this chance."

"I know. He's so excited." She watched a bird swoop

from the top of a golden aspen to alight on the green branch of a fir. "I'm going to miss him."

"I know. I will, too. He's a good kid. So, how about that sandwich? What kind did you bring us?"

"My grandmother's pimento cheese." She opened her basket and pulled out their lunch. "Fruit slices. Carrot sticks."

He waited, and when she said nothing more, he actually whined a little and reached for the basket. "No chips? No peach cobbler?"

Savannah laughed and slapped his hand, then tossed him a bag of corn chips. "You have to eat the carrot sticks before you get cobbler."

"Nag."

They ate their lunch in companionable silence. Once he'd polished off his meal, Zach wadded up his napkin and shot a paper basketball into the picnic basket. When Savannah finished, he climbed down from the picnic bench and offered her his hand. Their fingers laced, they walked toward the safety railing at the edge of the point and stood, gazing out at the valley below. Zach said, "This is a special place."

"It's beautiful."

"True, but that's not why it's special." He faced her, gently touched her cheek. "It's special because this is where I met you."

She melted, even as her heart began to pound. *This is it. He's going to ask me to marry him.*

"That's sweet. You're sweet, Zach."

His expression rueful, he said, "That's me, Mr. Sweet. Better than Barney Fife, I guess."

Savannah shook her head and laughed at them both. "You never were Barney Fife. You've always been Andy Taylor. Tall, smart, sexy Sheriff Andy."

"You thought Sheriff Taylor was sexy?"

"Absolutely."

"He wasn't a little too . . . good?"

Savannah clicked her tongue and teased, "Now, Sheriff, a man can never be too good."

He leaned down and kissed her, long and thoroughly, and Savannah melted against him, her heart soaring. When he pulled away, those gorgeous blue eyes of his stared down into hers. "I love you, Savannah Sophia Moore."

"I love you, too, Zach Turner."

He kissed her again, quickly, then said, "I have something for you. I wanted to give it to you up here."

Of course. She should have realized it. How perfect that he'd give her a ring here where they began. "Okay."

He reached into his pocket and pulled out a . . . not an engagement ring. Savannah gasped, brought a hand to her mouth.

It was a dirty, ragged muslin bag with a dirty, ragged blue ribbon. "Zach. You found it. How did you find it? Where?"

"I just happened to see it one day when I was out walking on the ranch." He handed it to her.

She clasped it to her chest. "Just happened to see it. Right."

"Maybe I went searching for it on the ranch. A few times."

"A few times? A few hours? Hours and hours and hours?"

He shrugged. "It was important to you."

"Oh, Zach. Thank you." She went up on her tiptoes and pressed kisses against his mouth, his cheeks, his nose, saying, "Thank you . . . thank you . . . thank you."

Finally he grabbed her face between his palms and gave her mouth a hard, carnal kiss. "You're welcome."

Once she was steady on her feet again, he let her go. "This was nice, Savannah. I'm glad we could do this."

"Me too."

"You ready to go?" He turned and started walking back toward the picnic table.

Go? Now? She stood staring after him, her mouth gaping open.

He picked up the picnic basket and his walking stick, then turned to wait for her. "Savannah?"

"Go? Now? Like this?"

"Um . . . yeah? I admit I'm getting a little tired."

"But . . ." She put her hands on her hips. "What about my ring?"

"What ring?" He honestly looked puzzled.

The jerk. "My engagement ring!"

Light dawned. "You thought I was going to give you an engagement ring today?"

"Yes!" she exclaimed, stepping toward him. "It's been three weeks, Turner! What's the deal? Three weeks ago in front of your family, your brand-new family, you toss out the word *wife* and then you never bring up the subject again? For three whole weeks?"

Savannah knew she was sounding a bit like a fishwife, but she didn't really care. "Then you bring me up here. To the place we met. What was I supposed to think?"

"Oh."

She waited a beat. "That's all you have to say for yourself? 'Oh'?"

Zach lifted his face toward the sky and sighed long and loud. "For crying out loud, Savannah. Think about it. Think about who you run with. I have some pressure here. This is Eternity Springs! The last marriage proposal that happened in this town was done from a hang glider above a field of roses that spelled out the words 'Marry Me.' I may not have Jack Davenport's money or his larger-than-life CIA-agent background, but I can darn well throw down a romantic marriage proposal that'll make you swoon and give you a fairy-tale story to tell our grandchildren someday. Only you're going to have to cut me a little slack. I'm recovering from a near fatal gunshot wound, here, and you need to pay attention to the verb tense. That's *recovering*. Not *have recovered*. You need to be patient and give me time. Because just like marriage is a two-way street, proposals are a two-way street. It's my proposal, too, and when it happens, I want more than romance. I want down-and-dirty, toe-curling, sweaty, steaming, screaming sex. So, honey, you're just gonna have to cool your jets for a few more weeks while I get my strength back. Got it?"

Savannah swallowed hard and considered fanning her face. "Yes, dear."

"Good. Okay, then. Are you ready to leave? I have to go meet my mother."

"Yes, dear."

Savannah fought a smile, knowing her eyes were twinkling as she walked up next to him, appropriated the picnic basket, and slipped her arm through his. "Zach, can I ask you one question?"

He sidled her a suspicious look. "Just one?"

"Just one. I promise."

"Okay. What is it?"

"Are you taking your vitamins?"

"Damn right I am." His lips twitched, then he leaned down and pressed a sweet kiss against her cheek. "Come on, Peach. Let's go home."

At two o'clock that afternoon, grasping Savannah's hand in a viselike grip, Zach stepped up to the door of Nightingale Cottage along the bank of Angel Creek on the grounds of Angel's Rest Healing Center and Spa. He rapped on the door.

Footsteps approached. The door swung open. A trim woman with auburn hair dressed in jeans, boots, and a University of Colorado sweatshirt opened the door. She had wounded blue eyes, high cheekbones, a thin straight nose, and full lips that needed some color.

She was short. Five foot three, five foot four at the most. Did he have the right cabin? How the hell had this woman given birth to four sons well over six feet tall and a daughter who stood five foot nine in her stocking feet? "Mrs. Romano?"

"Yes?"

He swallowed hard. Savannah squeezed his hand reassuringly. He cleared his throat and said, "I'm . . ."

He couldn't say any more. He had a boulder of emotion in his throat. Trying again, he said, "My name is—"

Her gasp cut him off. She took a step forward. Placed her hand against his chest. Touched him. Then the hand traveled up to his face, warm and soft.

"Giovanni. Oh, sweet angels above. You are my Giovanni."

ACKNOWLEDGMENTS

My thanks to the entire team at Ballantine for their fabulous support: Libby McGuire; Gina Wachtel; Scott Shannon; Linda Marrow; Lynn Andreozzi and the art department; Janet Wygal and the production department; my editor, Kate Collins; and Junessa Viloria. A special thanks to retired sheriff Mr. Jim Brand and my legal team in Boston, who assisted me in the development of Savannah's criminal history. To Nic Burnham, Mary Dickerson, Christina Dodd, Lisa Kleypas, and Susan Sizemore—Eternity Springs lives because of you. Thank you.

Read on for a preview of Emily March's next novel
in her Eternity Springs series:

MIRACLE ROAD

When Hope Montgomery's gaze snagged on the date in her curriculum planner, she sucked in a sudden breath: March 15.

She closed her eyes and absorbed the hurt. This was the way it happened now, four years later. Rather than being her constant companion, the pain would slither up and strike when she wasn't prepared and braced for it.

" 'Beware the Ides of March,' " she softly quoted.

She shut her planner and set it aside, then reached for her coffee. Her hand trembled as she raised the china cup to her mouth, but she concentrated on savoring both the smell and the taste of the aromatic, full-bodied brew. Using her senses helped anchor her to the present, and besides, the coffee at Angel's Rest was truly sublime.

Nevertheless, she teetered on the brink of tears until Celeste Blessing swept into the old Victorian mansion's parlor saying, "I'm so sorry I'm running late, Hope. It's been one thing after another today. First we had a plumbing problem in the showers beside the hot springs pools, then one of our guests suffered a death in the family, the poor dear, and I helped arrange emergency transportation home. Finally, my sister phoned, and I'm afraid I lost track of time."

Hope stood and smiled at the woman whom she'd come to view as the matriarch of Eternity Springs. The vital, active, older owner of Angel's Rest, Celeste wore black slacks, a gold cotton blouse, and a harried smile.

"Celeste, I love your new haircut," Hope said.

"Thank you. I do, too." Celeste lifted a hand to fluff the short, sassy style, her blue eyes twinkling. "One of my guests told me I look just like Judi Dench. He's an old flirt, and I think he was hoping for a discount on his bill, but I'll accept the compliment."

"As well you should," Hope agreed. "He's right."

"Thank you, dear. I'm going to tell my sister you said that." Celeste wrinkled her nose as she added, "She told me I was too old for this style."

Hope couldn't help but smile. She had met Celeste and her sister when they'd rented the beach house next door to Hope's rental the summer before last. She could picture Desdemona saying that to Celeste. "How is Desi doing these days?"

"She's well. Busy, but then, aren't we all?"

"Is she still traveling quite a bit?"

"Constantly. As a result, we don't have the opportunity to see each other as often as we'd like. I'm trying to convince her to visit Eternity Springs sometime soon. She asked me to tell you hello and to blame her for my being tardy, but we're both to blame. It was downright rude of me to ask for a ride to the baby shower and then not be ready on time. Please forgive me."

"Don't be silly, Celeste. We have plenty of time. Besides, your front desk worker gave me a cup of spectacular coffee and I used the time to my benefit and looked over some of the paperwork Principal Geary gave me this morning." Hope picked up her purse and slipped the strap over her shoulder. "Can I help you carry anything?"

"Thank you. I have a few gifts in the kitchen."

Celeste led Hope down the hallway toward the kitchen. Upon entering the cheery room, Hope stopped and laughed. The kitchen table was covered with gaily wrapped and ribboned packages and bags, all in nursery themes in shades of a beautiful baby blue. "A few bags?"

"It's the latent grandmother in me, I fear. I just love buying for little ones."

Hope's smile grew bittersweet. "I do, too."

They loaded the gifts into Hope's crossover SUV, chatting about the presents they'd chosen. Hope was excited about the baby shower. This would be her first visit to Jack and Cat Davenport's mountain estate, Eagle's Way, and she looked forward to seeing it. She'd heard it was fabulous.

They picked up two more passengers for the drive, Maggie Romano and her daughter, Gabi. An attractive widow in her early fifties, Maggie was the newest full-time resident of Eternity Springs, having moved here at the beginning of the summer to be nearer to two of her adult children. Gabi was the town's deputy sheriff, though with her long legs, high cheekbones, and her mother's beautiful blue eyes, she could have been a model if she'd wanted. Hope was in the early stages of friendship with the Romano women. She liked them both very much but, considering her history, she was cautious about letting anyone get too close.

Celeste Blessing had been the lone exception. Being around Celeste was like slipping into Angel's Rest's inviting hot springs pools—sans the sulphur smell—on a cold winter's night. She simply made Hope feel better. She'd planted the seed about moving to Eternity Springs during those beach house days, then nurtured the notion with phone calls. Once Hope expressed real interest in making the change, Celeste had championed her to the principal and the school board.

The four women made small talk as their trip commenced. Gabi began relaying a story about the sheriff's office dispatcher's unfortunate experience with online dating, and with the laughter the story elicited, the melancholy that had lingered within

Hope after the unfortunate lesson-planner incident began to dissolve. She turned onto the road that climbed out of the valley, and her spirits rose along with it.

They were halfway up the ridge when Maggie observed, "I've not been up this road before. What a spectacular view!"

"Isn't it lovely?" In the front passenger seat, Celeste twisted around to speak with Maggie directly. "This is one of my favorite Gold Wing rides. Up here I sometimes feel like I can reach into the sky and touch heaven."

"Maybe I'll have to get a motorcycle," Maggie mused. "We could form a gang, Celeste."

Gabi let out a groan and buried her head in her hands as Celeste laughed out loud.

It was a beautiful, late-summer afternoon. Temperatures hovered in the mid-seventies. Snow-capped peaks climbed up to a sapphire sky dotted with puffy white clouds. The road wound around a mountainside to reveal an alpine meadow carpeted with wildflowers. "Oh, how gorgeous," Hope observed. "What are those purple-blue wildflowers called?"

"Gentians. They're one of my favorites," Celeste said. "Up near Heartache Falls they . . . Oh dear."

Hope braked to a stop as they came upon a small herd of bighorn sheep congregated on the road in front of them. Celeste clucked her tongue. "These animals are becoming my nemesis. This is the third time they've delayed me this month. Sarah Murphy will have my guts for garters if we're late to the shower."

"We have plenty of time," Hope assured her.

"Yes, but Sarah is not her usual cheery self these days. I need a distraction. What's the latest on your project, Maggie?"

Gabi rolled her big blue eyes and groaned for a second time. Her mother sniffed with disdain, then beamed at Celeste. "Actually, I have exciting news. Jim Sutton has accepted my offer for his great-grandmother's Victorian on Aspen Street. With a little renovation, it will make a perfect B&B."

"That *is* exciting news," Celeste said.

"Congratulations." Hope's brows knit as she tried to place the house. "On Aspen, you say? Which house is it?"

"The yellow one between Fifth and Sixth."

Maggie must be referring to the dilapidated three-story whose faded, flaking paint sometimes floated on the air like dandruff. Hope pictured an overgrown yard, broken shutters, rotted ginger-bread trim, and plywood-covered windows.

"It needs a little work," Maggie added as if reading Hope's mind.

"And Murphy Mountain is a little hill," Gabi drawled.

"Now, honey . . ."

Gabi slipped on a pair of designer sunglasses.

"Zach is quaking in his hiking boots. I heard him tell Savannah to be quick and hide his tool belt."

"I promised I wouldn't ask your brother to help," her mother protested. "He's the sheriff, for heaven's sake. He doesn't have time to be my handyman."

"I'm the sheriff's deputy," Gabi whined. "Why am I instructed to report for cleaning duty first thing Saturday morning?"

"Zach gets newlywed dispensation."

"He's your favorite."

"Right now, yes."

The exchange surprised Hope. In her experience, mothers denied the existence of a favored child even if the charge was true. Taking her attention off the bleating roadblock that was finally beginning to move, she glanced into the rearview mirror to observe the Romano women.

Gabi caught her look and flashed a grin. "It's okay, Hope. He's due for it."

She wanted to ask why, but she wasn't that nosy. Celeste obviously didn't share her concerns. "Being a newcomer to town, Hope probably doesn't know your family history. Tell her about Zach, Maggie. She loves happy endings as much as I do."

"It is a happy ending, isn't it?" Maggie sighed with pleasure, then explained. "I'll share the short version, Hope. Our family is dealing with a rather unique situation. I got pregnant with Zach when I was fifteen and I gave him up for adoption. Gabi and her brothers tracked him down and we've been reunited in the past year, so I have a lot of pent-up love to shower upon him."

Oh. A lost child, found. Hope's throat grew tight.

"Mom has always been a big proponent of sibling equality when it comes to parental favoritism, so my sibs and I understand it's Zach's turn," Gabi added. "That doesn't mean the rest of us won't complain about it. Especially under current circumstances. I can't be your handyman, either, Mom. It's too big a job. You need a contractor—shoot, you need a miracle worker—if you're going to turn that broken down behemoth into a bed-and-breakfast."

"I know, Gabriella. I actually have something different in mind. Someone different. I know a man who is good with his hands who desperately needs a project. A worker who needs a miracle."

"A miracle? Who do you know who needs . . . Oh. Lucca."

"He's one of your twins, isn't he?" Celeste asked Maggie. "The one who coaches for Colorado?"

"No. That's Anthony. Lucca took the Landry University Wildcats to the Sweet Sixteen last March. Then he . . . well . . ."

"He wigged out," Gabi said, a bite of temper in her voice. "He quit his job and took off, didn't tell the family where he'd gone. He acted like a total jerk and it hurt us. I'm warning you, Mom. It's going to take some time for me to forgive him. And what makes you think he'll come here anyway? According to Max and Anthony and Zach, he's perfectly happy lounging in his Mexican beach chair and getting drunk on tequila and he has absolutely no intention of ever coming back."

Maggie squared her shoulders. "He's my son. I have not begun to utilize all the weapons in my arsenal. He will come."

Hope followed college sports, so she'd picked up the connection between her new friends and the well-known collegiate basketball coaches early on. She admitted to Googling for more information. What Lucca Romano had done was publicly crash and burn and alienate the power brokers in his professional field.

Hope recognized that he'd suffered a tragedy. She sympathized with his pain. She didn't respect the way he'd chosen to deal with it. Quit everything, quit on everyone, and run off to become a drunken beach bum? It demonstrated a distinct lack of character as far as she was concerned. His mother must be so disappointed in him.

"I hope you're right, Mom," Gabi said. "But I'm afraid you're going to be hurt."

"He'll come. Now, look at that beautiful iron sculpture up on our right. It's an eagle in flight. How graceful."

"That's our Sage's work, a gift to Jack."

"So this is Eagle's Way?" Hope asked. "We're here?"

"Yes. With three minutes to spare, thank the dear Lord."

They drove through an open gate and along a road that wound through a meadow painted with wildflowers. The large, sprawling house was built in the traditional mountain log home style, with windows facing what had to be one of the best views in Colorado. "Wow," Hope said.

"Wait until you see the inside," Celeste said. "And the patio and pool area. Gabe Callahan is a landscape architect, and what he created is perfect for such a heavenly spot."

Jack Davenport stood on the front steps, and he waved at Hope to pull her car onto a circular driveway where Cam Murphy, Gabe Callahan, and Colt Rafferty stood acting as valets. "Hello, dears," Celeste said, climbing from the car. "I'm surprised to see you here. I thought the girls decided they wanted a traditional females-only baby shower."

"We're just here to provide muscle," Jack said. "As soon as everyone arrives and all the loot is hauled inside, we have a date with fishing rods and the creek."

"You have a lovely home," Hope told him.

"Thanks. We do love it."

Just then the front door opened and Nic Callahan called, "Thank goodness you are here! Sarah and Kat are ready to get this party started."

"Are we the last to arrive?"

"Rose is running late, but she had a patient. She's asked us to start without her."

Hope stepped into the great room and her gaze was torn among three gorgeous sites: snowcapped mountains displayed like a fine-art painting through the wall of windows; a glowing Cat Davenport holding her sleeping four-month-old son, Johnny, in her arms; and Sarah Murphy, sprawled in an overstuffed easy chair, her feet propped up on an ottoman, a grumpy scowl on her face and a baby belly so big that Hope wondered if she might be having a litter rather than a single baby boy.

"Sarah, you look beautiful," Hope told her.

"You are a liar, Hope Montgomery, but I appreciate the effort."

"How do you feel, darling?" Celeste asked.

"Fat. Grouchy. Ugly. Fat. My back hurts. I haven't seen my feet in weeks. My former neonatologist so-called friend tells me I could go another week, curse her black heart."

The physician in question, Sage Rafferty, rolled her eyes. "I'm not your doctor, Sarah. I gave you my personal opinion, not my professional one."

Sarah pouted then turned to Nic. "Sage is right. I should have asked you instead of her. You're a vet. I'm a cow. When should I head for the barn and lie down on the straw? Or would I stand up? Do cows have their babies lying down or standing up?"

"Mother," Lori Murphy chastised, her expression long-suffering. "Just stop it. The baby is healthy and you are healthy and you look lovely."

"Your father called me a whale!"

As one, the women in the room gasped.

"No he didn't, Mother." Lori explained to the others, "He called her a great white because she'd just bitten his head off for accidentally sloshing coffee onto the kitchen floor."

"It was clean. I want a clean house when I go into labor. But I shouldn't have snapped at him, and he spoke the truth. Big fish, big bovine . . . what's the difference? I'm fat! Why couldn't I have a little bump like Kat had? I'm bigger than Nic was and she had twins! I'm a blimp and I'm ugly and I'm too old to be doing this. What woman has her first and second children more than twenty years apart? I can't do this!"

"Sure you can." Nic Callahan crossed the room to sit on the arm of Sarah's chair. "And I thought this was supposed to be a baby shower, not a pity party."

Sarah's lips quirked. "Can't it be both? I'm one-hundred-and-twelve months pregnant."

"I'll bet you didn't sleep last night, did you?"

"Not much. Between the heartburn and his constant kicking and the fact that he has his butt right on top of my bladder . . ."

"You've never done well when you're short on sleep."

"Newborns don't sleep. I'm going to be a terrible mother."

"You're a wonderful mother," Lori protested. "The best. And this time, Cam will be around to help."

Sarah sniffed. "I love you, Lori. And I love your father and my friends. I have a wonderful life. I don't know why I'm being such a witch."

"It's the late-pregnancy hormones," Sage said.

"I hope it *is* hormones and not the new me. But my emotions are a mess. I'm happy and excited, but I'm also anxious and nervous and worried. Frankly, I'm scared to death."

"Of course you are," Nic said. "That's normal."

"She's right," Ali Timberlake chimed in. "Every mother-to-be is a little bit afraid."

You should be afraid, Hope thought, though she wouldn't dream of speaking the warning aloud.

"Don't be so hard on yourself, Sarah." Cat took a seat in a wooden rocking chair, then shifted her infant son to lie against her shoulder. "What you have to remember is that the risk and worry are worth it because the reward is so great."

"Excellent advice," Sage Rafferty said. "On that note, I say we get down to business." With a flourish, she gestured toward a table piled high with gifts. "Presents!"

Sarah's eyes went misty. "There's a mountain of them. You guys went crazy."

"A little," Celeste admitted. "But it's so much fun to buy for babies."

"At the rate we're reproducing, someone should open a children's store in town," Nic observed.

"Is that an announcement?" Gabi asked.

"Bite your tongue," Nic responded as Ali handed Sarah the first gift to open.

Hope enjoyed the afternoon. She liked these women, and she appreciated the way they welcomed newcomers into their circle of friendship with such genuine pleasure. She didn't know if it was a small-town thing or particular to Eternity Springs, but either way, she felt as if she had found the people who were meant to be in her life and the home she was meant to have.

She'd found a new life—a good life—to replace the one that had been stolen from her.

And when she watched Sarah Murphy ooh and ahh over three-month-sized overalls and took her turn cuddling little Johnny Davenport, she reminded herself to be thankful for what she had. Positive thinking took work, but Hope knew that it was work worth doing. Negative thoughts could be dangerous and destructive and lead a person to consider dangerous, destructive acts.

She remembered that bleak afternoon when she'd thought about taking her own life. She'd wanted to die. She'd felt like she deserved to die. But after giving the idea serious consideration, she'd realized that she couldn't do it. Because somewhere deep inside herself and against all odds, Hope still harbored hope.

Sometimes dreams came true.

Sometimes an infertile couple gets their little Johnny, she thought as she gazed down into the precious face of the cooing baby in her arms. When Sarah opened a hand-knitted baby blanket and burst into tears, it proved that sometimes long-lost lovers return to create the family that was meant to be.

So why couldn't it happen to her? She couldn't live her life in a constant state of waiting. That way lay misery, depression, and wicked thoughts. But if she kept her thoughts positive, continued to put one foot in front of the other and move forward on this road of life, well, then, who was to say she couldn't have her own miracle someday?

Jack and Kat Davenport had their new son. Cam and Sarah Murphy were married and awaiting their second child. Maybe someday she would get her miracle, too. Maybe someday, Holly would come home to her.

Sometimes kidnapped children were found. Sometimes miracles did happen.

PB FICT MAR Romance
March, Emily
Reflection point
$7.99   9/13